PRAISE FOR SHATTERED GLASS
GLASS AND STONE - BOOK 1

Perilous Safety Series
Perilous Cove (Book 1)
Storm Song (Book 2)
Desperation Falls (Book 3,

Glass and Stone Series
Shattered Glass (Book 1)
Glass Revenge (Book 2)

I0679324

GLASS REVENGE

RICH BULLOCK

RichWORDS PRESS

REDDING, CALIFORNIA

Book cover design by Robert Henslin

Published by RichWords Press

V 9/23av/24

DEDICATION

For those willing to forgive…
when it's the last thing they want to do.

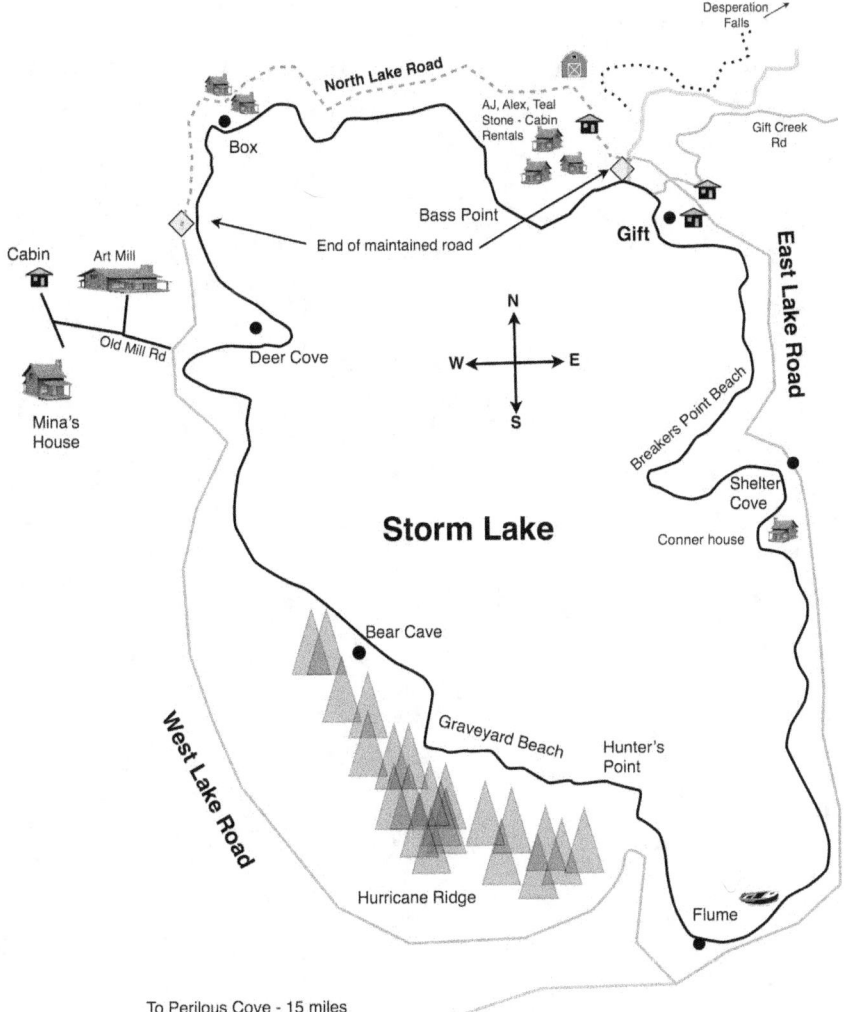

Desperation Falls

North Lake Road

AJ, Alex, Teal Stone - Cabin Rentals

Gift Creek Rd

Box

Bass Point

End of maintained road

Gift

East Lake Road

Cabin

Art Mill

Old Mill Rd

Deer Cove

N

W   E

S

Mina's House

Storm Lake

Breakers Point Beach

Shelter Cove

Conner house

Bear Cave

Graveyard Beach

Hunter's Point

West Lake Road

Hurricane Ridge

Flume

To Perilous Cove - 15 miles

GLASS REVENGE

CHAPTER ONE

Berlin

MINA GLASS JUGGLED her ringing mobile as she unlocked the door of the two-bedroom flat in Berlin, Germany, and pushed it open.

"Glass," she said, automatically switching to the German convention of answering a call.

"Palomino! Are you back?"

No matter how many times Mina urged her roommate to use her nickname, Kristen ignored her. She loved Mina's full name.

Mina rolled her suitcase through the opening, sighing in ecstasy as heat flowed around her. She opened her heavy coat and leaned over the radiator, shivering from the shock of returning to the Berlin winter after the hot Florida sun.

"We're going dancing at Platz," Kristen continued without yet confirming Mina was even in the country. That was so Kristen. A former fashion model from Croatia, she was six feet tall and an advanced economics major. Gorgeous *and* smart. If she wasn't so nice, Mina would hate her.

"Come join us!" a male voice shouted in German in the background. A girl laughed and replied in what sounded like Italian.

Kristen shushed them. "*Please* come, Palomino."

Platz was the hottest new club among dozens sprouting up in the Kreuzberg district, and a favorite gathering spot for young alternative internationals and expats.

The radiator's rising heat spiraled deep into her lungs, warming from the inside. Another hour of this would be heavenly.

"Palomino? Are you there?"

"Sorry," Mina said, blinking. She was dozing standing up. The throbbing in the front of her skull had started somewhere over the Atlantic. "I just walked in and need to go to bed."

"But it's still early," Kristen pleaded.

"Sorry," Mina repeated. "Past my bedtime tonight. You guys have fun."

Kristen said she probably wouldn't be home tonight, then disconnected. The Platz crowds didn't typically disperse until dawn.

Mina inhaled the heat for a few more minutes before pushing off the wall and heading for her bedroom.

Visiting her dad at his Florida movie location had been pushing it, especially after her recent bout of bronchitis. But other than Skype calls, they hadn't seen each other in over six months. So when he said he had free time...well, she couldn't say no. Now, after a two-day visit bookmarked by interminable ten-hour flights, she'd come to a realization: she was sick of hiding.

The threats on her life had abruptly stopped four years ago—permanently, she hoped. Maybe it was safe again.

Kristen said Mina had a case of seriously delayed homesickness. Probably true. More likely it was the dreary German winters, the different holidays, the endless mental translations of street signs and menus, the metric system, the smell of the city. She wanted to wade in the Pacific Ocean at Malibu, lie on the warm sand, listen to waves thump against the shore while seagulls squawked and fought over tossed scraps, wear flip-flops all year if she wanted, and stop at In-N-Out for a burger and chocolate shake.

Mostly, she wanted more time with her dad. They had spent every Thanksgiving apart for six years.

"Jet-setting is so fun," she mumbled as she brushed her teeth.

The sheets were cool when she slid between them two minutes later. At least bedding felt the same whether here or at home.

She closed her eyes and willed sleep to claim her. Meanwhile, she watched memories play on the inside of her skull like a drive-in movie: swaying palm trees, driving on the twisting freeways with their green signs, planes descending over the city on approach to LAX, and Randy Newman's "I Love L.A." cranked on the stereo. And hearing the old names: La Brea, Chavez Ravine, Westwood, Hollywood, Venice, Mulholland, PCH. And not I-5, but *the* 5, *the* 57, *the* 134. East Coasters never understood that Southland quirk.

Germany and other places in Europe and in the US were beautiful, even magical, but they lacked one thing—familiarity. Her history was in Southern California.

She sighed. Maybe it was time to return.

Mina cracked one bleary eye enough to see it was still dark beyond the bedroom window blinds. Then she turned to the red numbers on her clock and groaned. Four and a half hours was not enough sleep. She needed ten. Or fifteen.

After staring at the ceiling for another hour, she gave up. Her class with Turkish artist Serkan Karga began promptly at 8:00 a.m., and he did not tolerate late arrivals. She showered by the glow of the nightlight, clutching the last shreds of rest while the water sluiced away travel grunge.

Karga's class was challenging, and Mina needed liquid energy. Immediately. She toweled off, wrapped herself in her heavy white robe, and padded to the kitchen with eyes half closed.

As she passed the end of the L-shaped breakfast bar, the coffeemaker's glaring red power button caught her by surprise. It had always been green. Had Kristen bought a new machine? In the same instant, the red dot swung right and disappeared. Coffee machine power switches did not move.

Mina dropped to the floor. A microsecond later, a silenced bullet struck the tile countertop above where she'd been standing. Other shots followed, sending bits of tile and wood flying through the air as she rolled farther into the kitchen. Without slowing, she reached up and grabbed a knife from the block by the sink, then ducked down and put her back against the breakfast bar cabinets. Would the thin wood stop the slugs?

As near as she could calculate, the shots had originated from the front door area. Someone had come inside as she shuffled into the kitchen, and she hadn't heard them. She shucked her robe and stuffed it into the corner, choosing to be naked instead of encumbered by the bulky garment, which was also a large white target.

The knife she'd chosen—an eight-inch chef more blade than handle—wasn't the best. She gripped the back of the blade, weighing the balance. With her left hand, she lifted a saucepan from the cabinet's lower shelf.

The firing ceased, but the laser pinpoint swept right and left on the far wall as her assailant moved closer. Cautious, not knowing whether Mina was armed. If he or she reached the kitchen, Mina would be dead in two seconds.

She watched the red dot, estimating the angle of the approach, then heaved the heavy pan over her head and across the breakfast bar.

Without hesitation, she rolled right, coming up into a crouch in the completely exposed opening to the kitchen. But equally visible to her was a man pivoting left as he instinctively followed the path of the saucepan. It crashed against the living room window and fell to the floor.

The dim light from the window showed him dressed in black from his boots to his balaclava. Not wearing a protective vest was a mistake.

He recovered from the distraction, and the gun barrel swung back toward her. Mina cocked her arm and threw the knife with all her strength. The tumbling steel glinted once before rapid muzzle blasts split wood from the cabinet at her right. A punch knocked back her right arm, then the laser seared across both of her eyes, igniting her vision into a hot mess. But no shots followed the laser's path.

Mina twisted and stretched blindly for the remaining blades in the knife block, exposing her back to the man. She could almost feel the hot red dot tracking up her spine as she freed another blade. Would she feel the bullet pierce her flesh, sever her spine? If it entered her brain, would she blink out like a burned-out light bulb? Would she be aware that she died?

But no bullet came. Instead, she heard a heavy crash. The red dot was gone.

Unwilling to claim victory, Mina ducked back behind the protection of the cabinets, sucking in air with silent, open-mouthed gulps. Needle-like tile shards pierced her bare feet as she crouched, gripping the knife. Waiting.

Her training emphasized regaining control of her body quickly during a fight. Adrenaline choked the body's fine motor skills, and she needed that finesse if she had to throw again. Easy to understand in class, but incredibly hard to do with hot blood running down her right arm.

Hearing was affected in high stress, too, and she strained for the slightest sound beyond the blood roaring like a waterfall in her ears. Only thirty inches of cabinets separated her from the other room. What was happening there?

Burning gunpowder signaled her sense of smell had returned. So did the metallic odor of blood. *Her* blood. She resisted checking the wound. It wasn't a priority.

When her thighs began cramping, she gripped the edge of the counter and pulled herself up an inch at a time. Enough morning light now filtered through the window to reveal the man's dark form. He had fallen backward and lay spread-eagled. The gun was a few inches from the fingers of his right hand, its laser dot shining cheerily, low on the wall to the right of the front door.

Mina gingerly made her way around the end of the bar, pausing only to pick the worst of the tile shards out of her feet, never taking her eyes off the black figure.

He lay atop the remains of her destroyed coffee table, the fingers of his left hand clinched in the long fibers of their Australian sheepskin accent rug—Kristen's favorite. The knife's black handle was the only part visible, sticking straight up an inch below his sternum. It moved slightly.

He was still alive. She should call 112, the emergency number that would summon an ambulance. Instead, she retrieved the pistol. It was too dark to determine the manufacturer, but it was a compact semi-automatic with a sound suppressor doubling its length. She ejected the magazine and held it up to the sparse light. Small, .22 caliber, with a glint of brass in at least two holes. Two rounds remained, maybe more. She reinserted the magazine, slapped it home, and racked the slide in case the chambered round had been a misfire. If he was using subsonic ammo, a .22 could be unreliable in a semi-auto.

Keeping the tip of the silencer a few inches from the man's ribcage in case he was playing her, she yanked two full spare magazines from his belt clip. He opened his eyes at the contact, but Mina stood and stepped away. She dropped the near empty magazine and replaced it with one of the spares. Then she jerked the ski mask off the man's head.

If he was surprised to see a nude woman pointing his own gun at him, his face didn't reveal it. His chest contracted in a wet, rumbly cough. Red seeped from his lips and trickled down each side of his face, turning his countenance into a macabre grimace.

"Who sent you?" she demanded. He gave no response. She repeated the question in her limited Spanish. That brought a bloody grin, like the Joker in Batman movies. He opened his mouth as if to say something, or perhaps spit at her, but his eyes widened momentarily. Then the muscles of his face went slack, and a last gurgling breath was all that came forth. She watched as the knife handle ceased moving.

Three sharp knocks made her jump a foot, and she almost shot through the front door.

"Hello? Are you ladies okay?" The three knocks repeated.

Mina recognized her neighbor's German accent, a thirty-something man who hosted frequent girlfriends and semi-loud parties. He'd been hitting on Kristen lately, and Mina pegged him as a player. Fortunately, so did Kristen.

Mina stepped closer to the door. "Yes. Sorry. I dropped the coffee carafe, then some mugs. I'm so clumsy."

"Are you injured? Do you require help cleaning?"

Mina looked over her shoulder at the destruction, more evident as the morning light increased. Except for the flying saucepan and the man falling onto the table, the fight had been amazingly silent. But cleaning up would take a while.

"No, that's all right." Her shoulder was beginning to throb. "I'm not dressed yet."

After more assurances and thanks—undoubtedly extended because he was picturing her undressed—the man changed tactics.

"What happened to your door?" The slab rattled as if he were testing it. "The wood frame looks to be damaged."

Mina's heart raced. She hadn't yet thought about how her attacker had gained entrance. Before she could come up with a reason for the damage, the neighbor provided her with the answer.

"Did someone try to break in?"

"Oh. Yes, we think so. Kristen found it that way yesterday and called for a repair."

After assuring Mina he would check on them after work today, he left. A few seconds later, his apartment door closed with a muffled thump.

She let out a breath and leaned against the wall, thankful her apartment was at the end of the building. No neighbors on the other side. And for once, Mina was abundantly glad Kristen liked to dance. Better that she might get a little drunk tonight than dead.

CHAPTER TWO

MINA SAT on a chair a few feet away from the dead man and picked the last of the ceramic tile splinters from her feet.

When they were out, she walked to her bedroom. Bloody footprints on the carpet were the least of her problems. She placed the gun on the bed and dialed a number on her cell phone, a number stored only in her brain.

"Da," the alert female voice said. Mina realized it was still the previous evening in Los Angeles, as if traveling back in time before all this had happened.

"This is your former student, the one with the wounds." The phone had the best encryption available, but Mina's training was to be careful.

"This tells me nothing. Many students have wounds, especially when I finish with them."

Even with the brusque reply, Mina relaxed hearing Alexandra Pavlovna's voice.

"My hair is lighter than any other."

"Ah." Alexandra's tone lightened. "It's been too long."

"Yes," Mina agreed, wishing this could be a casual conversation. "Perhaps I could come for a visit. It would be nice to—*get away*—

from Berlin." She added the emphasis like Alexandra and her husband, Mike, had instructed if she ever needed help. At the time, it seemed like she was test reading one of her father's thriller scripts. "But first I have to clean my apartment here."

"Is big job?" The Russian accent had thickened.

"It shouldn't take more than...*one hour*. But I also have to call a repairman to replace some broken tile in my kitchen."

"I might know someone," Alexandra said.

"I was hoping." Mina's knees began shaking, and she sank onto the bed, relieved she was no longer in this alone. Or maybe it was the blood loss from her arm. "Unfortunately, I'm also not feeling too well. Nothing serious, but I might need a clinic soon."

Mina suspected the next Russian words she heard were swearing. Years ago—after the first attack, and while Mina was taking self-defense classes from Alexandra—Mike had jokingly made a pact with Mina to determine whether his exotic new girlfriend was former KGB. Mina had never gotten a single clue from the Russian. But whatever Alexandra had been in her old life, Mina was glad for her connections and resources.

After they disconnected the call, Mina's hands began trembling—another aftereffect of the adrenaline. It made typing out the encrypted emails on the small screen difficult. She first sent her address so Alexandra could dispatch a physician to the apartment. A second email included detail about the tile and repairs needed, including photos of the scene from every angle and close-ups of the damage. From the cautious voice wording, Alexandra knew Mina had to *get away*, and *one hour* designated a lone attacker. The cleaning reference made it clear there was a mess to make disappear, including a body.

Shortly before 7:00 a.m., a stooped German woman looking like any kindly Oma appeared at the apartment door. She introduced herself simply as "the doctor," and spared only a raised eyebrow for the dead man on the floor. Mina led her into the bathroom where the light was better, and the woman quickly went to work.

The bullet had gone through the outer fleshy part of Mina's arm, about four inches below her shoulder and half an inch deep, missing bone, but damaging muscle. The local anesthetic the doctor used numbed her from upper chest to wrist, relieving the stinging pain.

The fact Mina had been naked at the time of the shooting meant no bits of fabric contaminated the wound, but the bullet and gunpowder residue were bad enough. After a lot of probing, flushing, and stitching, the doctor gave her a shot of antibiotic and some pain pills, plus more antibiotics to last the next several days. She was given strict orders not to move the arm too much for a week.

Before taking her leave, the doctor insisted in helping Mina through another shower, efficiently cleaning away sweat and blood like she was scrubbing a naughty hound after a romp with skunks in the woods. Mina's skin was red and tender afterward, and she revised her earlier impression of a kindly Oma. After a few minutes passed, however, she realized the woman did her a great service. The proximity of death on her skin was gone, replaced by raw cleanliness and a floral scent that distanced Mina from the earlier battle. At least physically. She understood now why rape victims took scalding showers afterward.

The doctor left, and Mina barely finished pulling a loose sweater over a sleeveless top before another knock came. Two women entered wheeling a commercial-size laundry cart, its deep bin lined with thick plastic. Another cart held cleaning supplies and a small steam cleaner. Two men followed a minute later with buckets holding a variety of tiles and repair supplies. One of the men powered on the living room stereo, tuning it to a light rock station loud enough to mask their work. Fortunately, Mina's curious neighbor would have left for work by now.

A young man entered last and locked the door behind him.

"I'm Jay," he said, "and I'll be your assistant in your relocation."

Assistant? She hadn't thought to ask for help getting away, but was glad Alexandra had.

Jay wore heavy, dark-framed glasses, and his hair was buzzed short on the sides and long on top, lifted in a careful wave. Combined with the layered clothing and trimmed beard, he could pass as a hipster from one of Berlin's universities. Maybe he was. Who knew where Alexandra's contacts recruited help for this kind of work?

However, a closer study revealed Jay wasn't all he seemed. His neck was the same thickness as his head, and the clothing didn't fully hide the width of his shoulders, nor the bulge under his left arm. This wasn't a skinny-jeans student.

"Here is our checklist," he said, turning a clipboard toward her. His accent was Eastern European, but she couldn't place it, which was probably intentional.

Jay looked around the room. "You have a housemate?"

"Yes. Kristen Pavić. She was out at a club and is staying with a friend." He wrote Kristen's name on the paper.

After a quick but thorough interview, Jay's list expanded, and included everything from removing all personal items and clothing, to canceling the rental agreement.

Jay said he'd take care of Kristen. For an uncomfortable moment, Mina was afraid they meant to permanently do away with the girl, but Jay explained that Kristen would be *encouraged* to take an extended vacation in Sweden or some other relatively distant country —starting today. All expenses paid by Mina, of course, including a daily stipend and bonuses payable at three, six, and twelve months if Kristen remained hidden away. He wrote down Kristen's cell number, and made a call to yet another associate, speaking so rapidly that Mina didn't even try to figure out what language it was. Alexandra's *"might know someone"* was turning out to be a whole lot of someones.

Mina turned to her closet. She always traveled light, and her suitcase was still packed. Jay returned and helped her load a second suitcase. When Mina came out with her coat, the body was gone, along with every shard of the coffee table and the throw rug.

"We go," Jay said, slinging her laptop bag over his shoulder and rolling the suitcases toward the front door.

Mina paused and looked back on the apartment. One man was fitting a new tile into place on the counter, while a woman with a painter's palette and small brush touched up two holes in the far wall. The second man was emptying the refrigerator and pantry, unceremoniously dumping milk, eggs, produce, cereal, crackers, and canned food into the thickest trash bags Mina had ever seen. It was like living an episode of *The Blacklist*.

But no matter how perfect the repairs or how many gallons of cleaning products were used, nothing would ever be as it had been. The stench of death in this room would linger in her memory.

At least Kristen hadn't been here to witness her housemate dispassionately watching a man die. It might be months before Mina could meet up with her and try to explain what happened. And how would her friend react if she learned tonight wasn't Mina's first kill? Both were self-defense, yes, but that wasn't something you dropped into casual conversation over streusel and a coffee.

It worried Mina that she didn't feel more about the ending of a human life. Shouldn't there be guilt? Regret? Mina held her hands out. They were steady again. She was washed clean on the outside, dressed nicely, and could be leaving for Serkan Karga's art class, where she would sit and draw gentle curves without so much as a waver.

Perhaps her lack of remorse was balanced by the dully pulsing wound and the cuts on her feet—and the grim reality it could be *her* body in a black plastic bag wheeled out in a laundry cart.

She turned to Jay. "If the police come and investigate my disappearance—"

"They will find nothing," Jay said, smiling proudly at the workers. "This is the A-Team."

Except this wasn't an 80s television show where the heroes always won and even the bad guys miraculously dodged all the flying bullets.

The second woman finished spritzing a clear liquid on the carpet, then switched on the steam-cleaning machine. Pink froth rushed up the clear attachment head. Here was the real world, where bad guys *did* die. And good people, too, sometimes. But not tonight.

She was foolish to think the person driving the threats from the deceased Viera drug family had forgotten her. This was a dramatic escalation, and the important thing to figure out right now was how this man found her. Also, did he know her new identity as Palomino Glass?

There was one way to find out, and perhaps she could use Jay or another of Alexandra's contacts to run a test. Wherever she ended up in the next few days, she would use her credit cards, give her name, be visible. And then she would wait and watch, see if another killer came to find her. It was time to stop this before more innocent people like Kristen were caught in the middle.

"Ready?" Jay prompted.

Mina gave a single nod. It wasn't as if she had a choice. Today was a time of loss: friendships, the apartment, her art studies, and the false illusion of safety that geographic distance had previously brought. All gone.

Today she had to run away for a while longer. She sighed. At least no one she cared about had died this time.

Mina stepped through the apartment door and closed it behind her. Jay was halfway down the hallway with the suitcases, and she hurried on hurting feet to catch up.

She would use the next weeks or months to plan, to prepare, to make sure her dad was safe.

Then she would take the fight to the person who wanted her dead.

CHAPTER THREE

Six weeks later - London

"Welcome to Ballards on Thames, madam. Your reservation name?"

"Palomino Glass." The front desk clerk typed a few strokes, then accepted her credit card. Mina had used the card and her name dozens of times in the four weeks since making herself publicly visible again. It still felt unnatural and scary to suddenly be high profile, but in the month and a half since the attack in Berlin, no one had tried to kill her. Yet.

That was the morbid greeting each morning between her and Karl Voigt. His job—and that of his team of four men and two women— was to make sure no one got close enough to try. Sometimes inappropriate humor, like cops laughing at a crime scene, was what allowed Mina to face the day.

Jay had introduced her to Karl when he handed her off at Berlin Central Station. The man was another of Alexandra's hires—billed to Mina, of course. He and his team were her new security detail.

Instead of boarding a train in the station as expected, Karl had led her to a pair of Mercedes SUVs. The 1,000 kilometer drive to Paris gave them ample time to get to know one another.

Looking back, Mina realized the journey across the German and French countryside was her time to process. On these hills, hundreds of thousands of men had died, but those deaths were distanced by passing decades. Her encounter in Berlin was a new, raw gash across her thoughts.

Karl proved to be a good listener, the kind who knew what killing a man close up was like. And the two men sitting opposite held military-grade weapons in a way that disabused all uncertainty about the proficiency of the other team members.

Mina also found Karl astute at strategic planning. Two weeks after leaving Berlin, Mina surfaced from hiding. They began systematic testing to see if her identity was compromised.

"The American Bar and Grill is on the second level," the desk clerk said, bringing Mina back to the present. "It overlooks the River Thames." He smiled and returned her credit card. The room keycard went to the bellman, who had her luggage on a cart. "James will show you to your suite. Please let us know if you need anything at all."

When the elevator doors opened, James rolled the cart into the center of the elevator car. Mina followed, taking the opposite side. A moment before the doors closed, a hand forced them open, and a man entered on her side. His too-large, off-the-rack herringbone suit would have made Kristen gag. A red and black tattoo peeked beyond the cuff of his left sleeve.

Before the doors could close again, a man and woman stepped in, taking a position in front of the man. Mina used the distraction to squeeze behind the cart to the rear corner on the bellman's side. She pulled the cart tight against the rear wall, creating a barrier between herself and the three others.

Finally, the elevator began to rise. The woman leaned close to her man, smiling and whispering in his ear. Two lovers, making plans to go out. Or, more likely—considering the way she was playing with his silk tie—stay in. Only Mina noticed the pistol in his right hand, hidden from the others by his woman's hip.

The elevator stopped at the third floor, and the stranger exited. The doors slid closed and the car moved upward again.

Mina let out a breath, and the male of the remaining couple slipped the gun into his shoulder holster. The woman, Annika, one of Karl's team, turned and smiled at Mina. While Annika's pretend lover, Wil, preferred his 9 millimeter, Annika favored knives, and carried at least two daggers in wrist scabbards hidden under the sleeves of her evening dress. She moved like a panther, as Mina knew from sparring with her after her shoulder healed sufficiently. The training was far more effective than any physical therapy.

James the bellman, facing forward the whole time, had missed the drama.

Three days later, the weather turned, and not for the better. Rare snow flurries and not-so-rare mist obscured the Thames from Mina's window. Like a raincloud over a cartoon character, bone-chilling cold dogged her from city to city. Here it was again, dropping white flakes that had children gleefully scurrying around with tongues outstretched, hoping for a direct hit.

She turned away from the depressing sight. It no longer mattered. Mentally, she was done. They had been outside in the cold and rain for the last two weeks, trailing tourists to all the historic sights, visiting banks, riding the Tube, and in and out of too many stores and cafés to remember.

London was famous for having something like half a million closed circuit cameras, and her job was to be seen and recorded by as many as possible. Most of the cameras and their captured data were private, not government. That made it easier for determined hackers to mine the data and run it through facial-recognition software. Some owners hocked it directly to distribution services that paid well. TV shows had authorities tracking people through the city in real time. Good drama, but fiction. Still, the reality of rarely being *off*-camera was disconcerting.

Prior to London, she and the team had run the same exercises in Paris, Brussels, and Amsterdam. Her credit card became figuratively hot to the touch from frequent use. If someone was looking for Palomino Glass, Mina was screaming, *Here I am!* The danger was that even if her pursuer didn't find her, Mina's pictures were now out there for all to see. And after her years of staying as invisible as possible, this public parade felt completely wrong. But it was her first step in taking the fight to what she had begun to call the Viera Threat.

As was their habit at other hotels, Karl had taken the second bedroom in Mina's suite. Wil, Martin, Jens, and Stefan shared the suite next door, and Annika and the other female team member, Sara, had a room down the hall.

Each had his or her specialties. While Annika often dressed to turn heads when they went to clubs, Sara could appear plain or downright dowdy, and go unnoticed in any lobby or bar. The men passed for handsome, inconspicuous, or menacing, depending on the situation.

Karl pocketed his phone as he joined Mina in the suite's common area. "No hits for *Palomino Glass* except those traced back to Kristen in Stockholm." A cyber security company notified Karl if anyone searched for *Palomino Glass* or *Lilly Hawthorne*.

Mina had been forced to call Kristen and explain why she could never search for Mina again. If anyone knew they had shared an apartment or were even connected as friends, they would trace Kristen. Mina promised to call when the situation was resolved. It was a vow she planned to keep.

"Many searches for *Lilly Hawthorne*," Karl said, "but not in close proximity to *Mina*."

"I'm beginning to think they don't know my identity," Mina said, relaxing onto the sofa and toeing off her shoes.

"Six weeks with no activity *is* pretty convincing." Karl sat on a facing wingback chair. "However, there is no way to know for certain."

That was the problem.

"And I remind you," Karl continued, "we have nothing to tie this attack to your previous threats."

Mina had no doubts about that. What were the odds someone else was trying to kill her? Sure, that had been exactly the case years ago, but this time she was positive: the man in Berlin was connected to the Viera family. Would his boss hold off while regrouping? How could Mina ever be sure they hadn't discovered her new identity and just hadn't acted on the information?

"Six months would be more conclusive," Karl said.

"So would six years," she said, but by then her bank account would be a dusty bin. Well, not really. But suites at Ballards weren't cheap. She wasn't used to blowing this kind of money on beds, not to mention the team costs or additional resources like the cyber group. Her humble upbringing was rearing its head.

"What do you want to do next?" Karl said, rising and going to the wet bar. He took two bottles of water from the refrigerator and handed her one.

Mina used a long swallow to confirm her decision. "We'll wait a few more days and get a final report."

After that, it was time for action.

Mina looked up as Karl entered the common room at the end of the week. Since the London weather was abysmal, she'd eschewed going out and was playing Scrabble with Sara. The woman was born, raised, and schooled in Germany, and was beating the pants off Mina in the English version of the game. She was more than ready for an interruption.

"I have the latest report," Karl said. "More hits for *Lilly Hawthorne*."

"None for *Palomino Glass*," Mina stated.

"Correct," Karl said. "Of course we cannot be certain, but it appears your new identity is still unconnected to *Lilly Hawthorne*. Whoever is looking for you is searching for your old name."

This confirmed what Alexandra's contacts had discovered about the dead man. Through airline records and security camera photos, the Russian traced the man's travel backward from Berlin to Miami, then from Miami back to Los Angeles. It seemed he'd been following Mina's father, not tracking Mina directly. She and her dad had gotten sloppy.

Following Mina to Berlin was easy—he'd been on her same flight. His delay in attacking was probably the time it took to procure the gun in Germany. It didn't appear he had discovered her new name, or at least hadn't communicated it to anyone.

"Except they could be looking at my picture right now."

Karl nodded.

It was a risk to splash her face all over, but her choice from the beginning. Still, no one had come to kill her, so her new visibility didn't seem to matter.

Mina walked to the suite's view window. The weather front had passed, sweeping the light snow band toward Scotland. In its wake, the fog thickened to a gray curtain. The river was invisible—like her hunter. And for now, it seemed, *Palomino Glass* was invisible to the hunter too.

It was a good stopping point. The team alone was 15,000 dollars a week—a discounted price in consideration of Alexandra. Additional expenses included transportation, team member lodging rooms, meals, and the cyber contract. More money went as payments to a few people in Berlin to "forget" she and Kristen shared an apartment or even knew each other. Then there was Kristen's *vacation*.

The total for everything these last several weeks amounted to nearly a quarter of a million dollars. Thanks to the trust her mother, Ekaterina, left, Mina was far from poor, but this kind of outlay couldn't continue.

"Have you decided what you're going to do?" Karl asked.

Sara, evidently sensing the game was concluded, scraped the tiles into the box and placed it back in the credenza. Mina waited to speak until she exited the room.

"I'm going back to the US to get warm." She laughed with Karl for a moment, relishing the momentary lightness. Then she told him the rest of her plan. "It's time to become the aggressor."

Karl leaned against the wet bar and crossed his arms. "It would be difficult for our group to work in the United States. It could be done, but the weapons, the licenses…" He shifted uncomfortably.

Mina nodded. "I'm not asking you to go." Two of the team had families in Germany, and there was talk of bringing in replacements if this assignment extended much longer.

"Alexandra can find you another team there."

"Perhaps."

"It would be unwise to go on your own." His tone implied *idiotic* and *foolhardy*.

The most difficult part of all this was others putting themselves in danger to protect her. Only the fact these men and women did it professionally and loved their jobs justified it.

After Karl left to inform the team their assignment would end tomorrow, Mina made a flight reservation. Then she sat in a chair facing the window and the gray beyond. The immediate goal had been achieved. Her name hadn't been compromised, and no one had come after her even with her picture readily available. But although her new name appeared to be safe, it would be prudent to keep her face hidden again.

She was free to travel, live, and plan—as long as she and her dad remained separated. Someone was watching him. The cyber team cautioned that even computer video calls to him could be reverse tracked, leading the bad guys to her location. The best options were cell phones that bounced calls off different repeaters around the world, making it impossible to determine the origin.

That wasn't an issue right now. Dad's film company was off to northern British Columbia, where two independent projects of his were using the same sets. He'd be tied up for weeks.

She rose and went into the bedroom to pack. Tomorrow would be a travel day—by herself for the first time in over six weeks.

Going on the attack could take months to set up, and she wanted to be somewhat close to L.A. But first, she needed to sharpen her skills. The man in Berlin had surprised her. That could never happen again.

And Karl was right about one thing: she couldn't do this alone.

CHAPTER FOUR

"SEVEN YEARS," Evie Mendak said.

The only reaction was the tinkling of ice swirling in a tumbler some twenty feet behind her. Slade Ibanez knew what she meant, and why she'd called him here tonight.

Evie stood inches from a wall of glass that provided a spectacular view of Southern California's San Fernando Valley stretched out below. Mild Santa Ana winds coming off the desert had cleared the air, leaving in their wake a twinkling fairyland of street lights. Red and white streams flowed through the grids, hundreds of thousands of people coming and going. Traffic would lessen somewhat in the wee hours, then ramp up around three thirty or four. Everyone had to be somewhere. She loved the restless energy, the manic pace. So ripe for exploitation.

The Valley had been a real estate developer's dream since the boom and bust cycles began in the late 1800s. Back then, only men controlled and manipulated the land. Mulholland, Lankershim, Van Nuys—the powerful names were etched on the landscape like brands on the cattle that once roamed the valley and foothills.

But they were long dead. It was her time now.

"Seven years." Her breath fogged the glass for a few seconds, blurring the sparkling reds and whites.

Her house—built over a half century ago—was a genius of design. Its open concept living area rested on cantilevered steel beams jutting out from the steep canyon wall far above Ventura Boulevard. Darkness swallowed the seventy foot drop beyond the thin glass.

Obtaining the house hadn't been without effort. The previous owner's demise had been—unfortunate. For him, anyway.

The ice tinkled again. Slade wouldn't come any closer.

She pressed her right palm to the cool glass, fingers splayed, watching momentary condensation flare around her fingers. The housekeeper would spritz away the mark, of course, but the symbol would remain like a brand. This house was a representation of the power she wielded. Yet, even with all that power…

She turned. "Seven years." Slade stood as close as he dared, which was on the other side of a hand-carved wooden bar holding an ice bucket, glasses, and liquor bottles on a silver tray. Behind him, her steel and glass kitchen filled the wall. He might be afraid of heights, but no man intimidated him. She was no man, and he had the good sense to look away. While she took pleasure in his deference, it did nothing to ease the years of pain.

He sipped his drink, but didn't meet her gaze. "We were close in Berlin—"

"How do you know? All you got was one brief phone call. Have you found your man yet?" Evie didn't wait for him to answer. "It's been weeks. He disappeared, and so did she." All they knew was a voice message that Slade's man was trailing her to Berlin. None of his follow-up men had found a trace of what happened there.

He shrugged. "She has money, resour—"

"She is a murderer—"

"with money and connections." He drained his drink and slammed the glass on the bar.

Her lips curved slightly, not enough for him to notice. Vain assertion of his manhood. "I want her. Now."

"You've always wanted her, Evie. We're always looking. We spent nearly seventy thousand dollars last year alone." He spread his arms. "What has changed?"

Evie spread her own arms and leaned back against the window, relishing Slade's cringe as she trusted the glass with her weight. As fearful as he was of heights, his eyes never left her. They couldn't. Her sleeveless scarlet sheath hugged her body from neck to knee, its color in stark contrast to the surrounding blacks, chrome, and glass, like a road flare in the night.

Slade was her antithesis. Black silk shirt, black slacks, short-trimmed black beard, black hair swept tightly back and secured with a black leather thong. He could pass as a celebrity—and occasionally did when they attended an event together, paparazzi scrambling for pictures because they looked like they should be famous. While the Viera family had hidden from everyone, Evie's strategy was to hide in plain sight.

But release Slade's curls from the tie, smear his face with some dirt, dress him in thrift-store clothing, and he became another vagrant on a street corner, ignored by everyone while he kept watch. No one thought to take *that* man's photo.

Slade had been, in the past, her lover, and was in charge of most of her less legitimate income streams. Born in Mexico, he spoke fluent Spanish and was the go-between with her business contacts there. Although she was from an immigrant family herself, she hated traveling south of the border. The country was dirty and poor, and you couldn't trust the food or water. It was no wonder everyone wanted to come to California.

But Slade was also her employee, and right now, her knee-jerk reaction was to tell him to do what she ordered.

Yet in this case, he was correct. Ever since that night long ago, she had sought her family's killer, but she admitted there were many months—years, even—where she gave little effort to the hunt. What had changed to make it imperative now?

She could argue it had taken those years to rebuild the cartel after she was thrust into leadership of the family business. The deaths of the Vieras, as well as arrests of their most trusted workers, had decimated the organization. Other cartels and opportunists surged into the vacuum, gobbling up both suppliers and customers. It was only Roberto Viera's previous efforts with Evie to diversify into real estate—held in hidden corporations—that gave her the resources to continue after his death, to restore a semblance of control and begin anew.

The responsibility consumed who she had once been. Overnight, Evie *Mendez*, the moderately successful, unassuming, brown-haired Hispanic realtor from Orange County who quietly worked under someone else, disappeared. Evie *Mendak* emerged six months later, a licensed broker with a chic blond chin-length cut from one of Rodeo Drive's classiest salons, and clothing from Carini's. New car, new surname, new look, new business territory—she had even cast off her accent. The one thing she retained was access to all the dummy corporations and the overseas accounts.

Now, finally, a small army surrounded her. Men like Slade. And women, who could be as vicious as any male. Loyal? As much as money could buy. She wasn't naive.

But no, her success in business wasn't what motivated her tonight. It was the small shadow on an X-ray film, followed by a second screening showing more shadows, then more meetings with doctors. Control of one's life, she quickly learned, was an illusion, decided by particles too small for the human eye. In less than two weeks, her world flipped, priorities dissolved, replaced by a single new goal.

She strode toward Slade. "I'm giving you one million dollars to work with."

His eyes widened, then narrowed. "I—"

"It will be in your bank account tomorrow. Use the money. Use it all. When you bring her to me"—Evie reached the bar and leaned across—"there will be another million." She ran a manicured fingernail slowly down his black tie, stopping at his silver belt buckle. "For you."

After a perfect pause, she straightened, and poured herself a half a shot of whiskey. It burned when she tossed it back. The liquor probably didn't help her body prepare for the medical fight ahead, but the small defiance pleased her. Weakness was not allowed in her organization, and the slight discomfort in her throat was a bare precursor of what her family's killer would face. Now *that* would be a night of celebration.

Evie gestured toward the door and turned away from the man, back to the view of the streaming red and white lights. Millions of people out there. She wanted only one.

"Bring me Lilly Hawthorne."

After the door closed behind Slade, Evie returned to the single chair positioned so it faced the view. She lowered herself slowly. The doctor said it was her imagination, but Evie felt the disease eating at her insides, like the mice that scurried and chewed in the walls of her long-ago bedroom before Mr. Viera took her away to live with his family.

A low table at her left held a remote control, a bottle of water, and her copy of *Currents*, by V.M. Narrano. A button on the remote released plaintive alternative rock music from hidden speakers.

Evie slid the book onto her lap, fingering its pages absently as she watched the distant lights. She wasn't sure why Narrano's writings spoke to her sometimes and aggravated her at others. Maybe it was the way he boiled things down.

An hour before Slade arrived, she had finished reading the book's last chapter, "Looking Down." The writing was often poetic in nature, if not in rhyme, but she didn't need an English degree to divine its meaning. The passage was written from a mother eagle's perspective as she soared the updrafts high above the sun-heated granite cliffs of Yosemite Valley.

Trees are resting places, temporary perches from which to survey the land below. Rocks are hard, unforgiving, but home, safe, a solid foundation. Scurrying animals are sustenance, nothing more.

Currents… ah, they are freedom! To soar. To swoop. To dive toward my prey in victorious attack.

I am not as large as some creatures, but I am determined, strong, sharp of talon, and superior in sight.

I will seize every advantage.

I will prevail.

Evie picked up her pen and underscored the last two lines.

CHAPTER FIVE

Mexico

FBI SPECIAL AGENT Kaden Hunt gradually became aware he was in the bed of a moving pickup truck, tossing back and forth on a hot steel floor. Exhaust fumes and dust filled his nostrils, but he resisted the urge to cough. Even this was better than his murky recollection of a dank, reeking cell with bugs as big as his thumb roaming for scraps —or for a bite of his flesh if he dozed. Then the beatings, the endless questions, the hunger and thirst.

He tried to remember where he was, why he was here. He'd been drugged, he knew that much, endless cycles of half-awareness and oblivion. But waking this time was different. His mind was clearing rather quickly. Maybe they used a new concoction hoping to get more information from him. Or someone had screwed up and got the dose wrong.

The truck lurched over a rough patch, bouncing Kade an inch into the air. His head banged against the steel bed. How long had he been traveling? Where from, where to? Useless questions for the moment. Days could have passed since the last time he was awake. Weeks, or months.

When he opened his eyes, muted sunlight flashed and strobed through a covering across his eyes. A blindfold.

Latin music played on a cheap radio. A male voice joined the radio singer, loud and off-key. It didn't help Kade pinpoint his location, but at least somebody was happy.

After several minutes of jostling on the dirt road, he tried moving his right hand. It obeyed. He inched it upward, across his sunken stomach and the protruding bones of his rib cage. No one clubbed him unconscious, nor did the vehicle slow, so they must not be watching him too closely.

A new song began on the radio and someone turned up the volume. A second singer joined the first man, and they laughed as they attempted to keep up with the pro on the radio like a bad night at a karaoke bar.

Kade's fingers reached the lower edge of the blindfold and lifted it enough to see down his body. His bare feet were against a rusty steel tailgate pushed inward several inches from some previous accident. Dust rose behind the vehicle in a thick cloud. He pushed the blindfold higher. Overhead, a tan canvas canopy flapped on a rusty steel frame.

Judging from the small bed and layers of rust, the truck was old, probably a 70s or 80s Toyota or Datsun. Not too high off the ground. Not moving too quickly. If he could throw himself over the rear gate...

He had no idea where he was, not even what country, but from the snippets of Spanish he'd heard during short spans of consciousness, it was probably Mexico. It was a big country, with lots of places to hide a prisoner. But it could be Guatemala, Honduras, or anywhere south. If he survived the fall out of the truck and got away, could he stay hidden, find food, make his way back to the US? A broken arm or leg might mean his death. If he didn't try, that might also mean his death.

Cars or trucks going the opposite direction passed every few minutes. Not a busy road. But he couldn't see if another vehicle followed the truck he was in. They might be traveling in a small caravan for all he knew, and he could land in front of the next vehicle. Still, this might be his only chance. They were moving him for a reason, and judging from the searing pain of his back, that couldn't be good.

Kade took a few deep breaths of the exhaust-laden air, rolled on his stomach, and scooted down until he lay parallel to the tailgate. The men up front kept singing. He got to his hands and knees and, with a quick peek at the pickup cab's dust-covered rear window, he rolled over the gate.

The ground hit him like a dozen sledgehammers. He barely registered the retreating truck as he skidded on gravel and tumbled violently. As best he could, he kept his elbows and arms tucked around his head, but his knees and ankles flailed and pounded the hard-packed dirt, sending pain shooting through his hips and back. There was no counting the number of rolls before he slid to a stop in a churning cloud of dust.

The shock of the landing momentarily paralyzed his muscles, and all he could do was lie there and let the dust settle on his face. It might have been seconds or minutes of coughing and spitting out dirt and pebbles before he blinked enough grit out of his eyes to orient himself. Then he rolled toward the road's nearest shoulder, down a shallow incline and into some tall grass. He kept going as far as he could until he came against a bush and collapsed. Every passing second woke more pain.

"God. Please help me."

Phoenix, Arizona's Sky Harbor was one of the nation's busier airports, managing over 100,000 passengers per day. At 12:45 in the afternoon, arriving travelers surrounded Mina in the familiar mad rush toward baggage claim. She could never figure out the need to hurry, since they would all stand and stare at an unmoving carousel for ten minutes anyway.

But today she kept up with the crowd, sandwiching herself

between a pair of overweight businessmen in flapping suit coats. She kept her head lowered. Unfortunately, that gave her an exceptional view of the wide-body rear of the man in front of her. And why would anyone willingly wear a suit to Phoenix?

Unfortunately, she had one on too, an ill-cut black outfit that made her look like a woman desperate to compete in a man's world. The bangs of the short black wig tickled her forehead, and her scalp was already damp at the mere thought of going out into the desert heat. She pushed the slightly too big, square-framed glasses up on her nose.

At least Arizona was warmer than Europe. Although still February, the captain had announced the temperature as upper 80s today—an early heat wave.

She retrieved her bags from the carousel and Ubered to a boutique motel she found online that boasted twenty bungalows in a style reminiscent of Sedona. The host—a thin fiftyish woman named Deidre, who wore her gray hair tied in a long ponytail—led the way along gently curving, red concrete paths bordered by succulents and a variety of beautiful trees.

"You're right here in number seven," Deidre said, unlocking the door to one of the bungalows. Before entering, Deidre pointed down another path that ended at a huge, rustic-wood door about 150 feet away. "Canyon Pool is through that gate. It's quite a masterpiece of design. Not to be missed. We heat it year around, and today is perfect for a swim."

That was all Mina needed to hear. She changed into her swimsuit and headed out.

The big gate opened easily, revealing a long, irregularly-shaped pool set in what looked like a canyon of narrowing rock walls. She wove between man-high rocks in shades of red and orange that anchored the near end of the pool. The far end was a ten-foot wall of boulders. It glistened with dozens of small rivulets trickling down its face, each stream dropping the last few feet into the deep water in a musical backdrop that masked all outside noise. Large shrubs, leafy plants, and even ferns filled every cranny.

It was like she stepped into Arthur Conan Doyle's *The Lost World* —the 1960 film version she'd watched with her dad in his office. A dinosaur could be lurking behind one of the boulders, and surely Michael Rennie and Jill St. John were nearby. It was a little creepy that Mina was the only one here. The only *human* anyway.

She smiled, unable to resist looking up to see if a pterodactyl swooped overhead. If only her dad was here to see this. He'd call in a film crew.

She dropped her T-shirt and towel on a chaise and walked down the beach-style entry into the bath-temperature water. Swimming in Germany was nothing like the bright sun and warmth of the Southwest.

She swam hard for thirty minutes, then slowed and glided through the water, letting her muscles relax after the long flights and stress of the last few weeks. Phoenix could be humid, especially when the monsoons hit later in the summer, but today the air was dry, filled with fragrances from plants waking up from the previous cool days.

Mina wrung water from her hair before lying back and spreading it to dry on the chaise headrest. After the dreary European winter, her pallid body was nearly as white as her hair, but the lounger was shaded by a pergola constructed from twisted branches that fit with the theme.

Since there was no one else at the pool, she used the opportunity to make the phone call that would be her next step. Now that she was within driving distance of L.A., home pulled like a strong magnet.

"Kris Stone," the voice answered.

Mina smiled. "It's good to hear your voice. Really good."

"Mina?"

"Yep."

"How *are* you? *Where* are you?"

"Finally someplace warm. Phoenix. Are you in California?"

"Puerto Rico," Kris said. "Security for a Congressional junket. I don't even know what that means other than *money-wasting-trip-extraordinaire*. Technically, they're supposed to be surveying the hurricane damage and looking for ways to help. They're doing some of that, but between you and me, I think they come down here to scout future players for their fantasy baseball teams."

Mina laughed, and sank into the chaise. She should have connected with Kris more often. She missed their talks.

Kris sighed. "Seriously, though, this country is a mess. Two of the congressmen met with the governor this morning. Parts of the island are still without power and reliable water. We drove past kids sifting through mounds of debris with their bare hands. Our guide said they search all day for anything of value to sell for food."

Mina's heart tightened at the visual. She knew what it was like to grow up poor, but her childhood, as bad as it had been, was nothing like what Kris described. She felt guilty sitting by the pool.

"Sorry, didn't mean to bring you down," Kris said. "So, are you still studying art?"

"I may get a class in while I'm here, but mostly I've had to put it on hold."

"Your call came up as an unknown number on my phone," Kris said, her tone turning sober.

"I've changed the number a few times."

"More threats?" Kris was aware the notes had stopped.

"I assume you're somewhere private so we can talk?"

"I'm off duty for a couple of hours, so I'm helping assemble food boxes at a distribution center. No one else in earshot right now."

"At least someone is doing some good."

"A little," Kris said. "But tell me, did something happen? Are you all right?"

Mina probed her right shoulder. Other than the entrance and exit puckers, the bullet wound had healed nicely. It had only been a minor bother while swimming.

"It's a bit of a long story," she said, donning her sunglasses as the sun moved below the edge of the pergola.

"I've got nothing to do but watch the Caribbean sunset." Kris's tone sounded anything but relaxed.

Mina told her about the last several weeks, then her plan to go on offense.

"I'm going to need some help. Is this something Omron would do?"

"Mina, this is crazy talk."

"I know it's dangerous…"

"Suicidal is more like it," Kris mumbled, more to herself than to Mina. "You could go somewhere else."

"No more hiding," Mina said firmly.

After a moment, Kris said, "Does your father know about this?"

"Don't play the child card, Kris. I'm no longer a teenager. Besides, what we've been doing is no longer working."

Kris sighed. "Yeah, I hear you."

"So…?"

"Well, you could contact Tanner at Omron. He's the boss. But we function in a security role, not offense. And after losing people last time… Honestly, you'd probably be better off working with Alexandra."

"That's problematic. She and Mike are expecting."

"A baby? The Mad Russian is preggers?"

Mina laughed again. A long time ago, Kris did some training with Alexandra and claimed she still had the bruises to prove it.

"She failed to mention it when I called in a panic, but Mike sent me an email after things settled down a little. The baby is due this summer, and I guess it hasn't been the easiest pregnancy." She thought she heard Kris say something about Karma.

"Okay," Kris sighed. "Well, if Tanner balks at your scheme—and he will—you can still count on me. And Mina? Please, be careful."

Mina gave her word. Then said, "I'm going to need some expert tech help. Cyber stuff. Do you know anyone?"

"Legal or illegal?"

"Well…"

"Let me make a call. I'll be in touch."

After they said goodbye, Mina gathered her things and headed to her bungalow, her skin tingling from UV exposure. Inside the room, she called the front desk and asked for phone numbers of tactical training ranges. She could hone her shooting skills and ask around about instructors. Former military were always the best.

She thought about what lay before her. One way or another, this would end before fall.

In the interim, she had to stay alive.

CHAPTER SIX

KADE CREPT along a five-foot-high wall constructed from stacked rocks. On this side, giant broadleaf plants provided him cover from the wide-open field. The setting sun gave him a good view of the hacienda on the other side. The structure was partially surrounded by the wall, making an enclosed compound that might have once been a safe place for kids to play.

When he first saw the stone building from a mile away, it appeared to be a church or small chapel, and his hopes soared. A church could provide sanctuary and safety.

But as he hiked through fields to get closer, what he thought to be a bell tower became a crumbling chimney, and the stained glass windows became raw openings, passing air, but no multi-colored light. From his current vantage point, it appeared abandoned, nearly a ruin.

He'd learned yesterday that some of these old buildings were used for livestock. Someone could be here checking on animals.

If used as an animal shelter, there was often water—that was the good part. The bad was that any water was likely a slimy cattle trough with untold things living in it, or a stagnant ditch the beasts stood in while drinking.

For the present, at least, all the walls and plants remained stationary, and no foot-long beetles crawled up the walls or around his legs. He shook his head. That didn't mean hallucinations wouldn't return. The drugs had done a number on him, and dusk was the worst time of day. He learned that last night when the shadows lengthened and moved, releasing all manner of evil. Kade pressed his fingers against his eyelids, willing the world to stay real —just a little longer.

The pressure on his eyes felt good for a few seconds, letting him forget the pounding headache and waves of heat that had him alternately sweating or shivering. An infection, probably, but it felt the same when one of the devils came for him. He remembered snatches of interrogations, threats, and beatings. That lingering terror was enough to keep him moving after jumping from the truck yesterday.

He shifted his weight on the crooked branch he'd found for a crutch, wincing as he gripped the rough wood. His left hand was red and hot, swollen nearly double normal size. Probably broken from the fall out of the truck. That was only one of many wounds. Everything hurt—his face, scalp, knees, back, and especially his bare feet. The pain kept him sane for the moment, but his injuries were growing worse with each passing hour.

The red sun slowly hid behind a mountain, softening the sharp shadows. Gloom quickly descended. It had been a tough day of constant movement, and he longed for a pile of hay where he could rest. He forced himself to wait until full dark. Food and water were necessary to stay alive, but more important was safety. He breathed in the sweet, greenery-scented cooling air.

Maybe tomorrow he could find a church and get help without alerting local law enforcement. While there were many honest officers in Mexico, they all had chains of command and reporting requirements. Someone might have an ear into anything unusual occurring in the area—such as a banged-up gringo.

He wished he could remember what led to his capture. It was some kind of assignment with the FBI, and he recalled others in a team. But no faces or names. Funny that he could remember the beatings, but not his team. Considering his interrogation, though, that was probably a good thing.

After water and food, his priority was getting back to the US. He'd gotten a clue to his location yesterday when a truck passed as he hid in an old orchard. It had *Monterrey* painted on the door. Later, he found two yellowed newspaper pages trapped in some weeds that had *Monterrey* printed in the header. He could have read more of the paper if he'd paid more attention in Mrs. Alvarez's Spanish 1 class in high school, but it was enough to surmise he was near Monterrey, Mexico, southwest of the Texas border. A lot of US companies did business in Monterrey. He just had to find one.

Pain spiked through his hip. He straightened, wincing as his feet found every sharp stone. He moved a few feet to a patch of grass and leaned against the wall. Supposedly, day three was the worst for pain after an accident. If yesterday and today were precursors, tomorrow was not going to be a happy time. Both knees and ankles were the size of grapefruit, and he worried about the grinding in his pelvis and the growing numbness in his legs. Even worse were the dizzy spells that tilted the horizon.

All he really wanted to do was lie down on a soft surface and sleep. Maybe a couple of painkillers. And clean water. And meat. A hamburger. An In-N-Out Double-Double with grilled onions. And french—

A clattering noise had him ducking into an agonizing crouch as someone opened a gate nearby. He must have dozed standing up, because stars shone in the darkness above, and he could barely see his hands.

A dog barked, and Kade stopped breathing. People were bad, but a dog…

Go away!

The barking grew closer, then became frantic.

Kade straightened and prepared to hobble away, but a huge dark shape rounded the rock wall a few feet away. Someone sat on top of…the dog? Kade tripped and fell headlong into a cactus, screaming as the needle-like spikes pierced his arms and torso.

The animal rose on its hind feet, pawing the air.

"No hospital," Kade repeated for the tenth time. He knew the word was basically the same in Spanish, but the farmer kept insisting on calling for medical help. The man's son—the young teenager who had surprised Kade an hour ago by riding up on a pony, not a giant dog—knew a little English. It sounded like he was explaining to the father Kade's wish that he call the American Consulate instead.

After their encounter at the ruin, the boy had summoned his father, and the two of them helped Kade back to their house and lowered him onto their lumpy sofa. It felt wonderful, but Kade doubted he could ever rise from it again. The barking dog from their encounter—a mixed mutt of only forty pounds or so whose tail never wagged once—sat a few feet away, keeping an eye on Kade.

The cactus needles weren't as painful as some of his other injuries, but they still hurt.

"*Uno, dos, trace…*" the man counted as he yanked out each barb with a large pair of tweezers.

"One, two, three…" the boy proudly translated for Kade's benefit —not that he needed a double reminder for each of the twenty-eight mini spears. He kept his teeth clenched until the last one was jerked free of his skin.

The man used a cloth and basin to cleanse some of Kade's wounds, turning the water a murky tan and red after only a few rinses. Between the painful ministrations, Kade dozed, his body collapsing in on itself after so much trauma and stress. Distant snatches of words and sentences whispered around him, but he couldn't tell, or at least remember, if they were in English.

At least once when he woke, it was dark and quiet. The boy sat in a chair nearby, reading or perhaps doing homework. He wondered about the boy's mother. Was she traveling? Dead? The boy fed Kade spoonfuls of soup, then Kade slept again. He dreamed of Lilly Hawthorne. It was a good dream.

Kade stirred as someone shook his shoulder.

"Señor. Can you hear me?"

He opened his eyes, grit rubbing against the insides of his eyelids. They needed hosing out. He grunted a reply, blinking away the grime as he had dozens of times before. Light streamed in one of the windows, bright and full of promises. Perhaps this was his lucky day.

"This farmer says you are an American. Do you have identification?" The rotund man leaning over Kade was in his forties, had thinning dark hair swept across his round head in a combover failure, and huge ears that dwarfed his face. He didn't look impressed with Kade's appearance.

Kade shook his head.

The man scrunched his brows. "You're not an American?"

"I…" His voice was wrecked, and he mouthed his thanks when the boy offered him a cup of water. After a few sips, he said, "I'm a US Citizen."

"But you have no identification."

"I was kidnapped. I'm Special Agent Kaden Hunt with the FBI."

The man's eyebrows shot nearly to his receding hairline. He pulled out a cell phone. "Let me make a call." He pushed a key on the phone and walked outside.

Even if Kade could have heard the man clearly, he couldn't have followed the rapid bursts of Spanish. He rested his head against the towel serving as a pillow on the arm of the sofa. Washing the towel was easier than cleaning blood off the furniture. Every movement generated waves of pain, so he closed his eyes and waited out the phone call. His body shook with chills one minute, then broke out in sweat and fever the next. Either he was sick from drinking from irrigation ditches and animal troughs, or he was going through withdrawal from whatever drugs his captors used.

"Sí, sí."

Kade opened his eyes when the man returned to the room, still holding the phone to his ear. His eyes darted between the farmer and Kade as he dabbed his brow with a white handkerchief.

"Are there others with you?" the man asked. "Can they come here?"

Vague memories of demanding questions surged to the surface. *"Where are the others?" "Who is your contact?" "Tell me what you know."*

Kade shook his head, as much to rid himself of the memories as to answer the man.

"Okay," the man said, looking at his watch and nodding. "Una hora." He ended the call and rattled off something in Spanish to the man and boy. Then to Kade, he said, "Someone is coming for you in an hour."

"Who?" Kade began pushing himself up from the couch, groaning as his pelvis crunched. "Can't you take me?"

"No, no!" the man said, backing away. "I must go now. You wait. One hour." He turned to the man and boy and held up one finger. "Una hora." With that, he practically ran out the door. Seconds later his car engine roared as he sped away.

The farmer looked at his son and shrugged, then repeated the gesture to Kade before leaving the house—probably to go back to work in his field.

But the boy's mouth was set in a firm line. He wasn't buying the consulate man's explanation or hasty exit any more than Kade.

Fifty minutes later, the boy reined his pony and small cart to a stop near the top of the hill behind the farm. Kade lifted himself onto one elbow from his bed of hay and a coarse blanket. The ride had been anything but smooth as the boy drove along rutted switchbacks up the hill, but the horse seemed used to the task. So did the boy.

The dust cloud stirred up by their rapid pace settled, and quiet enveloped their small party. They were surrounded by rows and rows of vines heavy with grapes—the reason for the stacked plastic crates that surrounded Kade in the cart. When the boy climbed down from his higher seat, they were completely hidden from the valley below, but could still see the house through the tops of the vines.

The chills were back, and Kade's teeth chattered under the hot sun as he waited.

"Mirar," the boy said, pointing toward the far end of the valley. A large dust trail billowed from two black SUVs speeding down the main road leading to the boy's home. As they grew closer, Kade spotted a white pickup in the rear, all but obscured in the dust cloud. A ratty canopy covered the pickup's bed.

Kade pointed to the pony and put a finger to his lips. "Keep him quiet." Kade whispered, even though they were a good distance away from the house. "Silencio."

The boy grabbed a handful of the hay and fed it to the animal, who seemed content to rest after the hard climb. Then the boy took one of the bins and started filling it with large bunches of grapes.

Below, the three vehicles reached the house. Doors opened, and several men climbed out. Even from this distance, Kade could make out the black rifles they carried. They entered the house.

"You go," the boy said, pointing to the vineyard. He handed Kade a drink container with a Nike swoop logo on the side, and a cloth bag with strap handles long enough to go over Kade's neck. The bag was filled with grapes. "Go," he said again, motioning toward the rows on the other side of the path and made shooing motions with his hands. Then he turned his back and began filling a basket with more grapes.

Kade slid out the back of the small cart as gently as he could. The boy's meaning was clear enough. If the men came up here, they would find the teenager harvesting grapes and filling the cart. He would say he left Kade sleeping at the house and didn't know where the injured man went.

Still barefoot, Kade wound his way through the old vines, using a leafy branch to obscure his footprints. The most direct path over the hill was straight away from the trail the boy and cart were on. It also put the most greenery between him and anyone who might come up the road.

Thirty minutes later, he stopped and took a sip of the water. He'd forgotten to ask the boy's name, but he offered a prayer of thanks for him. Perhaps someday he could return and thank the young man for saving his life.

Although he still wasn't sure of his location, the fact that the bald man from the American Consulate came so quickly confirmed Kade was indeed near Monterrey. The consulate was supposed to help Americans, but he couldn't risk another encounter with someone who would betray him. He'd have to try for the US border on his own.

The fever intensified as he trudged along, and each footfall jarred his brain like a hammer to his skull. He squinted into the brightness, keeping the hot afternoon rays burning the left side of his face as he limped north.

CHAPTER SEVEN

DIARRHEA STRUCK late in the day after Kade left the boy, each gut-wrenching bout leaving him sweating and dizzy. The water container was empty, so he finished the grapes as he walked. Liquid was critical to ward off dehydration.

When he reached the edge of another vineyard, he reloaded the bag with as many grapes as it could hold, and stood filling his churning stomach while watching the sun descend toward the horizon. Darkness brought safety from suspicious eyes, but also danger from fences, ditches, and roadways. If it was cloudy at night, he couldn't navigate using the stars for direction. Resting during the dark hours made more sense.

He didn't know the weather here, other than the days were hot and muggy, making him long for a hat. His two nights outside were cool, but not cold. At least he probably wouldn't freeze to death, but that didn't make sleeping outdoors without shelter desirable.

After the sun set and last light was nearly gone, Kade found a pump house shed at the edge of a field. The door had disappeared sometime in the past, leaving remnants of rusty hinges on one side of the opening and a latch on the other. The interior was entirely taken up with silent equipment. Still, it was shelter from the evening breeze. He made do by lying across the open entrance, his back against the pump's concrete base still warm from the day. He wasn't sure he could get to his feet in the morning, but he had to sleep.

Shivers came in staggered waves, traveling from his toes to his scalp. Two minutes later, fever replaced the chills and he scooted away from the pump base which was suddenly too hot. How long could a human body survive being broken and sick? Deep inside, he knew tomorrow was crucial.

Sometime later, he woke in the dark, shaking from a nightmare of being dragged from his cell and beaten by faceless men.

"Where are the others?" "Who is your contact?" "Tell me what you know."

During each of those times, he sought out the figure lingering in the shadows: Lilly Hawthorne. Mina Glass. Silently encouraging him to hold on as fists bruised his ribs and whips ripped his flesh. He knew she was a figment, a fabrication of his drugged mind and ruined body, but she was so real, and he held tight to her image.

Kade fought off the lingering memories. He'd been a fool to let her go. If he got out of this…

At first he thought himself drenched in sweat, but then something hit his face, then again. It was raining, and his ragged clothes were soaked through to the hard earth. Cold air from the weather front swirled around him as the rainfall increased. His shivering grew worse.

Moving was essential to avoid hypothermia—if he could get up. He gritted his teeth and forced himself to his hands and knees, then to his feet. Impenetrable darkness stretched in every direction. Raindrops pattered his face and body, and created a soft shushing on the nearby plant leaves.

Although he needed to move, he couldn't just set off walking into the night. Keeping one hand on the small structure, he hobbled around it until he reached large pipes that blocked his way. He turned around and circled the other way until he came to the same pipes. He reversed again.

He wasn't sure how long he kept moving, but eventually the rain and wind stopped, and he lowered himself to the muddy earth. It was then he knew he'd never make it to the US border without help. Trusted help. For that, he needed a phone. And that meant risking himself again to strangers.

It was that or die.

By the time the sun peeked over the hills, Kade's shivers had increased to the point he was afraid he might break a tooth. A clanking noise roused him enough to spot two workmen using tools on a section of pipe about fifty feet from where he lay. Unable to speak without biting his tongue, he began crawling toward them.

The exertion cleared his head—or maybe it was the pain. Whichever, his blood pounded in his ears when he saw the men gathering up their tools and putting them into the back of an off-road utility vehicle.

Lying on his side, he lifted his left arm and began waving. As the men climbed into the vehicle, one glanced his way and pointed.

Kade dropped his arm, exhausted from the short journey. His teeth still rattled in his head, but he had to stay conscious. If these men called the authorities, he was dead.

Or worse.

CHAPTER EIGHT

BEEPING noises were the first thing Kade recognized. He opened his eyes to muted lighting, chrome bedrails, and the soft cream walls of a hospital room. Curled in a chair to his right was his mother. He must have made a noise, because she was at his side in seconds.

"Kade?" Her brows were scrunched together with worry, relief, maybe anger.

"Where...?" he managed. She raised the bed so he could sip from a glass.

"Houston, Texas," she said. "You've been unconscious for days." And then the tears flowed. "Oh, Kade. They told us you...you..." The tears choked away her voice as her fingers hovered over his face, his hair, as if she were afraid to touch him.

He was already being drawn back under when his dad came in a few minutes later, followed by his little sister, Rowan. His father's mouth was tight with control, but gave nothing away. Not so with Rowan. As soon as Kade saw her expression, he knew things were worse than he thought.

"I want a mirror," Kade told his father the next afternoon when it was just the two of them. His parents had been cryptic about his injuries, the doctors even more so. This morning, one of the nurses had adjusted an IV feed when he demanded answers and became agitated. It was lights out after that.

He was more aware now, enough to notice the increased gray in his dad's hair and the deep lines in his mother's face.

"And I want to know how long I've been gone." When his father hesitated, Kade said, "Dad, I need to know."

His dad sighed, then said, "You disappeared over six weeks ago." Then, he cleared his throat. "The FBI told us you were dead."

"We had a memorial service for you," Rowan said the next day when they were alone.

"Really?" He hadn't thought about them doing anything like that. "How was it?"

"Kinda sad," she said, "but the food was excellent." The corner of her mouth quirked.

They laughed, but emotion brushed the surface, and her voice held the same shudder as their mom's. Six weeks. He couldn't imagine the pain they suffered, the first weeks of not knowing, then believing he was dead. What was it like to accept that and try to go on with life?

As they talked, he realized how much he'd missed of Rowan's growing up these last few years. Even as a preteen, she showed an abundance of confidence in everything, especially sports. Now twenty-one, she was a beautiful young woman with a bold approach to life.

Their twelve-year age difference was a disadvantage. She'd been busy with high school and college, and his career with the bureau—at least his specific assignments—tended to be all-consuming. Important work, yes, but he regretted time away from his family.

Maybe a near-death experience was always a wake-up call, an opportunity to reevaluate and make changes. Family was important.

He didn't remember his first words that day when his mom accepted his collect phone call from Mexico. Just hearing her voice was such an intense relief it felt like half his pain went away right that moment.

Now, thanks to medication, the pain truly was at a low level, a dull constant reminder of his body's trauma. This morning, for the first time, he realized how much weight he'd lost. His arms were limp skin hanging on bones, and his legs were two thin branches between his bandaged hips and wrapped feet. They looked like twin Q-Tips under the sheet. He still hadn't seen himself in a mirror.

"I guess I look pretty bad, huh?"

"It's gonna be a while before Hollywood calls," she said, the vertical line of concern on her brow so like their mother's.

"Can you find me a mirror?" His father had managed to avoid fulfilling Kade's request yesterday. Perhaps his sister was an easier sell.

Rowan bit her lip. "Are you sure?"

He nodded. She hesitated, then left the room and returned a minute later with a handheld mirror.

He took it from her and turned it toward his face.

"They say most of it will heal," she said, but her voice lacked conviction.

Kade knew why. He studied what he could see of his scalp, his face, his right ear, his chin. The skin looked like it had been scraped with a cheese grater. Those were evidently the *least* damaged areas, because bandages covered most of the left side of his face. His skin was red with a bad sunburn on top of it all. He breathed a sigh of thanks for modern pain medications.

The doctor assigned to oversee his treatment had been by earlier and told him they operated as soon as he arrived at the hospital, putting pins in his broken pelvis. They splinted his broken left hand and immobilized his broken ankles. Nothing could be cast because of the road abrasions. The doctor was cautious about his mobility and pain in the joints after he healed, but one thing the man was certain about: it was a miracle Kade had been able to walk at all when he escaped.

"They're planning plastic surgery," Rowan said. "Got anyone special you want to look like?"

He gave her points for trying to make light, but she wasn't fooling him. He couldn't see his back, but the doctor had mentioned there were a lot of overlapping scars—evidence of severe whippings that split the flesh again and again. Some stripes had healed badly; others were still fresh. No plastic surgery could fix that. And there were other torture scars. Some of those memories were becoming less fuzzy. That wasn't a good thing.

"George Clooney?" he suggested.

"Umm," she said, putting a finger to her lips and tilting her head to the side. "Clooney might be a stretch. I think more like Morgan Freeman."

"Ouch, Rowan. Give a guy a break when he's down."

His sister sank into the chair, her bravado draining out of her face as her eyes grew shiny.

"Hey, sis. It's over. I made it back. Now I just have to get well."

"It was a drug cartel, wasn't it? Was it the same one you fought protecting that girl, Lilly Hawthorne?"

Hearing her name from Rowan shocked him. He'd never told his family about his relationship with Lilly, if he could call it that. She and Kris Stone had stopped in Boston to see him after his transfer, but the visit had been brief, only a couple of days. Lilly had changed her name to Palomino Glass by then, and was on her way to Paris to study art. He never introduced her to his family.

And afterward, although he and Lilly spoke on the phone or video many times in the following months, their nine-year age difference bothered him. Actually, it was more the fact she was just out of high school at the time and only three years older than Rowan. The distance across the Atlantic made it easier for him to pull back a little, and when his work assignments widened the gap, he didn't fight it.

Yet always present just below the surface was that same unexplainable pull he felt on that first visit to her in the hospital after her kidnapping. It took him a long time to admit it was attraction on a deep level, and by the time he realized what it was, too much time had passed to fix things. Lilly had moved on with studies, travel, and new friends. And he…well, there was always a new, pressing assignment with the FBI. It was true: guys were idiots. He, the top dog.

"You're thinking of her, aren't you?" Rowan said quietly.

He didn't try to deny it. Simply nodded. Everything had changed with this last assignment. Somewhere in Mexico, Lilly Hawthorne had resurfaced in his subconscious mind and become his focal point. The beatings and interrogations were indistinct, thank God, but her image was seared in his mind. He recalled the shape of her nose, her eyes, the cadence of her speech, and the two tiny freckles under her left eye. She was a big part of his survival.

Where was she now? Still in Paris? He should have visited her there. He needed to find her and explain.

As soon as he got well.

"Mr. Hunt?" a nurse said from the doorway. "There are two men here from the FBI who would like to speak with you."

CHAPTER NINE

"KADEN HUNT?" The bigger of the two men approached Kade's bed and reached out to shake his hand. Then, after seeing the bandages, awkwardly pulled it back. "I'm ASAC Amory. I work out of the DC office."

The Assistant Special Agent in Charge wore the regulation FBI suit and tie, polished black shoes, and trimmed hair. In spite of his ruddy complexion, any perp could spot him in a crowd in under a second. Amory introduced the other man as Mr. Fowler in an offhand way that communicated his subservient position.

Fowler, several inches shorter and as many years older, wore a suit similar to Amory, but it was cut perfectly for his trim frame. He was classically bald on top with a ring of gray hair around the back. He carried a briefcase, and looked as if he'd never seen a field day in his life.

"We're glad to have you back, Mr. Hunt," Amory said.

It didn't escape Kade that Amory hadn't referred to him as Special Agent. He supposed that wouldn't be appropriate for an agent declared dead.

"We've been looking for you for a long time, haven't we, Fowler?"

Amory swiveled to the other agent, but then back to Kade before Fowler had an opportunity to agree or contradict.

"Was it the agency that told my family I was dead?" Kade asked. It was nearing time for his next pain medication, and his body was growing twitchy, like too much caffeine after an all-nighter. He shifted, trying to get the weight off his sensitive left hip.

"Well, uh, yes," Amory said. "We received a report from a source in Mexico that you had, uh, expired. The Executive Assistant Director for Human Resources thought it best to move ahead—for your family's sake, of course." He shrugged, as if it were the obvious decision.

Maybe it was. But Amory made it sound like they had been sitting around waiting to hear something. Had anyone been actively looking? Did they try to confirm his death from a second source?

No, that was unfair. Of course they had.

Amory shifted his weight from leg to leg under Kade's gaze. At first the man was a little too upbeat, but now he presented as nervous, perhaps wanting to be anywhere but here in Kade's room. Kade understood that. Some in the bureau did better speaking to family and victims than others.

However, speaking to a fellow agent shouldn't be a problem. Something was off. Amory's cheery demeanor felt artificial. Most would ask about Kade's escape—that's what *he* would do—but Amory hadn't even asked how Kade was feeling. Maybe he'd received a briefing from the doctor.

"My memory's a little fuzzy on what happened, ASAC Amory. Can you help me out?"

"Sure, sure. What would you like to know?"

Again Kade thought Amory a little too anxious to please. "What was my mission when I disappeared? Maybe it'll help jog my memory." He remembered it was an opportunity for a big assignment, something in conjunction with DEA in Los Angeles and San Diego. Everything beyond that was a blur.

"I'm afraid that's classified, Hunt. You're no longer in the need to know."

"I see," Kade said, suspecting the answer was tied to the dropping of his title in the bureau. "Can you tell me where this operation took place?"

"Afraid not, Hunt. You know how it is."

Kade didn't know, but he was putting the pieces together.

"Are you here to debrief me?"

Amory shook his head. "Old news, I'm afraid. No longer relevant."

Behind Amory's back, Fowler flinched at his partner's choice of words. It was quick, but Kade caught it. No matter that Kade put his life on the line, he was no longer on the team, and that meant no longer privy to information—not even about what he experienced firsthand.

"Then I guess my last question is, why are you here? Or is that classified too?" He couldn't stop the sarcasm from creeping into the question.

Amory rocked on his heels and glanced at Fowler in a way that telecast his unease. Amory would be a disaster in an interrogation situation.

Fowler cleared his throat and stepped forward. He set his briefcase on the food tray table, snapped open the brass locks, and removed a sheaf of papers.

"We're here, Mr. Hunt, to process your severance from the FBI."

Kade's face heated. They weren't interested in any results from the operation, or how he ended up being taken captive. Had other agents or assets been captured? Tortured? If there had been other team members who got away, maybe they already knew all this. Or perhaps this approach he was seeing today was the level of effort they put into finding him. If Amory had been the one in charge of the operation, no wonder it went south. Kade could hear the man's incompetence dripping on the hospital tile floor.

"What if I want to stay on with the agency? The doctors are optimistic about my full recovery." It wasn't really a lie. The docs *were* encouraging, at least about his survival. As for regaining his full physical abilities, well, they were more guarded about that.

Amory glanced at Fowler, then retreated a step more. A clear passing of the lead if Kade ever saw one. The little man was taking charge.

"I'm afraid that's not an option, Mr. Hunt," Fowler said. He tapped the papers. "You'll find everything in order to reverse the unfortunate declaration of your passing, as well as checks for your back salary and accrued vacation. You'll receive twelve months of medical insurance plus a stipend for living expenses while you're in recovery. An especially generous package, if I do say so." He actually rocked on his heels a couple of times before catching his self-satisfaction.

Kade tried to take it all in as Fowler thumbed through the papers and passed each stapled set to Kade. He didn't look at them.

"I don't understand," he said. "Why don't I have the opportunity to continue with the bureau? My performance reviews have been excellent."

"Yes, of course," Fowler said. "Unfortunately, this decision came from top levels, so there's nothing I can do." He picked up the papers and tapped them into a neat pack, then set them down again and continued on as if Kade hadn't interrupted his presentation. "There is, of course, the standard confidentiality agreement regarding your part in the operation. You agree not to discuss your activities or the bureau's part in those activities."

"If I knew what those were," Kade said, directing the words at Amory, who turned to stare out the window.

"We have a notary waiting in the hall when you're ready." Fowler laid a pen on the table beside the papers, then snapped the clasps on his briefcase. He held it in front of him by the handle, waiting.

Fowler was standing too close to the bed for Kade to see whether he was impatiently tapping the toe of his shoe. Kade purposely stared at the man for a full minute, but received no response. A bureaucrat doing his job, regardless of circumstances or the unfortunate impact on people's lives. Those weren't important. Only the successful completion of the task at hand mattered.

As distasteful as Fowler was, Amory was worse: an *incompetent* bureaucrat. Maybe that was too harsh, but Kade had always been able to spot a phony. Like every organization, the bureau practiced the Peter Principle, and had its share of people promoted one step above their competency. Kade had to wonder how many levels above competency Amory was.

"I would like a review of this situation," Kade said.

"Not possible, Hunt," Amory stated. "Just sign the papers." Fowler picked up the pen and offered it to Kade.

The nurse arrived and went straight to the heart rate monitor. The beeping had increased in frequency. "Everything all right, Mr. Hunt?" she asked, checking the screen. "Do you need more pain medication?"

"Let's wait a few minutes," Kade said, taking a deep breath. The ache in his left hand had intensified, and he forced himself to unclench his fingers as he observed the two men. "Nurse, I wonder if you could call my parents to come in?"

The nurse left after admonishing the two men to keep their visit short.

"Why do you need your parents, Hunt?" Amory said.

"Because legally I'm still dead, Mr. Amory." The man bristled at Kade's drop of his agent title. For men like him, title, rank, and seniority were everything. "I'm not sure my signature would count for much."

"There's no need for that, Hunt," Amory said, dropping all pretense of civility. "We have the papers right here that certify you're still alive."

"Plus," Kade said, "I want to ask my father to locate an employment attorney."

The nurse returned and said his parents were on their way. She took a position by the monitors.

Amory wasn't through. "We can get this all done right now. You'll walk away with a check." Amory didn't even realize the stupidity of his words. Kade wasn't walking anywhere for quite a while.

"I think that's enough, gentlemen," the nurse said, getting

confirmation from Kade. "Mr. Hunt needs to rest." She spread her arms to usher them out.

Before moving, Fowler reached for the unsigned papers. Kade put his hand on them. "I'll hang on to these. Look them over. That is what you want, right?"

The men stepped back, but hesitated at the room exit.

"Goodbye, gentlemen," the nurse said, and closed the door in their faces. "Those two are a piece of work," she muttered as she administered the next dose of medication. "Not that it's any of my business."

Kade's eyelids grew heavy as the pain slithered back to its lair in Neverland. But even the strong medicine couldn't remove the bad taste in his mouth.

CHAPTER TEN

Eight weeks later

"COME ON, GLASS, MOVE, MOVE, *MOVE!*"

Mina sprinted along the gray building, out of breath from a hundred-yard run and zigzagging around a dozen low walls. Without slowing, she dove to the ground, rolling twice to her right and coming to a stop in a prone shooting position. Only the rifle muzzle and the right side of her face extended past the building's corner. Dust swirled and burned her nostrils as she held her breath, sighted, and squeezed the trigger. The AR-15 bucked twice against her shoulder as each .223 bullet left the barrel and struck the cardboard target ten yards away.

She swung a few degrees right and snapped two more at the more distant second target, then carefully fired again at the third black figure, half hidden behind a bush at a hundred yards.

After that sixth shot, she rolled left behind the safety of the structure.

Before she had a chance to take a breath, her instructor shouted, "Get going! Bad guys ain't gonna wait for you to sunbathe!"

She scrambled to her feet, fighting the stiff tactical vest strapped with four extra magazines, a seven-inch fighting knife, and a set of four throwing blades. Across from her position was another wall with doors mounted every ten feet. One of them opened, revealing a dummy pointing a gun at her. He was only twenty feet away, and her two rounds punched holes high in the thorax.

A second door opened and a target popped out on a spring. Mina pivoted and pulled the trigger, but nothing happened. While her brain was still processing the misfire, she instinctively released the rifle, drew her Glock 19, and fired four times while crab-walking right.

"You're hit in the right arm!" her instructor shouted. Mina dropped the pistol. Per their protocol, her right arm was now useless. A second later, another door opened revealing a female target clad in tactical gear and holding a rifle.

"Shots fired!" the instructor yelled, indicating the female was shooting at Mina.

She rolled onto her "injured" right arm, at the same time pulling out one of the throwing knives with her left hand. Throwing left handed was her weakest skill, and the knife bounced harmlessly hilt-first off the target's vest. But Mina's next blade caught the woman on the side of her throat. Seizing the opportunity, Mina drew her KA-BAR fighting knife and rushed forward, plunging it deep under the lower edge of the target's vest.

A buzzer sounded, concluding the modified run and gun exercise. Mina wrenched the knife free and rotated 360 degrees, seeking any new threat from her crouched position. *Never think the fight is over.* She learned that the first day with this instructor.

"Not bad, Glass. At least you didn't die—this time."

Coming from Rowdy Haines, that was high praise. She dropped onto her butt and leaned against the building façade.

The range master where Mina first went shooting had pointed Haines out as a trainer. The man was a mountain, close to 300 pounds, with tattooed biceps as large as her thighs. His skin was the texture of an angry horned toad. Most days his personality matched it.

A former United States Marine, Haines "...*did unspeakable things*" —at least, that's what the bio on his website boasted. Mina didn't know if he was blowing smoke about that, but when it came to combat scenarios, everything he taught her was practical and made perfect sense.

When she first introduced herself at the range, he growled, "*Go away.*" Instead, she stepped forward until her chest nearly touched his belt buckle, looked up, and said, "*Make me.*" That got her a smile and a handshake. Or maybe it was a returned challenge.

He'd done his best to break her for the last two months. Four days a week, sometimes five, whenever he wasn't training "*some CIA spooks*"—his words. By week two, she believed everything his bio stated was true, and probably much more that remained classified.

Typical run and gun exercises were repeated over and over, focusing on accuracy and a faster time. While that might be fine in competition against other shooters, Haines didn't believe that was best for real life, or for Mina.

After the first session so he could get the feel of her abilities, every run-through he devised was unique. Different doors opened, targets were set at varying ranges, and she never knew when a gun would misfire. It was up to her to pick which weapon best matched each encounter.

Some events were at night using laser pistols, others were with a team of four or five—mentally taxing due to having to make sure she didn't shoot an innocent.

A month ago when the temperature dropped into the 50s, he hosed her down with cold water and let her shiver in the desert breeze for fifteen minutes. Then he sent her through three run and guns with blinding flash bangs and smoke bombs obscuring the bad guys. It was grueling, especially after he drenched her again and muddied up the ground before the final round. She slipped and fell several times, burying the muzzle of her rifle in the mud once. The only way to clear it was to put the barrel in her mouth and suck the mud out. Slightly unnerving, but she'd had to recover quickly and come up fighting.

Everything after that night seemed easier. She learned to be her best when the situation was at its worst. *"That's when you win, and they lose,"* Haines drilled into her. Still, as much as she appreciated the progress, she was thankful it was too warm to freeze or snow.

The stiff vest cut into her stomach as she tried to rise.

"You all right, Glass, or you want I should call 9-1-1?"

She wasn't convinced he'd do it even if she *were* dying. "I've had worse," she croaked on the dry desert air. Haines laughed and extended his right hand. They grasped wrists and he hauled her up from the hard clay.

The bulky vest was a necessary evil too. The weight, heat, and even the reeking sweat-stink from other wearers before her were all part of her conditioning. *"There is no comfort in combat,"* Haines growled. *"Let the other guy get comfortable while you kick his ass."*

"Are we going again?" she asked, dusting off her tactical pants.

"Nah. That's six times through, and it's pretty hot today."

Her jaw dropped. "Since when has my comfort been a concern?" she said, jumping to catch up with him as he headed to the cars.

Haines raised his eyebrows. "Not you. *I* don't want to get overheated. I have a date tonight. *That's* when I want to get overheated...if you catch my drift."

Mina extended her palm toward him. "TMI, lover boy. Don't ruin my boy scout image of you."

He laughed again. They reached his truck. He folded down the tailgate and ran a cleaning rag over the AR while she removed her noise-cancelling earbuds. A few of their sessions were without hearing protection, because guns were louder than people expected, particularly indoors. Being surprised by a gun's sharp report wasn't good, and self-defense situations didn't lend themselves to leisurely prep time to find earplugs.

Cool air washed over her back when she released the buckles of the vest and it fell away from her wet shirt. He took it from her and tossed it into the bed of the truck. Next came the tactical belt with the holstered Glock and extra mags. The big knife and throwing knives were hers, picked up at a local pawnshop.

Haines locked the guns in cases, each padlock clicking loudly in the quiet of the desert. Their vehicles were the only ones at the shooting site today, but it wasn't uncommon for a few of his buddies to drop by. All were former military, quick to give another a hard time about which branch they were from or in what hellhole they'd fought. Usually Mina remained silent, watching and learning. Their reliance on each other, the bond they shared, made her aware of how alone she was in facing what was ahead.

"I'll be gone next week," she said, coming to a decision.

"A sudden trip?"

"Property hunt. Maybe moving altogether if I find the right vantage point." She was dithering about what to do next. *Make up your mind.*

Haines didn't look up from stowing his personal sidearm. The instructors always carried. "So, this is our last week?" Was that a hint of disappointment from him?

"Yeah." Decision made.

"You gonna be all right?"

She'd given him a few hints of what was coming so he wouldn't baby her in training. She shrugged. "We'll see."

He turned and leaned against the lowered tailgate of his pickup, crossing his arms and staring toward the mountains, their peaks bright from the fleeing westerly sun. "When's this going down?"

"Summer. Probably July." The 14th, if all went well. Her mother's birthday. She leaned on the tailgate beside him.

"Legal?"

Mina smiled. It was the same question Kris had asked. "Let's call it *off the books*. Self-defense. Ending the threat."

He nodded, rubbing a hand over the coarse stubble that was a constant feature of his jaw. "Some of the guys...well, we get bored these days, you know? We're always looking to do something interesting. If it's a good cause."

She was silent for a minute, the only sound a jet passing high above. "Paid?"

"Highly."

Professionals, then. "They as good as you, Haines?"

He laughed at that. "Ain't nobody as good as me, Glass. Don't you know that by now?"

It was her turn to laugh...but she didn't. Rowdy Haines was one of the good guys, a man who had served his country, risked his life, willingly given up part of his soul for the sake of the nation.

Mina pushed off the truck and walked a couple of paces, then turned to face him. He met her gaze. It wasn't that the humor in their banter had died, rather like sobriety was now layered on top.

Men like him—and women—became who they needed to be for the job their government asked. Then, when they came home, tried to step back into a society that had no need for many of their skills. It became their responsibility to change back, to fit in, to slough off all they'd worked so hard to be. That wasn't so easy.

In a far smaller way, Mina had gone from a subsistence-level childhood to being adopted by *the* Hollywood power couple, however, she'd never felt completely natural in that world. Her experience was far from what Rowdy Haines and his military buddies had endured, but it gave her a toehold on the wall of understanding.

Some men and women served, got out, and went back to relatively normal lives. For Haines and his friends, their experiences had carved them into people who *couldn't* just go back. They were fundamentally changed, but found a way to forge a balance between everyday life and occasional episodes of supreme challenge.

And now he was willing to gather a team of like-minded guys and help her. But it was important they understand the risks before going all in.

"They *need* to be as good as you, Rowdy." She hadn't used his first name before, and it captured his attention. "I don't want anyone *else* dying for me."

That got his attention even more.

It also earned her a smile.

CHAPTER ELEVEN

"I'm just saying, Glass, you're gonna hate Seattle."

Mina ignored Haines as they walked to her truck in the parking lot of the discrete bungalows, her home for the last month. She stowed the final small box behind the seat of her 1989 Toyota pickup and closed the passenger door. The sun hadn't topped the mountains yet, but the night cooling had fled. She flapped the front of her T-shirt to get some air moving.

"You sure this heap will make it all that way?" Haines said, sliding her other suitcase into the bed and shutting the tailgate. Together, they stretched the vinyl tonneau cover and snapped it around the bed's perimeter.

"Don't dis my new truck," Mina said, but she noticed a few of the snaps were tearing out of the material. She hoped it would survive the trip.

"New? This thing hasn't been new since Reagan was president."

Mina shot him a look. Her third day in Phoenix, she found the pickup languishing on two flat, cobwebbed tires in front of a house a block from the motel. Its dash and seat covers were cracked and blistered after years under the unrelenting sun. She bought it on a whim and had a mechanic go through it top to bottom. An upholstery shop replaced the dash, seat covers, and carpeting. After a detail shop finished the interior, it smelled like it just rolled off the dealership lot. She would have had it painted after she got settled.

The little truck had a factory sunroof and a vintage cassette deck complete with a box of tapes. Sitting in it for the first time reminded her of her mom—her old mom—reading about the three bears, where Baby Bear's things were just the right size for Goldilocks. The truck fit her.

"Why don't you just do your planning from here?" Haines said. "Grayson and his wife have that guesthouse."

"I've got things to do in Seattle, Haines." But the real reason she didn't want to stay with Jim Grayson was that he was one of their team possibilities. Mina didn't want to meet the wife of one of the men who would risk his life for her. If something went wrong…

She climbed into the truck and started the engine. Haines squeezed his head and one massive shoulder through the open passenger window as the radio came on.

"Good morning, Arizonans! Well, the Valley of the Sun is earning its reputation early this year. We're looking at a high of 102 today, and 104 tomorrow. Time to break out the sunscreen and those door handle wraps so you don't get burned."

Mina turned down the volume and pointed at the radio. "That's another reason, Haines. If I wasn't leaving, we'd be out on the training range this afternoon and this heat would kill me. Or you would."

He laughed it off, and said, "Call me when you have your base set up. I'll text you details about the team and their skills." He held out his massive paw.

Mina took it, but didn't let go after the simple shake. She pulled herself across the seat and surprised him by kissing him on the cheek. "Thanks, Rowdy. For everything."

He nodded, his face reddening a bit. Then he dug in his pocket. "I've got something for you." He handed her a plastic square about two inches on each side. A small spring clip was attached to one corner. "It's a fob for your truck keys."

She turned it over in her palm. Fused beneath the smooth plastic of each side was a picture of an angel. But this wasn't some Renaissance age, golden-haired, pink-cheeked cherub with a halo. The stunning female in profile had her eyes closed in complete serenity. A complex dark gold comb held her raven hair back from the side of her face, and her long black eyelashes rested on perfect skin. Luxurious feathers of blacks, grays, and whites covered four massive wings that swept forward, cradling her body and extending above her head. The monochrome feathers stood out against the background pink hues of a morning sky.

"It's beautiful." She immediately envisioned a full-sized version sandblasted into a glass panel. For her future home, if she survived the next few months.

"My grandmother believes in angels," he said, his voice rough in a different way from his standard growl. "Says they kept me safe and brought me home each time."

"Thank you," Mina said. Instead of hooking it to the ignition keys, she clipped the angel on the rearview mirror arm.

Haines backed out of the truck window and cleared his throat. "You take care, Palomino Glass. Don't get dead before we get there, promise?"

It was her turn to nod.

Then she was pulling away. In her rearview mirror, right above the beautiful angel, Rowdy Haines walked to the center of the motel driveway and waved. In response, Mina lifted her right hand.

If all went well, there was only one person who would *get dead*.

CHAPTER TWELVE

Adversity builds strength, and strength overwhelms adversity.

FLAME OF HOPE, BY V.M. NARRANO

EVIE SAT behind the desk at her Hollywood office. Deidre Wilson, her assistant, sat across from her, reporting on everything Evie had missed while out with *"the flu."*

The truth was worse than influenza: appointments at Cedars-Sinai Cancer Center, meetings with doctors and discussing new treatment options now that the first rounds hadn't worked.

"The Mansfield property passed inspection, but the buyer wants the pool resurfaced," Deidre said. "He claims there are cracks. That's an Olympic-sized pool, and it would cost a fortune. The seller is balking. Angelique is mediating."

Evie stared out the window, her mind reeling with chemo drug names, radiation doses, treatment schedules, and surgery options that could leave her incapacitated for days or weeks.

"Steven wants to call in an engineer to do an analysis on the hillside above the Brainer estate. That could take weeks and hold up the listing."

Weren't doctors supposed to be optimistic, cheering the patient on? Hers were anything but.

"Mason Carlisle turned in her resignation," Deidre continued. "That was no surprise after I spotted a billboard yesterday with her picture and *The Carlisle Group* plastered underneath. She's going into direct competition with us, despite the non-compete clause in her contract. Do you think we should file suit?"

"I'm sorry, but I have to advise you to get your affairs in order." He was the least optimistic of the doctors, so maybe that was good. Down deep, she feared he was also the most realistic.

Affairs. How did one even begin such a task? She had no family to bequeath things to, no one she really cared about.

Magda, Ernesto, Tommy, and Roberto stuck together because they were family. And when their father grafted Evie into their fold, they included her. In return, she grew up, studied finance and real estate, and worked for years putting layers of protection in place for their investments and real estate holdings.

Now they were all gone, and there was no one left to care about *her.*

What did it matter if her bank account was balanced or her car payment made? Her house would be sold to the highest bidder, her clothing and personal belongings fought over or sent to shelters.

In the beginning, this kind of independence was what she wanted. Now…she was alone.

"Evie?" Deidre was tapping a folder on the desk. "Are you feeling all right?"

"Sorry," Evie said, suppressing a laugh at the absurdity of the question. She sat up straighter. "Yes, what?"

"We need your decision on the Bennet commercial property. Seven buildings. Are we going to sell it en bloc, or set it up as individual listings? Personally, I think separating them is the right way to go. I calculate we could make an extra million if we maximize each sale. Do you agree?"

Did she? An extra million made no difference at this point. Outside of their work together in the office, Evie knew nothing of this woman. Did she have aspirations of one day filling Evie's position? Perhaps she wanted to travel abroad, have a family, divorce her husband. Was Deidre even married? With stark clarity, Evie realized she cared nothing about any of this. Not this woman. Not this office. Certainly not about cracks in a swimming pool.

Only family mattered, and Lilly Hawthorne had taken everyone from Evie. She'd been right to set Slade personally on the hunt.

She rose from her chair, instinctively picking up the stack of work folders to take with her. She shook her head and tossed them back onto the desk. One slid off the edge, scattering Deidre's carefully organized papers across the Berber carpet.

"I'm leaving," Evie said. She kicked her briefcase aside, then gathered only her purse.

"But...what about the Bennet property and the others?" Deidre rose, fumbling more folders as Evie headed for the door. "Evie?"

Evie stopped at the doorway and turned to her assistant. The office, once her domain, was only walls, furniture, and a potted palm. Weight lifted from her shoulders.

"Do whatever you want," Evie said.

"But I can't do all this by myself," Deidre whined.

"Adversity builds strength, and strength overwhelms adversity," Evie whispered.

A line formed on Deidre's forehead. "What?"

Evie turned away and strode across the lobby, ignoring hellos and goodbyes from employees. There was one thing left in this life that mattered, and she had a phone call to make.

It was time to send another message.

CHAPTER THIRTEEN

IN THE TWO weeks since Mina arrived in Seattle, it hadn't stopped raining for more than an hour. Of course, locals called it drizzle and claimed media bias about the city's damp weather. How many interviews had she watched where experts tried to convince themselves it didn't really rain that much in Seattle, and the real culprit was clouds and bleak days?

Mina swiped water from her face as she sprinted to her condo. She'd signed a two-year lease on a sunny day a couple of years ago, lured by the location on a west-facing hillside with a view of Lake Sammamish. Mostly, it was an admission that she could never return to Los Angeles, but the condo's modern style appealed to her, and it had been perfect while she set up her glass studio in a nearby industrial area.

Summer was spectacular, but by the end of the first full month of a dreary fall, she admitted to being a weather prima donna. Lake Sammamish's brilliant blue had become a permanent slate gray, and the condo's view windows were streaked with moisture or out and out rain. While an effective shot in one of her dad's movies, the wet glass depressed her, and more art classes while drying out in southern Italy sounded perfect. All of her studio equipment went into storage, and she found a professional woman to take over the lease payments.

Although she had intended to return to Seattle the following summer, she just *had* to see Paris again. And then a chance introduction to Kristen had her heading to Berlin. Two years had flown by. Then the woman who subleased the condo had bought a place of her own, and Mina's home sat empty.

Her cell phone rang, the display showing *Kris Stone*.

"Hi, Kris," Mina said, setting down her bags on the counter. "I just got back from the electronics store. I think I got everything Proxy recommended." Proxy was the code name of a hacker Kris had recruited. According to Kris, Proxy was a *technical wiz dedicated to securing justice for those who were wronged*. Maybe a little superhero, but it sounded good.

"Perfect. Proxy said plug your new phone into its charger, then turn it on. Text her the IMEI number on the box and she'll do the rest."

The *rest* was tying the phone to an encryption network that automatically bounced any outgoing calls off a series of repeaters around the world. Mina didn't know the magic behind it all, but was assured the originating location of the call was completely hidden. It worked the same for incoming calls.

"Now—" Kris said, but her next words rattled like a handful of syllables in a steel barrel.

"Where are you?" Mina asked. Two days ago, Kris was at a job in Texas.

"Sorry." The connection cleared, but still had occasional garbles. "We just landed in Dubai with a small site survey team, but I'll be back in the states in a few days. I was asking if you found a new place."

Arab Emirates was probably twenty plus hours travel time from California. Omron International was living up to its name.

As Kris predicted, Tanner had turned down Mina's proposal for Omron to help her confront the Viera threat. Losing three men the last time had been a huge blow to the company, and she couldn't blame him for saying no. But it had all worked out. She met Haines the next day.

"I'm leaving in a couple of days to check out possibilities," Mina said. "Hope to have something soon." Actually, Mina's requisites were simple: studio space, living space nearby, and a creative environment. Close to Los Angeles, but not too close.

"I'll be done with this assignment next week, so let me know where to find you. What about the team this Haines guy is rounding up?"

Mina could tell by Kris's snippy tone she still wasn't a fan of Rowdy Haines, nor of having a bunch of strangers running around. The braggadocio on his training website hadn't helped one bit.

"He texted yesterday. He's got two. Plus himself, of course."

"Then that makes two total," Kris muttered.

Mina laughed. "I'm telling you, Kris, Haines is a good guy. You'll be impressed."

"Uh, huh. So, what about your plan to draw this Viera threat out?"

At least Kris had stopped calling it *"your* stupid *plan."* Maybe she was warming to the concept. "Still working that out."

"You don't trust me enough to tell me? Or do you think I'll say it's nuts?"

Mina sighed. When the taunting part of the plan executed, *everyone* would think she was nuts. Especially her father—who she still needed to call.

Her phone rang again an hour later when she was unbolting the gun safe in her master bedroom closet. Normally, she went days without a call, but today was a regular telethon. *Fin Silvan* showed on the display.

"Hi, Fin. Good to hear from you." After serving as one of her bodyguards back when the Vieras attacked, Fin resigned from Omron and became head of security for her father.

"Hi, Mina. How is Berlin?"

"Actually, I'm at my condo in Seattle. What's up?"

"Some bad news, I'm afraid."

Mina sat back, besieged by memories from seven years ago, and the more recent ones from Berlin.

"We received another message yesterday. I thought you'd like to know "

"What did it say?"

"Essentially the same as the others: *Tell Lilly Hawthorne I haven't forgotten.*"

The messages—threats—had been sent regularly to her dad for a year or so after the Vieras died. Then they grew more sporadic, showing up five times over the next two years. They stopped about four years ago. Mina rubbed the tight spot on her forehead. First the attack in Berlin, now this.

"It's probably nothing, Mina. And don't worry, we're tightening security around your father."

It wasn't *nothing*, not after Berlin. She didn't want to tell Fin about that attack, but she had to make sure her dad was safe. "I...received a message, too, Fin."

His voice took on a hardness borne of years of security work. "What did it say?"

"Let's just say it was direct and crystal clear." She chose her words carefully. "Someone followed Dad to Florida, then saw me and tracked me to Berlin."

"What happened? Are you safe? I can organize a team."

"No," she said, putting strength behind the word. "I hired a team to get me out of there. And I have a team here in the states." A slight exaggeration. Haines wasn't technically with her, but he was coming soon. And Kris too.

"Mina—"

"Fin, you know how Dad gets. He'll hire an army and pack me off to an igloo in Nome. I'm not doing that. Clear?" She'd never been this direct with Fin, but this was important to her.

A sigh came across the line. "What do you want me to do? Your father needs to know."

"I'm giving up the condo here in Seattle. I'll call him as soon as I get settled in a new place. I'm safe, and I know he's heading out again on a shoot, right? I don't want him to worry."

"We're leaving tonight for Toronto," Fin confirmed. "Are you sure?"

"I'm in touch with Kris Stone. We have a plan. It's still rough, so give me a little time to flesh it out, okay?"

Fin reluctantly agreed to let her lead the communications with her dad.

"And please, Fin. Keep him safe."

Mina retrieved her Seecamp .32 caliber semi-automatic from the box. The palm-sized gun was as clean as she left it before heading for Italy. She loaded one magazine for the pistol, then four spares. Kris had laughed at the weapon's diminutive size when she first saw it, appalled it didn't even have sights. The little gun was designed for close range defense, but Mina had won Kris's respect during a shooting contest.

Even after all the time away, the little gun felt at home in her hand, a result of hours and hours of practice. However, it was visualization that filled the time between live shooting sessions.

She closed her eyes and pictured the scenarios.

In restaurants, she kept the exits, kitchen, and bathrooms in view while she ate. She mentally rehearsed everything, prioritizing first movements, memorizing innocents around her, and constructing exit plans.

Grocery stores often provided overhead mirrors for sighting down aisles. Parking lots, with all their places to hide, were especially dangerous. Driving required constant vigilance. Who were in the cars to her left and right? Was the SUV in front slowing down to block her in? How long had that silver sedan been following? Where was the nearest turn or freeway exit? All that in addition to avoiding the normal crazies on the road.

She had twenty different settings memorized, everything from restaurants to sidewalks to movie theaters. Even a church. Like a skier visualizing a giant slalom race, Mina's head turned and tilted with each movement through a room or area. Her body registered the weight transfer between her legs, noting the subtle air pressure change as she shifted directions. Knees ready for a sudden feint or jump, head on a swivel seeking a threat, ears alert for an out of place sound. Always aware. Searching for what didn't belong, what wasn't right. And if something was found, rolling onto her shoulder, drawing her gun, targeting the threat, squeezing the trigger. Then move, move, move. Never stay still.

Variations involved knives or weapons found in the imagined scene: vases, lamps, chairs, books, rocks, branches. She pictured dodging between trees in an all-out sprint, diving into freezing water, or turning and charging her attacker. Anything unexpected that might give her an advantage.

Mina opened her eyes, seeing the closet, the wrench, the gun in her hand. She waited while her heartbeat slowed and returned to normal.

Normal. That's all she ever wanted.

It was all second nature now, but she would be glad when Kris and the guys showed up to give her some downtime from perpetual guard duty. She stood and pocketed the pistol.

Until then, staying alive was all on her.

"Good job, Kade."

Kade adjusted his crutches under his arms and maneuvered across the physical therapy room while his therapist, Kenny, kept a light grip on his belt. Holding the crutch grip with his left hand in a cast wasn't easy.

"How are the ankles?" Kenny asked.

"Painful." They had healed enough to put weight on them for brief periods, but the tendons and ligaments were still inflamed. Part of that was due to malnutrition and dehydration during captivity. A weakened body took longer to heal, and his doc said it might take months for them to calm down. But overall, even short trips across the room like this were better than being confined to a wheelchair.

"Are you still icing?" Kenny asked as always. Accountability was the man's superpower.

They worked for an hour each visit, concentrating on balance as well as strength. Due to his broken pelvis and resulting time in bed, he'd lost muscle mass.

Unfortunately, the PT appointments were often superseded by trips to his plastic surgeon or nutritionist. Most mornings, simply getting out of bed and dressed left him panting and in need of a rest. All normal, according to the doctors. To Kade, it was anything but normal, and his progress was frustratingly slow.

At least his back was better. The beatings left long, overlapping cuts that healed into an ugly lattice of scar tissue. Daily stretching exercises and massages were required to keep the skin loose and raised keloids from developing. Those treatments were fun, especially at first.

"You'll be ready for the Boston Marathon," Kenny said, always the encourager. The race was only a few months away, and he had participated the last two years.

Kade had never been much of a runner, but marathon madness took over the city every April. It was impossible not to entertain the notion that one day he might just do it. He should have done it last year. The way his body was now, it might be forever out of reach.

But during all the workout sessions here and also at his dad's gym, he kept a different goal as motivation for getting well: reconnecting with the girl he'd let slip away. He wasn't ready yet—unless he was going after the sympathy vote, and he wasn't—but with Kenny's help and hard work, he'd get strong and healthy.

Then, no matter where he had to travel in the world, he'd find Mina Glass. He just hoped it wasn't too late.

CHAPTER FOURTEEN

MINA DOWNSHIFTED INTO THIRD GEAR, guiding her Toyota down the narrow ravine that marked the entry to the coastal town of Perilous Cove, California. Without a generous helping of dynamite—something she was sure the infamous tree-hugging residents would never permit—these near-vertical rock walls would forever guard and protect this part of the coast.

Perilous Cove was high on her list of possibilities. The other towns from the Bay Area south on Highway 101 were either too far away from L.A., or didn't have the creative vibe she sought. Any farther south was just too close to her enemy. She wanted someplace nearer her dad, yet far enough from L.A. to give a modicum of protection while she worked out the details of her plan. It wouldn't do to have the Viera threat find her before she found them. After the confrontation, the matter would be settled. Either she would survive and live and work wherever she wished, or...not.

Ahead, the walls fell away and the road opened up, revealing the million-dollar view shown on post cards and in travel books. The Pacific Ocean's deep blue stretched forever, its surface marred only by soft lines of shifting currents on one of those perfect days without fog or haze.

Mina slowed as she passed a dirt turnout on her left where several artists had set up easels, paints, and stools. Splashes of color on canvas nearly drew her in, but the limited parking at the viewpoint was already past capacity.

She lowered her window, allowing the briny fragrance of the sea to pull her onward, down toward town.

She had history here. One summer her parents rented three side-by-side beach houses for a couple of weeks. Mina was thirteen and still a relatively recent member in the family. What it had *not* been was a vacation. An endless rotation of important guests from the movie industry flowed through, mostly moneymen. Each new batch required a lavish party, live entertainment, and expectation from her parents for Lilly—Mina's name back then—to be seen, not heard.

The only person who noticed her was a forty-something guy with a beer belly who patted her butt one night in the buffet line. She turned to face him, holding an eight-inch carving knife in the same business-like manner she once used to fend off her real mom's boyfriend. This guy beat a retreat and avoided her the rest of his visit.

It taught her that evil dwelt not only in poor trailer parks, but in the circles of the rich and powerful as well, and to never let down her guard.

As she wound down the hillside and turned onto Harbor Street, she remembered the times she and her mom strolled these sidewalks and snooped in the shops, Ekaterina in disguise, of course. Mina viewed the village through older, more critical eyes today. Only a few blocks long, the main street was one of those with buildings along only one side, giving each one an unobstructed view of the harbor. Some edifices had obviously stood for a century or more, their wind-etched trim softened by dozens of coats of paint.

Beyond the little marina's forest of boat masts, the curving finger of the manmade breakwater protected the harbor from the intermittently volatile Pacific. The northern end of the rock barrier connected to Perilous Point, which was dominated by the lighthouse perched at the brink of the bluff. The tower gleamed white against a clear blue sky.

Mina slowed as she passed several art galleries, clothing stores, eateries, realty offices, and gift shops. Tourists strolled along the sidewalks, peering at windows displaying seafaring antiques, colorful kites, and an abundance of dolphins, mermaids, and lighthouses. She spotted a hanging sign that said *Last Drop*, and deftly parallel parked the little truck in the next available spot.

Mina exited, walked around to the sidewalk, and faced the ocean. She breathed deeply. Salty air, pizza, and coffee. Besides the enticing aromas, the air was filled with the ringing of cables on aluminum masts as boats rocked gently in the harbor. While the water here was decidedly colder than Malibu, the familiarity of everything else eased the tension in her shoulders, and her lips turned up in a smile. It was good to be back. Well, as close as she could get—for now.

She trailed her fingers along her truck's red hood. The paint left a chalky residue on her fingertips, and she brushed them on her jeans. Before leaving Seattle, she asked a detail shop about buffing it out. The attendant nearly laughed.

"I'll get you fixed up soon," she promised, noting the bug-spattered grill. "Maybe a paint job."

"Nice truck. I used to have one of those."

A tall, white-haired man stood in the doorway of the coffee shop. White stubble softened his chin, as if he hadn't shaved in a couple of days. His blue eyes reminded her of every Paul Newman movie she'd ever seen, which was all of them. Plus, it was always nice seeing someone with the same color hair as hers, even if he was probably in his seventies.

She grinned at him. "Thanks."

"Visiting our slice of paradise?" he asked, sipping from a mug the size of a German beer stein. He wore a dark brown apron embroidered with *Last Drop* on the front.

"Actually, I'm looking for studio space. I do sandblasted glass art." She stretched her arms wide. "Big, messy stuff."

"Ah…an artist." He smiled. "Well, this *is* an artist community."

"That's what I've heard. And I need a place to live." *And space for my small army.*

A string of a dozen tourists snaked between them on the sidewalk, interrupting their conversation. As soon as they passed, she moved closer to him.

"I figured the town barista would know all the gossip and what places might be available."

He rubbed his chin. "Well, I won't admit to the gossip, but as to the space…" He pulled the screen door open. "Come inside and I'll buy you a cup of coffee."

Rich aromas of freshly ground beans, vanilla, and chocolate flooded her senses as she followed the man through the tiny space to an equally tiny bar with a half dozen round stools. None of the seats were occupied at the moment, though all the tables were full. She slid onto the stool he indicated and watched as he lifted a pass-through section of the counter and slipped behind.

"I'm Conrad Langworth, owner of the Last Drop. Friends call me Connie. How about one of my specialty brews?"

"You're the boss," she said.

He tipped his head in her direction. "And you're a quick learner." He smiled and turned to the carafes and machines behind him. Sixty seconds later, he shot a dollop of cream on a mug and placed it in front of her.

She blew across the steaming cup while he topped off his own mug. At her first sip, the flavors collided on her tongue, and her eyes widened. Almond, cinnamon, hints of cherry and chocolate, dark roast coffee. And something else that she couldn't quite…

"Chili powder," he provided, leaning on the bar. "Fools them every time."

She took another sip, relishing the incredible combination. "Maybe you shouldn't be so quick to divulge your secret ingredient to strangers. I might market this and make a fortune."

"Oh, I never give it out to strangers. Only to friends and neighbors. 'Course I'd need to know your name to say we're truly friends."

She extended her hand. "Palomino." His hand felt warm and dry, with a grip anything but old. She sensed vitality and joie de vivre.

"No last name?" he asked, his eyes narrowing a little, as if trying to remember something.

She arched a brow in her best imitation of her mother. "I'm an artist." She tossed her hair and lifted her chin. "Artists only need one name."

Connie laughed. "Well, Palomino, it's nice to meet you."

"Actually, since we're now friends, call me Mina," she said, relaxing as sea air blew into the shop with a pair of women.

"Back in a minute," he said, and went to take their orders.

She followed him with her eyes. It wouldn't be impossible for him to recognize her from the news reports, even though she changed her name and left Los Angeles soon after finishing high school.

After arriving in Paris, she cut her hair, too, but it made her look like a pixie. Not good. Coloring it made more sense, but she hadn't been able to do it. So it was long again and remained its natural color, as white as Connie Langworth's.

Fortunately for her, *Access Hollywood*, *E!* and every other entertainment news show had been laser-focused on actor Chad Holt's kidnapping those years ago. The cameras followed him through rehabilitation for his head injury, and celebrating his just-in-time recovery to begin shooting *Blood Moon 2*, the second installment in his film trilogy. By the time the third *Blood Moon* film released two years ago, the kidnapping and shootouts were ancient history. Her role in the drama was on the cutting room floor.

She hoped.

Still, Perilous Cove was only a few hours away from the city, and lots of people who might have seen news photos of her moved north every year to escape the congested southland. Connie might be one of those transplants.

But it was too late to back out.

Mina shook her head. That sounded like a bad movie line. Her dad would have the head of any writer who stuck that turkey into one of his screenplays. Of *course* she could back out, disappear again, move to Katmandu or someplace, and make it virtually impossible for whoever was carrying on the Viera threat to find her. An option.

But it wasn't what she wanted. Hiring Haines and coming here guaranteed things were going to get messy. She was counting on it.

But just like in movies, timing was everything, and Mina wanted this timing on her terms. She needed a base and time to prepare, or the wrong people might die.

Her hand shook, and she accidentally slugged back too much of the scalding brew. She quickly reached for the glass of water Connie offered her and sent it chasing after the hot coffee.

"Thanks," she gasped, wiping her chin with a napkin. "Sorry, I—"

His hand covered hers on the counter and he caught her gaze. "Hard as it is, it's good to remember. Life is precious, but it's not easy."

He broke his knowing gaze with a wink, then removed his hand and went to work on a drink for another customer, giving Mina time to take a deep breath. Connie Langworth might be getting up in years, but evidently there was nothing wrong with his memory.

She sighed, appreciating his sensitivity, even if he had misinterpreted the focus of her thoughts. The injuries she sustained seven years ago were horrible, but those were in the past. Harder was remembering those who died protecting her and her family. Her biggest worry was accidentally creating new tragedy that would haunt her and others.

"Hi, there. Do you need a refill?"

A girl had taken Connie's place behind the counter. She had the brightest, curliest red hair Mina had ever seen outside of an *Annie* remake. Also the widest smile. She was tying an apron around her waist.

"Oh," Mina said, pulling her empty cup closer. "No. I'm fine."

"I *love* your hair," the girl said, bouncing on her toes while openly staring and corralling her own mop with a lime green scrunchie. "Is it naturally white?"

Only if nearly being blown up as a kid was natural. Even the doctors couldn't explain why it changed from brown after the trailer explosion. Did that make it natural? Before she could answer, Connie Langworth returned.

"I see you've met my newest employee, Starfire Conner. Star is practically a native of Perilous Cove."

"Yep," the girl said, "ever since my parents dropped me off here when I was three."

Mina couldn't help wonder what *that* story was, but the girl didn't elaborate.

"Star, this is Palomino," Connie said. "She's a glass artist, new in town, and looking for studio space."

Mina shook the girl's hand while Connie excused himself to the back room.

"Do you make jewelry? My sister, Mandy, does. You should see some of the great stuff she turns out." Star prattled nonstop about turquoise and silver, qualities of stones, where to buy the best supplies, and how to mix black elements to set off the colors.

Recently, Mina had been developing a new line of jewelry called *Pana's Dream*, in honor of her high school friend. It was something far different from her much larger projects.

Connie returned and chased Star off to wipe down tables and fill napkin dispensers.

Mina leaned forward and whispered, "She's adorable."

Connie sighed. "And unstoppable. I wish I had her energy. She was in here pestering me every day for almost four weeks before I broke down and hired her."

"A determined young lady."

"The final straw was a ten-point prioritized plan for business improvement."

"Is it working?"

He winked. "We'll see."

Mina laughed as Connie slid a piece of paper to her.

"Unfortunately for you, businesses in town are doing well for a change. Space is at a premium, especially for a big studio like you're talking about." He tapped his finger on the paper. "But I think this might fit your need. And it's not far. And while you eat your breakfast, I'll tell you a little about the lake."

"You serve breakfast?" Mina said.

A timer dinged, and Connie plated a large scone and slid it in front of her. "Wild olallieberry mint."

Mina stared at the huge pastry. She might have to walk to the lake to work off the calories.

CHAPTER FIFTEEN

AFTER HER COFFEE, Mina exited the Last Drop and stepped into a wall of late-morning fog. The lighthouse was gone from view, and the gray obscured the furthest boats in the harbor. The stiff breeze lifted her hair, and she breathed it in, savoring the salt and seaweed, and perhaps a touch of the wild that lay beyond the breakwater.

For centuries, explorers set off in waters like these—sometimes in conditions like these—willingly losing themselves for the promise of a new land or a new route. For some the promise was elusive, and they returned in failure or not at all. But for the ones who prepared well and persevered, treasure awaited.

Mina understood their need to go. The smell and sounds of the sea spurred the imagination, called those who sought fame, fortune, and adventure. Their motivation came from deep within, when they could no longer remain content where they were.

In a way, the Berlin attack was her push, a clear signal comfort and safety had disappeared like the lighthouse in the fog. Her reward would be no less monumental than what awaited those early explorers—providing she prepared well and persevered. Even then there was no guarantee.

A shiver caught her by surprise. Although foggy and damp, the day wasn't that cold. She hoped it wasn't a portent of what was to come.

Water dripped off the door handle as she unlocked the truck. Maybe living at the coast wasn't such a hot idea. With the engine going and the heater fan on high, she dialed the phone number on the slip of paper Connie Langworth had given her.

Bibs at Bibs' Beauty Barn in Deer Cove

The call went straight to an answering machine. Weird. It was only noon—unless they closed for lunch.

Her truck easily climbed the hill out of Perilous Cove, quickly bursting through the fog layer and leaving it below. The artists at the viewpoint were gone. No sense painting the gray that blanketed everything from shore to the western horizon. By the time she took the turnoff heading inland, brilliant sunshine had her switching off the heater and rolling down the windows.

The gloriously warm air scrubbed the truck's interior, slightly dank from three hours on the coast. Blindly fishing in the box of cassette tapes, she pulled one out and inserted it into the player. Joni Mitchell's "California" from her *Blue* album filled the cab. Mina grinned, taking the song as a confirmation of her plan.

Fifteen minutes later, she arrived at the tiny burg of Flume, set at the southern end of Storm Lake. The Chain Gang restaurant—a biker hangout if the number of motorcycles in the parking lot was any indication—appeared to be the busiest establishment, although a marine store with power boats and jet skis for rent had several families browsing the small lot.

A directional sign stood where the road forked. Left to Deer Cove. Right to Shelter Cove and Gift. A smaller, newer sign had been added below: Desperation Falls 7.5 mi. An arrow pointed right.

Desperation Falls. She knew that name from the Los Angeles Times Newspaper feed that came to her phone. The daily news allowed Mina to feel close to her dad, wherever she was.

One news story from over a year ago stood out to her above the rest: A young girl, gruesome murders, and a psycho killer. Even in Italy and Germany, the sensational story had been a hot topic among

Americans. Mina might not have paid it much attention if it hadn't reminded her of her own ordeal. The people involved were strangers, and Mina had never had a mental image of where it had all gone down. Until now.

She put on her blinker and turned left, relieved at putting a little distance between her and Desperation Falls.

The two-lane road wound behind low, rugged hills for a few miles, and it wasn't until she got closer to Deer Cove that the hills fell away and the lake came back into view. Rustic cabins and a handful of amazing log homes hid among tall pines and majestic oaks, some with commanding views across the sparkling water toward the far shore.

According to Connie, Storm Lake wasn't quite the artsy coastal community Mina had envisioned for her studio, but he assured her this Bibs woman had something worth a look. The lake probably didn't attract as many tourists as the beach community did, and being off the beaten path a little would be better for her security until the Viera threat was stopped.

She passed a cute cabin that had flower baskets hanging on the porch. Kids' bikes and colorful plastic toys littered the patch of grass along one side. Idyllic, innocent. Yet evil had struck here.

It wasn't this community's fault some madman had come. Dr. Cain, her psychiatrist years ago after the attacks, emphasized over and over that evil came in the form of people, not in places or things. Mina knew that was truth, but she would never walk beside a parked white van again. And if she saw one on the freeway, she either sped up or slowed down to gain some distance. Police sirens still gave her goose bumps, although she tolerated cop shows where bad guys were cuffed and hauled away.

Mina braked at a curve where a short bridge crossed a creek, the beginning of Deer Cove. A carved redwood sign stated the town lay at 1,475 feet elevation, and was home to 1,256 people. Connie said the population soared during summer months when second homes, RV parks, camping sites, and rental cabins filled to capacity. Even more people drove in for day use.

"Looks like summer begins in June," she muttered, crawling along behind a string of cars, pickups, and rented four-wheel tourist bicycles clogging the road leading into the town center.

A view of the marina on her right was soon blocked by businesses that lined both sides of the narrow street: Deer Cove Mercantile, a vintage clothing store, several galleries, a sporting goods store with colorful wake boards on a rack out front. Even at 11:15, there was a line outside the Crab Shack restaurant self-proclaiming *World Famous Fish and Chips!* Her stomach reminded her that the scone at the Last Drop had been a long time ago.

Before she could consider food, she wanted to connect with this Bibs woman. And she also had to find a place to stay for the night. By the looks of things, this place was as busy as Perilous Cove. The back of her truck wasn't out of the question. She had a sleeping bag with her. Dad would be horrified, but at least here at the lake she wouldn't be drenched in morning fog.

Most of the vehicles ahead of her peeled off by the time she reached a swimming beach on her right. The grassy area featured play sets, picnic tables, and pole-mounted grills. The grass sloped to a sandy beach that disappeared beneath sparkling blue water. Even from the road, she smelled hotdogs, mustard, and suntan lotion. Kids chased each other around tables and trees. Mina slowed again for some beach-bound tourists crossing the road, then accelerated out the north end of town.

After a brief open area with nice lake views, Bibs' Beauty Barn appeared on the left. It was a charming example of a classic western barn, with a tall center section and matching low side wings. Dark wood shingles covered the roof, and the wood siding was silvered with age.

Not as classic was the modern red fire truck, lights flashing, blocking the entrance to the parking lot. Mina braked and turned left at the road just before the barn and pulled onto the gravel shoulder. She climbed out and walked along a decorative split-rail fence until she found a break that gave access to the lot. A dozen women milled around the blacktop in front of the business, several draped in colorful smocks, their hair in curlers or highlighting foil.

Mina made her way between parked cars into the chaotic scene in front of the rumbling fire truck. A fat hose stretched from the truck and disappeared into the sliding barn door, and a fireman carried a large portable fan into the building.

Loud voices drew her attention to the far corner of the structure where an aproned younger woman with purple hair used a garden hose to wash an older woman's hair. Another woman stood nearby babbling about how "...if you don't get that treatment out, Mildred's hair is gonna fry!" Mildred—Mina assumed she was the woman whose head was being drenched with the hose—was blubbering about her ruined anniversary dinner.

Mina thought she caught the distinctive odor of skunk, but then again it could have been chemicals for Mildred's perm.

"I'm afraid we'll be closed for a bit, dear."

Mina turned to an elderly woman who had come up beside her. She was shorter by an inch than Mina's five foot two inches, and shaped like a beach ball. Spiked, short white hair tipped in bright purple was held in place by a stiff gel. It took years off her overall appearance, but Mina guessed the woman around eighty.

"Actually, I'm looking for Bibs."

The woman's eyes sharpened. "Bill collector?"

"I was given her name by Conrad Langworth—about a studio rental property?"

"Irene!" The woman's piercing shriek backed Mina up a step, and one of the firemen stumbled over his boots in his rush from barn to truck. "Take over! I've got an errand!"

A smaller woman who clutched two skeins of yarn and knitting needles waved cheerily in response.

"You're Bibs?" Mina asked the stout woman who was clutching her arm and turning them toward the street.

"I am. That your truck? We'll take it." She glanced back at the mayhem. "Mine is kind of...blocked at the moment."

"What's going on?" Mina asked as Bibs pulled her between the cars and along the fence. A sheriff's four by four drove up and angled in beside the fire truck. "Did you have a fire?"

"Oh, no. Just a little…wildlife incident. C'mon." She tugged harder on Mina's arm, practically dragging her toward the truck.

"Are you sure this is a good time to leave? It looks—"

"Never better," Bibs insisted as she hoisted herself into the truck. "So you're Palomino? Connie called. Cool name."

With a final glance at the commotion at the barn, Mina started the engine.

"Straight ahead for a bit," Bibs said while tugging to stretch the seatbelt across her bulk. As soon as they moved beyond the barn, Bibs pointed to the open field behind it. "Right there is where we have our big Halloween party each year. People come from all over for the barbecue, games, and music. A real family affair."

"Oh. That sounds nice."

"Going to throw a Fourth of July shindig this year too. Lots of food, music, and fireworks on the beach. Married?"

"Me?" Mina had been nodding to Bibs' description of the party, but quickly changed to a shake of her head. "No, I'm—"

"Single men love barbecue, you know. You won't want to miss those parties."

Okay, then.

"This is Merle's. You can turn around here." Bibs pointed to a driveway. A hand-painted sign stretched between two tall poles. *Merle's Grading, Hauling, Firewood.* Yellow tractors and other machinery littered a graveled area flanked by piles of cut wood as high as houses.

"Isn't this the road to the studio property?" Mina asked, obediently using the driveway for a three-point turn.

"Nope. Just wanted you to see the field where my party is. We're heading back through town to the mill," she said, as if that explained everything.

Mina shook her head. Maybe Bibs' best mental years were behind her. Far behind.

Bibs lifted a fist full of Mina's hair, examining it. "Amazing. How did you get it this white? Doesn't look dyed. You know, we could add some raspberry peek-a-boos. Maybe dip the ends in black or a little cobalt. Make it pop. You'd really stand out."

Mina kept her mouth shut. The woman had been inhaling beauty products too long. And standing out was the last thing Mina wanted.

"Come by the shop and we'll fix you right up."

Town hadn't changed much in the ten minutes since she last drove through, except if anything the line for the Crab Shack was longer than before. Her stomach growled again as they passed.

Just across the bridge at the beginning of town, Bibs ordered her to take an immediate right along the stream on Mill Road. Mina hadn't even noticed it before. There was evidence the road had been widened recently, and the surface was hard-packed gravel.

"Merle's work." Bibs indicated the road as if reading her mind. "Good man if you need anything heavy and sweaty."

The mental picture seared into Mina's brain before she could banish it to the bottom of the lake. Did Bibs imagine this sweaty Merle guy escorting Mina to the July 4th party? She shook off an involuntary shudder, concentrating on following the curving road that played peekaboo with a stream on the right for a few hundred yards before it disappeared.

Ahead, the road changed to rutted dirt and went straight up a hill. Mina braked, wary about proceeding. A realty sign lay in the brush.

"Turn here," Bibs said, pointing to the right. A thriving manzanita had blocked the view of a driveway.

"What's up the other road?" Mina asked as she turned onto the driveway.

"Couple old abandoned houses quite a ways up. Used to belong to one of the old logging families. They've been empty for years. I expect broken down or vandalized." The old woman shook her head and muttered, "Too bad what happened there."

Mina shot Bibs a look, but before she could ask more, the freshly graveled driveway led them under some majestic oaks. The mature trees created a canopied tunnel of dappled light and shadow that ran for the length of a football field. She leaned over the steering wheel, peering up at the sight.

"This is amazing." It reminded her of France, and she imagined strolling along here in the cool shade on hot summer days.

Then the road turned again and widened into a small parking lot in front of a two-story, shingle-sided building at least seventy feet long. The siding had weathered naturally, and it ranged from blackish-brown in the shaded areas to light silver where the sunshine bleached it.

"Welcome to the old mill," Bibs said, a hint of pride in her tone.

CHAPTER SIXTEEN

WHILE THE STRUCTURE appeared many decades old, the roof had been replaced with dark red metal, the type seen in snow country. The color stood out against the deep green of the oak trees, and the overall effect pleased Mina.

But it was the surrounding landscape that transformed the building into something spectacular. Stone planters lined the parking area, each packed with brilliant petunias and marigolds. Olive trees rose from a large undulating lawn at the right of the building, each tree surrounded by beds of gladiolas, leafy hostas, ferns, and amaryllis. Dozens of other flowers and shrubs produced a kaleidoscope of colors.

"Oh, my," she said as she stepped from the truck. "This is..." *way more than I was looking for*. She had plenty of money—her mother had seen to that—but being frugal was burned into Mina's nature, and not something she wished to change. Taking care of this place... Her hopes dipped a little southward even while tasting the intoxicating floral perfume that hung in the air.

"Pretty nice, huh?" Bibs stood with hands on her wide hips, beaming. "A yuppie from L.A. thought he'd make this into a tasting room for his wines. Lost his shirt on the whole caboodle. Sold his vineyards east of here and moved back to Malibu."

Mina was still trying to conjure up the definition of *caboodle* when Bibs hustled up the meandering cobblestone path toward the entrance.

"The place was in foreclosure for two years 'cuz nobody wanted it," she shouted over her shoulder. "Too far removed from town. I picked it up for a song, and I've got big plans. Come on, I'll show you the inside and explain how all this works." With surprising agility, the old woman hopped up the wide steps instead of taking the gently sloping wheelchair ramp.

The planks, when Mina reached them, were gouged with age from countless workmen's boots, but solid and unyielding. The nine foot front door was more recent, a carved relief of grapes and vines, subtly colored against the dark wood. Bibs swung the door open and disappeared inside. Mina stepped through the doorway and stopped.

High, rough-cut beams spanned the building front to back, and crossed supports connected them to the open rafters high above. But the hand-hewn wood was anything but dark and dirty. Everywhere she looked, soft honey-colored surfaces shone. The exposed ceiling wood had been stained slightly darker, but indirect lights gave it life and contrast. In a word, the interior was stunning.

"That yuppie spent thousands having these beams pressure washed, sanded, and sealed," Bibs said, standing with one hand on her hip as the other swept the ceiling. "Part of the reason he went bankrupt. But I'm glad it was him paying for all the work, not me."

Mina wondered if yuppies still existed, but didn't let that interrupt her perusal of the space before her. The distance from the front door to the far wall was approximately forty feet, but it was longer right to left. The wall on her left separated this space from the rest of the building, but Mina turned right and stared. The end of the structure was an A-framed wall of glass panes stretching from peak to floor that looked out onto the lawn and gardens. Two sets of French doors opened to a patio where an ancient, twisted olive tree stood on a small mound, positioned perfectly in the glass like a still life painting. Three picnic tables on graveled areas around the tree's perimeter waited patiently for families to spread checkered tablecloths and unpack baskets of food.

Reluctantly, she turned away from the view. Not all of the room was as pristine as its ceiling. The far wall had rectangles for large windows, but several had been removed and were leaning against the wall. One frame was missing its glass and lay flat on a large worktable constructed of sawhorses and plywood. An electric sander sat on the floor near it, and was being used to refinish the water-stained wood. Sawdust swirled around her shoes with the incoming breeze.

"Had some vandalism while the place sat empty," Bibs explained. "And we're doing some updates for the showroom here."

Three small sections of flooring had been cut out, exposing pipes and electrical underneath. And there could be more holes if the squares of plywood scattered around were any indication. Extension cords snaked every which way between boxes of electrical wiring, plumbing fittings, nails, saws, drills, and two overflowing toolboxes. A commercial floor sander was parked in the corner.

The windows were spaced between eight-inch vertical pillars. Mina ran her hand down the satiny wood, feeling undulations that testified to the tree's former life. While the window frames needed work, the pillars were finished and in good condition.

She turned in a slow circle. The bones of the structure were solid, seriously overbuilt in fact. She wondered how old it was and started to ask when she spotted Bibs outside the back wall on a large deck. She gestured for Mina to come out.

The room's dividing wall had a doorway in the far corner, and Mina passed through into a short hallway that contained several doors, two of which were marked as restrooms. One door led outside. Sweet air and water sounds greeted her as she stepped onto the deck, which extended about fifteen feet over a ravine.

"This is Conner Creek," Bibs said, hanging over the railing and pointing to the stream twenty feet below. "It's the largest of three water sources that feed Storm Lake." Then she turned and pointed along the side of the building. "And that's the main attraction that everyone comes to see."

Mina looked the direction Bibs indicated. "A waterwheel."

"Yep," Bibs said, bustling past her.

The wheel was mounted against the side of the building and extended a few feet above the deck, which had been constructed around it. Water flowed from a flat-bottomed trough mounted higher along the side of the building, and splashed into the wheel's wooden buckets. The weight of the water drove the wheel forward and down in smooth rotation.

"We've got the flow set to just a trickle compared to the old days." She indicated an adjustable wooden gate near the end of the trough. "This wheel cranks it up to let more water through. More water equals more power."

"You said this was a mill?" Mina asked. Her eyes followed the trough as it disappeared past the end of the building and continued uphill into the trees.

"A sawmill. It and another mill processed all the timber harvested around here. 'Course after they got the flume built down to Perilous Cove, they just floated the rough logs down to the big mills there. More efficient than hauling cut wood down the mountain by wagon. The other mill up here got torn down, but they kept this one active to provide lumber for local construction. Don't know why they didn't tear this one down eventually, but I'm glad they didn't."

"Does the creek run year around?" Mina asked, following as Bibs led them back inside.

"Occasional dry times can bring it to a stop, but you should see it after a good downpour." Bibs opened another doorway off the hall and stepped into a living room. A sofa and two mission-style leather chairs faced a wood-burning stove, and a flat-screen television hung on the wall beside it. Magazines littered a coffee table constructed from twisted tree limbs and glass. "This is the living quarters. There's a kitchen through that door over there, and the other door leads to the bedroom suites—one on this floor and one upstairs. I'll show you."

Suites?

Bibs shooed Mina through into a nice-sized bedroom with the same polished floors. A window overlooked the front parking area, but a trellis with vigorous climbing roses provided privacy. She opened a door that led to a full bathroom.

"These have all been redone with granite counters and new fixtures. A lot nicer than *my* bathroom," she chuckled. "The upstairs bedroom is the same, only bigger and with a view out over the creek. If I were you, I'd pick that one. There are also two small bedrooms off the hall behind the kitchen and a common bathroom."

Mina hadn't been expecting four bedrooms or living rooms or granite bathrooms. This was set up for a whole family. "I'm afraid there's been a mistake, Bibs. I'm looking for workspace for my glass etching business. It's a messy process and—"

"That's comin' up. Follow me." Back out in the hallway, Bibs turned deeper into the building and opened a well-sealed door. It led into a different world.

Whereas the front of the building—except for the current renovation work—could be an upscale dwelling, there was no mistaking the intention of this equally sized back half. Beams and rafters that matched those out front were dark with age in here, rough-hewn, and unfinished. But Mina noted they were free of cobwebs and dust. The floor was smooth and stained a golden tone, but the polish had worn through in places.

A half-dozen sturdy work tables were distributed around the large area, and freestanding panels made out of two-by-fours and pegboard divided the room into workspaces. Some had easels with canvases in various stages of completion, where others had boxes of stained glass, jewelry-making supplies, or piles of fabric. One bench had at least twenty woven baskets of several sizes and colors.

A corner of the large space had been walled off as a separate enclosure with windows on the interior walls. Mina cupped her hands against the glass to see inside the room within a room. At least a dozen woodworking machines lined the space, including a table saw, band saw, lathe, sanders, and a drill press. Sawdust had been swept into a neat pile at the base of a lidded fifty-five-gallon drum.

"Roy does some furniture building," Bibs offered as explanation. "He was my first renter about four months ago and set up this shop. This is the main work area for a co-op of local artists. They rent their spaces. You will, too, but you'll get the majority of the building. Once we get the front room finished, it will be the display area and we'll open it as a store. But here's what I want to show you." Bibs started down a flight of stairs at the far side of the room. "I thought you might like the space below this one."

The descent ended at yet another door. It opened into a space that ran under the workroom immediately above, but this didn't have the dividers. Bibs flicked switches and light flooded the area. Large windows on the creek side showed the side of the waterwheel, and looked out under the deck to the creek. Massive wood blocks just inside the wall held one end of the wheel's rotating axle. A wrought iron railing was screwed to the wood floor, preventing anyone from getting too close to the spinning shaft. The floor was a patchwork of filled holes, marking equipment mountings of long ago.

"This is where the drive gears for the sawmill were located. Belts ran through to the floor above to the big blades and machinery. Logs came in the back end, and finished lumber came out the front where the garden is now. All that's gone, of course, and the waterwheel is just for show."

"Do tours come down here?" Mina asked.

"Not anymore. Now that I've got paying artists, we can't have kids tromping through everyone's workspaces, so we limit them to the outside deck and grounds. There won't be any more around until school starts in the fall."

Bibs leaned against the railing, watching the waterwheel turn. "My father and *his* father worked for this mill. Delivered horse-drawn wagons of lumber all around the lake. It stopped operations about the time I was born, so I never got to see it in action. Must have been something, though. Giant blades singing as they sliced through the logs, sawdust flying everywhere." She nodded at the memory that wasn't really hers.

Mina wandered around the room until she came to the building's end wall, where a ten-foot-wide sliding barn door hung from a steel rail.

Bibs unlocked the padlock and leaned her weight against the handle. The panel slid smoothly aside, revealing an exterior concrete pad with covered roof extending out from the building about twenty feet. "You can't see it from the upper parking area, but another driveway curves around and down to this lower level, right up to this sliding door. Connie said you work with some heavy glass. There's no raised threshold here, so you can roll things in and out."

Overall, the room was like a walkout basement, with large, operable creek-side windows near the waterwheel for generous light and air. It was cooler than the rooms above, perfect for the heat her small kiln pumped out. She could build a sandblasting booth along the windowless wall for small jobs, and roll the big projects outside for blasting. Yes, this could work. In fact, it was far larger than she required.

"There are some conditions on me renting this to you," Bibs said, hands locked behind her back, rocking to and fro.

Mina sighed. There always were.

Her cell phone rang and she checked the display. It didn't indicate an automatic forward from her Palomino Glass business number. Only a few people had her direct number, and this wasn't one of them. But with Proxy's filters in place, she decided it was safe to answer.

"Excuse me, Bibs." Mina walked out onto the covered loading dock. Where the day had been warm minutes ago, a chill climbed her bare arms. "Yes?"

"Palomino Glass?" The voice was mechanical, sounding neither male nor female. Perhaps computer generated.

Mina didn't respond.

"It's Rowdy Haines, calling from Phoenix."

It sounded nothing like the man Mina knew. She hoped Proxy had gotten her phone set up as promised so no one could track her.

A click sounded on the line, then, "How's this? Do I sound normal now?"

She recognized Rowdy's deep voice, and relaxed. "Haines. Are you trying to give me heart failure?"

He laughed. "So you like my new voice-disguising app?"

"Pretty effective," she said, sinking onto a low wall, "and still not funny." That earned another laugh. "What's up?"

"The guys are ready, but they're wanting details. Where are we setting up headquarters for the op? And when are we coming? Give me a time and place. I got things to do, you know."

She grinned at his gruffness, then glanced at the yawning doorway. The massive building had studio space, living quarters for a few people, and relative isolation. The only drawback was there would be other artists and customers here during the daytime. That wasn't ideal. But maybe…

"You still there, Glass?"

She realized it was time to pull the trigger, so to speak. The training, the recruiting, the preparations—those were done or on schedule. Yet she hadn't fully committed, hadn't done anything that couldn't be undone. Was she stalling?

"Glass! You alive, or did somebody shoot you already? Don't tell me all my hard work was a waste of my time!"

Mina was smiling as she walked back into the old mill a few minutes later. The building was huge, far bigger than she envisioned or needed for herself alone. Maybe it was just right.

Bibs still leaned on the rail by one of the creek side windows, staring out at the slowly turning waterwheel.

"Bibs, I'll take it."

The woman turned in surprise. "But—"

"I want a two-year lease."

"You don't even know the cost or details."

"And I want the living area—all of it. I do have some requirements, but if you agree, I'll sign the paperwork today."

CHAPTER SEVENTEEN

THE NEXT MORNING, Mina finished half a banana, carefully wiped clean the granite in her new, completely bare kitchen, then walked out onto the deck. She unrolled her workout mat and began her morning stretches, a routine she'd kept up since finishing rehab. The exercises kept most of the old pains away—in her body, at least. She sat with legs out straight, leaned forward, and relaxed until she could hook her hands around her feet.

As soon as she had left Bibs' Beauty Barn yesterday with the signed lease papers in hand, Mina called her moving and storage company in Seattle, and set things in motion to have the truck with her bed and belongings here late tonight. Doubling their fee ignited their initial lack of urgency.

Then she'd driven to nearby Mission Peak and purchased beds, chests of drawers, lamps, night stands, throw rugs, and other furniture to outfit the bedrooms and common areas. That delivery was coming Monday next week. Unfortunately, the large order caught the eye of the store manager, who rushed out to personally thank Mina. This close to Los Angeles, she wanted to stay under the radar when possible, at least until her plans were in place. But life was full of risks.

She'd stayed up late, unpacking linens, small appliances, and groceries.

Mina exhaled, letting her forehead touch her knees. After a night on the bare bedroom floor, she was anxious to get her own things, particularly her bed. Besides her kiln and truck, it was the largest thing she owned.

She held a downward-facing dog position for the prescribed count, wincing as her left heel relaxed toward the deck and pulled her hamstring.

Finally, she stood, set her feet wide, and clasped her hands overhead. Then she slowly leaned left as her torso stretched tight along her right side. *Ouch.* Maybe she should have spent the night on the front seat of her truck instead of on the hard floor.

Her cell phone rang, playing the ringtone she set for Kris.

"Hi, Kris." She held the phone in one hand and switched the stretches to the other side.

"Mina. I'm back in San Francisco for a two-day job. I promise, it's the last one. Did you find a place?"

"I did." She continued her stretches.

"And that would be...?" Kris prompted.

Mina grinned. Knowing Kris grew up in Mission Peak, she couldn't resist a little fun. "A perfect spot. Small town, a beautiful lake."

"Arrowhead?"

"A little farther north. Storm Lake."

"Are you kidding me?"

"Why, is there something wrong with it?"

"My brother, Alex, and his family live there."

"Really?" She hadn't known Kris had family here.

They chatted for a while about the mill. Kris had never been to it, but knew where it was.

"So," Mina said, "when are you coming?"

She sighed. "Probably a week or so. I wasn't expecting you to jump this close to the fire so soon." Kris explained her landlord recently completed some major improvements on her complex, then announced he was raising the rent by 25 percent. "I'm looking for a new place to live. I've got this next job, and honestly I need the income."

Rent was insane anywhere around Silicon Valley and the San Francisco Bay Area. Mina had a thought. "What if you moved here? I've got a lot of room—or will have once this whole situation is over and the guys are gone." Again, she was projecting her future without the constant threat.

Their talk was cut short due to another call coming in for Kris, but she promised to think about it and call soon.

Regardless of Kris's uncertain arrival, Haines and his team were coming in a couple of weeks. Mina wanted to have everything ready.

Her back twitched from the stretch, and she straightened. The warming air lifted her hair with a fragrant swirl of sycamore, oak, grasses, wet stream rocks, and rich earth. She inhaled deeply, the familiar scents of the California hills calming her spirit.

Many of the places she saw while traveling around the world were spectacular and majestic, but nothing had ever felt quite right. For a while, she wondered if there was something wrong with her, that if she stayed in a place longer, maybe she would adjust. Other people did. Eventually she realized part of the problem was that she had no history in those places, nothing to act as an anchor. She took another deep breath, closed her eyes, and slowly exhaled.

Yet, those reasons were only the *lacking* of something she sought. This place had a compelling pull, like gravity. Specifically, a familiar sense of expectancy. An energy like nowhere else. It pulsed with creativity, like on some of Dad's movie sets as hordes of staff labored to produce something meaningful and beautiful. She felt it at the beach with the unrelenting power of the Pacific pounding the shore. She even felt it on the Southern California freeways—an itch to *go*, to *be*, to *move*—even if some of the drivers were seriously crazy.

More than anything, this place felt like home. It *smelled* like home.

Finished with her routine, Mina locked up the living area. No sign of the carpenter this morning, but Bibs promised the work on the retail space would be done by what she proclaimed as the

Independence Day Weekend Grand Opening Extravaganza. With the fourth falling on a Tuesday this year, many would make it a long weekend at the lake. Some would take the whole week.

Calling her dad would be a wise move before the day got going. He wouldn't be pleased she moved so close to L.A. Her lips curved into a smile. He'd get over it. Nathan Hawthorne was a fair but stern taskmaster on the sets of his film productions, but after all, she was his only daughter. Only child, for that matter. Stubbornness ran in the family, even if she *was* adopted. She decided the call could wait until after Kris arrived. Dad would be relieved to hear her former bodyguard was in residence.

Mina exited the building by the front door and struck out along the gravel path that curved around the big olive tree toward the creek. According to Bibs, Merle had built a footbridge that crossed over to the north side of Conner Creek and joined a new walking path leading to town.

She found it easily. The handicap-accessible surface was hard-packed decomposed granite all the way to the footbridge. On the other side, she continued on smooth, black asphalt. The path followed the gently descending water as it gurgled over rocks. Happy birds flitted between the beautiful oaks like a Disney movie.

Bibs was committed to making the mill work as retail space as well as studio, so the shortcut to town was a necessity.

The path ended at an inviting little patio with benches overlooking Conner Creek where it flowed under the main road bridge and into the cove that began the marina. Mina jogged across the street to the waterside businesses. A few of the hundred-year-old storefronts showed the scars of age, but most wore updated paint in colors that highlighted their character. Benches along the sidewalk invited shoppers to sit awhile, and wine barrel halves in front of every store brimmed with colorful flowers. Clearly the business community made a concerted effort to attract tourists.

The scent of coffee tickled her nose and determined her direction. She passed Deer Cove Mercantile with its fluttering kites inside high transom windows, and resisted the pull of Ami's Armoire, which was filled with some amazing clothing she vowed to peruse in the future. Farther on, the mouthwatering aromas of Peg's Waffle House would have drawn her in if she hadn't eaten at home.

"Can I interest you in a sample coffee?"

Mina stopped short. She'd traversed several blocks completely lost in thought, and now stood in front of the source of the compelling aromas she smelled earlier: DC Coffee. Connie Langworth's blue eyes shone in the morning light as he extended a round tray with a dozen small paper cups.

"Connie? What are you doing here?"

"I'm the new owner of DC Coffee," he stated, his chest expanding a little. "Bought it a month ago. We're branching out."

"Is this one of Star's business improvement items?"

He laughed. "No, I already had this in the works. But it's on her radar now, believe me."

"This is how you knew about Bibs' new adventure with the mill."

He nodded. "She and her sister, Irene, stop in once in a while—*if* I have something on sale." He shook his head. "That woman loves a bargain."

Mina could relate. She regretted telling Bibs the mill rental price didn't matter. Mina selected one of the cups and sipped. Coffee, plus everything else that tasted good in the whole world. The man had a knack.

"So, are you going to be up here often?" she asked.

"Soon. I'm grooming Star to run the Last Drop for the rest of the summer while I get some new equipment installed here and do a little remodeling. Got some other young people lined up to staff both shops. My old bones are getting tired of the damp coast." He drew a deep breath. "I do love this dry mountain air."

Mina stifled a laugh. Today was shaping up to top a hundred degrees. That would dehydrate anything, even bones. But she had to agree, especially with the scent of brewing coffee on the morning breeze. She glanced inside. DC Coffee had more room than his place in Perilous Cove, and featured a freezer case with a dozen flavors of ice cream in addition to the coffee and scones.

"We'll add sandwiches when we can handle the load," he said, passing out cups to a family of five and chatting for a few minutes. After the group tasted, they all headed inside to order full-sized versions.

She wasn't surprised. Connie was a natural salesman, and he seemed to genuinely enjoy people. "Looks like you've got another winner."

A man with unkempt dark hair and beard passed them. His white canvas painter's pants were torn at the knees and splattered from hundreds of paint jobs. Even in this heat, he wore a long-sleeve, faded chambray shirt. Scuffed leather sandals were covered in dust, as were his feet, as if he'd walked a long way on dirt roads. He carried a dark satchel, protectively clamped to his chest by both hands.

"Hi, Mike," Connie said. "Would you like a sample?"

The man—Mike, apparently—shook his head, and continued into the small patio just beyond the shop that provided outdoor seating.

"I'll bring out your regular in a few minutes," Connie called. That brought the man to a halt. He looked back to Connie and gave a nod. Then his gaze locked on Mina.

She was struck by gray eyes so light in color they looked like something out of a sci-fi movie. They were set deep in his tanned face, hooded by bushy brows. For a moment, Mina caught a feeling of a mind teetering on the fence between brilliance and insanity. She barely suppressed a shudder before he broke their gaze and strode to the table furthest from other people.

"Who is that?" she whispered to Connie.

"Everyone calls him Old Mike. The previous owner told me he comes by most days. Always sits by himself."

The man took a notebook from his satchel, opened it, and hunched over it as he began writing in a careful, cramped style.

Mina leaned close to Connie. "What's he writing?"

"No idea," Connie said. "He buys a large coffee, cream but no sugar, and his money is always good. I slip him a muffin or specialty cake once in a while."

"You're a good man, Conrad Langworth. That's why you succeed in business."

"Speaking of business," he said, "how's the new studio?"

She sighed. "Lots to do. My equipment is arriving tonight." Of course, that was only a small part of everything coming up.

"You'll do fine. Come inside and I'll make you a Cappuccino Blast."

"What's that?"

"My new invention. Let's just say that after you've had one, you won't need lunch and you'll have energy till midnight."

Great. Another two-thousand-calorie Langworth concoction. She would have to walk around the whole lake if she kept this up. Or swim it.

She glanced at Old Mike, who was scribbling furiously, but then a flyer pinned to the bulletin beside the door caught her attention. A group called the Tadpoles was meeting tomorrow at 11:00 to swim. Everyone invited.

CHAPTER EIGHTEEN

AFTER HER TOWN EXCURSION, Mina spent the afternoon downstairs in her new workshop, sweeping away cobwebs and dust. The living areas were already clean, so until the movers arrived, she didn't have a lot to do. What Bibs said about the abandoned houses kept tickling her imagination. *"Too bad what happened there."*

She grabbed a bottle of water and headed out again, walking down the long driveway. The shady stretch of the oak canopy truly was beautiful. Where the driveway met Old Mill Road, she turned right.

The battered signpost still lay in the tall grass where she'd seen it. In fact, judging from the covering of dust, it looked like it had been on the ground for months or years. Evidently the realtor wasn't aggressively marketing this property. Mina used a clump of grass to brush away some of the grime.

Lake Realty. Unique Properties, Land, Opportunities!

There was no realtor name, only a phone number. The listing, if it was still active, was probably foisted onto the most recently hired agent, the lowest man or woman on the totem pole.

It took Mina a full fifteen minutes of energetic hiking to reach the top of the hill where the road turned left through a stand of pine. Here, the surface was smoother, not carved by rain running down the tire tracks. She followed it into the trees where it split. An overgrown path too narrow for a vehicle went off to her right, while the more substantial road continued left. It looked more promising, so she took it.

Although she was only a couple hundred feet higher than the mill, the mix of trees changed with the elevation, oaks giving way to more of the tall pines that stretched to the blue sky and imbued the air with their sharp fragrance. A hundred yards farther, she emerged into a clearing.

Before her was what must have once been a stunning house—the one Bibs said belonged to one of the lumber barons.

From one of her art classes about architecture, she knew the turret and rooflines classified this as a Queen Anne style home. This particular structure didn't have the ornate scrollwork and corbels found on fancier Victorians. It was more what might be found on a Western cattle ranch. She instantly appreciated the balance of practicality in its simple style that still flaunted the owner's showcase of wealth and prominence at a time when labor was cheap and craftsmanship reigned.

The main structure was two full stories, but small windows near the top of the gables and steep-roofed turret indicated an attic as well. A deep, curving porch began on the right front corner, wrapped around the turret on the left, and continued to the back. The porch's low-pitched roof connected to the house between the first and second stories. Eight round columns supported the overhang. A perfect place to sit on a hot summer day, especially with a few large ceiling fans turning lazily.

Mina climbed two stone steps, but hesitated before testing the porch planking. A couple of ragged holes, one right where she would step to enter the front door, indicated severe rot. If she fell through and was injured… She backed down the steps. Entering from this side would have to wait.

She skirted the left side of the house, peering across the porch into the broken first floor windows. Empty rooms were filled with leaves and trash, and she caught a glimpse of a staircase leading upward. Other than every window being broken, it didn't look like the place had been vandalized much, probably due to its isolation on the mountain. Kids these days were more into first shooter video games than throwing rocks.

Dozens of roofing shingles littered the ground, and she wondered how much damage had been done by yearly storms. The whole interior could be a rotten, moldy mess.

The rear of the house had a smaller porch about twenty feet across. Scraps of silver window screen hung in shreds where it had once been enclosed. The flooring here appeared in better condition, but some of the planks sagged ominously, as if waiting for an unsuspecting human foot. She stayed off them too.

Fifty feet behind the house was a Western barn similar to Bibs' Beauty Barn, except smaller in stature and with only a single side wing. Off to the barn's side was a tiny shed that could be a pump house for a well. Overhead electrical wires came out of the pines behind the barn and connected to a tall pole, but the wires that would have continued to the house had been disconnected and hung at the top of the pole in large loops.

Mina hiked the rest of the way around the house, and then turned to face it full on. Its last paint job was a long time ago, and whoever did it must have gotten a sale on white. But she could envision it in a pallet of complimenting colors. It would shine like the vintage jewel it had once been.

The driveway, mostly obscured by weeds, leaves, and strewn branches, curved around a garden area. A birdbath leaned precariously in the center of the circle, its shallow bowl filled with debris.

Then Mina turned away from the house, and her jaw dropped open. Past the outer edge of the driveway circle, the flat area began a steep slope downward. Through tall pines, the entire length of Storm Lake sparkled, deep blue against oak-covered hills and clear sky. She pivoted back to the house, then back to the lake. Every front-facing room and even the porch had a spectacular view. No wonder the lumber baron chose this location. With some judicious trimming of the overgrown trees that probably didn't even exist in the 1800s, this house would be…

"Home."

The word had come unbidden, unimagined, spoken in the silence of the mountain, as well as in her soul.

Mina took a step back, but she couldn't escape the majesty before her. When she turned again to the decrepit house, the word lingered. *Home*. It sank its teeth into her being like a living thing.

"Yeah," she answered the thought. "Probably the way a million termites are sinking their tiny teeth into the foundation, walls, floors, and rafters right this second."

A light breeze chose that moment to swish through the pines, adding to the peaceful ambience. With work—a *ton* of work—the house could be as it had once been. Even better. High-back rocking chairs lining the repaired porch. Friends and family eating together, kids playing in the yard and chasing around the circular drive.

Her kids.

She didn't push the thought completely away. But with how she was forced to live her life, with what was coming, a family might not be in the script.

As unbidden as the word *home*, the image of FBI Special Agent Kade Hunt suddenly flashed in her mind. She hadn't seen him in years, but he was hard to forget.

Agent Gray Eyes she had named him when he bent over her broken body on the streets of Los Angeles and saved her life. He'd used his shirt and hands to slow the blood pouring from her body until paramedics could rush her to the hospital. In turn, a few months later, she did the same for him. But the blood bond, as powerful as it seemed then, couldn't hold them together.

Kade was bothered by their age difference—her eighteen years and fresh out of high school to his twenty-seven—and felt it was too large a gap, regardless of their obvious attraction.

She begged to differ. On her way to Paris to study art months later, she stopped to visit him at his new assignment in Boston—properly chaperoned by Kris Stone at the insistence of Mina's father.

She'd gotten her hopes up. Then his planned visit to Paris at Christmas didn't happen. His work with a serial killer task force took precedence above everything else. Mina was going to fly to his location in the spring, but her schedule of classes got crazy and they couldn't find an open window of time. Honestly, it was her fault as much as his. For two months, she studied with an artist in a rural area between Paris and Lyon, where cell coverage was spotty at best and the artist believed electronic devices robbed the soul of creative energy.

When she was available, Kade wasn't. When he had opportunity, she was tied up.

And that's the way it went for the next eighteen months. They emailed, texted, and talked on the phone, but that wasn't enough with the Atlantic Ocean between them. At one point they went three weeks without communicating, and she knew they were over before they got started.

When she talked to Kris about it, her response was a shrug and *"His loss."*

Mina blew out a cleansing breath. Yeah, but that didn't keep her from wondering what might have been.

She took one last look at the house. The late afternoon sun had moved behind the roofline, silhouetting the house's outline. The turret gained majesty, casting its long shadow across the driveway and to the trees beyond, and she could picture oil lamps being lit in the rooms as the family prepared for the evening meal decades ago.

Kade would be about 34 now. Her 25th birthday was in October. That gap no longer sounded so large. As Kris said back then, the man was an idiot.

Not that she thought about him that much anymore.

She sighed, reluctant to leave this house. Then she began the long hike back to the old mill.

When she reached the bottom of the road, she paused, staring at the downed realtor sign. It was a crazy idea. The place was a wreck. And judging by the roof, rotted porches, and sagging lines, likely unsalvageable. It would, at minimum, cost a fortune.

Mina used her cell to take a picture of the realty sign and phone number, then texted it to her attorney and financial advisor, Abigail Coddington.

It didn't hurt to ask.

CHAPTER NINETEEN

MINA YAWNED CONTINUOUSLY the next morning as she drove to Deer Cove. The moving company from Seattle hadn't arrived until nearly 2:00 a.m. By the time they unloaded and she got to bed, light was already seeping in the windows.

Traffic stopped as a driver two cars ahead attempted to parallel park in front of one of the stores. It wasn't the weekend yet, but all the local schools were out for the summer, and the sidewalks were filled with people. Clearly, she was going to have to do more walking and less driving during the busy months. Or get a bike.

A block ahead, she caught a glimpse of Old Mike coming down one of the side streets on her left. He was dressed in different but similarly scruffy clothing, clutching his satchel in front like something precious as he crossed Main Street with other pedestrians. True to form, he headed straight to the DC Coffee patio.

The traffic moved again, and a minute later she lucked out and found a parking spot at the swim beach at the north end of Deer Cove not far from Bibs' Beauty Barn. She rested her forehead on the steering wheel. Last night had been a killer, and she was second-guessing her grand plan to swim this morning. Napping in the sun sounded better, but since she wasn't doing daily workouts with Haines, she needed to stay in shape.

She sat up straight and slapped her cheeks. "Wake up, Mina." Alexandra would have slapped harder. Haines would have kicked her in the butt. It was almost eleven o'clock and she needed to get a move on. She stashed her wallet under the seat, and struck out with only her towel and truck key.

Before her lay a scene from a Norman Rockwell painting. Dads tended grills and moms spread tablecloths or blankets. A group of older kids splashed in the water, while younger ones trailed long streams of bubbles as they ran. Four college-age guys were sitting on top of one of the picnic tables, jamming on guitars. They sounded pretty good. Off shore, a rope line of yellow and white floats marked off the shallows for a kids' swimming area, monitored by an older teenage boy on a wooden lifeguard platform.

The flyer Mina saw said the Tadpole group met here three times a week for swims along the northwest shore where boats seldom ventured. Swimming had been a major part of her rehabilitation at her home in Beverly Hills—until it was destroyed. But lake swimming was new to her, and going with others seemed like a good idea.

She located a cluster of four men and three women in their fifties and sixties standing at water's edge on the north end of the beach. They were pulling on swim goggles used by serious swimmers, so she made her way over and introduced herself. They were excited to have a newcomer, especially someone so young, and went on and on about her white hair, her smooth complexion and, of course, the scars on her legs. As she always did, she passed those off as an old accident and changed the subject back to swimming.

"We swim up to Box, then turn around and head back," one of the women, Maria, said. She was medium height and had a lean, sinewy body.

Mina was about to ask what "Box" was, but everyone began wading in. Water swirled up her bare legs, refreshing but not cold.

When chest deep, she dove under. Any lingering weariness fled as the cool liquid momentarily shocked her scalp.

She took up the rear, pacing herself with an easy overhand stroke, pushing herself a little to maintain contact with the others. For older people, they were fast, and daily laps in her parents' pool were quite different from open-water swimming. There was no quick break for each turn at the end of the pool, just a long, constant grind that soon had her heart racing.

After about thirty minutes of the tiring pace, they stopped at the base of a black rock bigger than a house. Its flat edifice rose straight up from the waterline, as if its bottom sat on the lake floor a hundred feet below. She hoped it was anchored well to the shore, because it seemed to lean over the swimmers as they treaded water and rested. The top of the rock appeared fairly level—hence its name, she guessed. A few modest cabins dotted the hill north of the monolith, and the trees probably hid more. With a shiver, Mina turned away, choosing to stare out at the length of the lake. Although the sun was high overhead and heating the surface, cold from the depths swirled around Mina's dangling feet.

"Is it the rock that's called Box?" she asked the baldheaded man named Paul who had been introduced as the de facto leader, "or is Box a community? Sorry, I'm new here."

He smiled at her. "No problem. Box is sort of both, I guess. It isn't a town or anything, just some scattered houses and cabins in this area that gets its name from the rock. Some of the homes have great views from the hill up behind, and sometimes teenagers jump off the top. I did it when I was seventeen."

With her eyes only inches above the water, the sheer wall rose up forever. No way was she taking that plunge.

Paul grinned at her, evidently reading her disinclination to hurl herself from the height. "Amazing what you'll do when you've had too many beers."

It would take a dozen margaritas for Mina. Even then, someone would have to push her.

"Ready to head back?" he said after too short a break, and began leading the group south.

The return trip faced annoying six-inch wavelets created by wind and ski boats. It seemed she got slapped in the face every time she took a breath, and she fought to keep up with the others who didn't appear bothered in the least. The distance between her and the last Tadpole grew with each stroke no matter how hard she worked. By the time the colorful floats of the kids' swim area came into view, her arms flopped like noodles, and her legs dragged behind, useless logs. But she pulled as hard as she could, unwilling to be left too far behind.

The others reached the swim area and strode from the water as if jumping out of a refreshing shower, but Mina paused on hands and knees in the shallows, not sure she could stand. She rolled over onto her butt and managed to lift one hand for a few seconds to wave goodbye to Maria.

Maybe she could just crawl out of the water and lie on the sand for an hour. Or two. Actually, what time did it get dark?

A shadow blocked the bright sun. "Need a hand?"

She lifted her head. A good-looking young guy with bronze skin stood in the calf-deep water, reaching toward her. She clasped his outstretched hand and he easily pulled her to her feet, grabbing her arm again when she dipped on rubbery legs.

"Easy there." He helped her ashore. "First time out with the Tadpoles?"

She nodded. "I thought Tadpoles were slow little wigglers."

The boy laughed. "They've been taking that route up to Box and back for years. If you're not used to distance swimming, you did well to keep up."

"I did well not to drown." She staggered to a picnic bench and dropped down. "I'm so out of practice."

He sat beside her, laughing. "Every year in late July, they sponsor a swim across the lake to Shelter Cove—about a mile and a half. Some of them go round-trip."

No wonder they outpaced her. But she felt good keeping as close as she had. If she kept regular workouts, maybe she would be ready for the July swim.

"You're the lifeguard," she said, recognizing him from when she first arrived this morning.

He nodded. "Just filling in for a friend," he said. "I'm off duty now. My name's Quin Conner."

"As in Conner Creek?" Mina studied him. He might be a bit older than she first thought, and his brown hair had the bleached look of someone familiar with a lot of sun.

He grinned. "Yep. My dad is Ben Conner. His grandfather was one of the early settlers here."

She stuck out her hand, relieved her arm had stopped shaking. "Good to meet you, Quin. I'm Palomino Glass."

"Cool name," Quin said. "I figured that's who you were."

"How…?"

"Small town." He shrugged. "Like it or not, you're news. And with a name like Palomino…"

Palomino would hardly create a ripple if she still lived in SoCal. Celebs seemed to lose brain cells when naming their babies. There was likely an unfortunate kid named *Quinoa* by now. This boy was young enough he probably hadn't seen her story splashed across the Hollywood news. She hoped.

"I met a girl named Star Conner at the coffee shop in Perilous Cove. At the time, I didn't know about Conner Creek. Bright red hair. Any relation?"

Quin grinned. "My sort-of cousin."

Mina opened her mouth to ask what *sort-of* meant, but her stomach picked that moment to rumble ominously.

"Sorry about that," she said as Quin laughed. "Guess I'd better find some food."

He checked his watch. "I'm meeting my girlfriend for lunch at the Crab Shack in a few minutes. If you're hungry, you're welcome to join us."

Mina had yet to eat at the place, but after burning a few thousand calories on the swim, she deserved a reward. Her stomach growled again.

"I'll take that as a yes," Quin said.

———

As Mina climbed into her truck, her phone rang. The display showed her attorney's name.

"Hi, Abigail."

"Palomino." She always used Mina's full name. "I heard back from the realtor."

Mina sat on the seat and propped her left foot on the door hinge. "That was fast. Are they hungry for a sale?"

"I couldn't get a read on that, but he was quite surprised when I described which property I was interested in." She shuffled some papers. "He told me the house is pretty much centered on five acres. He's sending a parcel map for the area. It was built in 1881 by Theodore Mann, and is about 2,900 square feet of living space. It has a barn, a good well—he's sending me the specs on the well's capacity —and a septic system of unknown usability. He was quick to add there is no reason to think the septic shouldn't function adequately."

"That sounds like realtor speak for, it probably doesn't work as it should."

"Most likely," Abigail agreed. "Electricity is available at the site. He said the foundation is solid, but the house needs some repair."

Mina laughed out loud. She should have taken photos for Abigail. "Let me guess: Needs TLC, but it has a great location."

"That sums it up," Abigail said. "The listing price is $250,000, and that includes an adjoining one-acre lot with a small cabin on it. He didn't have details about the cabin, but said that lot could be split off. If so, the price for the house and five acres would drop to $200,000."

He probably didn't *have details* because the cabin was in even worse shape than the main house. She needed to check it out for herself. "How long has it been on the market?"

"Seven years."

"*Years?*"

"Correct."

"I don't know a lot about real estate," Mina said, but doesn't that seem like an awfully long time?"

"It does," Abigail said. "I'm not familiar with the area where you are, but a few months is a long time down here. It could be due to one of the old disclosure items I found."

"What's that?"

"The California Civil Code requires it be disclosed if there is a death on the property within the last three years."

"Someone died there?"

"Correct."

"But if it's been on the market for seven years, when did this death happen?"

"It's not on the current disclosure list, but I did a little digging. The previous owner was an elderly woman estranged from her family of two younger siblings, a brother and sister. She had no children of her own, and lived alone in the house. After her death, the brother and sister fought over who would inherit the property. From the couple of news items I found, there was suspicion the owner was poisoned, and that brought a lawsuit and countersuit from the siblings. No wrongdoing was ever proved, and the lawsuits were settled out of court.

"This all happened over twenty years ago. The other sister moved into the house, and she died there two years later. The brother became the owner and moved in. Seven years ago, he had a stroke. He's in poor health and wants the property sold."

A possible murder and a second death? No wonder Bibs said what she did.

"Even if it isn't on the current disclosure," Abigail said, "these things have a way of coming out, especially with two deaths. Many buyers are superstitious. Extended time on market could also reflect there are major issues with the property that buyers are reluctant to tackle. Or, perhaps, it's simply greatly overpriced."

Mina flicked at a persistent fly that kept landing on her leg. Now that she was drying off, it was getting hot out here. Still, she was intrigued by the property. Two hundred fifty thousand didn't seem too high considering the acreage and view.

"And, if I may," Abigail said, caution evident in her tone, "I'm wondering why you're so close to Los Angeles. Wasn't your plan to stay away from the danger here?"

The pesky fly landed on her knee, zipping off before Mina's hand even twitched toward it. "There's been a new development." She told Abigail about the attack in Berlin.

"Oh, my. Did the police—?"

"They weren't involved. I can't say more, other than there's nothing to worry about from Germany." Kris, and perhaps Mina's dad, would be the only ones she told about Alexandra's part in cleaning up the mess. Others could know about the attack in general, but the Russian valued her secrecy more than anything else.

"And you think it was still from the Viera family?"

Mina remembered the man's smile when she spoke to him in Spanish. "Positive."

"With this last man dead, will they leave you alone?"

"I'm working on that," Mina said, not wanting to get into her detailed plan.

Abigail asked if Mina had talked to her father about the attack and the house.

"I'll call Dad soon," Mina said, and changed the subject. "Let's offer $48,000 for both lots. Tell the realtor that's a generous $8,000 an acre, and that the house is a teardown—the cabin too—which they might well be. I'm betting he hasn't been up there in several of those seven years. But even if the house is restorable, at the minimum it's going to require hundreds of thousands of dollars of his *TLC*."

Abigail wrote down the terms and repeated them back.

"Also, I guess I need to have someone work on a thorough inspection and building permits," Mina said. "I've never done anything like this before. I don't know what I don't know."

"I think I can help with that," Abigail said. "I have a young man working for me now who grew up in Mission Peak. Before he joined our firm, he worked for the city manager there, so he's got contacts with the county. I'll put him on it."

"Abigail," Mina said, weighing the enormity of the tasks, "thank you for this. I really appreciate all you do...I hope you know that. And if you think of anything I'm missing, please let me know."

Abigail promised to be in touch, and Mina started the truck engine, her whole being tingling a little just from beginning the negotiations. A few minutes ago, it was a wild dream. Now it was real. She was actually making an offer. It was like bidding on an item on eBay, upping her max in the dwindling seconds as she competed with others. Only this was on super steroids. And if she won, she would own a wreck.

It was stupid taking on something like this right now. She'd just signed a two-year lease on the mill, and someone was upping their effort to kill her. If she *got dead*, as Haines called it, what would happen to this?

She shook her head. Absolutely crazy.

But bottom line, she wanted the house. It proved she *did* have future plans for her life. She needed that hope. Kris would probably call it faith. Maybe it was. Life was a crapshoot—things could go right or wrong in a heartbeat, and sometimes you just needed to go for it.

This was one of those times she wished she could ask her dad for advice. Not that she didn't trust Abigail—the woman had managed Mina's trust to spectacular growth, which is why she had the money to do this at all. But Dad would want to know where the house was, see pictures, send his own inspector, even plan to see it himself. It would become *his* project, not hers. He was like that. And that didn't even count that he'd totally freak when he discovered it was only 200 miles from L.A.

She pulled out of the swim beach parking lot and headed for town. Crapshoot or not, she was starving.

CHAPTER TWENTY

THE LINE WAS out the door of the Crab Shack when Mina drove by. She spotted Quin chaining his mountain bike to a rack on the sidewalk. Easy parking for him. The first vacant space she found was three blocks up a side street. She might as well left the truck at the beach.

After spending a minute towel-drying and brushing her hair, she pulled on a thigh-length cover-up, grabbed her wallet, and slipped into her flip-flops.

About half the places she lived while studying art had been in older parts of cities or towns, but not all of those were thriving communities with restaurants and other businesses within walking distance. Deer Cove was large enough to have a variety of stores and services, but compact enough to be called a village.

Once, while she lived in Paris, she walked arm in arm with a fellow student, a young man named Henri who lost his vision due to a kiln explosion a few years before. Amazingly, he still worked with pottery.

On that day, Henri challenged her to close her eyes and let him be her guide, to experience Paris as he did. At first, she feared crashing into a pole, or tripping off a curb and plunging into the path of speeding traffic. But Henri's voice was calming, hypnotic, and after about fifteen minutes she loosened her grip on his arm and relaxed as the blind man led her safely through sounds of automobiles, scooters, and workmen.

They passed conversations from sidewalk cafes and storefronts, and noted the difference between recorded music drifting from speakers and that from live performers on corners. He encouraged her to trail her fingers along the stone wall of a building, note the texture of a wrought iron handrail worn smooth by millions passing like herself, detect the heat emanating from a metro post baking in the warmth of the sun.

Some things were harder for her to visualize than others. But not the smells. Oh, the wonderful smells! Garlic and oregano became an Italian eatery, with red and white checkered tablecloths, spicy red sauce, and the bouquet of red wine. Butter, cinnamon, and chocolate transformed into a boulangerie. She had halted there, inhaling deeply, imaging in her mind bright display cases abundant with decadent pastries and confections waiting to be sampled.

"Please," she begged, pulling on his arm.

A laughing Henri held her back. "No, little one. Food comes later," he promised, and tugged her on.

They hurried past alleys where the smells were not so wonderful, and came to the shore of the River Seine, its fresh breeze occasionally tainted by a whiff of unfiltered French tobacco from other strollers.

Her toes stubbed on uneven cobbles on the old streets and walking paths, and appreciated the rare patch of squishy grass. She learned to distinguish the difference between the abrupt shade of a building and the subtler filtering by majestic trees with their softly rustling leaves and cleansed air.

Henri located a bench near a busy sidewalk, and they rested awhile, listening as accents from dozens of countries brushed their ears. The distant bells of Notre Dame, which she'd heard up close dozens of times, were more majestic as she imagined the sprawling city and its inhabitants all experiencing the same unifying musical notes from the cathedral.

Mina felt fortunate that her brief sightless experience allowed her to absorb the cosmopolitan energy of the city deep into her marrow in a way she never had with her eyes open.

"Next time, my Palomino," Henri said, "we *taste* Paris." He kept her hand tucked in the crook of his elbow, as if not wanting her to escape.

Mina laughed at the sincerity of his promise, almost anxious to explore the foods of Paris while unhindered by sight, while hoping he wouldn't require her to lick a lamppost or a wall. Henri remained a dear friend during her year in France, and she missed him terribly when she left for Italy.

Mina wished Henri were here, strolling confidently through Deer Cove, while she gripped his arm—her eyes closed, senses open, drawing in her new town with its unique blend of smells, textures, and sounds.

By the time Mina reached Main Street, Quin had disappeared.

Bypassing the Crab Shack's waiting customers, Mina stepped through the front door. Her mouth watered at the delicious smells of fresh fish, tangy lemon, and clean lake air blowing in through wide windows that opened over the myriad of boats crammed into the little marina. Her stomach kept up a never-ending demand as she approached the check-in desk.

"I'm supposed to meet Quin Conner here," she said to the forty-something hostess with naturally graying hair and a wide smile. "Do you know him?"

"Oh, sure," the woman said, pointing to her right. "Quin's in his usual seat, right over there by the front windows."

Mina wove between the tables, wondering how such a young man warranted a *"usual seat."* Then again, the primary lake tributary bore his name. She found him sitting next to a petite girl dressed in a white long-sleeve shirt. She wore a complex necklace of silver and jade high on her neck, almost like a choker, and the colors contrasted nicely against her tanned skin and short, jet-black hair. The two were head-to-head, oblivious to her approach—and to everything else around, for that matter. Mina stopped at the end of the booth and cleared her throat.

"Oh, hi," Quin said, jumping up. "Glad you could join us. This is my girlfriend, Teal. Teal, this is Palomino." He waited until Mina slid into the opposite side of the booth before he sat down next to the girl. Such manners. Not since Paris.

"Teal," Mina said. "That's a beautiful name."

"So is Palomino Glass." Teal said, smiling back.

A smartphone sat by Teal's water glass, and Mina sighed. There was no such thing as obscurity in the digital age. "You Googled me?"

Teal laughed. "Even better. I ran into Bibs an hour ago. She told me all about you."

Oh, boy.

She took some relief that Bibs didn't know Mina's background. Therefore, Teal couldn't know that Mina's adoptive parents were considered Hollywood royalty—until her mom died.

A waiter came and they placed their orders, Mina following Teal's recommendation of the fish and calamari combo basket, and then Quin excused himself to go to the restroom.

Mina turned to the open window, the breeze sucking the remaining dampness from her hair. Out of remembrance of Henri, she closed her eyes and reached out with her other senses. The noisy restaurant behind her faded, replaced by fresh water, sycamore, pine, sun-baked docks, bait both old and new, the slap of lines against sailboat masts, an outboard motor idling, revving, then receding. Her lips curved into a smile at children's distant laughter. "It's beautiful here," she said, her eyes still closed.

"It's home," Teal said, her voice so wistful Mina almost imagined it on the breeze.

Yes, that was it exactly.

After a few moments, conversations around her returned to normal, silverware again clanked, glasses tinkled, servers rushed. The spell dissolved. She opened her eyes and anticipated surprise and perhaps embarrassment on Teal's part at Mina's momentary lapse into her own world. Instead, she saw a reflection of understanding.

Then she noticed the girl had shrugged out of her shirt. Puckered scars in intricate patterns ran up both arms. A pattern of white raised scar tissue in a maze-like design wrapped her right shoulder, and a half dozen small tattoos and raised artwork peeked around the sides. Teal unstrapped the wide leather band of her watch, revealing more scars encircling her wrist. She slid an assortment of woven bracelets up her other wrist, exposing the scarred skin beneath. This girl had been held captive. Her eyes said so, too, if the binding marks weren't enough.

Mina wasn't sure what to say, how to react to Teal's deliberate provocation. Then, in an awful moment, Mina knew the truth. The news stories she read of the corruption in the Los Angeles District Attorney's Office, the mutilated body, the shooting at Desperation Falls here at Storm Lake. Teal was the teenage girl involved, the center of it all. As a juvenile, her name was never revealed, but the sensational story raced nationwide. A young teen held captive in L.A., miraculously escaping, only to be tracked by a psychotic killer to the aptly named Desperation Falls. Mina couldn't help glancing out the window. Right across the lake from where they sat in a fish restaurant.

"You can close your mouth," Teal said, as she slipped the shirt on again, the marred skin once again hidden. Then she smiled.

"I'm sorry." Mina shook her head. "I don't understand. Why would you choose to…"

"I wanted you to know. You see, I wasn't entirely truthful a few minutes ago," Teal said, casually buttoning a cuff. "After talking with Bibs, I *did* Google you. Well, not Google exactly. I don't mean to brag, but I'm pretty good online. It wasn't hard to connect the dots."

Mina's shoulders sagged, and it wasn't from the long swim. Was it truly this easy to find her? All the years of traveling and being careful rendered futile by a teenager with a smartphone?

"You've lived several places in the past seven years. I'd love to travel to some of them." Teal finished the last button on her shirt.

"How…?"

"Once I found a photo of you with your professional name, I used an online photo recognition site to search for similar faces. The app's still in beta, so not many people know about it. It's called M32K1. Anyway, your high school yearbook picture came up—with the name *Lilly Hawthorne*. You're older, but you haven't changed that much."

Mina sank back into the chair. If the swim had sapped her physical energy, this news drained her very spirit. Scenarios of packing her things and breaking the lease on the mill filled Mina's head, accompanied by the sinking loss of this place she was beginning to think of as special—perhaps a refuge.

She fought to speak around the lump in her throat. "How long has this…software app…"

Teal toyed with her water glass. "The FBI and others have had stuff like it for years, but this is the first site I've seen where it's coming to the public. The developers are promising a release date of September 1st. But even though I'm a beta tester, it's going to cost a pile to actually buy. Way out of my league."

Teal's matter of fact attitude surprised Mina. She wasn't gloating or acting like a stalker fan of Mina's mother, Ekaterina Orlov.

"I'm not sure I understand," Mina said. "I mean, why did you even think to look me up?"

"I'm still a little cautious whenever someone new moves to the lake," Teal said, leaning forward, "and I research everyone." She shrugged. "Call me paranoid."

That was the basic preparation Mina had learned from Alexandra. *You can never be too careful.*

"You can never be too careful," Teal echoed aloud.

Mina barely kept from jerking in her seat. Whether it was because of the familiar words without the Russian accent, or the fact this teenager understood what it was like to be hunted, Mina didn't know. Either way, it was sad someone so young had to live like this. But there it was. Perhaps they weren't so different—except Teal's attacker was dead. Whereas Mina's…

"Once I discovered who you were," Teal said, "I knew it was only a matter of time before you heard my story or figured it out for yourself. I wanted you to know now."

"Why?" The girl's ordeal was behind her. They'd caught the guy. Even if the justice system didn't carry out his death sentence, he'd never get out of prison.

Teal gave a slight smile. "There wasn't much information about you..."

Which was exactly as Mina wanted. Her father's PR people had paid handsomely to persuade reporters to bury her part in the story.

"...but enough to know you fought back. I figure you had training. I'm hoping you can teach me a few moves. Survival skills. You know, just in case."

Mina sat back. This girl wanted self-defense training? No matter how good Teal was with her research, she would never find mention of Mina's trainer. Alexandra Pavlovna was a ghost, and expert at moving through society without leaving a trace. Alexandra gave *low profile* a new meaning.

For a crazy minute, Mina wondered if she could get Alexandra and Mike to visit her here. The Mad Russian was a formidable trainer, relentless. Mina looked closer at Teal. Could this girl handle that level of intensity? But with Alexandra expecting a baby, any plans like that would have to wait for months, and that was providing Mina was still alive.

"And we can compare scars," Teal said. Her pixie nose and sprinkle of freckles across her nose didn't mask her intransigent seriousness.

Mina didn't know the details of Teal's story, but the scars—the visible ones—were real, and far deeper than the skin. Mina had been able to fight back against her attackers, but Teal had been held captive, restrained while her pain was inflicted. It was all Mina could do to suppress a shudder.

Yes, this teenager was made of sturdy stuff, but could she keep up with the rigorous training Alexandra demanded? Mina raised a brow in her best and most intimidating impression of the Russian.

"Perhaps." She might have thrown in a hint of a Russian accent. Teal might have returned the slightest smile. Mina liked this girl.

"Hey, you two." Quin slid in next to his girlfriend, grinning at them. "What did I miss?"

Teal looked at Mina and they both laughed. "Nothing," Mina said at the same time Teal said, "Everything."

Quin didn't seem to be put off by being an outsider to girl talk, and that made Mina like him even more.

But as Mina listened to the two young people plan their afternoon in seeming oblivion to the world's dangers, she knew her situation was quite different from Teal's. For Mina, there still the continuing threat from the Viera family. Although the three brothers and their sadistic sister were dead, someone was carrying on the family grudge. She needed to call Proxy and get a report. Had her team of hackers found anything?

CHAPTER TWENTY-ONE

MINA MUST HAVE CONSUMED a thousand calories in tarter sauce alone. At least the beer-battered fish was flash broiled in a wood-fired oven that made it as tasty as deep-fried but without the oil. No need to mention the mountain of spicy fries and dipping sauces that came in three flavors—though the taste of the third one was impossible to determine with her lips flaming.

While eating, Mina learned Quin used his boat to do deliveries all around the lake for Porter's Drug, a small, branch outlet here in Deer Cove for the larger drugstore in Mission Peak. He also gave rides to people needing to visit the lake's only medical facilities in Deer Cove. And she was impressed to learn the grocery store had a website where one could place an order and have it delivered, often by Quin Conner.

One thing Mina found they all had in common: Quin and Teal were also adopted. Quin talked openly about how his mother had disappeared when he was a baby, and not long after his father died, Ben Conner came into his life and eventually adopted him. Mina wanted to hear Teal's story, but the girl filled the time asking questions about the mill. Bibs had recruited her to work in the art studio's front room when it opened on the upcoming July Fourth weekend.

After their meal, Mina staggered down to the dock with the couple. Quin was dropping Teal off at her home across the lake. Teal climbed into the bow of Quin's small boat, then helped him bungee his bicycle crosswise with its wheels extending a little beyond each side. They'd obviously done it many times.

Mina returned Teal's wave as the aluminum boat cut through the calm water on its way out of Deer Cove. They were a cute couple, certainly more mature than anyone she knew when she was finishing high school. Maybe living at Storm Lake, away from the Southland's plastic craziness, allowed kids to mature at a faster rate. Or forced them to. Even in this idyllic setting, Teal carried a deep-seated wariness that carved lines at the corners of her young eyes when she appraised every stranger who came into the restaurant or passed on the sidewalk.

Mina turned and began the hike up the street to her truck, sincerely hoping Teal's lightning-fast discovery of her identity was a fluke. But when this M32K1 software became available to the public... Well, all bets were off. Her picture was virtually plastered all over European security systems. That may have been a mistake. How long would it take anyone to link up her old and new identities? Seconds.

According to Teal, not only could M32K1 track her practically anywhere there was a real-time camera—and they were everywhere —the company was also negotiating agreements with dozens of online photo storage sites. Virtually every photo taken with a smartphone contained metadata of GPS, date, and time. Find a face— even one in the background from an uploaded tourist's snapshot— and the software could build a map of when and where the photo was taken. You could track anyone's movements across the world.

Although she steered clear of security cameras after the tests with Karl and his team, she didn't exactly worry about them either.

The big unknown was if her enemy knew about this M32K1 software. Maybe they already had access to it and were tracking her right now. Tracking her to Storm Lake before her plan was ready would be a disaster.

Time to be more diligent.

Mina waggled the tension from her jaw and rolled her shoulders as she unlocked the truck, at the same time surreptitiously scanning the street. Five cars away, a middle-aged couple was getting into a Prius plastered with stickers about saving whales and the planet. He was bald, she waddled. Beyond them, two preteen boys on bikes chased each other around a yard, jumping off a sheet of plywood propped up a couple of inches on a two-by-four. Hardly assassins on the hunt. But a true assassin wouldn't appear obvious, would they?

"Paranoia is part of being prepared," Alexandra had instructed, and Mike had pounded *Situational Awareness* as the first and last tool in staying alive. It wasn't until she noted Teal's watchfulness in the restaurant that Mina realized how lax she'd become.

"Get your head in the game, Palomino, or you're going to be wearing cement shoes and sleeping with the fishes at the bottom of the lake." Old black and white gangster movies were some of her and her dad's favorites, and they'd spent hours watching them in his home office when she was a teen. Just because the stories were fictional didn't make them untrue.

Mina started the truck's engine. It sputtered a little, then evened out, missed a couple beats, then ran smoothly. The idle speed varied a little, up and down.

"Always keep your vehicles and weapons in top condition."

The exterior might be deteriorating, but she made it a point to keep the Toyota's engine and running gear in top shape. When Bibs had been in sales mode about the town, she mentioned an auto repair place.

Four blocks over on a back street, Mina spotted a Quonset hut constructed of heavy corrugated steel, like something salvaged from World War II surplus. *Deer Cove Auto* had been painted on the flat wooden fascia long enough ago that the white paint barely contrasted with the aged wood. Overall, the business appeared a little sketchy, but the small parking area in front held a hodgepodge of vehicles, including some near her truck's vintage. A man with his head in the engine of a pickup straightened as she pulled in, and began wiping his hands on a red shop rag. He wore a tattered ball cap backwards on his head, but his gray-blue mechanic's jumpsuit was relatively unstained. Above the right hand breast pocket, *MARK* was stitched in white thread.

After spending her lunch hour filling her mind with bad memories and possibilities of what could go wrong, she actually relaxed a little. Some people would find that weird, but for Mina, she felt aware and more prepared. The trick was to stay that way.

As she climbed out of the truck, she saw Old Mike walking on the other side of the street. Mark lifted his hand in greeting, and Mike returned it. He kept going without a word, but he did shoot a quick glance at Mina.

"Hi," she said to the mechanic. "I'd like to make an appointment for a tune-up."

CHAPTER TWENTY-TWO

Boston

"TAKE A THAWED Thanksgiving turkey and toss it off the back of a truck driving down a dirt road at forty miles an hour, then ask me to fix it. That's you, Kade."

"Thanks for the enticing holiday visual, doc," Kade said. He might never eat turkey again.

"I'm just saying, if you were that turkey, you're looking a lot better now."

When it came to reconstructive plastic surgery, Dr. Sadana was the best in Boston. He specialized in trauma cases, not boob jobs and butt implants. Kade appreciated that—and that he didn't have to sit by the next Buxom Barbie in the waiting room.

"Look up for me," the doctor said as he examined the skin graft on Kade's chin. After two rounds of grafts all over his body, the patches were healed. Except for skin color, the surgeries were nearly invisible.

Sadana's parents were from India, and he looked like the handsome young actor in *Slumdog Millionaire*. But he'd been raised in New Jersey. He had a cabbie's sense of humor, and an accent like

Paulie Walnuts on the *Sopranos*. Even after dozens of visits, Kade was still surprised each time Doc Sadana opened his mouth.

"Back of your head looks good too."

"Thanks for that, doc. Seriously." Doc Sadana had been able to stretch Kade's scalp tissue over the missing piece and stitch it together, eliminating the road rash bald spot.

Kade slid off the exam table and winced as he stood.

"Ankles still hurt?" the doctor said, stripping off his exam gloves and tossing them in the stainless waste can.

"Only when I put my full weight on them. The orthopedist says the alignment is good." The soles of his feet had needed thorough cleaning to get all the dirt and small stones out, but they healed fine and didn't bother him anymore. His ankles were another story. Babying them tweaked his knees, hips, and back, throwing everything out of alignment.

Dr. Sadana handed Kade his crutches, then leaned against the counter and crossed his arms. "Well, Kade, I think my work is done. Keep sunscreen on the new skin. Wear a hat and long sleeves. Give everything a chance to settle in. I promise you, my friend, it will only get better."

Kade accepted the handshake. "Thanks, doc. My sister is disappointed you didn't make me look like George Clooney, but I'm very grateful for what you've done. I hope you know that."

"Time for a selfie," the doctor said, and pulled out his cell phone. They stood side by side, smiling as he snapped a photo. Then Sadana put his hand on Kade's shoulder. "Call me if you have any questions or concerns."

CHAPTER TWENTY-THREE

Over seventy percent of the Earth's surface is Water. The universal solvent. Pure. Nourishing. Vital. Spiritual. Human bodies are more water than anything else.

INTEGRITY OF WATER, BY V.M. NARRANO

Evie stared out over the hazy San Fernando Valley, then read the quote again while sipping her water bottle. She'd looked it up. The human body was about 60 percent water. If she drank enough, could it cleanse the remaining 40 percent—flush out what was killing her? Some believed so.

She almost laughed at the thought of being 60 percent pure and spiritual. Maybe once—a long time ago. Before she'd grown up and learned how the world worked.

Still, she liked Narrano's writings. Through beautiful prose, the author trimmed away the world's clutter, revealing the essence and artistic underpinnings so often obscured by meaninglessness. But did that mean the author had the keys to life? How could one person know, really know, what was important? The way the world should be. The way *she* should be.

Evie thought of the reclusive author as male, but no one really knew for sure. The publisher wasn't talking, and a growing number of investigative reporters hadn't cracked anyone who knew the truth. As contrary as it was to her resistance to men dominating business, something in the writing conveyed leadership and strength different from every woman Evie knew. VM Narrano was a man, she was sure of it.

She thumbed through the pages of the thin book, one of six she owned and had read multiple times before he became the current sensation. Now he was everywhere, people elevating him to new world, mystic guru status and they had no clue who he was.

And wasn't that the fundamental genius? Like the book *The Secret* from years ago. Everyone was hinged on what the secret of *The Secret* could be. The hype had gone on and on.

Narrano's twist was he didn't conclude how people should act after reading his books. He stated his observations. There was no secret for everyone to follow, no *therefore, do this thing to be happy*, or *Next Steps*. No preaching of right or wrong.

That appealed to Evie. Narrano simply took her to a place of peace and left her to…what? Contemplate?

Well, not about how to live her own life. She doubted Narrano would approve of revenge. Contemplation could wait until she could no longer lift a hand to determine her own course. No, not even at that point. She wanted control of how she ended, not be some helpless invalid dying in a hospital bed.

Her phone signaled Slade's ringtone and she lifted it to her ear.

"Yes."

"I may have a lead. Well, something that could develop a lead."

Evie stood and drained the last of the water as she walked to her kitchen. She dropped the empty into the recycle bin, feeling better for pouring 16.9 ounces of purity into her body. Maybe it contained some of Narrano's spirituality. Couldn't hurt.

Her physical self might be plotting her downfall, but she wanted to accomplish one more thing before the end came.

"Tell me."

"I heard from a guy who works in our I.T. department."

"And?"

"He's found some new facial recognition software."

CHAPTER TWENTY-FOUR

PROMPTLY AT NINE o'clock the next morning, Mina dropped off her truck with Mark at Deer Cove Auto, then walked the several blocks to the swim area. Sunlight danced on the water, splintered by the occasional boat wake. Mina stowed her bag in one of the new lockers mounted like mailbox clusters on the base of the lifeguard stand. The combination was an easy one: her mother's birthday.

A pair of SUVs drove up, and kids and two moms climbed out. Two preteen boys raced past Mina, discarding flip-flops, T-shirts, and towels before splashing into the water in tumbling balls of laughter. The others piled ice chests and swim gear on a picnic table.

A muscular, deeply tanned young man she didn't know rode up and said hi. He chained his bicycle to the lifeguard stand, then spent a few minutes spraying on sunblock and opening the large umbrella that shaded the two canvas chairs perched on the flat platform.

Although the air was warming fast, the lake water painted chill rings around Mina's legs as she waded in. It certainly didn't seem to be bothering the boys as they thrashed to the platform floating a dozen yards out and climbed on top. She was probably still tired from the Tadpoles' grueling pace. The training with Haines hadn't done a thing for her swimming muscles, and she'd been so wasted from the run and shoot drills that she eschewed other training while in Phoenix.

At waist deep, she splashed water over her arms and shoulders, then she surged forward and dove under. The world above became a memory, muted light and sound as she swam a few yards underwater. Sunlight flickered on the sloping gravel bed, an ever-changing mosaic of geometric shapes. By the time she surfaced and turned her face to the sun, the water temperature felt merely refreshing.

With no one else to chase today, she swam slowly, alternating from crawl to sidestroke to backstroke to breaststroke, concentrating on form and on stretching every part of her body. The old wounds in her arm and chest never bothered her—they had healed completely—but her left calf and especially her hip still cramped after workouts. A cool-down stretch helped, and she vowed to do that when she completed the swim.

These minor aches were her small price to pay, her penitence and gratitude to others who had died or been badly wounded protecting her. She hoped the pain would never fully go away.

Ninety minutes later, Mina skirted DC Coffee as she walked through town. No sense adding back double or triple the calories she burned on her swim. Today's more leisurely pace had been a perfect blend of exercise without leaving her body limp with fatigue. She needed her strength to walk home, and then return later this afternoon when Mark promised her truck would be ready.

When she crossed the bridge onto the lawn of the mill, she spotted a dusty Jeep Wrangler in the parking area. Its red paint was a close match to her own truck. The whine of a power saw came from inside the building. The carpenter Bibs had promised.

She smiled at the contrast to her parents' old driveway in Beverly Hills. Parties there would find the circular drive lined with Mercedes, Bentleys, and flashy waist-high supercars whose speedometers exceeded two hundred miles per hour. She rode in one once—

unbeknown to her parents, of course—the digital speed readout flashing past 164 before they topped a low hill and went airborne. Her friend Pana had screamed so loud that the driver, a twenty-something actor, let off the gas. Mina and Pana were strapped into the single passenger seat. If they had crashed that night, they would probably have been buried in one casket.

Mina rarely knew any of her parents' guests personally, but that never stopped her from chatting with major movie stars. She always treated them like ordinary people, refusing to be cajoled into worshiping the orbits of their professional worlds. Her favorite breakthrough questions were about where they attended high school, their first car, how the air smelled where they grew up, and if they'd taken a long bike ride lately. Occasionally, ego rose to the surface and the guest walked away from her uninformed inquiries, but usually the big star transformed into a fairly regular person. Mina saw it her mission to ground them in the real world—at least temporarily, and as much as one could do at a party that was, after all, in The Hills.

She didn't miss the plastic entertainment industry, where shameless butt kissing prevailed, everyone wanting something from everyone else. She could never do what her dad did on a daily basis.

The saw noise cut off, replaced by pounding. It was time to investigate. When she opened the front door, she was shocked at how much had been accomplished this morning.

Yesterday when she returned home, the carpenter was gone for the day, but the floor patches were in place, sanded, and shiny with curing finish. But today...

Hand-built display cases were lined up a few feet out from the rear windows. They were constructed with clear glass notched into three-inch logs sporting the same satiny natural finish as the rest of the beams. A dozen rustic tripods were placed around the room, and overhead, three twisted limbs were suspended horizontally on chains and dotted with screw hooks for hanging merchandise.

Mina heard a clunk, and spotted a figure hunched behind one of the cases.

"Hello," she called, and was surprised when a blond woman stood. A quite pregnant blond woman. "You're not AJ, are you?"

"That's me," the woman said, wiping her brow with a leather glove, leaving a streak of sawdust behind.

"Oh." Bibs had said the carpenter's name was AJ, but she assumed that was a man. "I was expecting... Oh, never mind," she said, walking toward the woman. "I'm Palomino Glass."

The woman removed her right glove and extended her hand. "I get that a lot. Lena is my real name, but a lot of folks around the lake call me AJ. Keeps everyone on their toes when a blond woman shows up with a nail gun."

Mina smiled, glad Lena had a sense of humor about it. "Uh, I don't mean to sound biased or anything, but I saw the floors yesterday. Is it safe for you to be doing this...while expecting, I mean?"

Lena laughed and put a protective hand over her very round belly. "Yeah, well no worries there. My husband banished me to napping in the car while he applied the finish. Who was I to argue?"

"Oh, okay."

"Believe me, I'm milking this pregnancy for everything it's worth." She blew a stray hair off her face. "After all, it's his fault."

Mina wasn't sure how to respond to that, so she changed directions. "You've made amazing progress since I left this morning. These cases are beautiful." She ran her hand along the satiny wood.

"Well, I can't take credit for those, either. They come from a craftsman in Mission Peak. Stone brought them in an hour ago."

"Stone is the craftsman?"

Lena shook her head. "Stone is my husband—the one with the paintbrush."

"Wait," Mina said. "His last name—*your* last name—is Stone?"

"Uh, yeah. Sorry, I guess I didn't make that clear. Why?"

Mina laughed. So many hints strung together in totally the wrong way.

Lena cocked her head sideways. "I must be missing something."

"Me, too!" Mina said, shaking her head. "Sorry. It's just…I know his sister."

"Kris?"

Mina nodded. "She'll be here soon to stay with me."

That produced a frown from the blond carpenter. "Stone is going to murder her."

"Why?"

"He's been trying to get in touch with her, but apparently she's gone off the grid."

"She's been working out of the country on some jobs," Mina said.

"Well, apparently you're better informed than we are. Teal's been worried too."

"Quin Conner's girlfriend?"

"You've met her?"

"I had lunch with her and Quin yesterday at the Crab Shack. How does Teal know Kris?"

"Teal's my daughter," Lena said. "Our daughter." Her smiled broadened. "I've only been her official mom for about a year, but she's trying hard to whip Stone and me into parental shape. His first name is Alex, by the way, but everyone calls him Stone."

Mina nodded, connecting more dots. "Teal told me she was adopted."

"We kind of all found each other at the same time," Lena said. "It's a little unusual."

Mina filed away Lena's and Alex's names, vowing to make some notes later; maybe a wall chart. What with the Conner name popping up all over and Star being Quin's *sort-of* cousin, Mina was getting connection overload.

Then she realized what this meant: Teal's scars, the news reports about the shooting at the falls, and the blonde television carpenter whose husband had been murdered in Los Angeles. "Oh! You're… You were in L.A."

A shadow crossed the woman's face, but she nodded.

"Sorry," Mina said. "I'm just putting all this together. You see, I used to live in L.A. I've been gone for a few years, but I still heard about the former district attorney and his involvement here."

Lena sighed. "It was a difficult time. But I wouldn't have Teal and Stone in my life if it hadn't happened." She touched her belly again. "Or this little one. Life is strange, isn't it?"

Strange didn't even begin to cut it. There was enough tragedy and drama between the two of them to create an entire season on HBO. But the world didn't need another made-for-TV movie about horrific tragedies. Teal and Lena had suffered enough. To be a parent of a teen girl who'd lived through that horror took guts. And by every indication over lunch, Teal was becoming a beautiful young woman. If Nathan Hawthorne the producer ever suggested doing a movie about Lena and Teal, Mina would pull every daughter card in the deck to squash the idea.

Mina gestured around the room. "Show me what you're working on."

She followed along as Lena enthusiastically explained the plumbing and electrical upgrades, window replacements, and finishes used on the different wood surfaces. Mina didn't have the carpentry skills, but she knew and appreciated tools: air compressors for her blasting equipment, bench grinders and polishers, and lots of hand tools. Lena's results were no less artistic. When cleaned of sawdust and filled with colorful items for sale, this room would be fantastic.

CHAPTER TWENTY-FIVE

"THEY COUNTERED AT $88,000," Abigail said.

Mina was on the back deck, cooling off from a sweaty morning down in her studio sorting and shelving her equipment and supplies.

"What do you suggest?" Mina asked. The broker's counter was forty grand more than her offer.

"Well, your offer *was* $202,000 lower than their listing price. But since their counter was also far below list, that says they really want to get rid of it. If you want it for less, you could offer for the main house and five acres; not go for the cabin."

Mina hadn't even seen the cabin, but she wanted it all. Like before, it felt right. And that view...

"How about this," Abigail said. "We agree to $88,000 and ask them to pay for the well tests."

"Okay."

"I'll call them right now," Abigail said, and hung up.

Mina paced the length of the deck and back, then decided to walk to town. It could be late today or even tomorrow before she heard from Abigail, and Mina would go nuts with waiting. But no matter what the realtor countered with, she was buying the house!

Fortunately, Connie wasn't at DC Coffee to tempt her with something sinful, and she opted for a lower-calorie iced mocha.

"Would you like a free book?" the young man who was running the machines asked, pointing to a stack on the end of the counter. "Connie said someone left a box of them on the doorstep this morning with a note to give them away to customers."

There were several copies each of five or six different titles, all by the same author. Mina picked one of the thin volumes. *Creation & Restoration*, by V.M. Narrano. She'd heard of the writer, a national sensation—and a mystery because no one knew if the writer was male or female. The back cover text caught her eye.

Creation requires complete vision to craft something from nothing, while Restoration requires complete dedication to brush aside corruption and find lost beauty.

Wow. If that didn't speak to her present situation, nothing did. All of her art was creating, but restoring a house would be totally new. She just hoped uncovering beauty up on the mountain wouldn't require a bulldozer.

Mina had no sooner returned to the mill when Abigail's name showed on her phone display.

"That was fast," Mina said, sipping the last of her mocha. Connie Langworth had a skewed definition of *low calorie*.

"They accepted your offer," Abigail said. "We'll have the signed papers tomorrow."

Abigail had Mina's power of attorney, and the deed would be recorded in Mina's new real estate trust name, Panamania. It was Mina's nickname for Pana. "How soon will we… I mean…"

Abigail laughed. "Don't worry, Palomino. Since you're going ahead regardless of the significant work, I waived the inspection and asked for a seven-day escrow. We'll transfer the full purchase price into escrow tomorrow, plus a buffer for title search and other fees. No monetary delays that way." She explained that gave them tomorrow through Saturday to wrap things up, then the following Monday to record the title and get the keys—if there were any.

Even with her limited knowledge of how these things worked, Mina knew that was incredibly fast. Abigail said her assistant would shepherd every detail to make sure it closed on time.

"His name is Carter Perney, by the way. He'll be staying in Mission Peak throughout your construction process. I'll have him come up and introduce himself as soon as he arrives."

"Does he know any good contractors?"

Once again, Abigail had thought of everything. Carter was planning for a general contractor to stop by on Monday after the closing, and his crew was ready to begin as soon as permits were approved.

"Wow, Abigail. I can't thank you enough. This will be fun."

Abigail laughed at that. "I've never known a remodel to be fun. *Afterward*, maybe. Of course, this doesn't sound like a typical remodel."

That was truth. After Mina ended the call, she took a big breath. She'd done it. Bought a house! And not just a tract home with stucco walls and Spanish tile roof, but a mega project with unlimited potential.

The little book lay open on her lap.

Restoration requires complete dedication to brush aside corruption and find lost beauty.

She smiled. Yep, regardless of Abigail's naysaying, this was going to be fun.

The furniture delivery truck from Mission Peak arrived on Monday as promised, and Mina spent most of the day making up beds at the Mill, arranging tables and chairs, and stocking the linen cabinets. The walls were still bare, and the overall feeling bordered on spartan. But it was as good as she could do. Interior decorating wasn't in her wheelhouse.

On Tuesday, she hired Quin Conner to take her truck on a run to the Costco in Mission Peak and stock up on more supplies for when Haines and his team arrived. She had a feeling they would be pretty self-sufficient, wanted to do the easy stuff for them so they could concentrate on the plan.

In the afternoon, she loaded two four-foot squares of plywood scraps Lena had into her truck and drove up to the house. Her house —almost. The rutted road reminded her of Bibs' recommendation of Merle for projects like this. Maybe he could grade and level the road like he had down below.

She parked in front of the porch and climbed out, stopping to stare in amazement at her investment. Unfortunately, it looked just as bad as it had before. But not for long.

The plywood sheets spread her weight on the sagging porch boards, allowing her to safely get to the front entrance. She turned the knob and shoved the door open. Tentatively, Mina stepped inside. Fortunately, the floors inside were in much better condition than the porch, but still creaked with each step.

A narrow doorway at her right led into a small room that could have been used as a parlor or bedroom. The woodwork and trim didn't match the rest of the walls, making her think it was a later addition. It screamed to be opened up to the rest of the house again. To the left of the front door was a large space that was probably the main living room and dining area.

Partially hidden behind the parlor room, stairs rose to the right, turned left on a landing, then doubled back and continued up to the second floor. A full sheet of plywood covered what was probably a window on the landing's exterior wall. As much as she wanted to see what the upper floor held, the rotted carpeting covering the stair treads warned her away. No telling what was underneath.

She snapped several pictures with her cell, then started down the hallway. The old boards creaked ominously with each step and she sighed, stopping again. The house wasn't officially hers yet, so further exploration should wait until a professional could evaluate everything and make it safe. It wouldn't do to fall through the floor.

After a few more pictures, she retreated out the front door, shutting it and tossing her plywood squares back into the truck. She walked around the right side of the house. About halfway up was a large window she judged was the one on the stair landing. The window faced north, meaning it would receive plenty of light but no direct sun. Perfect for the creation she had in mind.

Her rush order of glass arrived by truck on Thursday. Six sheets three quarters of an inch thick, two more were quarter inch. She rolled them into the downstairs workspace on her vertical dollies.

Although it would be weeks before her house was ready to accept her creation for the landing window, she felt almost a compulsion to finish it.

She chose one of the thinner sheets that was seven feet high by five feet wide, then began drawing her design on white butcher paper laid across her worktable. At her right was her inspiration: the angel given her by Rowdy Haines.

The first drawing was a small-scale copy. When she was satisfied with it, she put a transparent sheet over it and traced it again. Once satisfied with that, she used a light projector to project the transparency image onto a sheet of transfer paper taped to her glass panel. Here again, she traced the projected image.

It was quiet in the mill, and when she finally took time to step out of the bright projector light, she realized the creek side windows reflected the bright interior like black mirrors. Surprised, she checked her watch: 1:17 a.m. She'd been working steadily for over seven hours.

Her back protested when she stretched, and her left hip made itself known.

"Time for bed." She turned off the projector and headed up the stairs.

When she reached the main floor, she detoured through the front retail space to check the front door lock.

Upstairs, Mina showered, then fell into bed with a smile. Things were coming together—at least here at the lake. But it was time to kick off her plan to draw out the person or persons behind the Viera threat.

CHAPTER TWENTY-SIX

Have confidence in your decisions. Don't rush, but don't wait too long. Inaction is an action, and indecision is always the wrong decision. It won't take you anywhere.

ON LIFE, BY V.M. NARRANO

As ABIGAIL PREDICTED, escrow closed on Monday. At 3:15 p.m., a Toyota Highlander pulled into the lot of the mill. Mina went out to meet the driver. Before she got down the steps, a white Ford F-150 parked beside the SUV.

"Palomino?" the man from the Toyota asked. "Abigail Coddington sent me. I'm Carter Perney."

He appeared to be about her age, and was dressed in khaki pants, deck shoes with no socks, and a dark knit shirt that hugged a flat stomach. He waited as she came down the stairs, then stepped aside to introduce the other man as Russell Howell, the general contractor.

Mina shook both men's hands. The contractor's was dry and leathery from daily use as expected, but Carter's grip surprised her. Not as coarse as Howell's, it was still rugged and strong, like someone who did a lot more than shuffle papers and type on a keyboard.

At Howell's offer to drive, they climbed into his pickup, and Mina directed them up the hill to the house.

"Wow, this is something," Howell said as he parked in the circular drive. "I've been around this county my whole life, but I had no idea this place was up here."

They climbed out and stood before the house.

"And you paid *how* much for this—" Carter started, then laughed as Mina cut him a glance. "Just kidding." He raised both palms in surrender. "Really."

She wasn't sure whether to believe him.

"So, Miss Glass," Howell said, "tell me what you have in mind."

"Palomino, please," she said. "But before we begin, I want to make it clear to you that my name is never to be mentioned. As far as you're concerned, Carter is the agent for the owner, which is a private trust. If I show up on site, please refer to me as Carter's assistant. We can talk privately anytime you need, of course."

"Got it." Howell nodded.

"My assistant," Carter grinned. "I like it."

Mina ignored him and described her plans for a full restoration. New roof, fix or replace the siding as needed, check the foundation, new windows and doors, then new paint with a coordinated color scheme.

Howell rocked back on his heels, but nodded.

"Other than right inside the front door, I haven't seen much of the interior. I'd like to keep as much of the style and craftsmanship as we can, but also modernize it, make it more open, widen the stairs or maybe move them entirely since they are right in the entry, refinish or replace the wood floors. I want a farm-style kitchen, new electrical, plumbing, and heating." She turned to Howell, who was making a few notes on a clipboard. "What do you think?"

He nodded. "Basically keep its character, but modernize everything, make it flow better, and don't ruin its style."

"Yep."

"I've done several like this, so I know the territory," he said, then led them on a walk around the property, viewing it from all sides. They checked out the barn which, other than some missing siding and roofing, appeared to be in good structural shape. He jotted down to add a metal roof to it. Howell continued around to the north side of the house. Mina pointed out a window halfway up the wall.

"I suspect that's the stair landing," she said, and Howell nodded. "I'm making a special window to go there, but I know the positioning may change if you redesign the stairs. Regardless, I'll get you the exact dimensions."

Howell made some suggestions for trim detail and the porch columns, and Carter promised to find someone who could tackle the landscaping.

"One more thing, Palomino," Howell said. "What are you going to name the house?"

"Name it? Like Windsor Castle?"

He smiled. "That might be over the top. But a house like this deserves a name. Something that reveals the character of the owner, the motivation that built it, or the future it will live into."

The contractor had no idea the house might outlive her before it was even finished.

"*Glass House* would be good," Carter said. For once he seemed serious.

"You can give it some thought," Howell said. "This is one thing you don't want to rush. But if you decide on something, it might influence parts of the design. Little touches, you know."

Howell whistled softly as he drove down the mountain back to the mill. Whether it was from the challenge of bringing the house back to its glory, or him mentally calculating all the many new boat payments he was going to earn, Mina wasn't sure. He promised to bring in a few guys tomorrow to do a full assessment, including interior, exterior, foundation, and all the utility systems. Then he would get back to her with a design proposal and rough estimate. He had a draftsman on his staff who could draw up the floor plans.

"Where are you staying, Carter?" Mina asked as they watched Howell pull out of the driveway.

"My mom lives in Mission Peak, so I'll probably stay with her for a while. She thinks I'm too skinny since I went off on my own, so I'll be well fed. I might try to rent a cabin up here to save drive time."

"Oh," Mina said, "I forgot to have us go look at the old cabin while Howell was here."

"I can meet him here tomorrow and do it," Carter said, rubbing his chin, "but I was going to meet my friends at the city building permit department—try to grease the skids."

"That's more important," she said. "Forget the cabin for now. We've got plenty to do with the house."

Carter promised to be back when Howell had his bid ready, then he climbed in his car and drove off. Mina decided Abigail made a good choice in Carter Perney.

Now, it was time for her to get moving on her main goal: staying alive. And for that, she would take the fight to L.A. She pulled out her cell and punched in Proxy's number.

"Yes," came the tiny reply, followed by several clicks.

"Palomino here. Is everything ready for tonight?"

"Affirmative."

If it weren't for the extreme seriousness of the situation, Mina would have smiled. Proxy was such a weird mix of geek and pop-oriented millennial. Sometimes the two styles complimented each other, but more often it was like the woman was born in two different time periods and spliced together. Or, knowing Proxy's abilities just a little, she could be reading her responses from two side-by-side generated scripts, purposefully intending to confuse everyone.

"Anything else?" Proxy asked.

"I can't think of anything. Just wanted to make sure. It's…kind of a big step."

"I understand," Proxy said, her voice hinting at compassion. "Believe me, I do. Once done, you can't go back."

Mina said goodbye, then sat down on the porch steps. *Once done, you can't go back.* Narrano should include that in one of her books.

Next, she called Rowdy Haines. He answered on the first ring.

"Glass," he said. "Good to hear from you. Everything okay?"

"It's a go, Haines. The message goes out tomorrow. I think you'd better call your team and get ready to come."

"Done and done, Glass. We'll see you by noon tomorrow."

"Tomorrow? Oh. You don't need to come that quickly. I thought you'd need a few days to prepare."

"We've been sitting around waiting for your call, Glass. If the message is going out tomorrow, we're coming. Think of things for us to do besides clean weapons."

She couldn't picture Haines cleaning anything except his guns and his truck. "You've got the directions?"

"Please." He sounded offended. Knowing Haines, he probably had GPS, hand-drawn maps, and an Indian scout.

She sighed, but didn't let him hear that. "It'll be good to see you, Haines." Really good.

"You too, Glass. Don't get dead before we get there." He ended the call.

Mina scooted down a step and used the upper one as a backrest. The heat of the day was finally relinquishing its hold, and a soft breeze brought the promise of a cool night. She closed her eyes, tasting the sweet air.

What a week. She bought a house and hired a contractor. And she hired mercenaries.

Because tomorrow she would start a war.

CHAPTER TWENTY-SEVEN

KADE LEFT the reception area and waited for the elevator. The doctors still didn't know exactly what types of drugs Kade had been given while in captivity, but from his description of symptoms, they suspected a variety of hallucinogens. Tests of his hair confirmed trace amounts of Rohypnol, and a blood test found Ketamine. Both were known as date rape drugs.

Rohypnol's effects were lack of muscle control, confusion, drowsiness, and amnesia. Ketamine had hallucinogenic properties, and could increase heart rate and blood pressure. Other effects were nausea, vomiting, numbness, depression, and amnesia. In high doses, it could have potentially fatal respiratory problems and produce out of body episodes. All that sounded like the story of his life—at least for those few weeks of captivity.

After Kade spent a month back in the US, his doctor declared him "*lucky*" that those and other probable drugs seemed to have done no deeper damage. However, he still woke in the middle of the night a couple of times each week, wringing wet, with shadowy, illusive memories brushing the edge of his consciousness. Sometimes parts of his body hurt or stung for several minutes after waking, as if his flesh remembered the abuse even after his mind had blocked it out.

The elevator doors opened. Two occupants moved aside as he made his way in. The lobby button was already lit, and the doors closed.

He'd had a few episodes during the daytime, triggered by a smell or a sound, or even a word spoken in Spanish. Those flashbacks were the worst, draining him of energy, and leaving him with almost crippling paranoia for an hour.

When the car stopped at the lobby level, Kade crutched his way through the clinic toward the main entrance. Spring snow fell heavy and wet, turning the circular driveway into a soupy muck. He spotted his sister's four-door Jeep Wrangler idling at the curb. Due to the flashbacks, the doctors hadn't cleared him to drive.

"How'd it go?" Rowan asked, whipping out of the clinic exit while he struggled to fasten his seatbelt. A solid wall of Boston's notorious traffic loomed ahead, and Kade nearly put his right foot through the floorboard as his sister nonchalantly cut in front of a car on her left and accelerated away from its blaring horn.

"I'm good for another 50,000 miles," Kade said, gripping the armrest, "unless I die in the next ten seconds. Aren't you going to turn on your windshield wipers?"

"Oh, yeah," Rowan said, switching them on to clear the nearly obscured glass.

Kade rubbed a hand down his face. She hadn't even noticed she was driving blind. His captors hadn't killed him, but his sister might.

"We gonna hit Dad's club on the way home?" Rowan asked.

His dad had moved Kade's mom and Rowan from Pasadena in Southern California shortly before Kade's transfer to the Boston office. Dad bought into a winter sports center that specialized in training future Olympians. The center had facilities in Newburyport, Massachusetts where his parents lived, and also in the White Mountains of New Hampshire. That move had been seven years ago, and during the intervening years, Rowan had become a regional giant slalom champion. She retired from competition a year ago before Kade made it to even one of her events. But he'd seen the videos. Aggressive and fearless. And he missed it all.

"I don't feel like working out," Kade sighed, "but I know I have to."

"That's the spirit," Rowan said. The rear wheels slid as she four-wheeled the Jeep around the curving ramp onto Highway 1 North toward Newburyport. Last summer she'd gone to a NASCAR driving experience event, then followed up with additional lessons when she thought she might like to race for a career. Their mother was not pleased, and she was thankful when other interests eventually caught Rowan's eye. Kade braced his legs as the Jeep drifted through the turn. Evidently Rowan hadn't totally let go of the sport.

He still was a few quarts low on overall energy, even with a strict diet, physical therapy, and gym workouts. The doctors all said it was due to the severe trauma his body sustained.

At his mother's insistence, he was also seeing a holistic doctor who specialized in cleansing the system of toxins, which, according to the man, included the pain medications and antibiotics given in the hospital. Kade had to admit to feeling better after beginning the treatments.

"So…" Rowan said as she sped around a slow truck, "I've been doing a little digging on your friend, Lilly Hawthorne."

Kade stared at her. She hadn't said a thing about Lilly since Houston. "I never—"

"I know," she said. "You talked about her in your sleep in the hospital. Those painkillers made you weird, bro." She cut him a glance. "Just sayin'."

"She never contacted Mom and Dad?" He didn't want to ask his parents about it, but it appeared Rowan was already in deep.

"No. I asked."

Kade rubbed his brow. So much for not talking to his parents.

"And all the references and photos I found were with her parents, Nathan Hawthorne and Ekaterina Orlov, or from that shootout. And, *hello!* Why didn't you ever introduce us to her? I mean, Lilly is practically Hollywood royalty. Or at least her parents are. Were." She waved her hand. "Whatever."

Another mistake on his part. Maybe if he had introduced her to his family things would have turned out differently.

"That's all you found?" he asked.

"Yep. Until I asked Gretchen. She's this girl I know in school—crazy-smart computer science major. Anyway, she told me about this new software application called M32K1 that matches faces."

"That stuff has been around for years," Kade said. Facial recognition was in use in many law enforcement agencies, especially international ones, and it was improving every year.

Rowan shook her head. "This one is different. It's still in beta, but Gretchen signed up as a tester. It uses all the public photos from practically every social media platform, plus many private security cameras in place all over the world."

"Why would those companies give out that data?"

Rowan rubbed her thumb over her fingertips in the universal symbol for money. "Gretchen says the company is paying big bucks for the rights. Plus, the company will trade tracking analysis back to the social media companies so they can do more targeted regional advertising. You know—like when you look at something on Amazon and a few minutes later an ad for the item shows up in your Facebook feed? The photo database is massive and growing. And the program will be available soon to the public. For a hefty price of course."

Kade couldn't help himself. "What...? I mean, did you find something?"

"Oh, yeah. Your Lilly—"

"She's not *my* Lilly."

Rowan waved a hand. "Whatever. Anyway, Lilly kept a low profile for years. Actually, she kept a *zero* profile, starting a few months after the attack in Malibu. I couldn't find one photo of her for over six years."

About the time she moved to Paris, Kade thought. Her identity change had worked.

"But then in January this year, she starts popping up all over the place. In Paris, Brussels, Amsterdam, and finally in London. I'm talking hundreds of pictures from store security cameras, banks, museums, traffic cameras, department stores. It's like she's trying to be as visible as possible. In a bunch of the shots, she's looking right at the camera, like it's a dare. No hats, no scarves, and no sunglasses. Six years zip, then she's showing up like William and Kate."

"That doesn't sound like Lilly," Kade said. "Are you sure it isn't a lookalike? They say everyone has a twin."

"Yeah, a doppelgänger. Well, this software claims 94 percent accuracy, and that's due to poor quality pics. And with all the excellent full-facial shots of Lilly, Gretchen didn't think it could fail." Rowan glanced over at him. "What's even weirder is that she dropped off the radar again. Four weeks of a zillion photos, then she's a ghost. Not one picture since then. You sure your girlfriend isn't a spy?"

"She's not my—"

"Yeah, yeah."

He wondered if he saw some of the photos if he could tell if it was really Lilly. It had been over four years since he'd seen her. Had she cut her hair? Changed its color? An ache to see the photos started in his chest.

"By any chance, did Lilly change her name?" Rowan asked.

Kade couldn't hide his surprise. "Why?" He'd never told anyone about her name change. He still thought of her as Lilly at least half the time.

"Because every instance Gretchen found in that recent burst of photos links her to the name *Palomino Glass*. But I swear, it's the same girl from the Hollywood pictures."

Kade stared out the window at the blur of falling snow. Something had changed for Lilly—for Mina—a trigger that had forced her out of hiding. But this sounded like intentionally provoking the enemy.

Or baiting them. *Here I am. Come get me.*

Would she do that? Set herself up to draw them out?

If so, he needed to find her, and not for the reason he originally planned.

CHAPTER TWENTY-EIGHT

We are not always in position to decide if life stretches long, or ends short of expectation. Living and dying are ends of a single cord.

BLOOD AND BONE, BY V.M. NARRANO

So OFTEN, it seemed as if Narrano was speaking right to her. Evie set the book aside when she heard the door of her house open.

"What do you have for me, Slade?" She didn't rise from the chair a few feet from the wall of windows, nor did he come closer. He should have, though, because the setting sun had lit feathery cirrus clouds in beautiful oranges and reds.

But this time, her staying near the windows wasn't a power play. She was just too weary to move. Her world had been rocked today at her follow-up appointment. No matter that she had prepared for the feared words, steeled herself against their power. They were the ones she had consciously expected, yet unconsciously hoped to avoid.

Two to four months.

All future opportunities were forever voided by those words of devastating finality.

Sunlight streaked across the glass, revealing dust and grime from morning fog and Santa Ana winds. It was time to have the window washers come with their gear. Was it worth doing one more time?

Two to four months.

"Did you drive on the freeway this afternoon?" Slade asked.

Evie glanced at his ghostly reflection where he stood behind her. What a strange question. But as a matter of fact, she'd come home from her doctor's office on surface streets because she no longer trusted herself at higher speeds. "Which freeway are you talking about?" L.A. and the valley were a twisted maze.

"Any of them. Maybe all of them."

"Have you been drinking, Slade?"

"Not yet." Ice tumbled into a glass, followed by liquid.

"You're not making sense."

"You didn't see the message. *Her* message."

Evie gripped the armrests of her chair and pushed herself up, hiding the pain that took hold in her bones and shot up her spine to her skull. She turned, but kept a supporting hand on the back of the chair, willing the dizzy spell to be brief.

Slade finished pouring whiskey into the tumbler on the bar, then drained half the glass. "It's on at least a dozen billboards that my men have found so far, and it's the same wording on every one."

"Tell me."

"They all say the same thing: *Look over your shoulder. I'm back, and I'm right behind you. – L.H.*"

A takeoff on the wording Evie had used in her initial threats: *Tell Lilly Hawthorne to look over her shoulder, I'm right behind her. She is a dead woman.*

Evie wasn't sure what to make of it. Lilly Hawthorne had disappeared after the Vieras died. She left town, and had obviously hidden in Europe. Why return now? There was only one answer.

"She's trying to draw us out, Slade." Evie walked to the bar, her bare feet sinking into the lush carpeting. Heels were part of her old life. She steadied herself on the stone countertop.

"A face-to-face fight is a bad idea, Evie. We want the element of surprise on *our* side, not hers."

Evie waved his argument away. "She might think she knows what she's doing, but we're the experts in this."

"She'll be protected," he said. "Harder to get to."

"With bodyguards, like before. That's all these Hollywood types know. But we have fighters." The flavors of the whiskey filled the air as he swirled the liquid. Her mouth ached for a taste, Narrano and his spiritual water be damned. But this was not the time. Instead, she got a bottle of water from the refrigerator and took a long pull, willing the liquid to flush away the cancer cells.

"Maybe." He didn't sound convinced. "This wasn't something she could do overnight. The posters need to be ordered and printed in advance. Then to buy that much space all at once..." He finished his glass and poured another two fingers. "This took planning."

Slade had always been more cautious than Evie, and when it came to business, she liked that in him. Unlike so many stupid men in the drug trade, Slade calculated the odds and weighed resources before making a move. And when he *did* move, it was decisive and overwhelming.

"The question is how to find her," he said. "Is she going to start driving the freeways in a convertible?"

"Well, it's obvious she doesn't know who we are—who *I* am. Otherwise, she wouldn't have to use billboards to reach me." Evie drank more water, but it tasted flat, lifeless. A mirror of how her body would be. *Two to four months.*

"There might be another way—what I mentioned the other day," Slade said. "Our I.T. guy told me about this new facial recognition software and database. It's still in trial, but they have hundreds of millions of photos. Probably billions by now. Their next step is matching the pictures with news stories. They know when and where every photo is taken."

"And?"

Slade sighed. "The beta testing signups for the software is closed, and our guy is unable to join the team. The final release will be in a couple of months, so we could—"

"No!"

Slade narrowed his eyes, appraising her.

Surely the effects of the disease were visible. *She* certainly felt it, even if others hadn't noticed. But Slade *knew* her. He'd see the lost weight, the darkening smudges under her eyes that concealer could no longer mask, the lack of energy, the fact she stopped going to work.

"All right," he said. "I'll have our guy find someone else in the beta test. We'll get in."

Evie didn't know why she didn't just tell Slade the truth. Maybe repeating the doctors' words gave power to the disease, acknowledging its relentless progress and finality. Just her hearing them earlier was enough for today.

"You heard me," Evie said, softening her tone. "I don't want to wait. Contact the billboard companies. Find out who ordered them, who paid."

"Already being done. I should hear in an hour or two."

———

Mina yawned, pushing up against the headboard and waiting through a series of random clicks as her call to Proxy connected, no doubt untraceably routed through switches around the world. Mina hadn't been able to sleep longer. She needed to know what was happening.

"So… The messages were put up yesterday," Proxy reported without preamble. She sounded way too chirpy for at least and hour before sunrise. Her voice changed, sounding less robotic, more normal. "They finished the last one before the afternoon commute."

"All fifteen?" Mina asked, rubbing her eyes.

"Fourteen," Proxy said. "The company had a truck breakdown, but the manager promised to get it done first thing this morning. I told him to forget it and take it off our bill."

Mina agreed. If fourteen billboards with her message didn't get to the right people, one more wasn't going to help. Each had the same pure white background with bold, black lettering.

Look over your shoulder. I'm back, and I'm right behind you. – L.H.

"The Hollywood reporters are falling all over themselves trying to determine the meaning," Proxy said. "Most of the online editions and blogs this morning are going with a promo for a new movie, a big budget action film with a female lead. Those are hot now."

"Let me guess," Mina said. "Amanda Seyfried or Keira Knightley?"

"Nope, they're old news. Keira Knightley is off in Scotland doing another costume period piece. They're predicting Charlize Theron or Gal Gadot. My personal fave is Scarlett Johansson. I mean, did you *see* her in *Lucy*? Whew! Talk about cold-hearted-rhymes-with-witch."

"This isn't a movie, Proxy."

"Oh, yeah. Sorry." She sounded a bit chagrined. "Just sayin'. But I'd pay to see that."

Good to know the Hollywood rumor mill was so reliable. Her enemy couldn't miss this return threat. "So none of the legit outlets are mentioning *Lilly Hawthorne*?"

"None yet. I've had web crawlers on the entire web all night, plus some specialized crawlers that can get to some sites that block them."

"Is that legal?"

"You don't want to know," Proxy said, her standard response. More clicks followed.

All Mina had gotten from Proxy was she had a team of people around the world that owed her favors.

The invoice for the billboards had been paid through a series of cryptocurrency accounts. The irony was that criminals used these types of accounts to launder money, and there were always new ones popping up. Mina was making use of their services to hide the origins of her payments. Not so much from the Vieras, but in case any legit authorities came sniffing.

"And the M32K1 software?" Mina asked. She could almost hear Proxy shaking her head.

"We can't get into it—yet. Those guys are cagey. Extremely serious security. I've got Snarkyboydog working on it." It was the first time Proxy had mentioned a name. Of course, it didn't mean any more than Proxy's own online persona, of which she probably had a dozen. Kris knew Proxy's real name, but never told Mina. Another story of hiding from the past. Or, in Proxy's case with her hacker friends, hiding from present-day enemies.

And even though Proxy couldn't get information directly from within the M32K1 database, she had set up constant monitoring of searches for *Lilly Hawthorne* in close association with *Palomino Glass*. There were many for *Lilly*, and quite a few for *Palomino* due to her glass business, which she had promoted everywhere she lived.

"So far, I've only found two instances of someone searching for both of your names," Proxy said. One was the day Teal and Mina met. "The other was in Massachusetts, a little over two months ago."

The only person she'd known there was Kade Hunt. Agent Gray Eyes. "I don't know anyone in Massachusetts."

Proxy said, "I traced the IP address and came up with a name: Rowan Hunt."

Kade Hunt's sister?

Mina felt like a bomb had gone off in her head. Kade had talked about his little sister, but Mina's visit to Boston was too brief to meet her. Why was Rowan Hunt looking for Lilly Hawthorne and Palomino Glass?

She toyed with the idea of calling the girl. But with the billboards up, there were more urgent priorities, such as discovering who issued the Viera threats.

"I'll give you hourly reports, and call immediately if something urgent comes up." Proxy signed off.

Fifteen minutes later, as Mina finished stirring cream and sugar into her coffee, her cell rang again. She checked the display, then took a hurried sip before answering.

"Now, Dad, don't be upset," she said.

"Are you kidding me, Mina? There are billboards all over the city. What got in your head to taunt these people like this after all these years?"

From his work on films, Nathan Hawthorne had always been an

168

early riser. Fine for him, but she wasn't used to getting up before sunrise. She stifled another yawn, but he sensed it.

"Are you still in bed? Isn't it 2:00 in the afternoon there?"

He thought she was still in Germany. She yawned again. She really should have called him to break the news in bits.

"More like 5:00—in the morning. As in, it's still dark outside, Dad." She couldn't help being a little snarky.

"Are you in Seattle? Why didn't you tell me?"

"When you stop asking questions, I might give you answers." It was Mina's favorite line from his latest movie, spoken by a sassy young female to the father character. That earned Mina a laugh.

"All right, young lady. I guess you'd better start from the beginning." That was the next line from the same script, but it's also what Mina did.

She told him about the attack in Berlin, downplaying her arm wound, but not about how she killed the man. She told him about enlisting Alexandra's help in cleaning up and escaping, and about the team that protected her for the next few weeks. He'd met her roommate, Kristen, once, so Mina explained her forced exile in Sweden.

Then she revealed her decision to bring the fight to the Vieras—or whoever was behind it all.

After a moment of silence, her dad said, "Go slower. I'm making notes for a new action film. It's going to take some revision to make it believable, though."

It was her turn to laugh. "Stop it, Dad. It isn't funny." From the time her parents adopted her at thirteen, Mina and her dad had bonded over movies. They watched hundreds of them in his home office, quoting lines along with the characters in familiar films, spotting flubs, and throwing popcorn at the screen whenever a character spouted a line of hackneyed dialogue, such as *I'm your worst nightmare, You go girl, Lock and load,* and the all-time worst offender: *Let's do this.*

"I'm serious, girl," he said. "This is going to be a blockbuster."

Mina rubbed sleep out of her eyes and opened the doors out onto the mill's deck. The cold morning air sent shivers up her arms, and she wrapped her hands around the hot mug. "You have a column for cast names yet?"

"Working on it."

"Not saying it's a good idea…"

"Of course not," he agreed.

"…but who do you have playing me?"

"Hmm. I'm thinking Scarlett Johansson. Or maybe Charlize Theron."

Mina cracked up. "That's what Kris Stone's friend said too." She told him about her contact with Kris—which made him feel better—and Proxy's help in getting a super-secure phone and in arranging for the billboards. He still wasn't enthused about the taunting messages, but at least he was listening. When she told him she moved from Seattle, his voice rose again.

"I think I'm afraid to ask, but… where are you?"

"Storm Lake. Near Perilous Cove."

"Mina, that's only a couple hundred miles from here. It's too dangerous."

"And I bought a house." May as well dump it on him all at once. She dropped a slice of bread into the toaster.

"You bought a house?"

She reached the kitchen. "You're repeating, Dad."

"Repeating? Why you little—"

"Hey, cut me some slack. It's like zero dark thirty outside."

"Don't say *like*. It makes you sound like an airhead Valley Girl."

"Time for a vocab update, Dad. No one knows what a Valley Girl is anymore."

"I'll fix it in post." It was his standard answer whenever he made a mistake. Anything could be edited in postproduction.

She pressed the button on the coffeemaker. It began its hissing and gurgling promises of good things to come. "You could drive up and have a cup with me. See my new house."

"After someone followed me to Florida? I don't think that's a good idea."

"Fin can arrange it for you. He knows the scoop."

"Fin? You talked to Fin? And don't tell me I'm repeating. I can't believe he didn't tell me. I'm going to fire his—"

"No, you're not, Dad," she said, speaking more softly so he'd understand she was serious. "He told me about the new threat you got. You didn't tell *me* about *that*, either."

A growl came over the line, but it was a guilty growl. At least that's how she chose to hear it.

"And I have a security team coming from Phoenix later today. I think you'll like them." She put her back to the railing, watching the water wheel turn slowly.

He sighed, making him sound older than his fifty-two years. "I miss you, Mina."

She missed him, too—and their rapid-fire dialogue bursts after watching old Jimmy Stewart and Cary Grant films where the characters talked so fast.

"It's just... Well, it sounds like you're preparing for a war." His voice grew soft like hers. "I hate this. I don't want you hurt too."

He was thinking of his wife, Ekaterina Orlov, the woman he loved. The woman who was Mina's mom for five short years—until the Vieras came after Mina and everything had gone so wrong.

It was one thing to *make* action movies, another thing altogether to *live* one.

"That's why we have to end this." She sighed too. But it wasn't a sigh of resignation, rather determination. "I'm tired of hiding like a rabbit in a hole, waiting for the next hunter with a shotgun to find me." Or a .22 semi-auto with a silencer, like Berlin.

Mina heard pages flipping—probably his old-style desktop calendar.

She smiled. He was such a contrast of the latest film technology and old school organization.

"I'm wrapping a project as a favor for McClausen," he said. "He's got pancreatic cancer."

"Oh, Dad, I'm really sorry." Joel McClausen was a longtime friend of her dad, and had directed him in a couple of movies when he was still acting. "He probably doesn't remember me, but give him my best."

"I will. Post begins Wednesday, so… How about next week? We'll have a good editing plan going, so I'll have some time."

"Done…and done." Another cliché.

"Aw, Mina, you're killing me!"

CHAPTER TWENTY-NINE

With Rowdy Haines arriving later, Mina drove to Cove Grocery to stock up on sandwich fixings, chips, steaks, potatoes, and a few large cans of ranch beans. She debated over lettuce and tomatoes. The other guys with Haines were named JD and Boomer. They didn't sound like salad guys, but you never knew.

She added enough lettuce, tomatoes, and carrots for at least one meal. If the other guys were the size of Haines, daily shopping trips were probably going to be a necessity.

Cooking was never her strength. Maybe she should think about hiring someone to come in to feed the guys.

"Hi, Palomino."

Mina turned to find Teal coming into the checkout line behind her. "Hey, Teal." The girl had a cart filled nearly to the top. "Looks like somebody's hungry."

"It's mostly a delivery for Mrs. Hamilton, but I'm stocking up for Mom too. With her working and the baby coming, she doesn't have much time."

An idea formed in Mina's head. "Say, do you know how to cook? I've got some, uh…friends coming to stay for a while, and I'm looking to hire someone to help."

Teal laughed louder, joined by the checkout clerk, a woman with a name tag that read *Midge*. "Only if they like Spam," Midge said.

"'Fraid I'm not much of a cook," Teal said. "Neither is Mom. Dad's okay, though—if you like everything barbecued. He tried cauliflower the other night." She stuck her index finger into her mouth in a gagging motion.

"Well," Mina said, "if you think of anyone, let me know." Until she found someone, it would probably fall on her. Then she smiled as an idea formed. If she fixed them barbecued cauliflower, maybe one of them would take over.

After unloading the groceries at home, Mina decided she had time for a swim.

The beach was typically crowded when she dropped her towel and kicked off her flip-flops. She waded into the shallows to get off the hot sand. A warm breeze rolled across the water, buoyant with summer fun. She stood for a moment, breathing in its promises. Water splashed on her legs and she looked down at a freckle-faced girl.

"Do you know how to swim?" the girl asked. She was seven or eight years old, and had neck-length curly blond hair. A small blue bucket dangled from her right hand, and she gripped a red plastic shovel in her left.

"I do," Mina said, smiling.

The girl shook her head, curls bouncing. "I can't swim, but I start class next week."

Mina leaned over and pointed north. "See that big black rock way over there? The giant square one?" The girl nodded, sighting along Mina's arm. "I'm going to swim all the way to it, and then come back."

"Wow," the girl said. "That's a long way."

"It is. But if you pay attention in swim class, you'll be able to do that too—in a few years."

A boy about the girl's age called that it was time for lunch, and the girl splashed ashore. She turned and waved to Mina, then ran toward a far picnic table surrounded by kids.

Mina kept up a stiff pace to Box and back, all the while thinking of the little girl and if Mina might one day have kids of her own. Her muscles were pleasantly sore when she returned to the beach. She spread out her towel and let the sun dry her as she went through some stretching routines. The old wounds protested as they always did, but the new one was less noticeable each day.

At her truck, she found a message on her phone from Haines saying the other two men's flight from Tennessee to Phoenix had been delayed due to thunderstorms.

"I can still come out as planned," Haines said when Mina called him back, "but I think they'll get out of Nashville later tonight or tomorrow morning for sure. Be easier if I picked them up at the airport."

She agreed it was okay to wait a day or even two until they could all drive out from Phoenix together.

She started the engine and backed out of the parking space. All around were families, thriving businesses, sunshine, and energizing views. Yet as Mina drove down Main Street, she felt a dark cloud just beyond the horizon. Haines's arrival would put her one step closer to the inevitable. And things that were inevitable weren't always good.

Evie was rinsing a glass at the kitchen sink when Slade came in.

"I have a lead on Lilly Hawthorne."

She turned, and when she saw the triumphant expression on his face, she grabbed one of the barstools and sat down.

"Tell me."

"Remember I mentioned our IT guy? Well, he got a facial match with that new software." Slade filled a tumbler with ice and poured two fingers of whiskey. "A security camera picked her up."

"Where?"

"Three hours north of here, in Mission Peak."

Evie had driven through the town a couple of times years ago, but it was too quaint for her taste. "And you're sure it's her?"

"It wasn't the best angle for the photo—you know how those security cameras are. But our guy says seventy percent probability."

"So it might not be her."

Slade swirled the ice in his glass. "Seven in ten is a pretty good shot."

Evie had to admit it was. If only *she* had as good of odds with the cancer. She should be rejoicing over the photo, but today hadn't been good. Something as simple as a shower shouldn't require a two-hour nap. "And that's the only photo?"

Slade drained half his drink. "Our man hasn't spent much time learning the software. If there are other pictures, he hasn't connected them to this one."

"There must be others," Evie said. "People can't hide anymore. Maybe some incentive…"

"I mentioned his daughter's school, the other carpool drivers, and their children. He's suddenly working overtime."

"Mission Peak is how big?"

"Forty, fifty thousand. I have men on the road now. They'll search every street, every business. We'll find her."

And without a miracle, Evie would be long dead by the time they did. She rubbed her right shoulder where the ache came again. Lifting her arm was becoming more difficult.

"We also know the law firm that handles her father's business investments," Slade said. "We suspected they do the same for the daughter, and now it's confirmed."

"Do we have someone on the inside?" After Ekaterina Orlov's death, it was rumored she left the daughter a large trust. Someone had to manage it.

Slade nodded. "One of the new interns at the law firm. Such an unfortunate situation. His little sister got into drugs, then prostitution. We're helping him out. For a price. Of course, he doesn't know it was one of our people who got her hooked—and hooking." He laughed at his own joke, finished his drink, and poured another.

"Good planning ahead, Slade. I'm impressed."

"He's worming his way into the team who handles Lilly Hawthorne's affairs. Shouldn't take more than a week or two."

Evie rubbed her forehead. Everything required so much time. If only she'd begun this quest in earnest a year ago. Still, anticipation rejuvenated Evie a little mentally, even if her body refused to cooperate. These were the breaks they'd been waiting for, and she had every intention of achieving her revenge before her flesh gave out.

She always envisioned fighting Lilly Hawthorne face to face, whispering in her ear, *This is for the Vieras*, right before she killed her.

The physical weakness wasn't fair. Even though the doctors told her this was consistent with the disease's progression, the debilitating symptoms startled Evie. She blinked away tears that stung her eyes. Her damn emotions were all over the place.

"Evie?" Slade's voice was heavy with concern. "What's wrong?"

Everything. Her muscles were letting her down. Her organs were sluggish. Her brain fuzzy. And no amount of Narrano's spiritual water was going to fix any of it.

The writer said all things work together for good. Well, if that were true, maybe she didn't have to be the one to pull the trigger or twist the knife. Having another do the deed wouldn't be as satisfying for Evie. But if she could just *be* there…watch the woman's life end. A good outcome justified whatever means were required. Narrano should put that in one of his books.

Evie pushed down the pain in her core and sat up straighter. "Send some people to search Mission Peak. Go door to door if you have to."

Slade tilted his head to the side. "I just told you, I have people on the road."

She pressed her fingers into her forehead, willing her brain to pay attention. "Sorry. I'm not at my best this morning."

"It's 4:30 in the afternoon, Evie," Slade said.

She said nothing.

He put down his glass and rose. "I'll call you when—"

"Slade," she said, reaching across the bar and putting her hand on his arm. "Before you go, I have something to tell you."

We are not always in position to decide if life stretches long, or ends short of expectation. —V.M. Narrano

CHAPTER THIRTY

KADE SLAMMED down the phone in his dad's home office. The cell coverage at his parents' house wasn't good, so he'd taken to using the landline.

"Not going well?" Rowan asked, pausing in the doorway. She had her own apartment she shared with a roommate, but stopped by every couple of days to see how he was. He suspected her visits had a lot to do with their parents' washer and dryer.

"Understatement," Kade said. "All my contacts with the FBI are closed up tight."

"Well, I guess it's expected after siccing a lawyer on them."

"Hey, I—" But his sister was right. Even though he wasn't suing the bureau, Amory and Fowler had been furious that Kade hired an employment attorney to review the termination papers. As with any attorney, the man had to justify his fee, so he came up with a long list of things to negotiate. He'd been worth every penny.

One former coworker did say Amory had been *reassigned*, usually code for sending someone far, far away as punishment for screwing up what should have been a straightforward assignment. Wherever the man ended up, Kade hoped it was below zero degrees—in summer.

"If I didn't know you better, I'd say you were stalling." Rowan crossed her arms and leaned against the doorframe. "Call her father. You helped save his daughter's life. It's not like he's going to refuse your call."

True enough. He'd met Nathan Hawthorne, but those were in times of severe crisis when authorities like Kade represented at least an illusion of protection. That illusion had shattered when the man's wife had been killed.

Now Kade was just a private citizen, not an authority—which could be good or bad, he wasn't sure. But he was also the man who, from Mina's perspective, had been the one to pull out of her life. Had she told her father? Probably. She was close to her dad. Nathan Hawthorne might greet Kade with a shotgun.

Anyway, he didn't have a number for Hawthorne. How did one pick up the phone and call one of Hollywood's top filmmakers? It would take a dozen calls just to figure out the next call.

"I've gotta go," Rowan said. "Want to meet up later for happy hour at Lazy Cat? Billie will be there, and she's asking about you. Again."

Billie Taylor, a vibrant brunette, was a friend of Rowan's roommate. He'd met her at Rowan's twenty-second birthday last week, and she more than hinted they should go out.

Rowan left with his promise to think about joining them. And he did think about it—for about two seconds. Not that Billie wasn't cute, but she was the same age as Rowan. His age difference with Mina now seemed inconsequential compared to Billie.

For the next hour, Kade called Los Angeles phone numbers. He finally tracked down Hawthorne's agent, but had to leave a message —probably for the assistant of the assistant to an intern. Same for Nathan's publicist. He even tried a few entertainment newspaper reporters, but they were only interested in helping if he had a story to trade. Two of them called him back twice within the hour, pressing for juicy information. If Nathan heard about that, or if one of the reporters printed a story about a former FBI agent trying to reach him, well...

Rowan's friend, Gretchen, was also digging electronically. Maybe she would have more luck. With Mina's pictures showing up in Paris, Amsterdam, and London, he wouldn't know where to start to track her down. She could be in any country in the world. In order to find her, he needed to talk to her father.

Kade thought about calling his main doctor again for approval to get a new driver's license. Hallucinogenic drugs caused occasional flashbacks, but he hadn't had an episode in a month. Primarily, it was two minor seizures during his early days in the hospital that prevented him from obtaining a new license. Of course, he no longer had a car, either. His parents sold his when they thought he was dead.

The doctors were also hesitant about him flying. Many patients had tracked rapid atmospheric pressure changes to the onset of a seizure. Unless he was willing to hire someone to drive him to L.A. so he could track down Nathan personally, staying on the telephone was his best option. He was reaching for the receiver when it rang.

"Hello?"

"I'm calling for Kade Hunt?" The voice was female, familiar, halting.

"Maggie?"

"Kade." Her voice was a whisper. "I can't believe it's you. They told us you were dead."

Several years ago, Special Agent Margaret Cartwright had headed up the team searching for JPK, the Jigsaw Puzzle Killer. Kade had joined the team shortly before the killer led them to several victims. In a bizarre twist, it had been Mina who ultimately brought the man down.

He laughed. "Well, I'm not 100 percent, but—"

"Kade," she cut him off. "They *left* you!"

There was nothing he could say to that. The FBI never left anyone, but that's the way this felt to him too. A hundred scenarios filled his mind as to the why. Most likely someone on the inside was on the take from the cartel that grabbed him. And his reward for survival had been the visit by Amory and Fowler. But they were mere tools.

What bothered him most was the impression the bureau wished him to disappear again. The clauses were written right into the severance documents: their payments in exchange for his silence. His attorney had ripped those to shreds and threatened to go to the press.

"They didn't even tell us!" Maggie's voice was low and deadly. "I was working a multiple kidnapping case in the Seattle area. I didn't know until I got your message an hour ago and started making calls. Believe me, Kade, I would have come. I would have—"

"Maggie, I know. It's okay."

She cursed a few superiors he knew by name, and several he didn't. He hoped she didn't run into any of them in the next few days. At her insistence, he recounted the little he remembered from captivity due to the drugs, and then about his escape.

"And you have no idea what the assignment was about?"

"Only that it began in Los Angeles and that there were probably others involved on a team."

She grunted an acknowledgement.

"So, I guess you're okay talking with me?" He explained no one else would speak to him, and he didn't want her career jeopardized by his contact.

"Technically," she said, the sarcasm dripping, I'm interviewing you about kidnapping rings in Mexico. My notes state you are unable to provide any useful intel. Besides, what are they going to do, fire me?"

He laughed at the irony. "Well, you know the bureau."

She laughed too, but it was still tinged with deadly intent. "Yeah, well, if they give me the boot I'll hire your employment attorney. Before I called, I heard from a guy in the Boston office that you did well by him."

That was true. During mediation, his attorney presented an impressive stack of doctors' statements regarding Kade's physical injuries, probable permanent memory loss, and needed ongoing medical treatments. He secured an additional eighteen months of medical coverage. Then he pressed the fact the bureau had accepted the report of Kade's death with no confirmation. The declaration of his death led to emotional suffering for Kade's family. It also halted the search that could have led to a rescue.

Since the bureau refused to provide any details about the mission, Kade's attorney was free to state the assumption as fact. Regardless, declaring Kade dead resulted in his need to replace personal possessions such as clothing, household items, and a vehicle.

Even subtracting the attorney's fee, Kade received a hefty settlement, far more than the original offer. The attorney had also stipulated the payment be divided into two installments over this year and next to lessen tax liability. Overall, it worked out well.

"Besides," Maggie said, "I'm thinking about retiring anyway."

"Seriously? You love your job." In his opinion, she was one of the bureau's best agents, responsible for tracking down some of the worst. He would work with her any day.

She paused a moment. "What I love is catching bad guys, Kade. But I'm not sure how much longer I can be inside their heads without them taking over mine, you know? I'm almost fifty, and I...well, I found someone."

"I take it you mean you found someone other than a psycho killer?"

"See? You've still got it, Kade." She laughed, then said, "He owns a horse ranch in Montana."

The job wore people down. Finding the Jigsaw Puzzle Killer had nearly broken them both, and few did it as long or as well as Maggie Cartwright. He smiled, envisioning her relaxed, riding a stallion across a Big Sky valley. She was a beautiful woman, with high cheekbones and a sexy ponytail of silky black hair. The Montana rancher was a lucky man, and he told her so.

"Now," she said, "before someone overhears me and tosses my butt off the premises, how can I help you?"

He explained his need for contact information for Nathan Hawthorne.

"That's all? No problem," she said, promising to email names and numbers. "And I'm going to do some digging about your assignment and what went wrong."

"Maggie, I didn't call to—"

"Can it, Hunt. This is for me. Someone screwed up, and I want to know what happened before I'm out of here."

"Sounds like you've moved beyond *thinking* about retiring."

A soft sigh came over the line. "Life's short, isn't it, Kade?"

It was his turn to pause, then he said, "It is." That was another reason he needed to find Mina.

He wished Maggie the best, and asked her to say hi to their former team members if she saw them.

Fifteen minutes later, Kade had an email with a dozen phone numbers to try.

CHAPTER THIRTY-ONE

Foundations give us confidence, a certainty even in the midst of crisis that things will stand.

A foundation can be friends, family, or spiritual, but by its very nature it supports from outside, not from within.

Our strength alone is not enough.

Never enough.

RETREAT TO EARTH, BY V.M. NARRANO

ROWDY HAINES ARRIVED at the old mill on Thursday. He drove his F-250 pickup with a man riding shotgun. Another man pulled in behind him in an old Dodge truck with a camper on the back. The driver parked it well away from the mill building. Since both the other men flew to Phoenix, Mina figured the Dodge also belonged to Haines.

"This is JD Forrester," Haines said, introducing his passenger. "Sniper." Then he pointed to the man coming from the old Dodge. "And this other dude is Boomer Poole. Explosives."

Mina shook their hands, then motioned them inside. With a name like Boomer for an explosives expert, maybe that's why he parked at a distance. She didn't ask.

After emptying half the refrigerator, the four of them sat down on the outside deck to eat.

"So," Haines said, sipping a soda. "The billboard messages are up, but you've got no confirmation this Viera group knows about them, right?"

"With just your initials as a signature," Boomer chimed in, "do you think they'll know it's you?" He was younger than Haines, early thirties, with a slightly trimmer build, and handsome in an action figure sort of way: two-day dark beard on a square jaw, and T-shirt stretched over bulging biceps.

Mina learned he was a bomb expert in the Middle East. He walked with a limp, and was missing the pinky and ring fingers on his left hand. Haines seemed to have absolute confidence in him, and that was good enough for her.

"They'll know," she said, and explained her billboard message was a close match to the wording of the Viera threats. Boomer nodded.

"So what's next?" JD asked. He was between the two in age, and had only been out of the Marines for a year. When he showed Mina photos of his wife and two toddlers, a boy and a girl, Mina nearly called the whole thing off right then. A knowing glare from Haines stopped her. They were well trained and knew the danger. She wondered if this type of operation, because of so many unknowns, was more dangerous than what they normally did. Or less so. There was no way for her to know.

"We'll prepare several scenarios," Haines said, as if reading her mind. "You mentioned your target date for the confrontation is July 14th. Why that day?"

Now it seemed arbitrary and capricious. That day had no firm connection to today's planning. Nor could she predict the Viera threat response would hold to that date.

"It's… I mean, when it was just me…"

"You picked it, Glass. Why?"

She took a breath and let it out. "Because it's my mother's birthday. She would be forty-two years old—if Tommy Viera hadn't killed her."

Boomer raised an eyebrow, and Haines sat back in his chair.

JD shrugged. "Works for me."

"First," Mina said, "we need to find whoever is behind this. Honestly, I was hoping to have that intel before you guys arrived."

"Don't worry about us," Haines said. "What's your plan for finding this person?"

"I've got a hacker contact working on finding the threat," Mina said. "Her network is digging into the Viera business records, emails, phone recordings from the government—"

"She can do that?" JD asked.

"Maybe I shouldn't have mentioned that one," Mina said, drawing a smile from each man. "She goes by the name Proxy. Her team pulled every arrest record of anyone associated with the Viera family, and they are cross-linking those names to addresses, and then those addresses to automobile registrations. She found shell companies, offshore accounts, and over three dozen buildings owned or formerly owned by the Vieras or one of their front companies. There are several other businesses as well. Even the FBI knew years ago those were used as fronts for their more illicit activities. The difference now is that Proxy and her friends are experts at correlating and analyzing all the data. They're building multiple databases and a matrix of social media friends and followers."

Proxy was more than earning her money on this job. Mina had no idea how many others the woman had pulled into the tasks, but it must be dozens.

"She's calling at five o'clock with a status update."

"Okay if we listen in?" Haines asked.

"She's expecting you."

"What are your ideas for where this showdown will happen?"

Mina had given that a lot of thought. It needed to be somewhere isolated so innocent people wouldn't be endangered. But she wasn't sure how to pick the right spot. That was another reason she needed these men's expertise.

"I guess it depends on what we discover about the identity or identities."

The confrontation couldn't be anywhere near Deer Cove. This was her new home, and she didn't want it tainted by Viera blood.

"All right, guys," Haines said. "The target date gives us a few weeks. Even if this Proxy woman is as good as Glass says, I don't see a bunch of keypuncher metro types hitting the streets of L.A. for recon. So we're going to be the eyes on the ground when she flushes out a rodent."

The men spent the afternoon moving in their belongings and gear bags. Haines took the downstairs suite, while JD and Boomer split the other two bedrooms. Kris Stone hadn't given Mina a specific arrival time, but it was going to get tight. She hoped they'd all get along.

Proxy called precisely at five, and Mina put her cell phone on speaker in the middle of the table. She introduced Proxy to the three men.

"I can tell you a little about us," Haines began.

"No need," Proxy said. "Reginald Haines Jr. Thirty-ninth birthday coming up on the 15th. Never married, but lived with girlfriend Stacey Alvarez in Chandler, Arizona, at 18810 North Avenue H for approximately a year and four months."

"Hey, now wait—" Haines began.

"Joined the Marines at eighteen," Proxy continued. "Two tours in the Middle East. I can give you rough dates and locations, but I had trouble getting the specifics on some Special Forces service. Honorable discharge after twelve years. I have his Social Security number, earnings for the last ten years and tax refunds for the same, driver's license number, bank account balances, vehicle VINs, and how much he spends on gasoline not counting cash payments. He frequents Albertson's and Fortney's Foods, Costco gas, Jackalope Bar, and about a dozen gun stores and shooting ranges. He eats out a lot. I also have his website host admin password. Anything you want me to change right now, Reginald? Add to your online résumé?"

"Don't you dare—"

"Most Sundays he cleans up—I'm assuming—and drives his grandmother, Marsha Haines, age 87, to Mass at St. Patrick's Catholic Church in Mesa. Father James doesn't approve of Reginald's chosen occupation, or his association with Jackalope Bar. You know, it's so helpful when church email servers use the default admin password. It's also amazing what you can get from Wi-Fi-enabled church security cameras and sound systems when they leave an open mic on the lectern or pulpit all week. I'd watch what you say in those confessional booths, Reggie. Sound carries."

JD and Boomer were still laughing about *Reginald*, when Proxy started in on JD.

"I think you've proved your point, Proxy," Mina said, grinning.

Haines pressed the mute setting on the phone. "Are you sure we can trust her, Glass? This woman is scary."

They all noticed the red mute indicator change back to green without anyone touching it. "Of *course* you can trust me, Reginald," Proxy said. "But you can never trust a mute button. Remember that."

Boomer, who wasn't married, asked for Proxy's photo. A picture of Gal Gadot dressed as Wonder Woman showed up on his phone. By the time they stopped laughing, even Haines couldn't hide a grudging smile.

"Why don't you tell us what you've found on the Viera threat," Mina said, getting them back on track.

Proxy kept her report succinct. Her group had collected a ton of data spanning the past several years, including court records, bail bondsman contacts, and defense attorneys, but they were prioritizing properties and vehicles that hadn't been transferred, and addresses of probable associates. They were weeding out the cars and real estate that had been sold. It was a long list.

"I'll email it to you," Proxy said. "Also, we're using traffic cameras to track every vehicle we discover. We're building a time-date map of their travels." She sighed. "That's a huge amount of data.

Whenever we can link a person to a smartphone, we're using GPS data to map movement. Then we mark where the movements intersect."

"Why don't you come here?" Boomer asked. "We can all work together."

Mina's mouth dropped open when Proxy hesitated, then said, "I'll think about it." From what Kris said, Proxy never revealed her identity to anyone, not even those in her hacker network. For her to consider coming here in person…

Boomer's handsome mouth turned up at the corners, and he lifted his right hand to JD for a silent high five. Of course, Proxy *would* have Boomer's complete history and tons of pictures of the man. She probably knew more about Boomer than his own mother. Talk about dating background check.

Haines and Proxy arranged getting new secure phones set up like Mina's, and then they worked on prioritizing those things that required ground observation. JD and Boomer made plans to leave for Los Angeles the next day.

"You're not going with them?" Mina asked Haines as they walked down the long driveway. The air had cooled to perfection with nightfall, and a soft breeze rustled the ancient oaks above their heads. Happy crickets sang in the darkness. Haines used a penlight to illuminate the path. Rattlesnakes were not uncommon here.

"Nah, they got it. Besides, I'm not leaving you alone. With all this snooping Proxy's doing, no telling when she'll stir up a pit of vipers."

Mina shivered, though it wasn't cold. More snakes. "Rowdy, do you think I'm doing the right thing? I mean, do you think I should just walk away, let this go?"

They walked in silence for a couple of minutes. But it was a comfortable quiet, and she didn't feel the need to fill it any more than he.

"Forgiveness is power, not for the forgiven, but for the forgiver," he said.

"Wow. You make that up, Haines?"

"Not me. Some guy named Navaro or something."

"Narrano?"

"Yeah, that's it. My grandmother reads his stuff. Has a whole stack of these little books."

"I think Narrano is a woman," Mina said.

"Really?" He stopped as they reached the end of the driveway. Now that they were out from under the canopy, there was just enough light for Mina to see him shake his head. "Nope, Naranno's a dude."

"How do you figure?"

Haines thought for a moment as they listened to the night sounds. "Because he hears and sees things like *I* do." They turned and started back toward the mill. "I grew up hunting and tracking. When I joined the Marines, I transferred those skills to tracking the enemy."

"And?" she prompted when he paused again.

"Well, this is going to sound sexist…"

"Try me."

"Okay," he said, stopping again. "I see it like this. A guy's mind is wired differently than a woman's. We're able to shut off the garbage around us and zero in on one thing. That's not always good, and sometimes we miss important things, like relationships. But it's how we can sit in a duck blind for hours waiting for a flock to come by, or drive a race car around four corners for two or three hours. Sure, women can do those things too. But most of the women I know tend to overthink things. Their minds are always going, and sometimes that gets in the way. Guys just shut it down."

"How does that convince you Narrano is male?" she asked. Rowdy Haines was surprising her on several levels.

"I can hear it in his words," he said. "The way he breaks things down to the simple, the bare minimum. Everything else is pushed away. That feels like the same concentration I have when I'm stalking a deer. Or a man," he added. "Except this guy Narrano stalks words and concepts."

"Wow."

"Told you it would sound sexist."

"No. I mean I had no idea you were so poetic." She bumped his arm with her shoulder as they continued walking.

"Yeah, well don't tell the guys. After Proxy's call, they've got enough ammo to torment me till I die."

As they reached the porch, Mina said, "You never answered my question. Are you saying I should forgive this person who is attacking me and threatening my dad?"

He shook his head. "That's something only you can decide. And even if there *is* forgiveness, that doesn't mean there aren't consequences for anyone coming after you. Nor does it mean they will stop."

He said goodnight, and left Mina leaning against the porch railing pondering his words. Consequences for her enemy could be jail or death, but she admitted that was wishful thinking. Death was far more likely. The man in Berlin died as a consequence of attacking her. And while his death ended that specific attack, it left her bearing the weight of the killing. Justified, yes, but brutal, ugly, and so final. In a way, his death tore off a piece of her soul.

Now she was planning the death and destruction of another enemy. But this wasn't just some ethereal force she was planning to end. It was a person or persons—real life human beings. Would that peel off more of her soul? How many times before there was nothing left of herself?

CHAPTER THIRTY-TWO

"I'LL DRIVE YOU," Rowan said, leaning against their parents' kitchen counter.

"All the way to California?" Kade set his cane aside. His left ankle still gave him trouble, but he'd been able to retire the crutches. Regrettably, the cane made him feel like an old man. "Do you know how far that is?"

She shrugged. "What I *know* is that you're cash flush, but aren't cleared to fly. I figure you'll hire a driver. If I do it, you can pay me instead. Besides, I want to see my friends in Pasadena again. We stay in touch, but I haven't been back since we moved. We're planning a girls' getaway."

Kade rubbed his chin. Even after leaving numerous messages, he still hadn't heard back from Nathan Hawthorne. Kade felt the man was stalling.

Rowan was right about hiring someone to drive him—and about being financially well off.

"You want me to ride in a car for 3,000 miles with you?" He shook his head. "Sorry, but I've seen you drive. We'd never make it alive."

She waved off his objection. "Spring's here and the snow's gone. Easy peasy." She snapped her fingers. "Hey, we can hit all those places that Guy Fieri goes to on *Diners, Drive-ins and Dives*. I bet there's an app for that." She pulled out her phone and began tapping.

While she hunted for a Triple D app, Kade weighed her offer. Her classes were wrapping up, and there were plenty of willing locals to fill in at Dad's club where Rowan worked. But more important, he'd missed too much of his sister's life. The simple fact she wanted to spend time with him meant a lot. Wild driver or not, the idea of a brother-sister road trip appealed to him. Not to mention that she was crazy-smart and had friends like Gretchen.

"Found it," Rowan said. She pressed the install button for the app, then looked up. "Okay. Now, about my pay. How about $200 a day for driving up to eight hours?"

"That's robbery," he said.

She tapped her index finger on her lips. "Okay, make it ten hours of driving each day. I'm sure I can get Billie to come along and spell me so we can go longer. Get there faster."

Kade scrubbed his face. He knew when he was beaten. "I'll give you $250 a day if you *don't* ask her."

"Done." She grinned and stuck out her hand to seal the deal. "When do we leave? I've got finals next week."

"I've got a few more P.T. appointments," he said. "How about the next weekend?"

Kade also had one more visit with his psychiatrist, Dr. Max Collier, before the trip. Since he thankfully didn't remember much about his captivity, he wasn't sure the sessions were absolutely necessary. His mom and dad thought otherwise, especially when they learned of his and Rowan's plan to drive to California.

Mostly, Kade and the doctor talked about coping if he *did* finally remember something. But they also talked about the physical scars that would forever be part of who he was, and how people would react to him because of those scars. And the fact that even though he didn't mentally remember what happened, his body did. It was a testament that terrible things *had* happened. That point alone was a lot to take in, and Kade promised to schedule future appointments when he returned from the trip.

Dad found someone to fill in for Rowan, and Kade used the days to work harder at the gym. Thanks to Maggie, Kade had spoken with two members of Hawthorne's staff. They both said he was deep into multiple productions, presently out of town, and would get back to him soon. Kade was reluctant to give his reason for contacting him— he didn't want to spook anyone with what could be unfounded fears about Mina's safety.

Kade wheeled his suitcase out the front door to Rowan's idling Wrangler. She helped him lift it into the back cargo area.

"I hope you won't have to do that much longer." He nodded at the bag.

"Hey, no worries." Rowan shut the tailgate door and they climbed in.

He'd gained back over half of his lost body weight, but was still taking it slow. The wrong foods or too much of the right ones often didn't agree with him, and came out, literally, in the worst ways. He was also trying to build muscle as he went instead of just adding mass. But it would be a while before he could toss a suitcase around. He hated being dependent on others.

He pulled out his phone. "I programmed in the route."

"I think we're going to have to change our final destination," Rowan said, accelerating down their parents' long driveway and turning left on Merrimac Street toward I-495. The tires squealed only slightly.

"Why?"

Rowan turned to face him, looking at him so long he was afraid she'd run them into a curb or parked car. But at her next words, he forgot all about her driving.

She broke into a huge grin. "Because I found Lilly Hawthorne!"

CHAPTER THIRTY-THREE

"Sorry, Kade, but I'm not sure you seeing Mina is a good idea right now. She's…well, she has a lot going on." Nathan Hawthorne's voice was breaking up. Kade and Rowan were climbing through the Rockies, and the cell coverage was spotty. But the message was clear enough. Hawthorne was a parent protecting his daughter.

Kade had explained his belief Mina was in danger because of the photo database, but it hadn't been enough to convince him to give Kade her contact info. He'd been out of her life for too long.

"I'll see her…soon," Nathan said. "I'll tell her we talked and give her your number. That's all I can promise."

Kade sighed. Hearing the cageyness in Nathan's response, he figured Mina had told him something about how Kade let their relationship drift apart. It didn't matter that Nathan might agree with Kade's reasoning as to their age difference back then.

How could he explain his renewed feelings for Mina when he didn't fully understand them himself? From the moment he laid eyes on her—crumpled on that street in L.A., blood pouring from multiple wounds—he felt connected to her. Then she saved his life, using her bare hands to stop his bleeding. Couldn't get much more intimate than that.

But it was more than saving each other. She came to him in the hospital, held his hand and coaxed out stories of his childhood, his family, his dreams and goals. Her interest in him revealed *her*.

Besides, his memories were no longer of her as a high school student. In his mind, she was a fighter, a fierce warrior who faced adversity that would have steamrolled a normal person. She overcame opposition and grew stronger with it. He wanted to know that person, how she had continued to grow, who she was today. She was the woman who had shown up during his darkest times in captivity.

Explaining that to Nathan, though…

Rowan grabbed the phone and transferred it to her left hand, away from Kade's reach.

"Mr. Hawthorne, this is Rowan Hunt, Kade's sister. Please listen. Your daughter is important to my brother. I have a friend who has found where Mina is within a very small geographic area. If my friend can find her this easily with this facial recognition software, then so can her enemies. We'll be there in two days—one day if we push it. I don't think it will take us an hour after we arrive to locate a beautiful young woman with distinctive white hair, do you? So…are you going to help us, or not?"

She listened for a minute, then recited Kade's cell number. "Thank you. We'll be expecting your text." She ended the call and handed the phone back to Kade.

"What did he say?" Kade was somewhat stunned by his sister's take-charge attitude. Maybe it came from the skiing competitions.

"He's texting you her direct number—and passcode, whatever that is."

"It's Psalm 23, verse 4."

"A Bible verse?"

"That's the code," Kade said. "'Yea, though I walk through the valley of the shadow of death, I will fear no evil: for thou art with me; thy rod and thy staff they comfort me.' It has to be the King James version or she won't pick up a call from a strange number."

He couldn't believe he remembered that. Despite his swiss cheese brain, it seemed most things involving Mina remained intact. So much time lost. So many opportun—

The right front tire slammed into a deep pothole hidden in the shade of a freeway sign, and Kade's head smacked the side window. Pain spiked across his temple and down his neck.

"Whoa, sorry," Rowan said, straightening the Jeep's path. "I didn't see that."

A sudden flush rose from Kade's gut, surging up his neck until his scalp was on fire.

"That passcode idea is actually kind of cool," Rowan said, boosting her speed as they climbed ever upward toward the Eisenhower Tunnel.

Hot, humid air filled his lungs. He adjusted the AC vents on the dash, but they didn't help. Nothing would keep the devils from coming to take him, question him.

"*Where are the others?*" "*Who is your contact?*" "*Tell us what you know.*"

Each question punctuated by another blow, another stinging lash.

His vision narrowed, and he lost the side of the road to his right, and then Rowan to his left. He shook his head, trying to clear the things that weren't real. But the choking air, the stink of his cell…

"Maybe I'll create a passcode."

"Ro…" His voice was barely a whisper, hoarse and cracked from lack of water. The road ahead began twisting, undulating, as if they were on a rollercoaster. He had to hold himself on the chair. If he fell off, they would start kicking him.

Stay in the chair. No matter how hard the blows. Don't tell them about other team members. No names.

"Sure would cut down on spammers."

"Ugh…" His knuckles turned white on the grab bar, but the road tilted more violently, trying to shake him loose, throw him to the dirt floor. They were going to fly off the edge of this mountain pass, tumble down a thousand feet. Then the kicking would begin. Steel-toed boots gouging flesh, breaking ribs.

A searing slash cut across his back, and he arched away from the seat. The leather sliced deep every time.

"Kade?"

A fist slammed into his face, and blood pooled under his tongue, metallic and foreign. He spit it out.

"Kade!"

A hand grabbed his arm, shaking him.

"Kaden Hunt. You say that is your name? Why are you here, Mr. Hunt? Who are the others?"

He couldn't answer with all the blood. He spit again. Another white-hot lash across his back, arching away from the burning that didn't stop.

"Talk to me, Kade!"

"Tell us what you know, or you will force us to continue."

The world tilted sideways, his body jerking against the restraints.

"I'm not... I don't remem—" He felt his skin open with the next slash to his back. Hot wetness like the time before, and the time before that. An open palm snapped his head left, then right. More blood. Ringing in his ears.

"I suggest you talk, Mr. Hunt—if you want to live."

"Tell me what's wrong, Kade!"

"Tell me their names!"

"Kade! Listen to me!"

"It's your choice: truth or pain."

The man, his white suit spotted by blood, faded in and out of shadows. Never a clear view of his face. What was his name? Alva. Or Alvarez. Alonzo. Someone had said it.

"Kade! Agent Gray Eyes. Are you all right?"

Lilly? A figure emerged from the shadow where the man in white disappeared. Her face was partially obscured by long white hair, but he knew the curve of her cheek, the length of her eyelashes. She came closer, reached for his hand, not quite touching. Her name was Mina now, and he couldn't reveal her new identity. Had to keep the secret. No names. Keep the secret about his men. Keep *her* secret.

Everything smelled hot like iron left in the sun, rusty from the salt air. Somewhere near the ocean. He strained against the strap tying him, but at least it kept him in the chair. It cut into his chest and he thrust his whole body into it.

"Throw him back in his cell." Alva-Alvarez-Alonzo was back. Lilly-Mina had disappeared. Where had she gone? How could he reach her? It was a secret. No names!

Ocean air. Foaming waves lapped against his face, filling his mouth. He was going to drown!

Something hard was wedged between his teeth. A branch, gritty with bark and dirt. Then it was wrapped with tough cloth, but he still tried to bite through it.

"Please help him."

Was that the boy? The one with the giant barking dog that was a pony. Grapes. Eating grape after grape.

"I've got his arms. You get his feet."

No. I'll fall on my face like last time. Then they'll kick me. Stay in the chair!

Couldn't they hear him? His back scraped on something hard, sharp, opening the old wounds until the skin flapped like torn cloth in the whistling wind. Had to escape from the moving truck. Jump onto the road.

"Lay him here."

Bright light blinded him for a moment, then a shadow covered it. Coming for him.

"Hold him!"

Rough hands gripped his arms and legs. He fought, but he was weak from beatings. More whippings would come. More fists and belts. Questions. Demands.

He must keep the secret. *Her* secret.

"Lilly!"

"Where are the others?" "Who is your contact?"

The wind roared by at irregular intervals, a thing alive that existed in pulses that pushed at his hair.

"Tell us what you know and we'll set you free."

Someone screamed, howling like an injured animal in the night.

But it was too bright for darkness. Too bright for shadows. But Alva-Alvarez-Alonzo was near, in the shadows. Always near. Waiting for him to break.

Lilly was there too, encouraging, urging him to stay strong.

Something pinched his arm. More drugs. They brought the giant beetles that crawled the walls, took away his memories. Took away *him*. But never Lilly. She was near. She would come.

Then everything—the bright light, the pulsing whistling wind, the pain—went away.

He went with it.

CHAPTER THIRTY-FOUR

"KADE? CAN YOU HEAR ME?"

It took supreme effort to open his eyes. His eyelids were so heavy. A tube was pushed between his lips.

"Drink."

He closed his lips around the tube and sucked. Cool water—a few drops at first—slid over his tongue and down his throat. He kept swallowing until the tube was removed. A warm washcloth brushed his forehead and his eyes. A motor whirred, and he began rising into a sitting position. By the time it stopped, he had his eyes open.

A hospital room, with two nurses. No, one of them was Rowan. Black streaks ran down her cheeks.

"Hey," he said. His jaw ached, and his tongue was tender. He reached toward her, then stopped. His hand had an IV needle inserted into a vein. Translucent white tape held it in place. "What happened?"

"Mr. Hunt?" the other woman said. "I'm Dr. Laya. Can you tell us what you remember?"

He did his best to describe the man in white, the pain that came with the whip and steel-toed boots, the blood in his mouth from being beaten.

The doctor nodded.

"I had a flashback, didn't I?"

"I would say so," she said, nodding. "Your sister told me a little about what you went through and your recovery. Have you had other episodes?"

"A few, but not for a while." And nightmares, but those were indistinct, and he woke with dread, not in a hospital. The previous flashbacks were never as vivid as this one.

"You scared me to death, Kade." Rowan's voice shook, and her chin quivered.

"How long?" he said, looking at the wall clock. It read 6:52.

"Two hours," the doctor said. "The EMTs gave you a sedative in the field. They were afraid you'd hurt yourself with the seizure."

Seizure? Then he remembered the thing in his mouth. He had tried to bite through it. No wonder his jaw ached.

"You should be fine, but you'll probably be weak for a while. We'd like to keep you overnight, just to make sure." She looked to Rowan, then back at Kade. "And with your permission, I'll call your doctor back home and get his or her opinion."

As much as he wanted to get back on the road, he wasn't sure he could move. It felt like someone had stacked a dozen lead-lined X-ray blankets on him, and he could barely manage to sign the permission form to contact his doctor. Rowan came to his bedside and took his hand, her hand shaking in his. Her expression convinced him staying in the hospital was for the best.

"Pull the chair over," he said.

"I've never been that scared." She collapsed on the seat.

"I'm so sorry, Rowan." His eyelids were growing heavy, but he fought it. She needed his reassurance.

"You were thrashing around, yanking on the seatbelt so hard I thought it was going to tear loose. Then you started spitting."

He rubbed his thumb over the back of her hand as the story spilled out. Her slamming on the brakes and skidding sideways onto the dirt shoulder. Flagging down two truckers who pulled him out of the Jeep and shoved a handy branch between his teeth. Others stopping who helped hold him down until the EMTs arrived. The cars swishing by only feet from where he writhed on the gravel. Her following the ambulance to the hospital in Silverthorne.

He apologized again, the words slurring on his tongue. A nurse came in to check his vitals, and suggested Rowan get something to eat.

It was nearly eleven o'clock when Kade roused again. Rowan was curled in the chair, her eyes open. Whatever her dinner, it hadn't renewed her energy.

She sat in silence for several minutes before he asked, "Did we get the text?"

Rowan shook her head. "When the men pulled you out of the Jeep, your phone fell on the ground. One of them...someone..." She pulled a wadded plastic bag from her purse and unwrapped it.

Kade's phone—or rather the pieces of it—spilled onto the bedside table. The screen was shattered and mostly missing. Bits of plastic and electronics fell from the case, which was bent about 45 degrees.

"I could take it to a store in the morning, but..." She shrugged.

He let the pieces lay where they were. Even if he got another phone, he would have missed the text from Nathan Hawthorne. And the phone numbers for Hawthorne were stored in the phone's memory.

"We'll go on in the morning," he said. If he had enough energy to walk to the car.

Rowan shook her head. "Mom and Dad are coming."

"You called them?"

"They're flying to Denver and renting a car. They'll be here tomorrow afternoon."

He sank back on the pillow. Being so dependent on his family again made him feel even more helpless than his injuries. "So, we'll be here at least a second night."

"Kade, don't you think we should go home? I mean...look at you. Are you sure this isn't going to happen again? Because no way do I want to go through it a second time. Or third, or fourth."

He didn't either. There was no telling what triggered this one. What would his parents say?

Maybe getting closer to Mina shook loose the memories. Although he didn't remember much about his captivity, she was the reason he'd gotten through it. But he also realized that version of Mina was a fantasy girl, one conjured by his drugged mind in the worst times, not the real one in California.

What would she be like? She might have a boyfriend. Surely Nathan would have said something if she were married. Kade might only be a distant memory of hers, an unwelcome reminder of the bad times that had taken her high school friend, and then her mom.

But whoever she'd become, Kade knew one thing. He had to see her.

CHAPTER THIRTY-FIVE

Some might think trees have no plans. Yet they grow tenaciously in crevasses, hang on to crumbling riverbanks, survive winds that strip soil from the earth, endure cold that kills other life. They bring beauty in their strength, conscious or not, and live for decades, or generations, or civilizations. Who can say they are without a plan?

TREES BREATHING, BY V.M. NARRANO

"Isn't this a great view, Dad?" They stood next to a tall pine tree at the edge of the circular driveway, looking east over the lake below. Well, at least *she* did. Her father, on the other hand, hadn't stopped staring at the wreck of a house behind her. She sighed, and turned to join him.

It did indeed look worse than ever. Most of the roofing was gone, falling in clumps from high above as four men pried off the last of it. The windows all had plywood coverings, and the rotten porch boards had been stripped away, revealing an age-blackened skeleton below. All of the round support columns holding up the porch roof had been replaced with temporary posts. She didn't have to ask what he thought.

"I wish you had asked me about this before jumping in."

"Why?" She knew the answer, but decided to punch a button or two.

"Because I... Well, this is such a..."

"Big project?"

"Mina," he waved his hand in an all-encompassing gesture, "it's practically a teardown."

"You don't think I can handle it?" She watched his face register his tactical error.

"I didn't say that."

"Think you could do it better?"

"Don't put words in my mouth, young lady."

"Cecil B. DeMille raised an entire Egyptian city out of the dunes in Guadalupe, California. It was the largest movie set ever built."

Dad's mouth twitched. "Don't lecture me on movie history, young lady. It was for the original *Ten Commandments* in 1923. What's your point?"

"If he can do it from a pile of sand, I can do this."

"Well, he *was* DeMille, after all."

"And I'm Palomino Glass, daughter of Ekaterina Orlov and her husband, a guy who is a pretty good movie producer."

"*Pretty* good?" He puffed out his chest. "I'm a master of my craft."

"Don't get cocky, kid," she said, waiting for his wince. It didn't take long.

He splayed his hand over his chest. "Mina, you're killing me."

She shoved his shoulder, knocking him off-balance. "Come on, Master Producer, I'll show you the barn."

After walking the property and hearing her plans, they sat on the tailgate of her old pickup and ate the lunch she had packed. There was a light breeze blowing, and the truck was parked in the shade of a huge pine. Its sweet scent brought a sense of longevity, from past to future, that reached far beyond her shaky present.

Dad patted the chalky red metal of the pickup bed. "What is it with you and rusty old things?"

"Oh, Dad, stop." She bumped his shoulder again. "You're not that old."

He laughed. "Walked into that one, didn't I?"

They fell silent, listening to the sounds of hammers, saws, boots on plywood, a hawk screeching overhead. Russ Howell had shown up as promised and begun the preliminary demolition while Carter Perney worked his magic on the permit process. The roofing permit was in hand—the easiest to get due to the urgency of protecting the property from further damage.

Mina lay back in the truck bed and watched a pair of high clouds tumble through the sky before dissolving.

"Are you worried about seeing him?" Dad asked.

He had told her what Kade said about his captivity and escape. Worried wasn't the right word. Anxious, maybe. Perturbed. Twitchy. Even a thick thesaurus wouldn't have enough words to describe her unsettled stomach, the sudden unexpected tingling of hairs standing on her arms, the ping-ponging memories of touching his skin, being soaked with his blood, gazing into his eyes.

Agent Gray Eyes. She had changed in many ways. But she knew who she was, who she'd become.

In her memory, Kade Hunt was exactly the same as he'd been years ago, frozen in time in both image and personality. But just as she'd grown, he wouldn't be the same either. No one could be after his horrible experience. How had it affected him? Would he be a stranger? Somebody she used to know?

"I shouldn't have sent your contact info without talking to you first," Dad said.

She shook her head. If there was anything she'd learned in the last several weeks, it was that life was too short, and that it could be cut even shorter in a split second. This was no time to keep things hidden.

"I don't understand why he hasn't called," she finally said.

"Maybe they had a breakdown. The way his sister made it sound, they might even be here by now."

Rowan. Her dad had talked to her, and talked to Kade too. So close. Why hadn't he returned her message and texts?

CHAPTER THIRTY-SIX

Clutter robs serenity, buries creativity, masks the obvious path. Order gives freedom.

THE ORDERED LIFE, BY V.M. NARRANO

MINA WOKE with her cheek mashed to her workbench. Her sandblasting hose and nozzle lay in a heap by the sliding door, tangled and dusty. Her airbrush, compressor, and paint table needed cleaning. And, although she did the blasting outside, the workshop floor was gritty with blasting media that had blown back in through the opening. Everything around her was a mess, but it was a satisfying mess.

And she was worse. The blasting suit never kept everything out, and fine grit stuck to her sweaty skin. She knew from experience it would take three shampoos and rinses for her scalp to feel clean.

Her dad had left last night after dark, beginning his long, circuitous route home, and she celebrated their visit by working most of the night. When so tired she feared making mistakes, she collapsed into an old desk chair she kept at her jewelry workbench and slept for a couple of hours.

Footsteps sounded on the stairs leading down from above and she rose and stretched. The door opened, and Rowdy Haines poked his head in.

"Hey, there you are." He came into the workshop. "Thought you got kidnapped."

"Don't joke, Haines. It's bad luck."

He handed her a mug of steaming coffee, and said, "No. Bad luck is the getting kidnapped part, not the joking." He stood drinking from his own cup while taking in the scene. "You look like crap. Been working?"

She groaned when the hot liquid filled her mouth. The brown energy went straight into her veins. Sometimes, just the smell was enough to get her jazzed.

"Just a little project that you inspired," she said, standing. "Want to see?" She walked to the wheeled cart that held the heavy glass pane vertically so she could work on either side. It was draped with a white sheet, her custom for any work not finalized. Once completed, it would require four strong men to lift the glass into a truck.

Haines came up beside her. "No...don't tell me you painted a picture of me?" He put his hand over his heart. "I'm so flattered."

"Get over yourself, Haines. But you *did* inspire this." She grabbed the edge of the sheet. "Ready?" Mina whisked the cloth aside.

For a moment, Haines looked as if he might drop his coffee. He stood and stared.

The overhead lights weren't at all ideal, so Mina moved one of her freestanding work lights behind the panel and turned it on. "Recognize it?"

"It's the key fob I gave you. The angel."

"Yep." The seven foot high panel towered over Mina, especially as it sat on the stand. Even Haines had to look up.

"You did this?"

She was a bit miffed at his wonder. "I can do more than shoot and fight, you know."

"How...?" He leaned closer, moving his head side to side. "It's painted?" He walked around the panel.

She explained the process of laying out the image, media blasting to etch the glass, then airbrushing paints onto the blasted portions. Because this was going to be a window with its bottom edge near floor level, the building code required tempered glass on the inside. The painted image would be protected between the panes.

The feathers of the angel's forward-sweeping triple wings transitioned from near black on the wings' leading edges, to grays, to white at the trailing feathers. The woman's stomach and breasts were sheathed in long, vertical white feathers. An intricate gold clip, the only color on her, held luxurious dark hair back from her face.

The angel was set against a backdrop of subtle clouds washed in soft pinks, yellows, and golds by a distant sunset. Her eyes were closed, black eyelashes resting on the porcelain skin of her cheeks, as if lost in the strains of beautiful music only she could hear. Although it couldn't be determined from this limited view, Mina envisioned her hovering high in the air, or maybe flying above the clouds, at peace with the world, the sky, and the earth below.

Every time Mina looked at it, her spirit calmed. The image promised hope and a future of peace.

She looked over at Haines when she thought she heard him sigh. "What do you think?" His opinion mattered to her. "It's not completely finished. I have to do a little more on—"

"Mina, this is..." His fingers hovered just above the surface. "My mother and grandmother would love this. I'm going to bring them out to see it."

That was all Mina needed to hear. And she knew right then that she would do smaller versions for Haines's mom and grandmother.

As she switched off the lights and they made their way upstairs, she wondered if angels really did protect people like the women in Haines's family believed. Just having the figure in her studio below made Mina feel better, as if the plain glass had become imbued with power strong enough to guard her house and those she cared about. Maybe the old stories held some truth.

Mina got in a nap before Carter stopped by after noon. She was waiting for him on the mill's porch, practically salivating at the sound of every truck climbing the hill. She wanted to be there at every phase, but had to keep a low profile.

"Howell and his crew are replacing the rotted porch joists, stripping off bad siding, and taking down the interior walls we plan to move," Carter said, leaning against a porch post. "They're also preparing for the new wiring and plumbing to go in as soon as we get building permits. And, of course, the new roof is on." He held up a rolled set of plans. "Meanwhile, I want to go over some details."

"Let's go downstairs to my workshop," she said, leading the way. Haines, DJ, and Boomer knew about the house, and she would tell Kris when she arrived. Other than that, Mina planned to keep her involvement a secret. There was a lot of buzz in town that something was happening at the old place, and people were talking about hiking up to take a look. Undoubtedly, some already had. She even heard there was a betting pool going for which Hollywood celebrity had bought the property.

Carter unrolled the large prints on her worktable. Some of the sheets were foundation detail, showing specifications to bring the structure's underpinnings up to code. Jacking up the whole house was adding a huge expense to the project, but it had to be done. Other pages showed plumbing lines for water and sewer, electrical routing, and details about the well equipment and septic system.

They discussed interior rooms and walls, kitchen layout, and the overall flow of the house. She was glad to see Howell's new plan for modernizing the interior stairs and railings, which allowed widening the hallway by a foot. The midpoint landing was still in the same place where her window would go. To get a sense of room size, Carter helped her chalk-mark dimensions on the workshop's concrete floor.

"I'll bring you some catalogues for light and plumbing fixtures, appliances, countertop options, and flooring. Paint charts too."

"Thanks, Carter. I couldn't do this without you."

"Hey, no problem. I love this stuff." He began rolling up the sheets.

"Carter…" She waited until she had his full attention. "I don't want you to worry, but we're getting closer to finding out who's threatening me." At least she hoped they were. "Just… Well, be careful. Let me know right away if you see anything strange."

"Like someone hanging around at the site who shouldn't be?"

"Exactly." She told him about the talk in town and that some curious locals might show up.

He nodded. "I'll tell Howell to keep an eye out. Maybe just say we've heard rumors of vandalism in the area."

CHAPTER THIRTY-SEVEN

"Kris!" Mina said into her phone as she heated a skillet. "I thought you were coming last week." The new frying pans and stove were giving her fits, but she was determined to master perfect sunny side up eggs.

"Sorry. Had another job. I knew with those gorilla Marines there you'd be safe."

Mina laughed and asked where the job was.

"Arkansas. Remind me to never go back."

"Why?" Mina wedged the phone between her neck and shoulder while she cracked three eggs into the buttered pan. None of the yokes broke. So far, so good. Boomer and DJ were back from L.A., and last night she had promised them breakfast.

"Well, I learned the official Arkansas bird is the mockingbird."

"And...?" Four slices went into the toaster.

"Do you have any idea what time mockingbirds get up in the morning?"

"I'm guessing too early for you?"

"Nope. Those critters never sleep. They just stay up partying and singing all night long."

"Sounds like some Marines I know," Mina said as the three guys came into the kitchen.

"Haines sings?" Kris said.

"Well, I wouldn't call it *that*." Kris's laugh was so loud, Mina had to pull the phone away from her ear. All three guys turned to look, and she flashed them an innocent smile. "So, when are you coming? All the guys are anxious to meet you."

"I'll be there tomorrow. I can bunk at my brother's. They have a screened-in back porch."

"That's good. It's a little crowded here."

"Not to mention that testosterone getting all over everything."

Kris promised to meet Mina for lunch tomorrow at the Crab Shack, and said goodbye.

"That the bodyguard chick?" Haines said.

"Yep, and she'll love you more if you call her that to her face," Mina said.

After two rounds of eggs—one too runny, the other slightly hard —toast, and a pound of sausage patties, Haines and DJ left to begin wiring video cameras around the mill property. Later, DJ was driving back to L.A. and staying with a friend in case they got a solid lead. He was also scoping out more of the properties Proxy identified prior to this latest call.

Boomer helped her clean the kitchen, then said, "I have some things for you."

He took her out to the old truck, unlocked it, and handed her a metal box a little larger than a briefcase. He grabbed a plastic bag. "Let's take these down below."

Mina followed Boomer down the gravel path that led to the big access door of her studio. They sat on the low wall there and he opened the box.

Inside were several rows of what looked like oversize firecrackers, red paper tubes that were larger in diameter than her thumb and about as long. Each had a fuse coming out of one end.

"These are my own design," Boomer said. "They'll produce a

loud bang, and if they're enclosed in something, bad things will happen to the container."

Mina scooted away from the box. "And just why are you showing them to me?"

Boomer laughed. "I'm not. I'm *giving* them to you."

He called the small explosives B-52s. Something to do with the amount of powder. They were his design, not technically legal, and very effective. On closer inspection, she found there were two colors of fuses.

"The explosive charge is the same in all of them," Boomer said. "Green fuses are 15 seconds. Yellows are 5. If you're holding one with the yellow fuse, get rid of it soon after you light it, or you might end up like me." He held up his left hand that was missing the outer two fingers.

"Did you...I mean, did these...?" Mina said, eyeing the colorful red tubes, then his hand. Then he was laughing again.

"Nah," he said, wiggling his remaining fingers. "I did this on a table saw."

Mina shuddered at that image.

"But," he said, "you have to be careful with these little babies, because if you're holding one when it goes off, it will hurt you bad. Light them and throw or run."

"And just what exactly am I supposed to do with these?"

He opened the plastic sack and dumped out a dozen butane lighters. "Hide a few B-52s around the mill, inside and out, in your truck. Make sure no kids will find them. Keep one in your pocket."

"My pocket? Are you nuts?" She already had enough scars. A bomb crater in her thigh would not be a good look.

"They're only dangerous if you light the fuse, Mina. Put a lighter with each stash. One of these can disorient an enemy, giving you an advantage, even if it's only a second or two."

He was talking about an attack coming here at the mill. "Boomer, we're taking the fight to them. No one gets this close."

He nodded. "I understand. But we know the bad guys are looking for you." He handed her one of the bomblets. "These are part of the defense contingency—like the cameras. Haines likes to be thorough. And when we take the fight to your enemy's turf, I'll be bringing something much larger than these."

Mina held the explosive, testing its weight, imagining its use.

The fight needed to be in L.A. Her mother's birthday was an arbitrary date, more goal than a must. Now that they had a solid lead, they were taking the fight south as soon as possible.

CHAPTER THIRTY-EIGHT

"Oh, man!" Kris said, snatching the last french fry before shoving the plate toward the waiter clearing their table. "I forgot how good the food is here."

The Crab Shack lunch was as good as Mina remembered, and she slouched in the booth, sluggish from the monster portions. She was taking half of her meal home, but Kris didn't have any trouble finishing her platter.

"Do you want to come by the mill and meet the guys?" Mina asked.

Kris shook her head. "If I don't get to Alex's, Teal will fire me as her aunt. How about if I come about six?"

"Should I warn them?"

Kris tightened her bicep in a Rosie the Riveter pose. "I'll be in my best fighting form."

"Now, now. I expect you to play nice."

"*Nice* is my middle name," she said sweetly.

Right after *Danger*. Kris could more than hold her own with most guys, especially verbally. This was going to be fun.

· · ·

Mina lifted her hand in goodbye as Kris pulled away from the curb and headed down Main Street. It was great to have her back.

Enticing aromas came from DC Coffee, and Mina headed in to grab some energy. Connie and a teenage girl were hustling behind the counter, serving the seemingly endless flow of tourists. She admired how he took time to talk and joke with each one.

"Plain," she said, when it was her turn.

"Plain?" He put his hand on his chest. "You wound me."

"Deal with it," she said, laughing and telling him about her lunch. "You're lucky I can fit anything in my stomach after that."

He asked about the preparation for the Art Mill grand opening. That was Bibs' official name, printed on flyers and posted in every store window in Deer Cove. Mina gave him a quick update while he filled her cup. There were a dozen people waiting behind her.

"Come by and I'll give you a tour," she said, stepping aside. "See you later."

The girl behind Mina ordered a Cappuccino Blast. Connie had added the drink to the menu board, showing two sizes: Little Mongo, and Big Mongo.

By the time Mina finished both her coffee and the walk back to the mill, her lunch had settled and she was bouncing with energy. She headed down to her workshop and began sorting a hundred or so pieces of glass into usable sets for her *Pana's Dream* line of pendants, earrings, and bracelets. Proxy's phone call came as she finished gluing the last of the work. A brief stint in the kiln would fuse the pieces.

"Got some news," Proxy said without preamble. "All the cross-tracking of vehicles paid off. I put together a 3D data grid, registration addresses, years, and names on the titles. Then we ran that against another grid of freeway cameras—"

"Proxy," Mina interrupted, "I really appreciate the hard work, truly I do, but I don't even pretend to understand your process. Could you sort of—"

"Cut to the chase? Sure. Here's the deal. We're looking for the places where several data points cross, hopefully multiple intersections. And…well, we found a good one."

"What is it? Did you find the person who took over for the Vieras?"

"I can't say that for sure, but he shows up again and again, like he's at least a high-level player."

"Do you have a name?" Mina held her breath.

"Not directly."

Mina sagged against her worktable.

"But…we've narrowed it to some phone calls to and from a guy named Slade."

Slade. Mina let the name take shape in her mind as Proxy talked.

"And get this. Some of the calls mentioned big payments from him. Recently. Like tens of thousands for information about… Wait for it—"

"Proxy!"

"Okay, okay. For information about Lilly Hawthorne."

Mina didn't hear what the hacker said the next several sentences about *no last name,* and *a visit.*

"Can you send me the information? I'll get it to Haines and the team. We'll sit down and go over it."

"Already on its way to Haines," Proxy said. "I've got all the guys' contact info."

Of course she did. Mina ended the call even while Proxy said goodbye, and took the stairs in twos.

"Haines!"

Ten minutes later, Mina, Boomer, and Haines were reading through each of the twenty-seven pages as they came out of the printer.

Haines traced the list of connections from page to page, while Mina started nearer the back. Boomer was scanning pages from a second copy as they emerged from the printer.

"Look at this," Mina said, pointing to an address that had eleven intersections of cars and phone calls, Slade's name tied to all of them. "This might be his home."

As Mina pulled up Google Maps, Haines put his phone to his ear. "DJ, we need visual on an address." He looked to Mina. "Is it a business or residence?" She turned her computer so he could view the satellite image. "It's a residence, DJ. Up in the hills. Mina's texting you the address and GPS coordinates."

Mina zoomed in on the property. The house sat on a hillside in the San Fernando Valley, somewhat isolated from the nearest neighbors due to steep canyons. Large palm trees lined the driveway and sides of the building, casting long shadows and hiding detail.

"High probability target," Haines said into the phone, "so don't get spotted. Yep. Give me a call soonest."

Mina clicked the magnify button until it wouldn't go any further, as if she could spot her tormentor standing in the driveway looking up at the satellite. He wouldn't be that stupid. Or would he? He might be good at concealing his financial holdings and personal ties to illegal activities, but that didn't make him a genius in everything.

"DJ's going to do a drive-by, see what the landscape looks like. He's got the ghillie suit with him, but if it's too much green, he's got contacts there to pick up another one in the right color."

She'd seen DJ packing the suit and asked him about it. He'd made it himself, sewing hundreds of frayed burlap strands onto a netting that was zip tied onto a base of camo jacket, pants, and hat. The tied burlap resembled dried grass. The bulk blurred the human form and blended into the surrounding vegetation—provided the suit was the right mix of colors.

And Proxy and her team would keep working their end to confirm—or to come up with an additional likely person or location.

How was this Slade related to the Vieras? A cousin? Or perhaps another brother no one knew about.

It would take DJ hours, maybe days, to get confirmation and, she hoped, a usable photo. But the location of the house was promising.

"No near neighbors," Haines confirmed as they studied it. "Hard to tell, but if the ravine is as steep as it appears, coming from below might not work. But that doesn't mean Boomer can't do a little work down there."

"Absolutely," Boomer said. "L.A. hasn't had an earthquake in a while."

Mina studied the house, its modern roofline, its trees and bushes, its black driveway that angled down along the hill and then made a sharp switchback. The desire to fly a drone up the canyon and peep in the windows was nearly overwhelming.

There was no assurance this was the right target, but Mina willed it to be. She was tired of waiting, tired of being hunted. The tables were turning, and everyone helping were now the hunters.

If Slade was the right person, then he had sent the threatening notes, and sent the man who had followed her to Berlin to kill her.

He was hunting her.

She traced the property outline on her computer screen. Now he was their prey.

"I leave for twenty minutes… and look at you two." Mina shook her head as she came into the kitchen and set down the two grocery bags on the counter. Rowdy Haines and Kris Stone were squared off over the kitchen island, slowly circling counter clockwise like two wild beasts assessing the other's strengths and weaknesses. Boomer stood nearby, grinning.

"Boomer." She snapped her fingers to get the man's attention. "There are two more grocery sacks in my truck." Boomer didn't move, just grinned at Haines and Kris.

"Oh, yeah?" Haines said, continuing whatever conversation they were having before Mina walked in. "I bet I can do anything better than you can."

"Not a chance, gorilla boy," Kris said. "You may be bigger, but I'm faster and nimbler."

"The groceries, Boomer?" Mina said, waving her hand. He still didn't move.

Haines stopped circling and crossed his arms. "Maybe we should have us a little contest? Find out who's best."

Kris mimicked his stance. "Bet I can outshoot you."

Mina hung her head. If there was anything Haines was proud of…

"You're on, punker girl." Haines leaned halfway across the island, hands flat. "How about shooting and swimming?"

Again, Kris matched his posture, leaning forward until they were nose to nose. "Twenty-five, fifty, and seventy-five yards, pistols only. Swim from Deer Cove to my brother's place across the lake. And then we bike back to Deer Cove. First one to stand up on the swim platform at the beach wins."

"Shoot, swim, and bike, then finish with a swim to the platform. Agreed." Haines stuck out his hand, and Kris took it. Of course, that resulted in push-pull tugging that migrated to an arm wrestling contest across the granite.

"Oh, good grief," Mina said. "I bought steaks and beer. Now, who's helping?"

That ended the contest, and began a new one as Boomer and Haines began arguing about who was better at grilling. They headed out to get the rest of the groceries.

"Well, I see you met Boomer and Haines."

"That big guy is a piece of work," Kris said, grabbing a Coke from the fridge. "I've seen his type. All talk."

"He *is* kind of handsome, though—in a rugged outdoorsy sort of way," Mina said, throwing on her best dreamy.

Kris's jaw dropped. "You and that gorilla? You have a…a thing going?"

Mina let Kris hang for a few more seconds, then burst out laughing. "Not me. Nope. No way." Then she dropped the zinger. "But I couldn't help notice the way you were admiring his biceps. I mean, what girl wouldn't—"

"Ha! Forget that. Somebody needs to take that ego down a few notches. I'm gonna kick his— Oh," she stopped mid-sentence. "Hi, Teal."

Teal came into the kitchen. "The guys"—she pointed over her shoulder—"said to come on in." Her eyes narrowed, darting between them. "What were you two shouting about?"

Kris waved it away. "Oh, nothing. Haines wants to have a little contest—"

"And Kris said she's going to kick—"

"Never mind," Kris said, giving Mina a look. "So, what brings you over?"

Teal's smirk showed the girl knew her aunt well, but she let her off the hook. "I'm running out of space at home for my artwork, so I brought some for the gallery. I want to get an early start on the display. See what looks best where."

Mina and Kris spent the next several minutes looking at Teal's art. Some were pencil or charcoal drawings, while others were watercolors. All were of local scenes: the marina in town, a cabin at her parents' fishing camp, the boat ramp at Flume, and several of the classic storefronts, including the Mercantile, the little church, DC Coffee, Shelter Cove Store, and even one of Mark's Deer Cove Auto. They were all excellent, and tourists would snap them up as memories of their visit.

To Mina's surprise, the majority were drawings and paintings of Desperation Falls. Some were realistic renditions providing great attention to detail of the rocks, plants, and water, while others were more fanciful, with colorful butterflies and birds, flowers, and misty rainbows.

Mina touched the girl's shoulder. "These are exquisite, Teal. I want this one," she said, pointing to an eight-by-ten watercolor of one of the fishing cabins. Two yellow Adirondack chairs added bursts of color to the rustic cabin's porch, and the six-pane front windows had faded blue curtains pulled back and tied. In the foreground, a fishing pole with a red and white bobber leaned against a dark green canoe.

"Really?" Teal grinned. "Okay."

"And this one," Mina said, pointing to one of the falls.

"That's my favorite, too," Kris said in a hushed tone.

In the twilight, the falls were a fantasyland of twinkling lights and color, as if a thousand fireflies conspired to illuminate every rock and bush. The water dropped in a silvery fall to the pool below, and a crescent moon wavered in the dark surface.

"Except I have a special request," Mina said. Teal's brows knit in question. Mina pointed to the falls painting. "I want this larger." She spread out her arms. "Maybe four feet wide by five feet high, in frameless style where the painting wraps around the edges of the frame."

"I've never done anything that big," Teal said.

"I'll buy the canvas," Mina said, "and I'll pay you five hundred dollars." Teal's mouth dropped open in shock, and Mina smiled. "In fact, I'll buy two canvases. If you paint two of these, I guarantee the second one will sell for the same price on the opening weekend."

While Haines and Boomer broke open a single beer each and cooked the steaks on the deck, Mina gave Kris and Teal a tour of her workshop. She showed Teal the projector used to enlarge images for whatever size glass pane she had. She promised the girl use of the projector for the falls painting.

Teal stayed for dinner, and they ate on the deck. The steaks were perfection, pink in the middle and crispy on the outside, and even Mina's corn on the cob came out juicy and tender. Rope lights around the perimeter of the deck cast a soft glow as darkness fell.

She sat for a minute, breathing in the sweet air as the others began clearing the dishes. Although she'd only been here a few weeks, this was right. The only thing missing was Kade Hunt. Where was he?

It took Kade three days to convince his parents he was all right to continue the trip to California.

He wasn't, of course—all right, that is. Not with this raging sore throat, coughing, and headache that threatened to squeeze his brain down to pea size. He blamed the sickness on the phlebotomist who drew his blood when he was in the hospital. The man's eyes and nose were red, and his voice sounded scratchy. Mask and gloves might help, but they couldn't contain every germ. Kade now suffered an unwelcome side benefit of his hospital stay.

The only fortunate thing about the virus was that it hit him after his folks reluctantly left for Denver and their flight home, otherwise they would have insisted on staying.

Rowan had extended their reservation at the motel, and she was out exploring the walking paths by the river that ran through Silverthorne. At least, that's what she said. He knew she was hitting the outlet shops.

Dr. Laya had consulted with Kade's doctor back home, and together they came up with the fact that there were sometimes no identifiable triggers for a flashback, and no guarantees about future occurrences. However, his past improvement physically and mentally were an overall good indicator of his progress.

Rowan hadn't been comfortable with the ambiguity, but as the days passed with no new episode, she was coming around. They had a thousand miles to go, two long days if they pushed, but he promised his parents they would take it easy for the rest of the trip. And he owed it to his sister.

He curled up on his side and pulled the blanket higher, waiting as another round of chills ran its course. When the worst of the wave passed, he picked up the bedside phone and dialed the FBI main number from memory.

"I'd like to speak with Special Agent Margaret Cartwright, please."

"I'm sorry, she's no longer with the bureau," the operator said. And of course, they could not pass a message or give him her personal contact information.

The chills returned like an unwelcome hitchhiker riding on the bad news. If his teeth weren't chattering so much, he could start over trying to locate Nathan Hawthorne again.

Maybe later.

Maybe tomorrow.

Or maybe they should just drive on.

CHAPTER THIRTY-NINE

Forgiveness is power, not for the forgiven, but for the forgiver.

V.M. NARRANO

SLADE HAD TRIED to talk her out of it a dozen times or more. *Going after the Hawthorne woman was crazy. She should rest. If there was no treatment, at least enjoy her last days.*

But there was no enjoyment for her as long as the woman who destroyed Evie's family lived.

They needed to get Lilly Hawthorne soon. She knew Slade wouldn't continue the hunt after she was gone. He had no stake in it. Maybe at one time in the past he cared enough for her to take revenge on an enemy, but now he was more concerned with money and power. No, the hunt would end with her, one way or another.

Narrano thought it best for people to forgive those who had wronged them. But if everyone did that, the offenders would prosper, overrun the world. Someone had to take them out.

Her cell phone buzzed, and she stifled a groan as she leaned over to reach it. Arms, legs, torso—everything hurt, as if she'd lost a boxing match or tumbled from a horse.

"I have news," Slade said. "If you're home, I'll come over."

"I'm here," she said, and hung up.

She rarely left the house anymore, and hadn't driven anywhere in nearly two weeks. The pain medications were too strong. Like an invalid, she was dependent on Slade and others to bring her what she required. Before long, whether she got Hawthorne or not, Evie would have to end this. But she wasn't at that point quite yet. All she needed was a break, a single piece of information that would change everything.

It could have been five minutes or two hours before the door from the garage opened and Slade entered. Evie roused from her stupor and watched as he went straight to the bar and fixed a drink.

She didn't get up—wasn't sure she could. He came warily closer to the windows, enough to take a seat on the far end of the leather and chrome sofa, marginally nearer her chair.

"Our inside man at the law firm came through," he said. Turns out, Lilly Hawthorne recently purchased a property. A house."

"Where?"

"A little place called Deer Cove on Storm Lake. Not far from Mission Peak."

"She bought it in her name?"

He shook his head and the ice in his glass rattled. "It's in a trust name."

"Could it just be an investment?"

"Perhaps, but I don't think so. The house is in the same town where she showed up on the security camera photo a few days ago."

"Another photo? You should have told me." Anger at being left out fueled a burst of energy. If Slade thought he was protecting her by—

"I *did* tell you, Evie." His voice was soft. "You don't remember? We agreed to send some men and women there to search for her."

The brief spike of energy fizzled as fast as it had come. Damn pain pills. She needed them, but she couldn't taste food, then couldn't remember if she'd even eaten. She didn't have the will or the strength to apologize to Slade, so she just stared at him until he sighed and continued.

"The photo was at a small grocery store in the town. It took several days, but my men spotted her at the store again and followed her back to where she's living. Probably a rental since it's a different address than the house she bought. They checked out the house owned by the trust and said it's being remodeled. They've seen her twice. It's her."

"When do we leave?" Evie wished her energy matched her determination, but it was what it was, and it wasn't improving. The doctors were cagey about timelines, but Evie got the clear message she wasn't going to exceed their initial estimates.

"It's complicated," Slade said. "She has guards."

Evie scoffed. "She had them before."

"It's different this time. My lead guy said they look like ex-military. They may be well equipped. We need to be cautious."

Evie felt her very bones rotting away as each minute passed. Every sunset was one fewer, and each was a bigger percentage of the days she had left on this earth. Caution was a luxury she didn't have.

"We have to move as soon as possible," she said.

Lilly Hawthorne was one offender who would not be granted forgiveness.

"Sorry it's taken so long," DJ said, his voice a whisper, nearly covered by insect noises and the wind buffeting the cell phone mic.

It had been days to get to this point, and Mina moved closer to Haines at the kitchen island so she could hear. He had his cell on speaker and conferenced in Proxy as soon as DJ called.

"I'm on the hill above the house. A hundred yards. Almost dark, but the sunset's behind me, so I have to be careful of movement until the glow fades."

"What's the layout around you?" Haines asked.

Boomer came in from his bedroom. He closed the door to the outside hall and locked it.

"Congested," DJ said. "I had to crawl about two hundred yards along fences of other properties. No lines of sight to other houses, but it's not an easy approach. I wouldn't have been able to do it without the wind blowing the grass and bushes. It masked my movements."

Mina looked at Haines. His mouth was in a firm line.

DJ continued. "I sent photos to Proxy of the man who just arrived—"

"Got 'em," Proxy said. "I matched them to everything else we found on the man. It's Slade. And get this: he's been linked by law enforcement in Mexico to the Viera's old cartel contacts. I couldn't find a last name. Or maybe *Slade* is his last name. "

"Is he related to the Viera family?" Mina asked.

"Inconclusive," Proxy said. "References to him don't begin until a few months after their deaths. One of my team is enhancing the photos. You'll have them soon."

Haines asked DJ about other approaches to the house.

"Limited. Either he knows what he's doing, or he got lucky with this place. It sticks out over an extremely steep canyon. If we take him here, we'll have to go in all at once from the road level. There are always at least two men with him, but they exit and enter the cars inside the closed garage, so there could be more."

"Alarms?" Haines asked.

"I've found two perimeter systems so far. You can't believe how steep that canyon is, Haines. I could hardly move down there without setting off a rockfall. Got to be at least one alarm in the house too. I'm going to try to check for driveway sensors as soon as it gets dark."

Haines rubbed his jaw and looked to Mina. "Might be better to draw him out somewhere—let slip information on where you can be found."

Mina stared at the phone as if she could see the house from DJ's perch high on the hill above it. "If we do that, he'll bring an army."

Haines nodded. "We only get the element of surprise once."

"Another option is calling in the police or DEA," Boomer said.

Mina considered this. It would keep everyone here safe, but there was no guarantee any charges would stick. If he had intel from inside any of the agencies, authorities would find an empty house.

"You stupid idiot." DJ's voice ratcheted up a notch, and they all looked at the phone as if they could see across the distance.

"Talk to me," Haines said.

Rustling obscured DJ's words for a minute. "Some guy towing a trailer is coming around the corner below me, between me and the house. One of his safety chains is dragging, throwing sparks all over the dry grass on the road edge. With this wind—"

Fire and wind were the devil's two rebellious teenagers—at least that's what one reporter called them when Mina lived in L.A. Nearly every year in Southern California, firestorms swept through houses, mobile home parks, and businesses, sometimes moving faster than a person could run. Some blazes stopped only when they reached the Pacific Ocean.

"There goes the first fire," DJ said. Seconds later, he reported a second blaze. They listened to DJ's description as the fires quickly spread, swirling in the capricious winds.

"The fires are coming my way," DJ said. "I gotta bug out." The line went silent.

Proxy said she would try to monitor any phone calls to, from, or about Slade, but with a fire, cell towers would become overloaded, making her task more difficult.

Haines scrubbed a big hand over his face and turned to Mina. "Wouldn't do for DJ to be spotted in the fire area wearing a ghillie suit."

She felt the same frustration he did. Just when they were closing in, everything went south.

Sirens sounded outside Evie's house, growing closer by the second.

Slade rose and drew his gun from his shoulder holster and went to the front door.

Something white drifted past the picture windows. Smoke.

"There's a fire on the other side of the road," Slade said, holstering his gun as he hurried back to her. "It's spreading up the opposite hill, and the wind is swirling and throwing sparks all over." He ignored his fear of heights, came to her chair, and helped her up. "We have to get out of here."

"My guns," Evie said.

"I'll get them."

He left her propped against the door to the garage as he rushed into her bedroom. She had nearly sagged to the floor by the time he returned carrying a lockbox. The air inside the closed garage was heavy and choking as Slade helped her to his black SUV.

Her sporty Mercedes sat forlorn on the far side. As Slade started the car and hit the door opener, Evie realized this might be the last time she saw the car. Even though she could no longer drive it, it stood as a symbol of independence and freedom all Californians cherished from the day they received their learner's permit until the grave.

Unfortunately, Evie was far closer to the grave end of the timeline.

Slade performed a quick three-point turn in the driveway. He switched on the headlights as he drove up to the main road in clouds of thick smoke tinted bright orange with close flame. Two fire engines lumbered up the hill.

The capricious Santa Ana winds cleared the smoke away even as they fanned the flames to blinding intensity. She recoiled from the heat coming through the tinted glass.

Slade turned onto the road, and she could see where sparks had ignited the brush under her house. Flames climbed upward in their quest for easy fuel. Evie's independence slipped further. Shortly, she would own nothing except scorched land, the clothes on her back, and her gun case.

But that would be enough. There would be no forgiveness for Lilly Hawthorne. Someone had to take out the offender.

Haines, Boomer, and Mina watched the fire coverage on the television in the living area. Within fifteen minutes, traffic helicopters had been rerouted, and video of the string of merging fires streamed live on Los Angeles news stations. Growing darkness precluded an aerial attack on the blaze today, but it didn't hinder the news choppers as they jockeyed for position high in the sky. Reporters' dire predictions were unnecessary as the bone-dry hills virtually exploded far below.

Mandatory evacuation notices crawled across the bottom of the screen, while cameras zoomed in on two homes reduced to horrific skeletons of blackened timbers and licking flames. With the billowing smoke, Mina couldn't tell if one of them was Slade's house. And DJ was still down there somewhere, desperately trying to get away from the fire without being seen.

"This will change everything," Haines said. "Even if Slade's house survives, there might be no cover left for an approach, and the area will be crawling with cleanup crews and contractors for months."

Cameras tracked endless lines of fire trucks racing along Ventura Boulevard, and turning up Mulholland Drive and Laurel Canyon Boulevard. These canyons and hills contained the eclectic dwellings of musicians and celebs, ostentatious mansions of the nouveau riche, and irreplaceable history. Jim Morrison, Carole King, the Mamas and the Papas, Brian Wilson, Joni Mitchell, and Linda Ronstadt—all had lived there and birthed the iconic music of the 60s and 70s. The fire crews would do everything in their power to save the homes.

Would they inadvertently save the man who wanted Mina dead?

CHAPTER FORTY

Mina tossed a ruined pendant onto the workbench and sat back. She'd rushed it, applying too much pressure to the electric drill. The small bit had snapped, its jagged tip carving a long scratch down the glass face. Bibs was predicting huge crowds and big sales, and Mina was trying to work ahead.

But the jewelry was just a distraction to stay busy. She already had two boxes of finished pieces ready to go, probably more than enough for the grand opening.

She thought about going up to the house, but a couple of the workers had asked Carter who the "blond chick" was. She would have to wait until they knocked off work. Besides, other than the roof, not a whole lot of progress had been made—not visible progress, anyway. Carter said they were a day or two away from final plan approval. Then things would take off.

But it wasn't the construction delay that had her antsy. Her real frustration was losing Slade. Haines and the guys were sitting on their hands, waiting for Proxy and her team to find a thread for them to chase. It wasn't like they could drive down to L.A. and hope to spot him.

Patience wasn't her strong suit. She'd run into Haines in the kitchen this morning a few minutes after sunrise.

"You've never been a hunter before, have you," Haines said, leaning against the kitchen counter while drinking a cup of coffee.

"I've always been on the other side," she admitted. "I hate this waiting."

He nodded. "The waiting happens for either hunter or hunted, but it's different."

"How so?"

"When you're the hunted, you prepare as much as possible, then you hunker down and wait for the attack. You know it's coming, and you know your territory. You're waiting, yes, but you're ready."

Haines finished his cup, then washed it out in the sink. "But when you're the hunter—and especially when you can't find your target—you're constantly working, planning, expending energy changing scenarios. Like this situation, the location of the enemy isn't certain, so you can't plan for every contingency."

It made sense to Mina. Defense was easier than offense.

Then Haines surprised her by taking both of her hands in his wet ones. "But there's an even bigger, deeper difference in the two sides, Mina. When you're being attacked, you are totally justified in doing everything you can to protect yourself and others around you. Your moral position is righteous. Your only other option is losing and dying."

Haines let go of her hands, dried his coffee mug, and put it in the cupboard. She wiped her hands on her jeans. She'd never heard him talk like this. Maybe lying in a sandy pit in the desert waiting for the enemy gave opportunity for such philosophical ruminations. Obviously, it was something he wanted her to consider.

"However, the hunter's role is not as morally pure," he continued. "Sure, the cause, the necessity, can be every bit as righteous, but at any time right up to the final act, a hunter can choose to walk away from an enemy."

"Let them live to attack another day," Mina said.

Haines shrugged in agreement. "Perhaps. But it's the difference between defending your life and taking another's life preemptively. You'll never know if he might have already decided to call it off and go on vacation to Cabo. One action is no choice, the other is a choice."

His words had weighed on Mina all morning as she worked on the jewelry. She stood and walked to the windows overlooking the creek, watching the waterwheel lumbering slowly beyond the glass. Normally, the splashing water set a perfect tone for her work, providing a beautiful background for creativity. But even its steady tranquility couldn't calm her thoughts.

She turned off the lights and headed upstairs. Haines was in the living area, honing a big knife, and suddenly, she didn't want anything that reminded her of death.

"I'm going swimming." Maybe exercise would clear her head.

He rose from the chair. "I'll go with you. I need the training to beat that chick." He slid the knife into a waterproof Kydex sheath.

After changing into their swimsuits, they exited the mill.

"Let's take your truck," Haines said. "Nobody will bother breaking into that junker."

"Watch it, buster," Mina said. "This isn't exactly the mean streets of Phoenix, you know. It's not like anyone's going to bother your precious four-by."

She knew his unstated reason was to be free to watch. His head was on a swivel, constantly checking in front, behind, and every side street as they drove.

A few minutes later, they locked their guns in the steel boxes she kept secured under the seat, then walked across the hot sand and waded into the cool water.

Swimming didn't foster talking, and she was left with her thoughts as they stroked toward Box. Unfortunately, her thoughts took her right back to their prior conversation.

In Berlin, she had killed a man—watched him die on her living room rug. It had been pure self-defense in reaction to his attack. His life or hers. As Haines said, justified.

But what if the roles were reversed—if *she* had been the attacker? What if she had learned of the man's plan to kill her and had gone to his hotel room hours before, broken in, and killed *him*?

Was a preemptive kill to save her life different than a self-defensive kill for the same reason? Did preemptive count as self-defense?

Box's black form loomed above her, and Mina stopped swimming, treading water. She was breathing hard, and Haines splashed up a few minutes later, red-faced. He turned over on his back and floated, his chest heaving.

"Holy cow, Glass," he said between breaths. "You trying to break an Olympic record or something?"

She hadn't even noticed how hard she'd been swimming, but the strain in her arms and legs, and the burning of her own lungs became evident.

"*...the hunter's role is not as morally pure.*"

Haines's words twisted through her brain as she led them back at a more leisurely pace. It wasn't too late to call it off. So far, she had invested only money.

But to go further, she would invest her soul.

"What are you staring at, bro?" Rowan asked.

They sat opposite one another at a picnic table at the north end of Deer Cove at a swim beach, eating sub sandwiches from a shop in town. It was the first food that tasted good since his cold, and so far it agreed with his digestive system.

Rowan's back was to the lake, and she twisted around. "Well, well. See? Told you she was here."

Mina Glass strode out of the lake like the newest Bond girl. Water sluiced from her black one-piece, and her hips swayed with every footfall. She had her face tilted upward to the sun, arms above her head as she wrung out her long, white hair.

She hadn't spotted him yet. Instead, she spoke to the man wading out beside her.

The man dwarfed her. Dwarfed Kade. Everyone. He wore baggy, nearly knee-length swim shorts, and they didn't fully hide the big knife strapped to his upper thigh. His eyes roved the tree line, the beach, then came to rest on the picnic table where Kade and Rowan sat. The man's arm shot across Mina's chest, positioning her behind him.

The man was perhaps fifteen yards from Kade, and Kade knew he'd be dead in as many seconds if he were the enemy.

"Mina!" Rowan shouted. She hopped up from the table and bounced toward the pair. "I'm Rowan Hunt," she said, ignoring the bodyguard and extending her hand around him to Mina.

"Rowan?" Mina hesitated, then took her hand.

Kade watched her expression change from wary to smiling. She looked beyond Rowan, beyond the big man, and locked eyes with Kade.

His heart stuttered in his chest as he rose from the bench and supported himself with both hands on the table. The bodyguard could have been pulling a gun and Kade wouldn't have noticed. His eyes never left hers.

"Kade." She spoke his name, a whisper that washed over him like a cool breeze.

They sat at a table for two on the patio of a coffee shop near the beach. Rowan somehow convinced the bodyguard, introduced as Rowdy Haines, to give Kade and Mina some space. He hadn't looked happy about it, but complied.

They didn't say a lot for the first minutes, and he couldn't stop studying her. Her hair was the same as he remembered, and the tiny freckles were there under her left eye. But there were differences from his dream vision that took him a minute to identify.

"You remind me of your mother," he said. "You look more like her now." Mina's cheekbones were slightly more pronounced, a refinement during her years past high school, and the beginnings of tiny lines at the corners of her eyes spoke of wisdom learned from facing the world.

She laughed. "You do remember I'm adopted, right?"

He smiled back. Ekaterina Orlov had been one of the most recognizable and beautiful women in the world, and Kade well remembered his shock the first time he met her in Mina's hospital waiting room. Yet after only a few minutes with her and Nathan Hawthorne, Kade realized they were there as parents, not famous movie star and film producer. They were good people.

Mina's hair was still damp and her face was free of makeup, but to him, she was more beautiful than ever. Even without direct blood connection with her parents, they had passed on the most important human characteristics to their daughter. Perhaps those characteristics carried beauty along as a passenger.

She asked about his limp and scars, and he told her about his mysterious assignment. He glossed over his weeks of captivity, but was a little more forthcoming regarding his escape and convalescence. She listened in silence until he ran out of words. When Kade looked down at his cup, it was empty. He didn't remember drinking it, or even what it was.

"This is kind of awkward, huh?" Kade said.

"I'll be right back," she said, rising and tossing their trash on the way inside the coffee shop.

Kade rubbed the scar tissue on his right cheek. Showing up like this was a dumb idea. He should have stayed in Massachusetts, written, given her time to—

"Drink this," she said, placing a large container in front of him. "Guaranteed to heal all wounds—" She faltered for a moment, her gaze flicking to the cheek he'd just been rubbing. "Or at least make you forget your troubles." She sat down, sipping a matching drink and closing her eyes with a moan.

He sniffed it, then tipped his cup and let the hot liquid wash across his tongue. "Wow," he said. "This is… What *is* this?"

"Cappuccino Blast," she said. "Created by the owner, Connie Langworth."

"My compliments to her." He took another drink, glad it was a large container.

"Connie's a him. Short for Conrad. He's the first person I met here. My first friend."

"Well, *he* has good taste—in friends. Coffee too."

She told him about her studies in France, Italy, and Germany, how she tried everything from sculpture to painting, mixed media, and even learned how to weld metal sculpture. She'd studied use of color for a month with a modern artist in Madrid, then another month observing art restoration at the city's most famous museum, Museo del Prado. In the end, it was glass artistry that fueled her creativity.

She leaned across the table. "Why did you come here, Kade?"

He told her about the facial recognition software Rowan's friend Gretchen was testing. How they had found Mina's pictures all over Paris, London, and other cities for a few weeks, then nothing. "Then Gretchen found another picture of you from here."

Mina sat up straighter at that. "I'm aware of the M32K1 software and my photos in Europe, but I didn't know about the picture from here."

For the next twenty minutes, she told him about the Berlin attack, the mad escape, then showing her face to the cameras to test if someone had connected her two identities.

"So," Kade said, "I see you have a bodyguard. I assume he's not the only one?"

She gave him a Cheshire smile. "He's not exactly a bodyguard. And neither are his two team members. They're more like an armed force." She went on to explain their role.

"You hired mercenaries? Are you sure you can trust them?"

She was quiet a moment, as if considering his question...or her answer. Then she nodded. "I hired mercenaries—at first. They've become friends."

A wave of emotion passed over her features, the smile replaced by regret, or resignation. Kade started to ask her about it, but she surprised him by repeating her previous question.

"Why did you come here, Kade?"

He began to repeat his answer about the photo, but she cut him off with a wave of her hand.

"You could have gotten me that information without driving 3,000 miles."

She was right, of course. Eventually he would have gotten in touch with her.

He sighed, so aware of the real reason. In his unconscious or drugged states during captivity, Lilly Hawthorne, Mina Glass, even more than his family, had been his anchor to the past and his hope for the future. Her image had burned into his mind like one of those ghost figures you stare at in bright light, then look into a dark corner where it appears for a few seconds. In the bad times when they came for him, he had only to stare at a dark corner and she would appear, exactly as he remembered her. The illusion never lasted long enough.

Today, unlike those bad days, she was right here, inches from him. His true fear was she had moved on. Or that he was too scarred.

"Kade?" she prompted, laying her hand over his on the table. He looked down at it.

Rowan would tell him to stand up, and then she'd kick the chair from under him, leaving no room for retreat. She'd tell him to go for it. Because really, what was the alternative? Leave here? Leave *her*?

He squeezed his eyes shut. His breath came in a ragged shudder, and he hated the way his emotions lingered so close to the surface these days.

Mina's hand tightened on his, and her image filled the dark corners of his mind.

"Because I couldn't stay away."

Her hand disappeared from his, and he heard her chair scrape backward. For a second, he thought he'd lost her, but then her palms cupped his face. He opened his eyes as her thumbs brushed away the moisture. She was bending over him, inches away, her gaze shifting between his eyes as if seeing everything behind them.

"That's a good answer, Special Agent Hunt."
Then she lowered her lips to his.

CHAPTER FORTY-ONE

IT SEEMED odd to hold the competition between Haines and Kris in the middle of waiting for information from Proxy, but the team's preparation was done, and sitting around at Deer Cove was agony on everyone's nerves.

The shooting part of the competition began at the range near Mission Peak to the south. Mina rode with Kris, while Haines, Boomer, and DJ took Haines's truck. Teal, Quin, and several others followed in a small caravan.

Mina fought back a yawn, glad it wasn't her in the competition. She and Kade had talked until midnight, then he and Rowan left to check into motel rooms Rowan reserved in Blue Rock Harbor, about halfway to Mission Peak. They were meeting them at the gun range.

Beyond being tired, Mina's mind was spinning with Kade's arrival. She barely resisted touching her lips again, but Kris was already giving Mina grief for the impetuous kiss.

But she wasn't sorry. It was a great kiss. And they had shared others before he and Rowan left last night.

Four years since she'd talked to him. Longer since they'd seen each other. Yet it felt like they bridged the gap in a few hours. There was much more to talk about, to share and discover, but everything felt right, like the last puzzle pieces fitting into place.

Narrano's quote this morning seemed especially appropriate.

Hold on to special times, special places, special people. As we change and move through life, we expect to find or recreate those again. New homes, new friends, new lovers. But sometimes those things are one-time only.

DJ had returned from L.A. while waiting for a lead to materialize, and he and Boomer set up the two stations at the shooting range. Kris and Haines had modified the contest slightly to pistols of their choice at 25 yards, then matching rifles at 75 and 100 yards. It was to be ten shots for each target. Mina squeezed her earplugs tighter as the shooters took their positions.

A hand touched hers. Kade. She turned her hand into his as Rowan grinned across at her.

Quin and Teal—official co-judges with DJ and Boomer—watched the targets through binoculars.

The shooting went quickly. Kris led by one point after the pistol round, and Haines bested her by one at the 75-yard targets. He led by a total of two after the 100-yard scores were added, and he rubbed it in on the walk back to the cars.

"Better not sink like a *stone*, little lady," he said. "You've got to make up a lot of *ground*."

Kris was grumbling as she climbed into the car with Mina. "He coughed just before my last shot. You heard him, right?"

Mina hid her grin and kept silent.

"That gorilla is as sleek as a brick," Kris continued. "I'll be across the lake and halfway back around on my bike before he even wades ashore."

Mina had seen Haines swim, and he wasn't bad for such a big guy. This was going to be fun.

When they arrived at the swim beach, the parking lot was overflowing, forcing Kris to park two blocks away on a side street.

"What in the world?" Mina said as they wound their way through people at the beach. "Are they all here to watch? I thought we were the only ones who knew about the competition."

"I have a feeling a certain Marine let the word out."

"Looks like someone issued a press release." A half-dozen vendor carts were set up on the grass, offering flavored ice, giant pretzels, hot dogs, and more.

"I might have told a few people," Kris mumbled, plopping onto a picnic table bench to remove her shoes for the swim.

"A few?"

"Well, I didn't want all the bets to go his way."

"You mean people are making bets on this?"

"Uh…"

Mina shook her head. "I swear, Kris, you two deserve each other."

Kris started to protest, but several people crowded close, wanting to know the shooting scores. Then Quin climbed onto the lifeguard platform and blew a whistle, the signal to get in position.

Haines and Kris stripped down to their suits and swam out to the floating platform for the start. They stood swinging their arms, loosening up for the mile and a half swim.

"Ready!" Quin shouted. He triggered an air horn, and the two competitors hit the water. They quickly cleared the floating rope ring and struck out across the lake.

DJ and Boomer joined Quin on his boat, and they raced ahead of the others to time the finish. Teal was already on the far side of the lake, waiting with the bikes at her folks' cabins.

Mina joined Kade and Rowan at a table on the DC Coffee patio and watched the receding flotilla of boats, canoes, and kayaks as they paced the swimmers.

"This place is like going to camp," Rowan said. "I love it here. I wonder if I can find someone to take me waterskiing?"

Mina had to admit, it was an absolutely perfect day. The dry air edged toward hot and smelled of grilling hamburgers and hotdogs. Kids yelled, dogs barked, and people laughed—all before the backdrop of the sparkling blue water. She leaned back, feeling the sun on her skin. If only her dad could capture this on film, package it for sale. People would pay millions.

This was how she wanted to spend her life. Was it too much to ask?

After forty-five minutes, a distant air horn sounded two quick blasts.

"That's the signal for Kris," Kade said. "Pretty good time."

They waited another eight or nine minutes before a single blast came for Haines.

"Kris has a good lead," Rowan said. "Is she a good cyclist?"

"No idea," Mina said. "But they are both stubborn and competitive."

Kade volunteered to stake out a picnic table at the beach while Mina and Rowan grabbed some takeout at the Crab Shack.

"So…" Rowan said as they walked to town, "you and my brother."

Mina was unable to hide a grin. "Hollywood meets the FBI."

Rowan laughed. "You're anything *but* Hollywood. Except the name. Palomino *is* kind of badass, like you should be one of the Justice League or Avengers."

"I could carry my media blaster and shoot sand in bad guys' eyes."

They stopped at the end of the line at the outside pickup window at the restaurant. There were only a few people ahead of them and the line was moving. Mina's stomach growled at the first whiff of battered fish and lemon.

"He's been through a lot," Rowan said, her expression serious. "And he's not through it yet."

"I know."

"It's just… You haven't seen—"

"Rowan," Mina said. "The first time I saw him—not a few days ago, but seven years ago—I was lying on the cold pavement in L.A. I was seventeen and shot full of holes, bleeding out, and scared out of my mind. I'd just seen my best friend murdered, and I knew I would be next. Then Kade was there, pulling off his shirt to stop the blood flow, calling for help, holding me. Promising I would be okay when he knew I might not be."

"Kade told me about that on our drive," Rowan said. "Well, not about the pulling off his shirt part."

"Did he tell you how he held my hand as the EMTs rolled me to the ambulance? How he bent close as I whispered my new name: Palomino."

Rowan blinked away moisture in her eyes. "That's when you changed your name?"

Mina nodded. "At that exact moment. I thought your brother might be the only person who would ever know. His gray eyes were the last thing I saw."

Rowan shook her head. "He didn't tell me all that."

"I was in and out of it for days due to surgeries, but he was always there in my subconscious."

They reached the front of the line, got their food, and headed back.

"So it was love at first sight?"

Mina smiled. "More like connection, but it was just as deep. He told me later that he visited me twice while I was in the hospital. Rowan, I swear I could feel him there, even when I wasn't awake."

"Is that enough? I mean, almost everything you guys have been through together has been crisis and trying to stay alive. That's not reality."

Unfortunately, it was for Mina.

They returned to the beach area, and Rowan scanned the tables for Kade. But Mina didn't have to search. She could feel his eyes on her, and she turned to meet his gaze where he stood at the same picnic table where she first saw him as she and Haines strode out of the lake.

Connection might not be enough, but it was one great foundation.

———

Her stomach full, Mina was starting to get sleepy when shouting and car horns started in town.

A minute later, a four-wheel ATV roared up with DJ and Boomer. They jumped off a couple of minutes before a huffing Rowdy Haines pedaled onto the sand. He threw down his bike at the water's edge and staggered into the shallows, shoes and all.

Kris rode onto the beach seconds behind, pedaling right into the lake and diving over the handlebars when the bike submerged. Her strokes were fast and furious, while Haines's were longer and more leisurely. He thought he had it won, but there was so much water flying, Mina couldn't tell who was in the lead. And with all the crowd noise, he might not be aware of Kris's close pursuit.

The crowd lined the water's edge, cheering as the two thrashed toward the platform.

"Looks like Kris is gaining," Kade said. Then one of Haines's big hands slapped the top of the platform, and he heaved himself halfway up, bending at the waist. He was pulling up one leg, when Kris surged up his back, grabbed his shoulders, and kept sliding right over him and onto the platform like a wet seal. She rolled once, then jumped to her feet and danced in a circle, arms high.

The spectator shouts grew even louder when Haines got to his feet and shoved Kris sideways off the platform. She cartwheeled before hitting the water. Haines faced the shore, both arms raised in victory.

Kris didn't stay in the water long. In seconds, she was back on the platform behind Haines. She jumped on his back, locking her legs around his waist and her arms around his thick neck. He spun in a circle, trying to dislodge her, but only succeeded in tumbling them both into the water, still locked together.

Everyone was still laughing a few minutes later when the two contestants waded toward shore. At knee depth, Haines scooped up Kris and slung her over his shoulder. He carried her ashore while she kicked and pounded his back.

"I thought you were going to *sink*, Stone," Haines said as he set her on her feet. He spread his arms wide, a picture of innocence. "I was just helping you out."

"You'd better think twice before you close your eyes tonight, mister," Kris spit out, wiping water from her face.

It took a few minutes to add up the scores. Kris had won the lake swim, but Haines had bested her in shooting and made up time on the biking. No one was exactly sure how to determine the winner of the last leg to the platform, so Teal, Quin, DJ, and Boomer officially declared the competition a tie.

By the grumbling in the crowd, it was obvious to Mina more than a little wagering had occurred. Others were speculating on next year's competition and if there would be a running leg added.

"I wonder if I'll be strong enough to enter next year," Kade said.

Mina glanced sideways at him. He was planning next year; she was wondering whether she'd be alive in a week or two.

At least she had a short reprieve. Mina had committed to be at the Art Mill opening in three days. There wasn't enough time to go after Slade before the July 4th weekend. And while one part of her wished Proxy's people would find a giant fluorescent arrow over L.A. pointing at their quarry, another part was beginning to wish it would never happen, that it would all go away.

She took Kade's arm as they walked up the beach through dozens of happy people.

Kade smiled at her. "Next year, Mina. You and me in this competition."

While she grinned up at him and tightened her grip, her insides were a lump of fused glass. What if they found Slade and it all went wrong? Before, it had just been her and her dad. The risk to eliminate the threats and attacks seemed worth it. Now she had new friends who had in an amazingly short time become like family. It was easy to envision a future. She had a house in this beautiful place, and a chance at a relationship she thought lost.

And if she died, then it truly *would* be lost. Forever.

Did she really want to go to war?

Hold on to special times, special places, special people.
    ...sometimes, those things are one-time only.

CHAPTER FORTY-TWO

Mina rubbed her face and squinted at the overhead fluorescent fixtures. They seemed to be getting dimmer. Or maybe it was her eyes. Up since 3:00 a.m., she was finishing the last batch of pendants for her *Pana's Dream* line.

Everything had been going well until one of her Kiln's heating elements burned out. She'd been willingly distracted by Kade, and hadn't noticed the oven's temperature drop. Almost thirty pieces were ruined and she had to discard them. A spare element fixed the problem, but now she was playing catch-up.

Thanks to Bibs, the Art Mill was the talk of the community. An eye-catching three-foot oval sign of sandblasted and painted redwood hung on chains from a simple log frame at the turnoff from Lake Road, and two smaller versions were at the mill driveway turn and on the lawn by the parking area. That woman had some pull to get those done and mounted so quickly.

The five-day grand opening spanned from noon today, Friday, through Tuesday July 4th at 3:00 p.m. Mina had seen only a fraction of the items from the fifteen artists, but Bibs promised everything from paintings and jewelry to clothing and furniture.

Besides the jewelry, Mina had finished two residential doors for a new house south of Deer Cove. For the laundry room, she etched a kitten jumping at clothes blowing on a clothesline. The door for the pantry had a bag of flour, wooden utensils, wine bottle, and grape vines. She'd seen others done like this before, but hers stood out due to the airbrushed color. The homeowner, a referral from Connie Langworth, had seen the finished doors and was ecstatic, and agreed to let Mina keep them temporarily for display as promotion for Palomino Glass Company.

Behind in her work or not, she didn't regret for a second the hours with Kade. She took him to breakfast at Peg's Waffle House, walked with him as he exercised his legs, and helped him up the stairs afterward when his ankles ached—which was all the time.

He expressed genuine interest when she showed him her art projects, both large and small. Unfortunately, Howell had moved the angel window up to the house for installation, but Mina promised to take Kade up to see it when the workers were gone on Tuesday.

With each time together, she learned a little more of what happened during Kade's captivity. Terrible things, vague flashes of memory, each corroborated by the marks on his body. When he showed her his back one day, she saw his hesitation, the fear she would find him damaged. She countered by peeling her shirt off her right arm and showing him *her* latest scar. They had a good laugh over that, especially when Kris walked in on them in the kitchen and saw Kade bare to the waist and Mina half out of her shirt.

Car tires crunched on the gravel driveway up in the yard, followed a minute later by Bibs' commanding voice as artists began streaming inside and setting up their displays.

"Time's up, Glass," Mina said to herself. She pressed her palms into her eyes again. Even her eyeballs were gritty, and she hoped she didn't look as tired as she felt. A shower would help.

She stood and stretched, then gathered the jewelry boxes into a cardboard box and trudged up the stairs to her living quarters. After showering and dressing in white shorts and a lavender T-shirt with her Palomino Glass Company logo, she headed to the retail area.

In the hallway, the door leading out to the deck was open,

admitting all the lake smells she loved. She paused there, breathing deeply. What she'd rather do was go for a swim, relax on a chaise on the deck, maybe grill a steak for lunch—if she had a steak, which she didn't since the guys had eaten them all. A bottle of Italian red to go with the nonexistent steak would be nice. She didn't have any wine either. Oh, well.

Daily highs were predicted to be around a hundred degrees all weekend, making for warm evenings, perfect for outdoor living and the fireworks show Tuesday night. But first, she had to get through today.

She sloughed off the fatigue, squared her shoulders, and pasted on her best smile. Those years of photo sessions with her Hollywood parents came in handy in times like these. She pulled open the door to the commotion of the front room, and her mouth dropped open.

Bibs stood in the center of the room, fists buried on hips hidden beneath a chartreuse muumuu the size of a four-man tent. She pivoted in a shaft of brilliant sunlight, surveying her domain.

"We open in fifteen, people." Bibs clapped her hands like a general commanding troops. "Let's wrap it up."

The fabric of her dress was like nothing Mina had ever seen. Every shiny surface in the room reflected the color, and it rendered the beautiful artwork displays somewhat drab in comparison. Bibs' white, spiked hair was newly tipped in celery green that oddly complimented the muumuu. It poked out above a gold headband.

"Quite a sight, huh?" Teal whispered as she hurried past the doorway, breaking Mina out of her trance. "If I ever get lost in the woods, I want Bibs with me. Search and Rescue couldn't miss her."

Mina barked a laugh that caught Bibs' attention. One plucked eyebrow lifted.

"Oops," Mina whispered.

Teal motioned toward an empty display case. "I've been saving this one for you." She had a large crate filled with rolls of black and silver satin, along with various sized wood blocks and cubes saved from Lena's woodworking.

Together, they draped and bunched the fabric artistically over and around the blocks, arranging each of Mina's creations on the best contrasting backdrop. Mina wove strings of LED seed-lights through the display and clicked on the switches. When she walked around the front of the case to see the result, her eyes stung as she read her hand-lettered card at the front of the case: *Pana's Dream.*

Delicate crosses, earrings, bracelets, and pendants, made from layered dichroic glass and softened in the kiln, changed color as the viewer shifted position. So similar to Pana, who had imparted light and fun wherever she went.

"Who's Pana?" Teal asked, coming beside her to admire the display.

Mina wiped under her eyes. "A good and brave friend—who died far too young." Teal stood quietly. It was one of the things Mina liked best about her. Unlike most teen girls, Teal didn't fill every silence with talking, texting, or whining. For a moment, they were cocooned, set apart from the hustle surrounding them.

Teal leaned her head close and whispered, "Pana would be proud." With a brief squeeze of Mina's shoulder, she headed off to help someone else.

Over time, the bad memories—Pana in the van, blood pooling under her, gripping the gun, dead—were superseded by ones of laughter, silly sleepovers, meeting for lunch at school or ditching to hit In-N-Out, and late-night phone calls to plan the next day's shopping or beach trip. Her loss wasn't as sharp these days, and that felt a little like betrayal, as if the importance of Pana's life was slipping away. Which is why she created *Pana's Dream.* A reminder of what was important.

Under the sign's heading, smaller print read: *Proceeds benefit the Pana Grant Foundation.* Mr. and Mrs. Grant had established it in their daughter's memory to help disadvantaged kids go to quality schools. Good had risen from the ashes of a terrible loss, but Mina would never forget that Pana's death was at the hand of Ernesto Viera.

Mina felt renewed thankfulness for her own parents. They had appeared in her life when she needed them most, when she was one of those lost, disadvantaged kids. They hadn't needed to be stars in Hollywood to change her entire world.

Then Tommy Viera came hunting Mina, and had gotten Mina's mom instead. The cocky Viera had been Mina's first kill.

She shook off the melancholy fog, closed her eyes, and took in the feel of the room around her. Lemon and pine cleaner, barely dry oil paint on canvas, wood oil, sweet air coming through the windows, happy voices, spicy aromas from the two food trucks Bibs contracted to feed the shoppers. Mina smiled, picturing it all. Henri, if he were here, would be proud.

"Doors opening!" Bibs announced, and a stream of people flooded the room like a Black Friday rush—except without the tussling over last year's discounted televisions.

"Ooh, is this yours?" a voice asked. An elderly woman was standing in front of one of three- by three-foot glass panels Mina had moved up last night and positioned on a sturdy table.

The image was a mermaid resting on a rock, her lower body submerged in the clear sea. Her face and upper body were hidden by long, blonde hair as she looked out over the water, and her broad, iridescent tail shimmered beneath the surface. A dozen colorful fish swam through twisting gray-green seaweed. The glass was an inch thick, which lent a perfect greenish cast to the painting, and was glued to a glass base. Backlit by one of the overhead lights, the image came alive.

Two other women were ogling the pantry glass door. For the next few hours, Mina had a never-ending parade of admirers asking about her glass art and jewelry. The mermaid—now sporting a SOLD sign —got most of the attention, though the other panel of running horses had sold too. She had three more orders for the mermaid and half a dozen follow-up promises for pantry doors. Who knew that was such a big market?

By the time 4:30 arrived, Mina was checking the clock every five minutes. Her feet ached, her stomach had collapsed against her spine like a deflated sack, and her ears rang from the constant hubbub. A dozen times, she had thought about sneaking out early.

Bibs announced the closing, reminding everyone they opened at 10:00 a.m. tomorrow on Saturday, and 1:00 p.m. on Sunday after church.

"Grab your stuff and let's go," Teal said, hoisting a small backpack over one shoulder.

"And just where would I be going when all I want to do is crash onto one of those recliners?" Mina asked, eyeing the sun-dappled deck. She thought there might be a mac and cheese in the freezer—if the guys hadn't eaten it too.

Teal hip-bumped her. "You're joining us for dinner." The girl pointed to the front porch where Lena Stone stood beside a broad-shouldered man in a tight black T-shirt and jeans.

"That's your dad?"

"Yep. The one and only Alex Stone."

The man's imposing physique was made potentially more menacing by his weathered face and crooked nose that had been broken in the past. If you were ever in a dark alley facing a bad guy, you'd want Alex Stone at your back. "And dinner plans are...?"

"The Wave Pizza in Perilous Cove. Best pizza on the planet." She snorted. "Not that you'll notice—I could hear your stomach growling an hour ago."

"That's when it *stopped* growling," Mina said. "I think it's dead."

"So I expect even tomato sauce on cardboard would probably taste good to you."

Originally, Mina planned to grab a bite with Kade, but he had come by earlier and begged off, citing something he needed to do with Rowan. At the time, Mina was too busy talking to three customers to do anything but wave as he walked out.

Before Mina could protest that she was too tired, Teal said, "You can follow us down to Flume, leave your truck there, and ride with us down to PC. We'll drop you at your truck on the way back."

"Let me tell Haines," Mina said. Pizza, especially the best pizza on the planet, sounded a lot better than a microwaved dinner.

After eating several pieces of undisputedly the best pizza on the planet, four or five buttery breadsticks, and a small salad as a nod toward something healthy, Mina staggered after the Stone family as they all hiked out to Perilous Point Lighthouse to watch the sunset.

It was one of those magical evenings where the wind died, the ocean went dead flat, and the world took on an unearthly stillness. When the sun's last glowing crescent disappeared into the sea, even the birds seemed to hold their breath. A collective sigh rose from the other observers on the bluff.

Mina wished she could capture sound and temperature in her art. Maybe that was the challenge for any artist.

On the walk back, Teal pointed out the house where Quin's cousins, Star and Mandy, lived with their parents Addison and Samantha Conner. Mina's brain was on calorie overload from gooey cheese and tangy sauce. Her confusion must have shown.

"Addison is the brother of Ben Conner, Quin's dad," Teal reminded her.

Mina again vowed to draw out an org chart to keep track of all the relations.

"Mandy also makes amazing jewelry," Teal said. "She sells them at a shop here in town."

"Oh, that's right," Mina said. "My first day in town I met Star at the Last Drop, and she told me her sister made jewelry."

Then Teal motioned for Mina to hang back and let Alex and Lena get ahead. "Quin says he's going to have Mandy make our wedding rings," she whispered.

Mina nearly stumbled as what Teal said sank in. "What?"

"Anything wrong?" Alex Stone asked, looking back from several yards ahead.

"No, Dad," Teal said with a perfectly straight face. "I think Mina's a little cheese-buzzed. Some people just can't hold their pizza." She grinned in perfect innocence, and the Stones laughed and began walking again.

Mina grabbed the girl's arm and dragged her close. "You're

getting engaged? Do you even have a driver's license?" Of course she did; Mina had seen her driving Lena's Jeep. But still…

"Chill, Mina. It's not happening right away." She seemed a little sad at that. "Besides, everyone knows we're going to be together."

"Do *they* know?" Mina inclined her head toward Alex and Lena Stone walking with fingers laced and heads together.

"Well…" The girl's brows knit slightly.

"And you're how old?"

"Seventeen," Teal answered, but then her face clouded, as if a shadow fell across their path. "I know that doesn't seem old enough."

Mina agreed. Even at twenty-five, she couldn't imagine being married. Then her thoughts slipped to Kade Hunt.

Teal kicked a rock with the toe of her tennis shoe. "I don't want to wait too long. There are no guarantees of life."

"Better go slow or you'll have a parental revolt on your hands." Even as she said it, she hated sounding like a parent herself. But getting engaged this young? Why, when *she* was seventeen, she'd been…

Mina stopped. At seventeen, she'd been in a white van with her dead friend lying beside her in a pool of blood.

Then Teal's wording dawned on her. Not no guarantees *in* life, but *of* life.

Pana's life ended at seventeen and, by all odds, Mina should be buried at Forest Lawn alongside her friend.

Teal grinned and waggled her bare ring finger in front of Mina, breaking her somber mood. The cuff of the girl's long-sleeve shirt slid back a couple inches, revealing the white encircling scars.

Teal Stone grasped life in a way few understood. And she had good reason.

CHAPTER FORTY-THREE

THIRTY MINUTES LATER, the Stones dropped Mina at her truck in Flume. They continued up the east side of the lake to their home, while she drove north on the west side. Now full dark, she watched diligently for deer lurking in the wisps of ground fog that sifted between trees and blanketed low pockets. Judging by the near weekly carcasses along the road, the creatures had a death wish.

By the time she reached Old Mill Road, she was squinting from the long day and nearly comatose from the rich food. She couldn't wait to crawl into bed. The oaks overhanging her driveway, so stately during the daylight, reached across with menacing arms as she steered along the graveled road to the mill.

The parking lot had overflowed with customers all day, forcing people to park along the driveway. To free up a space for tomorrow, Mina turned left on the access road that led down to her studio and parked in front of the big sliding door. Impenetrable night invaded when she switched off the truck's lights. Unfortunately, this door didn't have an exterior lock. Using a little flashlight she kept in the glove compartment, she made her way back along the path that led up to the main entrance.

It was just as dark on the front porch. Days were so long this time of year, and she hadn't thought to turn on the light before leaving. She made a mental note to speak with Bibs about landscape lighting.

Mina unlocked the door and stepped inside. The interior, although dark, was still warm from the day, and her body shivered at the transition from the cooler outdoors. At least Lena had placed a couple of nightlights on the far side of the room, and they showed the outline of the display cases enough so Mina wouldn't run into one.

She locked the door and headed toward the living quarters, but before she'd taken three steps, she tripped over some kind of bulky bag and sprawled face first onto the wood floor. Her little flashlight went spinning across the surface as she scrambled to her hands and knees.

Had one of the other artists left their bag? How had she not noticed it when she left earlier?

Before she could get to her feet, hands shoved her sideways. A hooded figure snatched the bag, but a strap had tangled around Mina's foot.

She kicked hard, trying to get away. Her foot connected with something solid, and she was rewarded with a loud *oomph!* Her heart banged in her chest as she backpedaled, dragging the bag with her. She caught a glimpse of a white face under the hood. A man.

The Vieras!

The man yanked the duffel at the same time she reached behind her back for her gun. She missed the pistol as she was twisted sideways. The bag's contents spilled, clattering across the planks. With one last effort, he tore the strap from her foot.

Mina had her gun out now, her finger sliding into the trigger guard and pressing on the sliver of steel.

The man jumped to the front door and wrestled with the deadbolt.

Another pound or two of pressure on the trigger…

The door flew open and banged against its stop. The figure disappeared through the wide opening.

Mina waited a heartbeat, staring at the gaping doorway, then removed her finger from the trigger. She scooted until her back was against the wall, panting as her lungs strained for air.

She should have screamed, yelled.

Where were Haines and the guys?

Cool air washed through the wide-open front door. The man could return any second.

Small items scattered as she scrambled on hands and knees to the door, shoved it closed, and locked it. Fifteen feet away, her flashlight shone a small yellow circle against a display case leg, and she scooped it up and retreated to the far corner of the room.

Then she remembered where Haines was. Since she was going out with the Stone family, she suggested the guys take the evening off, especially since the mysterious Proxy announced out of the blue she was coming in on the last flight tonight at the Mission Peak airport. Someone had to pick her up.

But they were supposed to be here before Mina returned. After taking a deep breath, she turned on the lights in the room. Rings, necklaces, earrings, carved figurines, and small paintings littered the polished floor. She turned on the rear deck lights and the ones on the front porch, then began making phone calls.

A few minutes later, blue and red flashing lights of a sheriff's cruiser lit the driveway trees. Its headlights swung across the building, angled so they illuminated the steps and entryway when the car stopped. A deputy stepped out.

Mina tucked the gun in the holster at the small of her back, opened the mill door, and walked down the steps into the glare. Before she could introduce herself, Bibs' 70s Buick roared up, scattering gravel as it braked to a stop. Bibs and Irene poured out and rushed to Mina, engulfing her in their arms.

"Are you okay, dear?" Bibs asked, dragging Mina toward the cruiser's bright lights and turning her around so she could get a better look. "Did he hurt you?"

Mina assured them she was fine. The deputy introduced himself as Drew Hansfield.

"Drew, would you go check out everything inside?" Bibs asked. It might as well have been an order from a superior the way the deputy tipped his flat-brimmed trooper hat and hurried inside carrying a large flashlight.

He returned a minute later to get Mina's keys for the living quarters. If that door was still locked, the burglar hadn't gotten into that part of the building—where the guys had an untold number of weapons and ammo.

"We used to babysit his mama," Irene said by way of explanation as they watched interior lights go on, one room at a time.

Mina recounted what happened twice to the two women as they waited for the deputy. She was beginning to shiver in the cool night before he returned.

"No one inside," he said. "The only room that looks disturbed is the front room. Why don't we go inside where it's warmer and I'll take your statement."

Irene held up a giant semi-automatic pistol. "I'm gonna put this back in the car so I don't have to lug it around. Want me to take yours too, Bibs?" Bibs handed her sister an equally large revolver.

Mina glanced at the deputy. His head was lowered and he was shaking it a little.

Bibs bustled about making coffee for them in the kitchen, while the deputy took pictures in the other room. The intruder had evidently filled his bag with dozens of items from the display cases, including every Pana's Dream piece that hadn't sold. They would have to make up a full inventory list in the morning when the other artists arrived, but as nearly as they could tell, most of the crook's loot spilled during his hasty exit.

Since much of the jewelry had been handled by multiple customers earlier in the day, there was no point in dusting for prints, so Bibs and Deputy Drew decided it would be pointless to secure the merchandise as evidence. Plus, that would severely limit sales tomorrow, their second day.

Drew checked the entire building again to make sure every door and window was secure. He showed Mina the suspected entry point —a window in the hallway leading to the outside deck was open.

"The perp probably unlocked it during the day when everyone was busy, then came back tonight," he said.

Mina leaned close as he demonstrated how the latch could be left open but still appear secure. It made sense the burglar entered from the back. That's why the front door had been locked when she came home. And by parking down below and walking up, she hadn't given him any warning.

Bibs promised to have an alarm installed by the end of the day Saturday, which reminded Mina to see if Haines's video cameras caught anything.

Before leaving, the deputy handed her his card. "My personal cell number is on the back. I'll come back tomorrow after you close and help you make sure everything is locked up tight."

"Oh, you don't have to do that," Mina said. "I'm sure we'll—"

"I'd feel better if I did," he said, stepping closer. "And if you need me before then, call me. Anytime." He tipped his hat, and was gone.

"Whew!" Bibs said, fanning herself with one of the store brochures. "Nothing like a man in uniform. I think he likes you, Palomino."

"Oh, I don't—"

"He's not married," Irene volunteered. "No girlfriend either." She leaned closer and stage-whispered, "They say he's partial to blondes, so with *your* hair, you exceed expectations."

Bibs tapped her lip with one purple fingernail. "I wonder if he's off work for Tuesday's fireworks show?"

About ten minutes after Deputy Drew left, they heard the growl of a roaring engine and more scattering gravel out front. Pounding feet followed seconds later, and Haines's huge form filled the kitchen doorway. He eyed Bibs and Irene, nodding a greeting. Then his gaze settled on Mina.

"You okay, Glass?"

"I'm fine." He'd been her second phone call, right after 9-1-1. She was glad he hadn't rushed in cradling his AR-15 while the deputy was still here.

"DJ and Boomer are checking the perimeter." He touched the bulge under his jacket and lifted an eyebrow.

She matched his gesture by touching the small of her back. He nodded in approval. Considering the firepower the two older women packed, she and Haines probably didn't need to be so secretive about carrying weapons. Bibs had said something earlier about there being a lot of snakes about. The woman wasn't talking about reptiles.

Maybe it was some innate instinct that she hadn't pulled the trigger during the confrontation. The man wasn't attacking her, just trying to escape. Still, it had been close. That scared her.

On the other hand, her hesitation could have been a fatal error. He might have turned on her any moment. Going into the dark building like that was right out of a chainsaw movie. The TSTL blonde: too stupid to live. That's what she got for being up half the night and then nearly drowning in mozzarella.

Bibs tried to direct the conversation back to Mina's date for the fireworks, but Mina wasn't having it.

"I already have a boyfriend," she stated. Of course, that sparked a new round of interest and You do?s from both women.

Mina couldn't believe Bibs hadn't heard about the kiss on the DC Coffee patio, but counted that as a freak stroke of luck. Now that the truth was out, it diverted the sisters from the subject of Deputy Drew and fireworks, but began a new line of interrogation.

She ushered Bibs and Irene out the door, assuring them that with all this manpower surrounding her, she would be perfectly safe until morning—which was coming soon.

The two women roared off in their Buick, and DJ and a young woman stepped onto the porch. Boomer followed carrying a suitcase. The bag had a distinguishing bandana tied to the handle. It was the gray-green of an old computer monitor, and printed with alternating lines of ones, zeros, and pirate skulls. Mina moved aside as they entered the building.

"Proxy, I assume?"

"Hi, Mina," Proxy said, smiling and extending her hand. "I feel like I know you."

That was truth. Proxy probably knew everything from Mina's shoe size to her dislike of curry. She was medium height, slim, and dressed simply in black yoga pants and windbreaker over a bright yellow tee. Her wet-look sable hair was swept back and down in a waterfall style, ending in a blunt cut mid neck. It stated *non-priority*, but was still chic. In fact, it looked like it might be a new cut. Now in better light, Mina guessed her to be her same age—twenty-five.

"I expected you to be older," Mina said. "Or younger. Or… something." Truthfully, she had pictured Proxy resembling the ultra-smart Abby on the *NCIS* TV show. Straight bangs and maybe a few tattoos. This woman looked decidedly normal, a young professional who could go to the grocery store and no one would notice. Mina longed for that kind of anonymity.

Proxy laughed. "Good to know my electronic persona is inscrutable." Then her expression changed to one of concern. "I'm sorry we're so late. It's my fault the guys weren't here. My flight almost didn't take off from San Francisco due to fog."

Mina couldn't help noticing how Proxy's openly shy gaze lingered a little longer on Boomer than the others, and how she moved almost imperceptibly closer to him. Boomer made a corresponding adjustment, closing the gap.

Proxy might as well have licked her lips. Mina hid a smile. Like a moth to a flame. Boomer Poole was a goner.

It took them a little while to get Proxy settled in the room Boomer had been using. He moved his stuff into DJ's room, and inflated an air mattress he'd bought in Mission Peak.

As Mina crawled into bed, she vowed never to come home to a dark building again. Maybe Lena or the guys could add some motion lights.

For the next couple of hours, she stared at the dark ceiling, every creak of the old structure had her ears straining. A light wind shook leaves from the oaks and sent them skittering down the metal roof on little burglar feet. She was immensely thankful for the full house.

If nothing else, tonight's incident was a wakeup call for being prepared. She couldn't afford to get comfortable. This could have been the Viera threat, someone invading her home like in Berlin. She had to stop this before they attacked again. Because if that happened, someone else might get hurt.

CHAPTER FORTY-FOUR

SATURDAY BEGAN with the artists scrambling to sort the items spilled from the thief's bag. Mina had spread them out on top of the display cases, and Bibs made a list of anything missing, which was thankfully short. They finished restocking the displays minutes before they opened for business.

The unfortunate part was Mina being immediately proclaimed a hero by the rest of the artists. When Quin arrived at noon to see Teal, he said the story in town was Mina had single-handedly fought off an entire burglary ring.

Two hours later, a television reporter from Mission Peak arrived with a cameraman. Haines made sure Mina was nowhere to be found, and the reporter shifted her coverage to the successful opening of the Art Mill. The story wouldn't run until tonight's five o'clock news, but word of the theft had spread by radio and social media, drawing new customers from all over the county. Most of the artists were selling as fast as they could restock their merchandise.

When five o'clock arrived, Mina's case was nearly empty. She had four more orders for the mermaid glass panel, two for variations of the running horses, and inquiries about a dozen custom works.

Palomino Glass Company was in for a busy year. Haines locked the main door after the last artist left, and joined her on the back deck.

"Looks like you're a success, Glass," Haines said, dropping into the lounger beside hers.

She closed her eyes. The noisy retail space had her ears ringing worse than after one of Haines's training runs. Starting next weekend, she planned to hire Teal as official sales representative for Palomino Glass in the retail shop. Then Mina could hide downstairs in the peaceful work space.

Conner Creek gurgled over rocks below, and a breeze wiggled the leaves above in a soothing lullaby. "Ah. I'd pay for more of this quiet. Oh, wait…I *am* paying for it."

Haines laughed. "It's pretty nice here. A lot different than the desert." He laced his fingers behind his head. "By the way, we checked the security cameras. Nothing useful. We saw him break in, but he had on a ball cap and hoodie. Knew enough to keep his head down."

That's what Mina figured. Cameras were rarely much help, and they couldn't use motion detector alerts due to raccoons, deer, and the occasional bobcat that routinely roamed the porch and deck. The false alarms would keep everyone up all night.

"Brought you something," Proxy said, coming through the doorway with a platter of cut cheese, crackers, thick slices of salami, peaches, apricots, and strawberries. Boomer followed with a pitcher of lemonade and a stack of red plastic cups.

"That's it, girl," Mina said, stuffing cheese and crackers into her mouth. She chewed for a few seconds before she could speak again. "I'm putting you in my will."

"Boomer said you might not take time for lunch today."

Or breakfast. After downing half a glass of lemonade, she tried to pace herself.

"He helped me make the lemonade," Proxy said, smiling at the man by her side.

Mina stopped drinking and stared at the pair. Boomer didn't even notice. His eyes were locked on Proxy's, and he had a silly grin on his face. Mina cut her glance to Haines. He pointed to his own empty ring finger, then wagged his finger between Boomer and Proxy, then mouthed, *"Two months."* He gave a definitive nod.

Mina raised a brow, but didn't contradict. Proxy and Boomer were still completely unaware of the exchange. Maybe the little chapel in town would have another wedding reservation soon.

"Proxy," Mina said to break up the lovers' spell, "how did your setup go?" The woman reluctantly tore her eyes away from her man.

"Everything's good," Proxy said, switching from shy girl to full nerd. Her number one requirement was internet access, and the building's previous owner had brought in a high-speed connection for some failed business reason. Of course, Proxy had been aware of all that before ever coming here. She wasn't saying how she knew, but it involved searching the private records of the cable company.

Three laptops were up and running in her bedroom, and she had spent the day working with her online gang. She carried on for a few minutes about Wi-Fi, routers, repeaters, VOIP, satellites, and spoofing...little of which Mina followed. Boomer, however, appeared enthralled.

"But..." Proxy said, taking a seat opposite Mina, "we picked up some chatter. About you—or rather Lilly Hawthorne."

"What about Lilly?" Kade asked, coming through the door. Rowan followed.

DJ must have let them in through the front. He was patrolling the grounds since there were a few shoppers hanging out at the picnic tables. Mina folded her legs so Kade could join her on the end of the lounger. His brow was creased with tension, probably from too much time on his ankles.

Proxy looked to Mina in question as to whether to continue.

Mina introduced Kade and Rowan, then said, "From Slade?"

"Connected, yes," Proxy said. "I confirmed that his house was badly damaged in the fire. Not destroyed, but not habitable. From cell calls, we suspect he's moved to Burbank. It's a heavily populated area, so it's difficult to pinpoint which building he's in now. It's not on any of the Viera property lists. We're searching rental records and ownership deeds with his name or the dummy companies we know about. It's a long shot. Many leases are never put into electronic form."

"DJ and Boomer will head down Thursday morning," Haines added, "try to get eyes on him again if Proxy can narrow it down."

"Proxy," Mina said, "you started out making this sound like a bad thing. Isn't this what we want?"

Proxy nodded, but frowned. "The bad part is some of the recorded calls to Slade's phone originated from Mission Peak. There was a photo of you caught on a security system. I traced it back to a furniture store there."

"They used face-matching software," Rowan said. "Like my friend Gretchen used to find you."

"Sounds like," Proxy agreed. "I'm afraid they know, or at least suspect, you're in the area."

"Then you need to leave," Kade said. "Go somewhere—"

"No," Mina cut in.

"But…"

Mina held up a hand and waited a few beats until everyone focused on her.

"This isn't exactly as we planned, but we can use it. Maybe." The food was kicking in, waking her brain after the numbing day of retail. "Proxy, these cameras track my photo with date and time, right?"

Proxy nodded. "And GPS and a bunch of exposure and camera data."

"Then, can photos be altered and planted to make it look like I was somewhere I wasn't?"

"I could…" Proxy pinched the bridge of her nose, then nodded again. "I'll have to ask Snarkyboydog—"

Rowan snorted.

"He can edit the EXIF and other metadata, depending on the file format, of course, and reset the GPS. We'd have to Photoshop your pictures onto the correct backgrounds—street signs, mountains, buildings—and make the shadows match the angle of the light. Things like that."

"So," Mina said, "you can make me show up in L.A.? Maybe multiple places?"

Proxy's face lit up. "Oh, I see. How about we put you right in Burbank? A block or two from Slade?"

Haines nodded. "Make it look like you're closing in on his location."

"There are always unused movie sets at the studios," Mina said. She'd been in dozens of those over the years with her dad and mom. "One of those could be our site for the final showdown."

"Mina," Kade said, "are you sure?"

She looked at each of the people around her. Haines, with steely determination, subtly slid his left index finger along his right forearm until it rested on the tattooed Bible reference. Romans 12:19. Mina had looked it up.

"Never avenge yourselves. Vengeance is mine, I will repay, says the Lord."

They'd had a long discussion about it one night after he and the guys arrived, and it all boiled down to two simple questions: Does God take direct action against evil people, like zapping them with lightning or disease? Or does he work through ordinary people to deliver justice?

To Mina, it seemed like the vilest dictators tended to live long lives—unless someone, like the Allies in World War II, took them out. If this was the way God administered his justice and vengeance, then she was willing to carry it out.

Proxy brought her own intense desire for justice, and had developed a loose organization to rain it down on people.

Then there was Boomer's readiness, and Rowan and Kade's intimate understanding of how badly a mission could go.

All of them were far too aware of how this could turn out, Kade most of all.

Her eyes lingered on his, not really asking, but…

He reached over and took her hand. One gentle but affirming

squeeze. Even in the face of his doubts, he trusted her, believed in her. It was her decision to make.

Mina took a breath.

"I'm sure."

After dinner, and after Kade and Rowan left, Mina went down to her studio and assembled a few more pieces for Pana's Dream. As she waited for the kiln to fuse the glass and soften the edges, she mulled over the next week.

On Thursday or Friday—or as soon as Abigail could rent a house for them all—they would head to L.A. A motel was a backup choice, but not as desirable due to other guests. From there, Proxy would begin dropping photos of Lilly Hawthorne into security systems around Burbank while monitoring cell calls. DJ and Boomer would be on the ground with special tracking antennas, zeroing in on the call locations. The whole idea was to eventually draw Slade to an empty studio building or back lot.

As the kiln crackled with heat, Mina let her mind roam, thinking of a million things that could go wrong with the plan. She could be dead in a few days. Weirdly, that was the least of her worry. Her greatest fear was the same as it had been in the beginning: that someone else she cared about or loved would die. If that happened and Mina survived…

Well, it couldn't happen. She wouldn't put others in danger. They were there as her backup, not her front line.

CHAPTER FORTY-FIVE

SUNDAY MORNING WAS SLIGHTLY COOLER, but the forecast was for increasing heat over the next few days. By Tuesday night at the time of the fireworks, the prediction was upper 80s.

Mina rose and dressed in tan Capris and a green T-shirt topped by a gauzy white cover-up. The shirt and pants were loose enough that she could clip the holster for her .32 at the middle of her back.

It felt odd carrying a gun to church. Odder still was attending church in the first place. But everyone was going, and Haines refused to leave her alone. Besides, maybe going to the service would provide some moral clarity for her. Wasn't that the purpose of church?

Kade and Rowan picked her up, and they drove the short distance to the chapel. Rowan parked as close as she could so Kade wouldn't have far to walk. Mina climbed out of the Jeep and looked toward town. Even at 10:30, Main Street was clogged with cars and pedestrians. Beyond the marina, the distant roar of ski boats preceded skiers and tubers as they zipped up and down the lake. Tons of people, all here to have fun.

As she walked beside Kade up the stairs of the chapel, she wondered if people confessed sins they *planned* to commit. She couldn't help thinking of military chaplains leading prayer services before troops went into battle and killed the enemy.

Inside, she spotted Lena, Alex, and Kris Stone, Haines and the guys with Proxy next to Boomer, Bibs and Irene, and Connie Langworth. Teal and Quin sat with another couple—perhaps Quin's parents. Even Mark from the auto repair was there, for once not dressed in coveralls.

"This place is more crowded than town," Rowan muttered, then pointed to the back row on her left. "How about this?"

Mina entered the row first, followed by Kade and Rowan. She excused herself as they squeezed past a few seated people. As they made their way to the last available trio of chairs, she realized who was at the end of the row. Old Mike sat alone in the outside corner seat.

Tentatively, Mina sat down in the chair beside him, squirming her butt as close to Kade as she could without being too obvious. Kade's arm immediately came around her shoulders, so she evidently wasn't as subtle as she thought.

Old Mike didn't acknowledge her in any way. He sat with his face raised, eyes closed.

Expectant, Mina thought. His jeans were years beyond the blue of a new pair, but they were clean, as was his long-sleeve ribbed top. Although his hair was still a bit wild, it was swept back in a thick gray mane. With his classic Roman nose, tanned skin, and relaxed brow, he reminded Mina of Charlton Heston as Moses. If he had a staff in one hand, arms raised over the Red Sea...

Piano music began, drawing Mina's attention to the front of the room. The woman who had been sitting with Teal and Quin was at an electric keyboard. She played a medley of patriotic songs and military hymns, including "Anchors Aweigh," the "Caisson Song," "America The Beautiful," "God Bless America," and even Bruce Springsteen's "Born In The U.S.A." The congregation sang along to the words projected on a screen, and men and women stood during each of the military songs in honor for their respective service. Everyone stood for the national anthem.

The audience applauded and took their seats as the pianist transitioned into a new piece. The music slowed and became more evocative, and she began singing. Over the next fifteen minutes, her lyrics captured the pride and glory of battles, the mournful loss of comrades, the beauty of hard-won peace. By the time she finished with *Going Home*, the Largo theme from Dvorak's New World Symphony No. 9, Mina was wiping her eyes, and many people were openly weeping.

Whether they had lost someone in a war, Mina didn't know, but there was no applause after the last echoing strains, just sniffling, blowing noses—and memories.

Her mother had died as she fought to save Mina, and her tears flowed harder. She got to her feet, mumbling *sorry* to Old Mike as she stepped around his long legs. Kade rose to follow, his face full of concern, but she stopped him with a hand on his shoulder as she walked behind the row and exited the chapel as quickly as she could.

A little of the claustrophobic emotion eased as she breathed in the outdoor freshness and made her way to one of the four picnic tables on the lawn alongside the chapel. She cradled her head in her hands, wiping her eyes again and again at the magnitude of what happened in the past and what was to come—what was so close. The burden drove down her spirit, compelled her to run away, far from the fighting and struggle. Only an idiot would travel the path she'd set.

The bench sagged beside her. She didn't look—assumed it was Kade, or maybe Rowan. Someone she cared for.

A voice she didn't recognize spoke.

"Loss is different for everyone. But also the same."

Mina cut her eyes sideways. Old Mike sat beside her, leaning forward, elbows on his knees. His hands wrung one of his notebooks into a tight roll, as if truth might drip out. He stared straight ahead, at something in the far distance...or in the far past.

"I was thirteen when my mother passed," he said, his voice deep and resonate, full of emotion. "Dad took it real hard. Things were never the same for me or my brother and sister. No, of course they weren't. Because inside—down deep where everything that matters lives—we all changed."

Mina turned toward him when he paused for a moment, staring across the lawn at the boats rocking in the marina.

"When someone leaves," he said, "they not only take all of themselves, they take a part of each person they touched. The deeper the touch, the bigger the part that's torn away."

His head dropped, and a trembling right hand swiped quick and sharp under each eye.

"That taking is what makes us sad," he said. He paused at this, as if considering his words, then nodded once. "And that's okay. Because it's the taking that makes them even more precious to us... and it makes us who we are."

He stood.

Mina watched as he nodded again, twice this time, as if finally convinced of his own words.

"That's okay," he said. His right hand moved toward her shoulder, hesitated, then descended, patting her awkwardly. Twice. She stared at the hand for a second before it lifted and joined its brother still wrapped around the notebook. He clutched it tight to his chest.

Then, without ever looking at Mina, he walked toward the street, slightly hunched around his precious notebook. He crossed the road and took the path Merle had built that led toward the Art Mill. Each step was measured, matching the one previous, but his gait today was unhurried, almost contemplative before each foot touched the earth. So different from other times when she saw him scurrying through town clutching his leather satchel full of similar notebooks.

A calm descended on her, and her tears dried as she took several shuddering breaths. The minister was speaking now, and his words drifted from the open windows on the side of the little church. But none of those words, which were undoubtedly meant as comfort and encouragement, sank in like Old Mike's.

As she pondered them, she wondered if he had it completely

right. Yes, the taking *was* painful when someone died. But maybe the holes created from taking were filled with all they left?

She stared at the path where Old Mike had disappeared. Next time, she'd ask him.

Music and singing started, a hymn that was at once both familiar in melody and alien to her personal experience. She should probably go to church more often.

"Hey, Mina," Teal said a few minutes later. She and Quin walked hand in hand toward the table. "I'm glad you came." She evidently hadn't seen Mina skip out early.

Over the couple's heads, Mina spotted Kade at the top of the church steps, looking her way. She lifted her hand, signaling she was okay. After a last swipe at her cheeks, she turned to Quin.

"The woman who was playing and singing... Is she your mom?"

He grinned. "Pretty good, huh? She used to sing onstage. Not as much anymore. She had a band and everything. Maybe you've heard of Regen van Onweer and Elusive Hope?"

Mina had to close her mouth. "Are you kidding me? She's your mother?" Quin's grin spread even wider.

Regen van Onweer had been queen of symphonic metal in Europe for years, drawing crowds in the tens of thousands to her concerts that were beautiful, powerful operatic theater. Mina had always wanted to attend one of her concerts, but had to make do with online videos taken by others lucky enough to be there. Then there had been some kind of incident with a fan or something, and Regen retired—or so the story went. The band continued, but with a new lead singer.

Mina looked toward the church steps. The woman was standing with the man, and Mina tried to picture her with the long, black curly mane that had been her signature look. Her hair was a rich auburn now, cut below the chin in a smart style. So different, but the woman's regal posture was the same as Mina had seen in countless online videos.

"Does she play every Sunday?"

"Not every week, but pretty often," Quin said. "This was special today."

"And she performs at some of the lake events," Teal said, "like Bibs' Harvest Festival on Halloween."

Mina would have to come to church more often. And bring a wad of tissues.

Teal and Quin left to talk to some friends their own age, and his mother—the queen of symphonic metal— caught Mina's eye, and headed over.

"Hi, I'm Rayne Conner," she said, extending her hand.

"Palomino Glass. But most people call me Mina."

"I know. Quin's told me a lot about you."

"Oh. Quin's an amazing young man. He invited me to join him and Teal for lunch the first time we met."

Rayne laughed. "That sounds like him. That boy knows everyone living at the lake."

"I want to thank you for playing, for the music. It was...so moving." Earth shattering. Soul wrenching. Mere words of praise paled in comparison to what she'd heard.

"Thank you," Rayne said simply.

Perhaps she also had trouble expressing without the music. Mina knew many artists who couldn't describe their work without showing and doing it, as if the hands and brain had to be engaged for a complete message to form.

"I wanted to ask..." Rayne began, then hesitated. "I mean, I saw you talking with Old Mike out here." She gestured toward the forward-most window on the side of the building. It was a straight view from the keyboard to the picnic table. "I noticed you both slip out."

Mina nodded. "Well...he talked to *me*, anyway." She turned again toward the path where he had disappeared, feeling his presence lingering as if he were still standing near. Her hand drifted to her shoulder, his touch so tentative, yet oddly reassuring. "Truthfully, I was a little shocked."

"From what I hear," Rayne said, "he speaks to almost no one, other than a one-word answer now and then. I've certainly never seen him in conversation with anyone. But I've also found him sitting for hours at places all around the lake, writing in his spiral notebooks. Something's going on in that head of his." She paused, then said, "Would it be too private to ask what he said?"

Old Mike's message was personal, intensely so. But it wasn't necessarily private. After all, it was Rayne's music that had broken down the barriers, for both Mina and Old Mike.

"He talked about loss. That's it's different for everyone, but also the same. I think he meant we have that in common—as a human race."

Rayne digested this for a few seconds, but said nothing.

"But why me?" Mina asked.

"Perhaps he saw something special in you."

Mina had the impression that Rayne knew more than she was letting on. Had Teal told Quin about Mina's history? Had he shared it with his mother?

"Well, I should go," Rayne said. "When things settle down after the holiday, have Quin bring you over to the house. We'll kick back, and you can tell me about your art."

When things settle down.

Mina watched Rayne rejoin her husband, and wondered if things would *ever* settle down.

Maybe next time she saw Old Mike—if there was a next time—she would find words to speak back to the man. Or ask a question like what's the meaning of life?

Kade started across the grass toward her, smiling. Her heart sank as she churned through the what-ifs of the coming days. She had so much to be thankful for, so much to enjoy. The thought of losing even a small part of any of it was more than she could bear.

It's the taking that makes them even more precious to us...and that taking makes us who we are.

CHAPTER FORTY-SIX

KADE'S CELL phone rang while he was sitting on DC Coffee's patio sipping an ice-blended version of a Cappuccino Blast. He angled the display, squinting against the noon sun. It wasn't a number he recognized.

"Hunt," he answered, turning in his chair so he could watch a ski boat zooming up the lake. A pair of teenagers bounced behind on an oversize tube.

"It's Maggie Cartwright. Did you find your girl?"

He smiled. "I did. Thanks for your help."

"It's the least I could do."

"Maggie, it wasn't your fault."

She sighed. "I know, but it's still frustrating. I do have news, though. I found some information about what went down on your mission."

"I'm listening." Kade turned away from the lake. Nothing she said would take away what happened, but maybe it would help fill the holes in his brain.

"It was a small joint op. The field team was made up of a DEA guy out of the L.A. office, two L.A. County Sheriff deputies from their drug task force, and you. You were brought in because of your familiarity with the Vieras, limited as that was. The objective was to find out who was rebuilding the family business. Plus, you knew the territory."

No matter how hard he tried, Kade still couldn't picture a team. "Who was in charge?"

"A DEA man named Fletcher."

Kade shook his head, but nothing surfaced. "I don't remember him." How could people disappear completely from his memory?

"Well, here's where things get wonky," she said. "A few days before the mission, Fletcher was tagged for a quick trip back to DEA headquarters in Virginia. He called in one of our Special Agents from the L.A. office to keep the team on track, a man named Rollins who had been part of the early planning."

"The name sounds vaguely familiar, but I can't picture him."

"You probably didn't meet him in person. From what I understand, the four of you were in San Diego at that time waiting for Fletcher's return. Rollins was coordinating from L.A."

"Okay," he said, not quite seeing where Maggie was heading.

"You told me before that one of the men you met in the Houston hospital was Assistant Special Agent in Charge Amory. Well, Amory was working in the L.A. office, and Rollins was assisting him in a money laundering investigation."

"Amory said he was from the DC office."

"That's right. He was sent west to follow the money trail. But get this. When Amory heard that Rollins was also working with your team, and that you were ready and just waiting for Fletcher's return, he ordered Rollins to pull the trigger on the operation. My guess is he thought of it as a quick win. Exert authority over the DEA and capture some glory."

Imagining Amory doing that wasn't hard for Kade. He took a slow breath, trying to let it go.

"Most of the team work was to be done north of the border in L.A. and San Diego, but Fletcher had you set to meet some informants in Tecate, Mexico. On the go order, you crossed into Tecate alone, while the rest of the team remained on the US side. After several hours of no contact, they went looking, but you were gone. Fletcher was furious when he returned and learned of Amory butting in. He argued it was a DEA operation and Amory had no authority to give the go-ahead. Amory said the FBI was the head agency over the DEA and he had the right to make the call."

"Pissing match ensued."

"Pretty much," Maggie agreed.

Kade pulled up Tecate on his phone map. The town was over a thousand miles from Monterrey. How had he traveled that far? And why? Then he remembered that Ernesto Viera had died in Monterrey after being wounded in the shootout seven years ago, the same gunfight that nearly killed Mina. Perhaps that city was their southern base.

"Fletcher and the others pulled out the stops to find you, but you were nowhere. Eventually, Amory was recalled to DC."

"Did they promote him?"

Maggie laughed. "Glad you still have a sense of humor, Hunt, but no, they didn't promote him. After you showed up in Houston, he was sent down to meet with you. I got the impression retiring you from the bureau was his decision, and his superiors were not happy when they got wind of what happened. But once he'd screwed that up, they felt they had to go ahead."

"So he's in Nome, Alaska?"

"Even better. They demoted him and sent him to New York."

"Doesn't sound like much of a demotion."

"It is when you're at the lowest level and doing all—and I mean all—the grunt work no one else wants to do. It's no secret he'll never rise above his current level. Plus, have you seen the cost of living in New York? It's obscene. He'll be broke in no time. I think they're hoping he'll quit."

Kade shifted his chair further under the shade umbrella and propped his right ankle on the chair opposite. His icy Cappuccino Blast was gone, and the late morning sun was in full blaze. He hoped Rowan arrived soon. She was anxious to head down to L.A. to meet her friends, but had agreed to drive him to Mission Peak for some shopping.

"Sorry, but that's all I've got," Maggie said.

"Actually, that's a lot more than I expected to learn." Drugs could account for the gaps during his captivity, but the fact he didn't remember the team or Fletcher was a bit shocking. Maybe he had farther to go in his recovery than he thought.

"Anything else I can do for you?" Maggie asked.

"Can you send me Fletcher's contact info? I might remember something that will help him in the future." Proxy already had enough to bury Slade's organization, and now Kade knew who would make the best use of it.

"Will do."

"How's the Montana rancher?"

She laughed. "That's one special op that's going exactly as planned."

"You're the best, Maggie Cartwright."

"I always get my man."

As promised, Bibs closed up shop at three o'clock on Tuesday, locking the door as the last two customers left. Families were streaming into town for barbecues and the fireworks show at the swim beach. She turned and surveyed the nearly empty display cases, easels, and hanging racks. "Well, I'd say this was a very successful opening."

Thanks to the free publicity due to the burglary, they had doubled Bibs' aggressive *hoped-for* goal.

Mina helped the other artists sweep the floor, dust the tables, and clean fingerprints off the display cases for next Friday when they would open again at noon.

Teal was practically bouncing. She had sold all but one of her drawings, and the large fantasy of Desperation Falls went as quickly as Mina predicted. A shop owner in Blue Rock Harbor asked Teal for a dozen prints.

Mina, however, was more than done. The long days had her brain begging for quiet. As soon as the artists left the building, she retreated to the deck and collapsed onto one of the lounges, as had become her habit.

At best, she needed several days to design, cut, and fire new Pana's Dream pieces, and she should order glass from the art supply for the big mermaid and running horses panels. Those would take weeks to complete.

But hard reality stared her in the face: she might not get those days and weeks.

Thursday at noon, Proxy would begin inserting the doctored photos showing Mina in Burbank. DJ and Boomer were coordinating surveillance around the buildings and streets where Proxy suspected Slade's phone calls originated. On Friday, Mina and Haines would head down to a rental house Abigail found in Toluca Lake. Because of its close location to the movie and television studios, the rental was tiny, dated, and an obscene amount of money, but it put them within fifteen minutes of Slade.

Mina pushed the thought of the coming conflict from her mind. She closed her eyes and concentrated on the wind shushing through the trees along Conner Creek, its soothing peace and tranquility. She willed her body to relax, accept the gift.

It didn't work. She gave up and opened her eyes. While everything surrounding her was a beautiful harmony, her gut was anything but. The future was as gray as the worst fog at Perilous Cove, oppressive and energy draining, and she had to accept the reality that things could go badly.

"Having second thoughts, Glass?" Haines took the chaise next to hers, sighing as he lay back and closed his eyes against the sunlight dancing through the moving leaves.

The Marine didn't miss much. Her reluctance was showing more each day, especially since Sunday. Unlike right after the Berlin attack, holding on to the things she valued was now much greater than the risk of engaging the enemy.

She looked across at Haines, his rough features and powerful frame. Underneath the exterior was a huge heart. These people, even gruff Haines, were precious to her. She hadn't meant for it to happen, but it had. If *she* died, she'd be without feeling. Gone. Over. But if one of them died—these new friends who meant so much to her—the tearing that Old Mike talked about might well rip her right in half. She would never recover.

"I... I'm thinking Proxy's idea of revealing Slade's criminal activities to the authorities might be an option. At least as a start."

He opened one eye and studied her. "It was *always* an option."

She swallowed. Haines saw deeper into her than anyone. Readiness for missions and war had been most of his life, and with the preparation came the terrible possibility of losing men and friends. That loss couldn't be allowed to incapacitate a warrior in the midst of battle, otherwise the entire war might be lost. Grief must be pushed aside until after the threat was neutralized. Easy to say— much harder to do.

She experienced it in her previous combat with the Vieras. Some died while she and others fought on. It was only afterward, when the shooting stopped and the dust settled, that the horrible, unchangeable cost hit home.

"Maybe it would be a better way to go. See what happens."

Haines nodded. "I talked to Proxy a bit ago. Her team is impressive. They've gained access to financial records, bank accounts, and contacts for prostitution and trafficking rings. Nasty stuff. The evidence might be enough—if it's allowed in court." He paused for a few seconds to let that sink in. "But this is an extremely bad guy. No one will cry when he's gone."

He was justifying it for Mina, offering it up as a righteous kill even beyond her personal reasons. If they went down south and took this guy out, the personal threats would stop, and so would much more evil he propagated. There would be no costly trial, no years of appeals by high-priced lawyers, no chance of mistrial by a botched procedure or influenced juror. There might not even be a grave. After that, Proxy could dump her preponderance of evidence on the authorities' desks and let them round up Slade's underlings.

Kade had made his wishes clear even before this latest news of Proxy's success. Electronic attack won hands down.

Mina had tonight and tomorrow to decide. When Thursday came and her photos started showing up in databases, the hornets' nest would be irrevocably poked, and the plan would be in motion.

Quin and Teal came out onto the deck. They were holding hands, two carefree young people with the entire world before them.

"We're going to the beach to meet our parents for barbecue," Teal said, "then later over to ViceCream for ice cream. It opened this weekend. Do you want to come?"

Mina had seen the signs announcing the new shop. The theme was old time cops and robbers, G-men and gangsters. Ice cream wouldn't solve her dilemma, but it sounded perfect.

"We're grilling here first," Mina said, "but we can meet you there. You still going out on your boat?"

"Yep," Quin said. Dozens of boats would be converging on Deer Cove to watch the fireworks.

They agreed to meet at the ice cream shop at 8:30 and load up.

The teens left, and Mina closed her eyes again, blocking out the evil lurking beyond her new home. She and Kade would watch the fireworks from a blanket on the beach. Maybe hold hands like teenagers, and pretend they were also carefree.

For a couple more days.

CHAPTER FORTY-SEVEN

"Are you sure?" Slade asked. He stood by the door of Evie's motel room, card key in hand. Even her own room was no longer exclusively her own—just in case she stroked-out or something.

She inhaled, gathering her strength for the coming walk downstairs. The air was a soup of moldy air conditioning, cheap wallpaper, and pine cleaner. Of all the body parts to stop working, why couldn't her sense of smell have been the first to go? She wished again she'd rented a house.

"Stop asking me that." Evie levered herself up, pausing to catch her breath and steady her legs underneath before trusting them. "Get my bag." Even words were an effort, and she no longer had extras to soften the order.

Traffic through the San Fernando Valley, Calabasas, and all the way to Santa Barbara was heavy, stop and go half the time. After that it thinned, and Evie slipped into a frustrating half-sleep. Although a part of her was aware of passing golden hills dotted with dark green oaks, she was unable to open her eyes. Instead, she imagined them, wondering if the corners Slade drove around matched her mental map.

Sometime later when she could no longer stand the suspense of their location, she willed herself to straighten in the seat. The sun was low above the western hills, but it would be a few hours before full dark.

Evie blinked against the fog in her mind.

"Mission Peak," Slade said, anticipating her question.

The painkillers screwed with her nighttime sleep, leaving her bleary all day. But this was the one day she needed to be sharp.

"Have you called the team?"

"Five minutes ago. They spotted Hawthorne earlier in the town at an ice cream shop."

Millions of people liked ice cream, but the thought of Lilly Hawthorne enjoying life lit a fire in Evie. She lifted her purse onto her lap and reached inside. The handle of the revolver felt huge, but it hadn't grown from six months ago. Her hands were shrinking. Muscle and fat dissolving, same as the rest of her body.

"And this is interesting," Slade continued. "It appears she has a lover. Angelina got several photos of him, and our I.T. guy got almost an instant match. He's an FBI agent." Slade slowed for traffic as they wound around the town, then took the exit for the road north. "Or should I say, *our* FBI agent. She said he's injured and walks with a cane."

Evie looked at him. "He's the one who escaped?"

Slade nodded, his mouth a hard line. "Small world."

This was too good. They'd lost a lot of money on the agent, delaying the normal ransom demand while Slade's men tortured him for information about others going after her organization. They were transporting him to Monterrey to set up the ransom when he disappeared.

But his presence here was better than any ransom payment. Lovers, friends, and family were weaknesses, perfect for applying pressure. "Maybe we can use him," she said.

"I thought so too," Slade said. He handed her a thin folder. "Here is a rough map of the town. The second page shows where she's living. And the third page is the location of the house she bought. Some photos too."

Evie scanned the papers. She'd seen pictures of the old mill building, both from outside and in. Slade's people had been there for the last two days, posing as customers and walking the grounds, but they hadn't been able to access the living quarters without being seen.

But the house... Evie shuffled through a dozen photos of the structure that must have been abandoned for a decade or more. It stood by itself on a large lot up on a hill, an unpretentious Queen Anne with a wraparound porch, corner turret, and dormer windows. That it had seen much better days was obvious, but someone was working on it. Plywood covered some of the windows and lay across the porch access to the front door, and sawhorses, buckets, and a commercial rubbish bin sat off to the side.

Evie's lips curved into a smile. It felt awkward after so many weeks of pain, but the potential of this house amused her.

Tommy Viera had all but destroyed Hawthorne's home in Beverly Hills, and Roberto and Magda had done the same to her hideout in Malibu. But those homes had both belonged to the parents. Lilly Hawthorne had purchased this home for herself. The fact it was being brought back from such a deplorable condition attested to the woman's vision and commitment. This was a personal project.

How fitting would it be for the woman to die in this house, have it utterly destroyed by Evie?

"Stop at a hardware store and buy some gas cans." When Slade looked over at her, she said, "We're going to have a fireworks show of our own tonight."

Kade's ankle was killing him by the time they got back to the mill, and Mina draped his arm across her shoulders to help him up the porch steps.

"I should have dropped you off and picked you up," Mina said. "I'm sorry."

The closest parking place she had found to ViceCream was uphill four blocks away, almost as far as if they walked from the mill. Haines and crew had parked on the road north of the beach and walked back to meet them.

"It's okay," he lied, trying not to yelp as his toe banged the edge of a step.

The walk down to the shop wasn't too bad, but when they headed back to the truck Kade had stepped on a rock that rolled his right ankle, tweaking the weak muscles and tendons. Fortunately, Teal was still there and gave them a ride back to the mill in her mom's Jeep Wrangler.

"You're sure you don't need me to stay?" Teal asked.

"No, you go ahead," Kade said. "Quin's waiting for you. I'll be fine as soon as I get some ice on this."

"Okay," Teal said. "I'm going to leave the Jeep here. Now that town's a mess, it'll be faster on foot." She waved from the yard as she jogged down the path.

"You should go with her, Mina."

"No chance. I'm so sorry," Mina said again, and helped him through the front room to the private living area.

Kade groaned as they got him reclining on the sofa. "Oh, man," he said as she lifted his right foot and unlaced his tennis shoe. He hissed as she eased the shoe off, and sweat popped out on his forehead.

"It's swelling," Mina said. "I'll get the ice."

She was back in a minute with a dish towel filled with cubes. He held his breath as she slid the makeshift icepack under his foot.

"That feels good," he said, relaxing his leg onto it. "Thanks."

He hated that his misstep had ruined her good mood. This was the first time in days he'd seen her so relaxed, joking and laughing with Quin and Teal, sampling different flavors of ice cream, even feeding him spoonfuls from her *.38 Special*, triple-flavor cup. Kade had gotten *Al Mascarpone*, a creamy cheesecake topped with bullet-shaped black sprinkles. It had been fun while it lasted.

She ran to get him ibuprofen and water, then stood by the sofa wringing her hands.

"I'll be okay," he said, now that he could breathe again. The cold was working its magic. He needed both ankles examined by a doctor. They weren't getting better, and lately he was longing for his crutches. This would speed up the appointment.

The room dimmed as the sun sank further behind the hills, and Mina turned on the floor lamps.

"Do you want anything?" she asked. "Coffee, tea…" she grinned at him and spread her arms, "or me?"

He had to laugh, but she spoke the truth. He *did* want her. One of the hardest things he'd done in life was to walk away from her hospital room years ago so he could take his new assignment in Boston. Then, like an idiot, he fought their attraction, using their age difference as the reason. He now realized what they had together was too powerful to fight.

And he didn't want to fight it anymore. In the years before his captivity, four of his friends got married. At each wedding, the couples spoke a variation of the words, *till death do us part*. When he and Mina were together now—and even when they weren't—he thought more and more about making that pledge. To her, and no one else.

"What I want is for you to go enjoy the fireworks with the others," he said, and watched her grin turned to a frown. "Listen, Mina. This is your new home. You have friends here. I'm not letting you miss your first town celebration because my ankles are flakey."

"I'm not leaving you alone," she said. "I'll stay and make popcorn."

"No, you'll miss the show. Kris and the others are saving a space for you."

"For us," she corrected. Then her face lit up. "Wait, I know. You can rest while I run to town and get my truck. Then we'll drive up to the house and watch the fireworks from there."

Kade could see she was determined, and the truth was, he didn't want to stay indoors and listen to fireworks exploding behind the trees and hills. Even as a little kid, he *loved* fireworks, and always got as close as he could. The view from the house wouldn't be like sitting on the swim beach and watching them launch almost straight up over the lake, but he'd be with Mina. That was more important than sparklers in the sky.

She held up her phone as she moved toward the door. "I'll call Haines on my way to town and let him know what we're doing." She darted back, bent over, and kissed him. "Don't go anywhere, Special Agent Hunt," she said against his lips.

She broke the kiss and checked her watch. "We'll have to hurry. The fireworks start in thirty minutes."

"I think they just started," Kade said. She laughed as she ran out of the room.

He adjusted his ankle on the ice, growling against the pain. "Not going anywhere, that's for sure." He laid his head back, wishing the pills would kick in a little faster.

Maybe the pills worked, because a few minutes later he heard a bump in the outer room and thought Mina had returned.

But the man who walked into the living room Kade knew only by a photo.

Slade.

He was holding a pistol pointed straight at Kade.

CHAPTER FORTY-EIGHT

MINA JOGGED across the bridge over Conner Creek and followed the path toward town. As she ran, she dialed Haines.

"Glass? I was just about to send Boomer and DJ out looking. Where are you?"

She explained about Kade's ankle, Teal's ride back, and Mina's plan to drive them up to the house to watch the fireworks.

"Bad idea, Glass." He was interrupted for a second before he continued. "Proxy's team picked up some chatter. She just got the call before you called me. It's Slade. As much as they can figure out, it sounds like he was in Mission Peak earlier."

Mina slowed to a fast walk, processing the news. Slade was that close? But she was going to L.A. on Friday. They were taking the fight to him. It wasn't supposed to be the other way around.

"Proxy's here with Boomer," Haines said, "and she's in touch with some of her team on her phone and tablet. They're trying to sort through all the calls, but there's a lot of holiday cell traffic, so it could take some time."

"Haines, are you saying we're in danger?" Only background voices came through her phone for several seconds, and her cell beeped. She thought it was another incoming call, but then saw it was the low battery indicator. It hadn't been charged since early morning.

"Sorry," he said. "Some of Proxy's team members are evidently out at fireworks shows of their own, so they're off-line. She has limited resources tonight, and she's talking about heading back to the mill so she'll have her computers."

"So…the danger?" she repeated.

"We have to plan for it. We don't know if Slade has anyone already here."

She was more than halfway to her truck. Would it be better to keep going, or turn back to be with Kade? She decided the truck would give her needed mobility, and picked up her pace again.

"Okay," she said. The low battery beep came again. She veered off the path and took a shortcut to the back streets where her car was. "My cell battery is about to die, but it's better if we're all together. I think the fastest thing is for me to get my truck, retrieve Kade, then come meet you. I think I can be there in ten or twelve minutes. Where exactly are you?"

"North end of the swim beach."

"Are there any parking places left?"

"We'll find one, even if we have to drag a few cars away by hand. When you get here, I'll send DJ back for more armament. Can't send Boomer—he'll be enthralled once the firework explosions start." He was trying to lighten the situation, but his tight tone only emphasized the underlying seriousness.

"Be there soon." She hit the end call button to preserve the battery and increased her pace to a run.

The photos of Mina around Burbank were supposed to draw out Slade, make him believe he was the hunter when, in fact, he would be the hunted.

But it had suddenly turned around. Slade's presence would put everyone in danger, not just her and Haines's team. As soon as she talked to Proxy, she'd tell her to begin posting the photos right away —tonight. Maybe they would draw Slade back to the Southland where Mina and Haines could deal with him safely.

Sweat ran into her eyes, and she swiped it away as she skidded to a stop by her Toyota. The engine started immediately, and she made a squealing U-turn toward Main Street and the route back to the mill. She reached for the cell charging cord, but nearly ran over a jaywalking mom, dad, and two little kids carrying chairs, a cooler, and two teddy bears. The man gave her a dirty look as he hurried his family onto the far sidewalk.

She wiped sweat again, hoping it wouldn't be as hot down by the water. When she turned onto Main Street and it became West Lake Road, she faced an endless line of approaching traffic. Hers was the only car heading the wrong direction. It was going to be tough driving back through town to the swim beach.

Kade nearly passed out as Slade dragged him through the mill at gunpoint, throwing Kade's full body weight repeatedly onto his sprained ankle. But he'd been through worse, even if he couldn't remember. His wrists were wrapped with duct tape, but at least they were in front, not behind his back.

Outside, a dozen armed men were spread out around the yard. They rushed back into two dark SUVs. Slade shoved Kade into the rear seat of a third one, then climbed behind the wheel.

The car was moving by the time Kade levered himself upright. He was facing a woman half-turned in the front passenger seat, covering him with a big revolver. Though her hand trembled, the muzzle of the gun didn't drift far enough for Kade to have a chance of escape. Dark shadows underlined each eye, and her face was gaunt, but he was sure he'd never seen her before. Not that he could remember.

"Special Agent Hunt," she said, her voice raspy and wheezing. "We were very disappointed when we lost you in Mexico." She took a few breaths, but didn't speak again. Her eyes unfocused a couple of times as Slade led the mini caravan to the end of the driveway. He turned right and began climbing up the hill toward Mina's house.

The other SUVs were somewhere behind, but neither had their lights on, and they were lost in the trailing dust.

Field training didn't cover every contingency, but one basic rule was *live to fight another day.* Or as one instructor said, *"If you die now, you're dead."* Some of the recruits had laughed, but he made his point by pretend shooting one of the trainees, then leaving him lying on the ground as the group moved on to the next exercise. When the "dead" trainee started to get up and follow, the instructor ordered him to stay where he was. *"You're dead. You can't do anything else. Dead is dead."* The man lay there for two hours, and the point was made. Dead men can't help anyone.

So, no matter what Slade had in store, Kade had to stay alive and keep alert for any opportunity. The man wanted Mina. So did Kade.

That was a fight worth having.

CHAPTER FORTY-NINE

We envision our future, our successes, our calculated outcomes. In reality, we control nothing.

ON LIFE, BY V.M. NARRANO

EVIE RESTED against the front of the SUV. The metal was hot from the drive, and a faint oily odor drifted up from the grill. It wasn't fair. Food tasted like sawdust, but she could still smell burning oil. She watched Slade drag the FBI agent through the rear entrance of the house and disappear inside.

Plywood sheets covered the porch deck, and some of the house's siding had been removed, exposing the framing beneath. Two stories of neglect and rot. Although battered and stripped of its beauty, the building had potential. Unlike her.

The slight exertion of climbing out of the car had stolen her energy and winded her. She eyed the two low steps leading up to the porch and wondered if she could make it. A small goal, yet momentous if achieved.

Weight loss in the last week had her skin riding on bone without benefit of padding, and the purse strap chafed her shoulder. She slid it off and opened the bag. There were only two things she needed. One was the gun, which she took out and laid on the hood of the car. The other was a small, clear plastic bag. It contained three capsules. She hadn't even asked what they were, and only knew they promised pure energy. It wasn't like she was going to become an addict.

She dropped the purse to the dirt, shook the pills into her palm, and tossed them into her mouth. It took her a minute to work up any saliva, and she bit through one of the plastic sheaths before they finally went down. The powder left a bitter taste on her tongue, but at least it was different from the bland nothingness that had ruled her mouth for weeks.

In less than a minute Evie's skin began tingling. First her tongue where the powder spilled, then her lips, nose, and eyes, like someone spritzed them with carbonated lemon water. A wash of heat shot up to her scalp, and every hair follicle awoke. The flush spread outward from her stomach. Her heart accelerated, thumping reassuringly in her chest. Foot by foot, her small intestines sparked and twitched as energy traveled their length, into her colon. For a moment, Evie thought she might wet herself as her bladder lurched, and she tightened her core muscles—jubilant she was able to do that once more.

Her chest expanded several times before she realized her lungs were pulling in fresh air at record levels, functioning again as they pushed oxygen into capillaries and red blood cells. Blood flowed through her renewed heart and flooded her starving arteries.

"Wow." For all the money she made from the Viera family business, she had never once been tempted to try any of the drugs her underlings peddled. But if she'd known it would be like this...

For the first time in weeks she was truly alive and aware. She held her hands out in front of her, turning and examining her fingers. The nails were yellowed and dull, but at least she could see them with sharp vision. For a crazy moment she considered applying a coat of polish. Just *wanting* to do it was a rush.

No time for that, but she bent over—another thing she could never have done moments before—and got her brush out of her purse. She began brushing her hair, lifting and stroking, curling it under and styling it with quick sure strokes. It could use a wash, but wasn't too bad.

Then she took the gun from the hood and walked to the porch, climbing the steps with renewed confidence.

It wouldn't last, of course, this new vitality. But she didn't need days, or even hours. Minutes were all she required.

Minutes for Lilly Hawthorne to find Slade's note. Minutes to come to the house to save her lover.

Minutes for Evie to end Lilly Hawthorne forever.

"Kade!" Mina shouted, throwing open the front door and sprinting through the darkening retail space. "We gotta go!"

She stopped at the door to the hallway. It was wide open, and she knew she had closed it when she left. When she found the door to the private living area also standing open, dread crept up her spine. She drew her gun and led with it as she leaned around the doorframe and cleared the room.

The sofa was empty, but the cushions were still dented from Kade's body, and the dishtowel full of ice was where his ankle had been. "Kade?"

Mina checked the kitchen, then all the downstairs bedrooms and bathrooms. She reached for her cell phone as she walked back into the living room, but realized she had left it in the truck. Then she stopped in her tracks.

An 8 by 11 sheet of white paper was pinned to the wall beside the door from the hall. She'd come right past it when she entered. Holding it was a blade from the kitchen knife block. The message was written with bold strokes.

LILLY HAWTHORNE. IF YOU WANT HIM, COME TO YOUR HOUSE BY 9:45. ALONE, OR HE DIES.

She checked her watch. Fifteen minutes from now. That was the same time the fireworks show was scheduled to start. With the traffic and pedestrians, she couldn't make it to town to get help.

Turning in a circle, she tried to think what to do. The guys' guns were locked in cases in their rooms, and they had the only keys. Her own extra ammo and throwing knifes were upstairs in her gun safe. She checked her watch again. A minute had ticked by. Fourteen left.

Pull the trigger.

Alexandra and Mike had driven that home. Make a decision... then act. Don't vacillate.

Mina ran back through the building and jumped off the porch. In her truck, she took precious seconds to call Haines.

"Come on, Haines. Pick up, pick up." He didn't. He probably couldn't hear it ring with the crowd. Or maybe he was manhandling a car. When his voicemail came on, she left the briefest message she could. "Slade kidnapped Kade. He's up at the new house. I'm going. Bring weapons!" She ended the call.

Thirteen minutes.

It took her another thirty seconds to compose a text message the same as her voice message. After she hit Send, she wished she'd sent it to others on the team. But her battery indicator beeped a last warning, and her phone shut down.

The truck's tires sprayed gravel in a wide arc as she slammed the gas and fishtailed out of the mill's parking lot. Not long ago, she and Kade had strolled under the canopy of oaks, relaxed and hopeful of a future.

Twelve minutes. That might be all the future Kade had.

At the end of the drive, Mina slewed through a hard right and powered up the hill. The road hadn't been fixed yet, and the truck's tires hit ruts and potholes at far too great a speed. She hadn't fastened her seatbelt, and she was repeatedly thrown against the driver door and cab roof. Her foot came off the gas pedal, then she mashed it to the floor as she regained her seat.

The green dash clock counted down another minute.

She hooked her left foot under the seat to keep her in place, and willed the truck to greater speed. The top of the hill came up fast. She skidded wide on the left turn. Rocks rattled the fender wells and chassis, and the truck bucked as the sliding rear end collided with a sapling oak growing too close to the road. Mina ignored the sound of wrenching metal and kept her foot pressed hard.

The engine roared and a hot oil smell sifted up from under the dash. Mina didn't slow. Kade was up here, defenseless with his injured ankle. She refused to believe he could be dead.

Ten minutes.

Mina cut the headlights and drove into the twilight. One hundred yards later, she slammed on the brakes and slid to the side of the road. She threw open the door, but reached back for one of Boomer's B-52s and the lighter she'd stashed in the glove compartment. She stuffed them into her pocket and began running.

CHAPTER FIFTY

DEEP TWILIGHT SHROUDED the land by the time Mina reached the Y where the road split—right toward the little cabin, left to the main house. She stumbled ahead, bent over, trying to catch her breath while clutching the stitch in her right side. Two thundering booms echoed across the lake, marking the five-minute mark before the fireworks started. The organizers wanted the maximum effect for their money, and they were waiting until the western glow disappeared. Mina praised them for their thoughtfulness. Darkness was her friend.

Sweat dripped into her eyes, burning and making it difficult to see. Although perfect for the imminent fireworks, the skinny crescent moon provided little help up here. The orb's reflection in the lake surface was splintered by dozens of boats motoring to the show at Deer Cove. Teal and Quin would be out there. Mina stumbled forward, forcing herself faster as her legs and lungs recovered on the flatter ground.

As she neared the house, a single work light mounted on a post shone outside the stair-landing window. Howell had set up the light this morning so Mina could view the angel window from inside later tonight. The single bulb spilled illumination across the whole north side of the building and pooled onto the ground. Beyond it, darkness ruled. That was what she craved. She would soon lose that advantage.

Mina kept inside the tree line to her right, picking her way counterclockwise around the house. The little pump shed provided her first solid hiding place. Twin red streaks climbed into the sky, followed by two booms.

Two minutes.

With the lake and Deer Cove on the other side of the house, the area here was in darkness. Yards ahead, the barn rose against the night, a black behemoth that blocked the stars. Between it and the house sat a dark SUV. It could only be Slade's. She patted the lump in her pocket. Perfect.

Mina bent low and darted to the barn and through its side door. She'd been inside several times, trying to visualize the future usage for the space. With some indirect lighting, rustic furniture, and carpets to cover the macadam floor, it could be a great venue for parties and entertaining. But that wasn't the image that she recalled now.

A cluttered workbench ran along the wall at her left, and she felt her way along it, fingers brushing the items as she tried to remember the location of what she sought.

There. At the end of the bench, her fingers closed on a screwdriver on the pegboard backing, and a small coil of sisal rope.

Another boom sounded over the lake. The one-minute mark.

A flashlight swept across one of the upstairs windows as Mina exited the barn and ducked behind the SUV. The person with the flashlight had just ruined their night vision, giving Mina a slight advantage for a few moments.

She removed the gas cap and wedged the back-flow flap open with the screwdriver. She stuffed one end of the coarse rope a couple of feet down into the hole, then pulled it out. Pungent gasoline fumes assaulted her nose. One more insertion and withdrawal ensured the whole rope was saturated with gasoline. Then she dug the B-52 out of her pocket and wedged it beside the fuel-soaked rope. Her hands were damp with gas, and she wiped them on her shorts, hoping she didn't ignite too.

Hesitation never wins. Pull the trigger.

"God, help this work." She cupped her hand around the lighter to block the light, and flicked the lever.

The little B-52's fuse sputtered and tossed off sparks. Mina began counting as she duckwalked to the front of the SUV.

1001. 1002.

It was then she realized she'd forgotten to check if this was one of the 15-second green fuses, or a 5-second yellow one.

Kade strained against the rope that held him to the newel post at the top of the stairs. With enough time, he could probably knock the post loose and get free, but Slade was hidden in one of the rooms down the hall and would never allow that.

The side of his head throbbed where Slade had clubbed him with the gun to get him up the stairs. A sound below caught his attention. The woman was standing at the bottom of the stairway, illuminated by the glow backlighting the angel window on the landing. Who was she? Slade's girlfriend?

She was hunched in on herself, like someone inhabited by sickness and evil that devoured both body and soul. If she cackled, it wouldn't surprise him. But witches didn't carry large revolvers. Then she had disappeared from sight.

He fought back the terror of being restrained—so familiar, so hopeless as they came to beat him time and again. But this was now. He had to think of a way to get free, be ready. Slowly, he moved the rope up and down on the sharp corner of the post, pressing as hard as he could. With each stroke, blood pulsed in his skull, sending his vision into a blurry kaleidoscope of color. If only he had enough time.

Mina would come. He had no doubt of that. He was the bait, and she was walking right into the trap.

CHAPTER FIFTY-ONE

1003.

As a child, Mina was fascinated by contestants on TV game shows counting seconds. Whenever she tried it, she rarely got within five seconds on a sixty-second countdown.

The fuse hissed and light flared in her peripheral. The gasoline soaked rope had caught fire.

1004.

If this was a yellow fuse…

Mina pushed off the bumper and sprinted toward the side of the house.

1005.

Mina stumbled as Boomer's little bomb violently splintered the quiet night. She turned at the building's corner and ran toward the lake.

A series of explosions set fire to the night sky over Deer Cove. Three giant red chrysanthemums were joined by green and blue. Flaming streams shot outward in sizzling trails that slowed and curved toward the water.

Behind her, a whooshing began, then a brightening. She glanced over her shoulder as she ran flat out.

The lakeside fireworks that had seemed loud suddenly became trifling, entirely eclipsed by the mega explosion at her back.

Night became yellow daytime, as if the sun rose all at once from behind the house. A fireball mushroomed into the sky, a red, yellow, and black roiling ball of heat and fury that illuminated the trees for hundreds of yards around.

Hot air washed over her, its power reminding her of that terrible night in Mojave years ago when her mobile home exploded. That blast had tossed her young body through the air, scorched her exposed skin, and sucked the oxygen away like a fiery dragon. Momma—her bio mom—had been inside. It was the night Momma left Lilly lying broken in the tan desert dirt, her body burned and broken. It was the night everything changed. The night when Lilly's hair turned white.

As the fireball rose behind the house, the black sky ate it up, and darkness rushed back in. Mina used the fading light to round the corner and leap onto the front porch. She crashed through the door, rolling left where she remembered the workmen had set up sawhorses with a plywood worktop.

"Help!"

Kade! His voice came from upstairs.

Violence of action.

Mike and Alexandra had drilled it into her. Overwhelm your enemy. Never let up. When attacked, most people hold back, thinking they need to save something for later. Or they are averse to severely damaging another human being. *"If you don't win as soon as possible, there will be no later. Attack with 110 percent. Bring unexpected violence, and never ever let up."*

She took the stairs two at a time. At the landing, the angel filled the window, lit from the outside work light. She put the image at her back and faced the next flight.

Kade was tied to the post at the top of the stairs, struggling furiously to get his arms free.

"Mina! It's a trap!"

A man dressed all in black came from behind Kade, raising his gun toward Mina. Kade head-butted the man's right shoulder as the gun went off.

Mina ducked reflexively. She recognized Slade from the photos. This was the man who sent the threats, the one who sent the killer to Berlin. The man somehow related to the Vieras.

He slammed his gun into Kade's head, and Kade slumped down on the post. Then Slade aimed at Mina. With nowhere to go, she hurled the screwdriver at him and ducked as he fired.

Slade was equally quick, dodging the tool as it clanged harmlessly off the upper hallway wall. He barked a short laugh and stood up, feet firmly planted. His dark grin spread as he raised his gun.

But Mina had her own pistol up now. She dove forward like an Olympic swimmer starting a race, arms extended, taking her first shot before she hit the hard steps.

The tread edges caught her body from chest to shins, each point of impact an electric shock of pain. She blinked away the trauma and targeted the man again, squeezing the trigger. His next shot went high as he staggered back. Mina scrambled up the remaining stairs on her hands and knees.

Overwhelm your enemy.

By the time she aimed over the top step, he was fifteen feet away, holding his side. He was hit, but his gun swung up when he saw her, and he began rapid firing.

Mina rolled right, banging into the stairwell wall. She aimed, squeezed. Rolled left. Aimed, squeezed, aimed, squeezed. Rolled right.

Shoot and move, like Haines's drills where she practiced this over and over. No thinking, just simple training. At each recoil of her gun, she expected to take her last breath on this earth.

She wasn't sure how many times the man fired, but her remaining ammo was gone long before she was ready, and her gun clicked empty three times before she stopped pulling the trigger. She ducked down, her breath coming in sharp gasps.

After a few seconds, she peeked over the top step. Slade was on his knees, his gun dangling from his hand. Mina held her breath, prepared to duck if he fired again.

Then he fell forward, face down on the filthy bare subfloor. He didn't get up. Didn't move.

Her breathing resumed, a momentary reward for eliminating the threat. It was done. But she had no time to wonder at the brevity of the battle, the finality of this confrontation. Kade needed her attention.

Something burned on the back of her left shoulder, and her butt felt like she'd been stabbed with a red-hot ice pick. She ignored the pain and moved to him. He was hanging limply against the ropes that bound him to the post. There wasn't enough light to see his wound or wounds, but she feared he'd been hit by one of Slade's wild bullets.

The knots of his restraints were impossible, his weight cinching them tighter even as Mina tore at them. She crawled to the dead man. A search of his pockets produced a switchblade, black-handled and wicked. She snapped it open and began sawing at the ropes tying Kade.

When the last length broke free, his dead weight toppled them both down the top couple of steps. He was face up, eyes closed, but the dim light was enough to see his chest moving. She tried to shove him back up onto the level floor, but he was more than she could lift.

Beyond Kade's feet, tendrils of smoke sifted down the hallway, alerting her to the new immediate threat. The exploding SUV probably splashed fuel and debris on the house. With some of the exterior siding removed and the interior stripped to bare framing, even a small blaze would take the building in minutes.

She began easing Kade shoulders-first down the stairs, protecting his head as it passed over each tread. Her right hand came away slick with blood. It might be from Slade clubbing him with the gun. It might be more. She kept pressure on the wound as often as she could, but it was difficult while pulling him at the same time.

"Stay with me, Kade."

Beyond getting him downstairs, she had no plan. Her hope was that many people would have noticed the SUV explosion over the noise of the fireworks and come to investigate. Kade needed an ambulance as soon as possible, and getting him close to the front door in case of fire seemed a good idea.

She tugged him down the next step. "I love you, Kaden Hunt. Just hold on. A few more steps, and then we can rest."

"How touching," a female voice said behind her.

Mina had Kade halfway down the upper flight of stairs. She stopped and turned, wincing at the stabbing pain in her left buttock.

A woman stood below on the far side of the landing, silhouetted against the lighted glass. Her gaunt frame seemed to rest against the angel's breast, the giant wings wrapping her in an embrace. Four bright holes showed through the angel's image from Slade's bullets.

"Help us," Mina said. "Call an ambulance."

The woman laughed, but it ended in a wheezing cough. She wiped her mouth with the back of her left hand, then cleaned it on her red dress. That's when Mina noticed a black revolver hanging loosely in her other hand. She made no effort to raise it, and her head fell forward. Whoever she was, she wasn't well. Had the man shot her too?

"Who are you?" Mina asked.

CHAPTER FIFTY-TWO

"SHE'S BEAUTIFUL," Evie said, lifting her head enough to tilt back at the angel. "Your work?"

"Please help us."

Evie shook her head. "I don't think so." She paused to take a breath, then another. Neither did much good. The trip up the half-flight of stairs had drained her. The drugs were wearing off sooner than expected.

"Who are you?" Hawthorne asked again.

Evie cared nothing about what the woman wanted. She deserved to die in ignorance.

And Evie's identity made no difference now—to either of them. Hawthorne would be dead in a minute. And at best, Evie wouldn't survive more than a few days longer. Maybe a couple of weeks. She could feel the disease eating its way into vital parts of her. Food no longer stayed down—or, if it did, her stomach simply refused the nourishment. Even Narrano's spiritual water couldn't help.

She stared at the woman on the stairs. Blond, pretty, healthy. Hate rose up, a hot fire that strengthened Evie's bones and muscles. She recognized the dark power for what it was, but she clutched it, embracing its rising eruption.

"You killed my family," she said, her voice not as forceful as she intended. It would have to do.

"Who *are* you?" Hawthorne repeated.

Blood dribbled down the stair riser behind her. The FBI agent was bleeding out, and the way the woman favored her left side, perhaps she was as well. Evie would have smiled, had she the strength. Slade hadn't killed her as planned, but he at least weakened her, evened the odds.

"Ernesto," she said, the name emerging as if by its own will. "Tommy. Roberto. Magda." It was good to voice their names again. Speaking brought them to life, and they deserved to be here to witness their killer's death.

"The Vieras," Hawthorne said.

They hadn't been perfect, but they were her family. All she had.

"You took them from me," Evie said. "Now it's your turn." She gripped the gun tighter.

"You still haven't told me your name. If you're going to kill me, at least tell me that."

Evie opened her mouth, but the words were suddenly snatched away. Something inside her opened, as if giant hands rent her lungs, stomach, and bowels in two.

Her vision narrowed, and she bent forward, trying to coax oxygen into her body. Her knees buckled, and she staggered forward a step to keep her balance. The container that held in life had ruptured, like a failed dam spilling its water into the valley below.

No. Not yet!

She had one more thing to do. One final task to accomplish. Using both hands, she lifted the revolver. The barrel of the big gun wobbled, rising slowly. Too slowly! She should have brought a smaller gun.

Her vision dimmed to half, but it was enough to see the woman before her.

Evie tightened her hold on the gun, felt the smooth grip against her palm and the ridged steel trigger beneath her finger.

Mina watched the angel's wings rise higher above the woman. No, it was the woman who shrank. Something had happened to her, a deflating, like a body-shaped balloon losing its air.

Mina pounced on the distraction, leaning back across Kade's long form and groping along the top stair. Where was it? Her fingers closed on the hilt of the switchblade.

As she turned back, the woman below raised the gun, its barrel trembling with the effort.

The switchblade's handle was clad in smooth plastic, slick with Kade's blood. Mina rotated it for a better grip, clenched it hard, and cocked her arm. The gun continued to rise, its barrel passing Mina's feet, her knees, her hips.

She concentrated on the woman's chest and, like a pitcher in a last-ditch effort to strike out the home-run hitter, began her throw with her shoulder. As her elbow and hand whipped forward for the release, she sensed the slippery handle squirting from between her fingers. The knife shot away too soon, sailing upward in a high, useless arc.

Mina's hand was suddenly empty, a powerless fist against a bullet.

An object flew through the air in front of the woman, a flapping mass of pages almost like the paper wings of a living creature. The woman raised her left elbow to ward it off as she pulled the trigger.

Fire erupted from the big gun, the blast a physical power that knocked Mina back by its sheer intensity.

She waited for ripping flesh, shattering bone, and pain. She knew what each of those felt like. But even as she toppled onto Kade's still form, none of those came.

The gun's recoil propelled the woman backward into the window. Sharp cracking filled the sudden silence, matching the splits radiating outward from the bullet holes in the glass. The fissures lengthened, severing the exquisite wings and shattering the hued sky.

The woman's face replaced the angel's as she fell against the window, joined with it.

The gun's barrel continued its upward path, until it pointed at the ceiling as the woman leaned back. Her twisted grimace dissolved, and her countenance relaxed as she merged with the image behind.

Then the window sagged outward and she went through, cradled in the shattering glass arms of the angel who carried her past the window frame and away.

For a crazy moment, Mina half-expected her to soar upward, disappear into the starry heavens.

A crash followed a second later, and jagged shards from the wooden frame rained down.

CHAPTER FIFTY-THREE

AFTER THE WOMAN FELL, Mina made it to the ground floor and found a flashlight one of the workers left. She shone it around the bare rooms. There was no one else there.

Getting Kade down the stairs left her woozy from the effort. The blood running down her leg squished out of her shoe and mixed with Kade's. Together, they left a wide, wet smear all the way across the floor to the wall beside the front door.

She sat down and cradled Kade's head in her lap, stroking his hair. He was so still. Blood seeped from the left side of his head where Slade clubbed him, leaking into Mina's pants.

Crackling gunfire sounded far away outside, automatic bursts followed by semi-auto fire. Of *course* Slade brought men with him. How many?

It reminded her of the final battle at the Malibu house. The bad guys had illegal, fully automatic rifles, while the good guys were limited to semi-auto legal ones. She closed her eyes and prayed the good guys would win.

A siren called out down by the lake, joined a minute later by a second in a duet of intertwining wails.

Mina stroked Kade's hair. From where she sat, she could see

through the kitchen to the back of the house. Fire rumbled and popped, projecting macabre dancing shadows on the interior ceilings. What was left of the SUV was fully engulfed. Upholstery, plastics, tires. That wasn't unfamiliar to her either. A man hired to protect her had died in a vehicle like that.

She rested her head against the wall. The fire didn't seem to be spreading to the house, so they were safe for now, at least from fire. But Mina had no weapon, no defense if Slade's men returned. The woman's gun had fallen with her, outside somewhere, near the body. Could she make it all the way out there and back?

The light at the back door dimmed as a man came through, silhouetted against the flame. He carried a rifle.

"Mina!" Kris yelled from the front porch. She came through the open front door on Mina's left.

The man in the kitchen opened fire, stitching a line of holes across the wall behind Kris as she dove under the same worktable as Mina had. The shooting stopped when his gun emptied.

"Kris!" Mina called. She could see her on her hands and knees under the plywood table. The thin wood wouldn't stop automatic fire. In the kitchen, the man ejected the magazine. It clattered to the floor. He inserted a new one.

Something dark slid across the floor and slammed into Mina's leg. A black semi-automatic. She snatched it up as the man released the rifle's slide, chambering another round.

To Mina's left, Kris came up on her knees and began firing into the kitchen. The man pivoted toward her.

Mina covered Kade's head with her left hand as she took aim and pulled the trigger again and again. The man staggered back, taking hits from the twin guns. He went down without getting off a shot from the new magazine.

Above the ringing in her ears, she heard engines roaring and tires throwing gravel as lights bounced through the windows, sending distorted rectangles skittering across the interior walls.

"Glass! Kris!" Haines's booming voice rolled through the open door. He came in leading with his gun and sweeping the room with its red laser dot and white tactical light.

"Here!" Kris called to Haines. "Man down in the kitchen! Armed!"

Boomer was right behind Haines, sweeping the other side of the room, then advancing on the kitchen while Haines covered him. "Dead," he said seconds later.

Proxy came in next, carrying a black semi-automatic handgun in a low, two-hand grip.

"Slade is upstairs," Mina said to Haines. "Pretty sure he's dead too."

Haines nodded, and began climbing, his gun and light leading the way as he cleared the stairwell above him in the same way Alexandra and Mike had taught her.

Mina leaned her head back. So tired. Her fingers continued to comb Kade's hair. Everyone would know what to do.

Kris's light traced the wide smear of blood from the bottom of the stairs to where Kade lay. "Oh, no."

Mina turned her face into Kris's light. "He won't leave me again. He'll be okay." She looked down and brushed Kade's dark hair from his forehead. His skin was so pale. "He has to be."

Kris didn't say anything.

CHAPTER FIFTY-FOUR

THE BOTTOM of the hill looked like an airplane crash site. Pulsating colored lights from a fire engine, the sheriff's SUV, an ambulance, and headlights from several private vehicles formed a patchwork of blindingly-bright areas and inky shadows. Engines rumbled and radio messages crackled across the normally peaceful junction at the bottom of the road leading up to Mina's house.

Mina hissed as the fireman EMT cleansed her shoulder wound.

"Sorry, miss," he said, and applied a bandage to protect the wound. He had already dressed the entry and exit wounds in her left buttock, but she could feel them soaking through with blood. The shoulder stung, but the lower throbbing was spreading to her whole left side clear up to her scalp. It had her panting.

She knew the scene up at the house was similarly chaotic. The only air ambulance available had lifted off from the house at least twenty minutes ago, carrying Kade to the trauma center in Mission Peak.

Sheriff Derrek Cabot, who was attending the fireworks with his family, had arrived within minutes of Haines and team securing the house and grounds. The lawman wasn't happy about all the weapons. It took some quick explaining and a call to Alex Stone to disabuse Cabot's initial plan to disarm everyone. The truth was the sheriff had limited officers, and no one was sure there weren't more bad guys lurking nearby.

A siren started up, and Mina watched a boxy ambulance bounce down Old Mill Road, lights piercing the night. It held two of Slade's men who were seriously wounded in a shootout when Haines and crew drove up the hill. After the battle ended, Haines had ferried the men down the hill in his truck, faster than having the big ambulances climb the steep grade. He had returned for Mina, and she was in line for the next ambulance.

She stretched across the rear seat of Haines's truck and gritted her teeth as the fireman prepared to change the blood-soaked pads on her butt. Her wounds were painful and serious, but her thoughts were on Kade. He should be getting treatment at the hospital by now. Maybe in surgery.

"How are you holding up?" Kris asked, leaning into the open door at Mina's head. At least a dozen bullet holes pockmarked the door panel, and foam bits and glass littered the seat and floor.

When tears filled her eyes, Kris squeezed her hand. It was far too familiar.

"He'll be okay, Mina. Look at all he's been through. He's really tough."

Mina brushed at her eyes and tried to ignore the discomfort as the EMT peeled off the soaked gause, focusing instead on Kris's recap of the events.

"Haines got your text a few minutes before the fireworks began," Kris said. "We saw the car explode up at the house right before encountering several armed men coming down the mountain on foot.

"The guys took out three of them," she said, "wounded three more. The others gave up. Except for the one who made it back to the house. I saw him run that way and took off after him."

Mina breathed again. "So everyone's all right." Alive, at least.

Kris nodded. "Well, except if Haines kills me later. He was pretty mad that I ran into the house without waiting for him."

"We'd be dead if you hadn't." She had saved Mina's life. Kade's too. "Where's DJ? I saw blood—"

"It's not bad," Kris said. "Bled quite a bit, but the sheriff has him guarding the bad guys until more help arrives."

Boomer had disappeared, but Mina was confident he was keeping watch from somewhere close—just in case.

Slade's third injured man was also waiting for the next transport to arrive. Emergency help was thin this far from the more populated towns. They planned to take Mina on that one too, but she hadn't decided if she would go. Being in an ambulance with one of the men who tried to kill her and Kade… Well, it didn't sit well.

A vehicle drove down the hill and parked next to them. Alex Stone climbed out.

After asking about Mina, he said, "Haines and I found two vehicles hidden up at the Y that branches right toward the old cabin. The battery cables are cut."

"Huh," Kris said. "That explains why they were on foot. But who cut the cables?"

Mina had almost convinced herself that the flying notebook pages that distracted the woman had been dislodged from the ceiling by Slade's shooting, but the sabotaged cars brought another odd piece of information to the situation. Those cables had been cut long before Haines and crew arrived.

"DJ speaks a little Spanish," Alex said, "and he got out of one of the men that they were instructed to let you pass. Each of them had a photo of you. They were to close the road to everyone else. Slade promised reinforcements were coming, but no one besides the men here has shown."

Mina raised up on one elbow. "Do they know who the woman was with Slade?"

"That Proxy gal is working on it," Alex said. "She took photos of the woman before the authorities secured the area."

The second ambulance arrived, and it suddenly became busy as the other man was readied for transport. By this time, Mina was hurting too much to refuse the ride. Kris promised to follow close behind with DJ.

The trip to the hospital was unsettling. The vehicle swerved and rocked, its siren blaring the entire thirty-minute drive to Mission Peak. While Mina's discomfort effectively muted the sound, no amount of noise or pain could block the memory of Kade's cool, pale skin, and that trail of blood down the stairs and across the floor. So much blood.

Old Mike had said, *"it's the taking that makes them even more precious to us...and that taking makes us who we are."*

But it wasn't okay. She didn't want to be anyone different than who she was, and Kade was already more than precious to her. More taking would tear out her core. Her heart.

She had to see those gray eyes again.

EPILOGUE

Four weeks later

"C'MON, MINA," Kris said. "Time to get ready."

Mina opened her eyes. Late afternoon was the hottest part of the day, and her bedroom at the mill was hot and musty. She should have napped down in her studio—or worked—but descending and ascending that many steps still constituted an Everest attempt for her.

Kris pushed open the door to the bathroom and a few seconds later the water started. "Get in the shower, girl. I'll come back in a few and help you downstairs."

Mina stood under the hot stream, washing her hair again even though it didn't need it. She might never feel clean again.

For the most part, the nightly replays had stopped. Each dream took new paths, offering might-have-beens in endless variety until she had difficulty remembering what really happened. Some of the fantasies had been so real she could have passed a polygraph.

Things improved when Proxy showed Mina the official crime scene photos on her laptop. How she gained access to them, Mina didn't know and didn't ask.

Proxy—whose real name Mina now knew was Deb Trent,

someone who occasionally worked with Kris's company, Omron, International—skipped past dozens of photos of the outside of the house lit by the morning sun. The back wall and porch were blackened from the SUV fire, but the structure escaped damage.

The next photos were inside the house. She shivered at the blood marking the floor from the foot of the stairs to the front door. The camera captured the red-black trail all the way to the top where Kade had been bound. Every stair tread was etched in her memory. Unknown to everyone at the time, a good portion of the blood had been hers, and up until a week ago, she still suffered fatigue as her blood replenished itself.

Proxy skipped through most of the forty pictures of the dead man in the upstairs hall. Thomas "Slade" Ibanez, 39 years old. Part of the reborn Viera family drug ring. The coroner's report—which Proxy also obtained—listed five .32 caliber bullet wounds stretching from the man's upper right thigh to his heart. Five out of seven. Mina had missed twice, but it had been enough.

But Ibanez hadn't been Mina's real enemy. Bad guy, yes, but not the one who wanted her dead.

She turned around in the shower, carefully lifting her left arm to rinse. Ibanez's bullet had skimmed the scapula bone on the back of her shoulder before doing a through-and-through of her gluteus maximus. Essentially, she'd been shot in the butt. The wounds had closed, but it would be a while before she could sit on anything other than the softest pillow.

Drying off was easier each day, and she managed to get most of the droplets before pulling on sweat shorts and a button-down shirt. Flip-flops completed her standard wardrobe just as Kris re-entered the bedroom.

"Oh, no," Kris said, shaking her head as she gave Mina the once-over. "I don't think so."

"What?"

Kris went to the closet and returned with a pair of white Capri pants, a green polo shirt, and white strappy sandals with a low heel.

"My butt's swollen," Mina said, eyeing the pants. "They'll never fit."

Kris gave the Capris a sharp shake and held them out. "Suck it up, Supergirl."

With her friend's help and a lot of tugging, Mina made it into the pants and the fitted shirt. Checking herself in the full-length mirror, she had to admit the white sandals looked far better than her black flip-flops, and her tanned calves contrasted nicely with the white pants.

"I might not be able to sit down in these," she said, turning to view her tight backside.

"Please," Kris said, her sarcasm dripping. "That's the first time you've *ever* filled out a pair of pants." Kris angled her own butt toward the mirror and frowned. "I think I hate you."

"Shall we go?" Mina said, starting for the door to the hall.

"Not without makeup."

Mina groaned, then hung her head in defeat. "I know, I know. Suck it up."

Kris smiled at her.

The mill was deserted when they left through the front door. As Mina turned to lock up, a sign in the window caught her eye.

Closed today for Private Event. - Bibs

"Do you know what's happening here today?" she asked Kris.

"What?" Kris waited by her SUV. She looked where Mina was pointing to the sign. "Oh, yeah. I saw that earlier. Nope. No idea about anything happening here."

Mina narrowed her eyes, but Kris hopped into the truck and started the engine. When they reached the end of the driveway, instead of turning left toward town, Kris turned right and started up the hill toward the house.

"I thought we were going to the Crab Shack," Mina said. She had skipped lunch, and her stomach was growling in anticipation.

"Got something to show you first," Kris said, giving her car more throttle as they climbed upward.

"Well, make it fast. I'm starving." Even with the puffy bed pillow beneath her, Mina was glad Kris took it slow up the hill. "This better be worth it," she said through gritted teeth. Kris smiled.

Before they got to the clearing where the house was, Kris steered to the side and shut off the engine.

"Why are we stopping?"

"You need the exercise," Kris said, exiting the truck and shutting the door. "Let's walk." She strode away before Mina got her door open.

"Kris? Wait for me." But Kris kept going while Mina navigated the uneven road surface like a tightrope walker, arms extended as she balanced on the sandals. She finally reached the clearing where the ground was smoother, and looked up. Her mouth dropped open.

The garden at the center of the circular driveway had a new border of beach ball-sized boulders that retained mounds of rich black topsoil. Gone were the weeds and wild grasses, replaced by artfully arranged plants that filled the space. In the raised center was a working fountain trickling water over the bowl's edge in an endless musical melody that floated across the yard.

A fieldstone path bisected the garden, beginning at the porch steps and continuing across the outer driveway. There, three steps down, a new round patio overlooked the lake. Benches formed a U around a low fire pit.

"Isn't it beautiful?" Kris said from Mina's right.

Stunning was the word that came to Mina. "Kris, how...?"

"Carter headed up the project, and a lot of people worked on it." Kris took her by the arm. "There's more inside."

As they walked along the curved driveway, Mina stopped again. Halfway up the north side of the house, a sheet of plywood covered the opening where the angel window had been.

Proxy had called the crime scene photos from this spot particularly gruesome. Haines labeled them divine justice.

Evie Mendak, who Proxy learned was taken into the Viera family

325

as a child, had been Mina's true enemy. It was Evie, not Slade, who picked up the pieces of the Viera family crime organization and rebuilt it. She was the one who sent the threats to Mina and her father.

In the photos, Evie lay on the ground on her back, her right leg bent slightly beneath her left, arms outstretched, almost graceful. With her eyes closed, she could have been described as peaceful... except for the two-foot shard of angel wing that pinned her to the earth.

According to the report, the falling piece of glass hadn't killed her. Evie Mendak's heart had stopped beating before she hit the ground, her body ravaged by aggressive cancer.

Confrontation with Mina or not, Evie would never have lived long enough to see July 14th, Ekaterina's birthday, and Mina's original target date. In a way, that was a relief. Mom's birthday would be forever free of the stain of hate and revenge.

Not Evie's vengeance, but Mina's. Her hate for the Viera threat had consumed her, and she hadn't liked the feeling. The darkness had eased when she decided to pull back on the attack and let Proxy begin dumping her mountains of evidence on the authorities' virtual desks. Ultimately, it hadn't worked out that way, but Mina was glad to have made the decision.

The words of V.M. Narrano rang true:

Vengeance and hate blacken the heart and rob the soul of peace, beauty, and compassion.

Peace now superseded the blackness of that night. Beauty was present too, in the reborn garden.

And the beginning of compassion. While she couldn't condone one thing Evie did in her life of crime and threats, Mina did understand being taken in by a family, then losing them. Evie's sins were her own, but Mina did, in a small way, feel sorry for her.

And what if their roles had been reversed? Evie adopted by Nathan and Ekaterina, and Mina by the Viera family.

A chill pricked the hair on the back of Mina's neck and she shook it off. Discussion questions for another time. Haines would love that one. Regardless, Mina knew her mom would be pleased that Mina struggled with the questions about self-defense. In the end, it was exactly that, not vengeance.

A sigh escaped her lips as she viewed the cleared and raked ground where the body had lain on a bed of angel glass. She hoped Evie Mendak found peace in her last seconds.

"Look who's here," Kris whispered.

Mina followed her friend's subtle head-nod. Back by the pump house, Old Mike stepped out. His clothing appeared the same as always: rumpled and marked with old stains, but not dirty. He looked at Mina first, then at the ground, then up at the plywood panel.

Mina took a few steps closer to him. "Your notebook is waiting for you on the deck of the mill. I wrapped it in plastic. You can bring it back to your place. I want to thank you—"

Before Mina could finish, Old Mike nodded and disappeared back into the trees.

"That is one strange dude," Kris said, shaking her head.

Two weeks ago, the sheriff's office returned a notebook found on the stair landing by the angel window. Its pages were bent and tattered from being thrown through the air. Mina didn't tell the deputy who delivered the notebook, but it matched the ones Old Mike carried every day.

Its pages were filled with neat printing—poetic descriptions of nature, beauty, life, and forgiveness. Some of the phrasings were startlingly familiar, and would be recognized by many, but she was the only one who had seen the contents.

Armed with that information, Haines began tracking Old Mike, and trailed him to the little cabin on her property. Haines checked it out while the man was in town one day.

Mina still hadn't seen the cabin, but Haines said it had a good roof and was in decent shape. He'd taken a few photos for Mina. The inside was simple and well kept, and showed signs that Old Mike had occupied it for some time—years maybe. The electricity and water—both fed from Mina's main house—didn't work, but there was a portable propane bottle outside with a line snaking in a window to a two-burner camp stove set on a table.

A scarred highboy dresser and a metal frame camp bed filled one corner of the single room. But the most interesting picture was of dozens of spiral notebooks that lined the shelves of a bookcase next to a rustic desk. Centered on the desk was one of the notebooks, two pens carefully aligned along its right edge. A hurricane oil lamp provided the only light.

Besides Haines and the guys, Kris and Carter were the only other people who knew Old Mike lived there, and Mina had no plans to alter the living arrangement. She would get the electric and water turned on soon.

"Come." Kris gently tugged Mina away, probably feeling the area below the angel window was a reminder of death and evil.

But that wasn't the case at all. Since that night, she often thought about Haines's mother and her belief that angels would protect her son when he was half a world away in battle. Mina wasn't sure if angels were real or if they even worked that way, but one thing was for sure, she had help that night.

She smiled as they climbed the steps to the porch. Maybe Old Mike was her guardian angel.

Temporary plywood still covered the area, but the dead leaves and sawdust were cleaned away. Kris pushed open the front door, then stepped to the side.

"Surprise!"

Mina started at the cheer and applause. Dozens of people stood under a huge banner that read, Welcome Home!

As the applause died down, the hugs began. First from her dad.

"I'm proud of you, Mina," he said as he held her. "You're so like your mom. Strong, beautiful, and a fighter." He pulled back, keeping his hands on her shoulders. "And this house is going to be spectacular."

She swiped at sudden tears. "Better than DeMille?"

"Don't get cocky, kid."

His publicist, Syl Straasberg, stood beside him. *Close* beside him— her hand tucked lightly in the crook of Dad's elbow. Syl had been Ekaterina's public relations agent, too, and had guided Mina through the nightmare of arranging her mother's funeral and managing the ravenous press. Mina raised a questioning eyebrow as her dad stepped back. He didn't notice, but Syl did. She gave Mina a slight smile.

Then Teal gave Mina a hug, followed by a slightly awkward side-arm one from Quin. Mina breathed in his suntan lotion, as familiar as anything at the lake.

"Mom wanted to come, but she's about to pop any second," Teal said. "We might have to jet out early."

Connie Langworth greeted her with a DC Coffee insulated travel mug. He tapped its side. "One of my cappuccino blasts. Don't drink it all in one place." With a wink, he stepped aside as a mountain filled the space.

"Good thing I trained you well, Glass," Haines growled. Then he swallowed her with his big arms. "You came through like a true Marine."

She laughed as he released her. "It's all because of you, Rowdy Haines." He nodded sagely, causing her to laugh even more.

Kris whacked him on the arm. "Sheesh, Haines. Humble much? You weren't the only one who trained her, you know."

Haines gave Kris a deadpan face, then burst into laughter at her appalled expression. She punched him harder, which earned an *ow!* Mina's brow lifted as Kris laced her fingers through Rowdy's meaty ones and pulled him away. She grinned sheepishly at Mina.

Bibs elbowed her way in and encircled Mina's waist with one plump arm, pulling her the other direction. "There's someone else here to see you." The others in the room parted like the Red Sea, making a path to the kitchen doorway.

Kade rolled out in a wheel chair pushed by Rowan. His right leg was propped out in front. He'd been gone for three weeks having some plastic surgery on the left side of his scalp where Slade clubbed him. The broken leg from one of Slade's bullets was healing well, and the cast would come off soon.

She went to him, grimacing as she dropped to her knees beside the chair. "One of these days, I want to see you not wounded."

He laughed. "You're one to talk." Then he said, "You're going to get your pants dirty."

She shook her head. "I don't care." She rose up, circled her arms around his neck, and kissed him. Whistles and cheers filled the room, and she only stopped when they needed air. She leaned her forehead against his.

"I'll be out of this chair in a few weeks," he said, "then I'll take you dancing."

"We can dance at our wedding."

He opened his mouth, but nothing came out for a minute. Then the corner of his mouth twitched. "We're getting married?"

"I'm not letting you get away again." She ran her fingernails through his hair. He might have shivered.

"Then I guess this is perfect timing," he said, and pulled a small box from his pocket. He opened it, and held it out to her. Inside was a ring with a small, clear diamond set in a white gold band. "I'd get down on one knee if I could, but—"

"Yes!"

"What?"

"I'm saying yes. Yes, I will marry you."

"I thought *you* proposed to *me*," Kade said.

"Whatever," she said, waving her hand, then holding it out, fingers splayed. "We'll call it even."

"Works for me." He grinned at her, and slipped the ring onto her finger.

When darkness fell and cold air washed up the hill from the lake, Haines and Boomer gathered wood from the construction scrap pile and started a fire in the pit. Then they carried Kade in his chair down the steps to the patio, while Mina followed with a camp chair and pillow. She set the chair as close to Kade as the wheel chair allowed and looped her arm through his. The dry wood crackled and popped, sending sparks rising like mini versions of the fireworks they all missed.

Boomer and Proxy huddled close together on the opposite side of the circle. He had moved his belongings out from Tennessee and rented a cabin on the other side of the lake in Shelter Cove, and a couple of days ago, Proxy asked Mina about renting one of the mill bedrooms.

The night air cooled rapidly as stars appeared one by one, and Mina was glad for the warmth of the fire. She leaned her head back as Kade toyed with her fingers. A mellow jazz CD played in a boom box up on the porch, sending music drifting across the yard.

Carter turned on dozens of strategically placed LED candles, transforming the new garden, trees, and house into a magical kingdom. The man could work miracles. If he weren't committed to working for Abigail, Mina would hire him to do the landscape design and permanent lighting.

Flickering firelight glanced off the diamond, and she held up her hand to catch the dancing flames. "It's so beautiful. Thank you."

"When are we getting married?" Kade asked.

"October," Mina said.

"That's only a couple of months."

"Are you having second thoughts?" She *had* kind of sprung it on him. More like told him they were getting married. Still, he brought a ring.

His voice was quiet, reflective. "I had years to work through those, Mina." He lifted her hand to his lips. "I just thought brides always wanted to wait like a year or something—to book the venue, get flowers, food, photographer, and…stuff."

"No more waiting," she said. *There is no promise of life.* "We can get married down at the chapel, and we have the flowers and room for the reception right here at our house."

The stars overhead had become bright silver pinpricks in the black canopy. In the coming weeks, the nighttime temperatures would drop more. They would need heaters.

"Outside if the weather's good," she said. "Inside if it's raining"—a mosquito whined around her ear, and she swatted it away—"and if the bugs are bad."

"I know some guys in Georgia who can get me a deal on some bug zappers."

"Do it." She shifted in the canvas chair, trying to get comfortable. "Oh. What about your parents?"

"Mom will be thrilled, especially if Massachusetts gets an early snow. She'll probably go property hunting while they're out here." He nodded toward the house. "And I think Rowan will be here for sure."

Carter and Kade's sister sat on the porch steps talking. There was no space between them from shoulder to ankle.

"Have you figured out a name for it yet?" Kade asked.

Candles lined the porch, windowsills, and shone from every upstairs window. It wouldn't be completed until early summer, but she saw the future. Friends new and old moved around inside, eating from tables brought in by caterers, talking and laughing. Even the unfinished turret stood proud and inviting, and she planned to transform its upstairs room into a reading nook. The house was exactly as she envisioned it, pulsing with life and energy.

And love.

Russ Howell said a name sometimes influenced design elements, but in this case, it was the other way around. No history of violence would ever again overshadow what they fought so hard for.

Now that she was getting around more easily, she would recreate the window for the landing. The angel represented protection, but perhaps more importantly peace and a need to forgive.

Forgiveness brings life and light to those who embrace its uplifting wings.

"I'm thinking...*Angel Ridge*."

Agent Gray Eyes squeezed her hand.

GLASS REVENGE

NOTE TO READERS

Thanks for reading *Glass Revenge*!

Please consider writing a review at your favorite retailer site. They help other potential readers, and advertisers look for how many reviews a book has. It's a competitive world.

I'd love to hear from you! Tell me what you liked or <gasp!> didn't like, and why. Your feedback will make me a better writer.

I have a great team of test readers and editors, and we work hard to catch every error before my books are published. If you find one that slipped through, please let me know. Just send a short phrase I can search for in the master document.

richbullockwriter@gmail.com

BOOKS BY RICH BULLOCK

Perilous Safety Series
Perilous Cove
Storm Song
Desperation Falls
Glass & Stone Series
Shattered Glass
Glass Revenge
Killing Callie
Lake Effect Series
Night Skyy

Nonfiction
Beyond Us: The Writings of V.M. Narrano
Wild Life: The Writings of V.M. Narrano

The Shortest Book On Marriage,
with Sheryl Bullock

ACKNOWLEDGMENTS

Jan Scanlin from Jan Scanlin Glass gave me initial inspiration for Mina and her glass art career. After a tour of Jan's studio and projects, I have a new appreciation for both the difficulty of the work and its amazing artistry.

Robert Henslin Design for another stellar cover. Rob's cover art is often the push I need to finish a book. www.rhdcreative.com

My wife, Sheryl, who puts up with long absences as I lose myself in my characters and stories.

And finally my beta reading team: Nancy Bailey, Patricia Bossman, Carol Dickerson, Lisa Gregory, Sis Hammack, Jennifer Haynie, Nita McCoubrey, Linda Murphy, Hannah Prewett, and Cathi Wofford. Their feedback and suggestions were invaluable.

ABOUT THE AUTHOR

Rich Bullock writes stories of ordinary people put in perilous situations, where lives are changed forever.

Fortunate to grow up in small-town San Luis Obispo, California, he developed an eye for settings that remind people of home. He lives and writes in Redding, California, where on most days he sees Mount Lassen and Mount Shasta.

www.perilousfiction.com

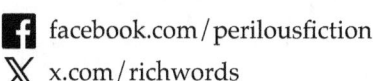 facebook.com / perilousfiction
x.com / richwords